9\03

Insurance Dictionary

What Means What When It Comes to Life, Health, Business, Home, Auto and Other Coverages

SILVER LAKE PUBLISHING
LOS ANGELES, CALIFORNIA

Insurance Dictionary

What Means What When It Comes to
Life, Health, Business, Home, Auto and
Other Coverages

First edition, 2002
Copyright © 2002 by Silver Lake
Publishing

Silver Lake Publishing
2025 Hyperion Avenue
Los Angeles, California 90027

For a list of other publications or for more
information from Silver Lake Publishing,
please call 1.888.663.3091. Outside the
United States and in Alaska and Hawaii,
please call 1.323.663.3082. Find our Web
site at silverlakepub.com.

Library of Congress Catalogue Number:
Pending

The Silver Lake Editors
Insurance Dictionary
Pages: 486

ISBN: 1-56343-749X
Printed in the United States of America.

ACKNOWLEDGMENTS

The Silver Lake Editors who have contributed to this book are Kristin Loberg, Christina Schlank, Megan Thorpe and James Walsh.

Many of the standard insurance policy forms referenced in this book are developed by and remain the property of the New York-based Insurance Services Office (ISO). Standard policy forms produced by ISO are updated and modified regularly. Our references—either direct or indirect—to the forms are intended solely to illustrate issues common to insurance. Check with an insurance company or agent or broker if you need current policy information.

Diligent efforts have been made by Silver Lake Publishing staff to provide timely and comprehensive terms and definitions in this dictionary. However, this dictionary is not put forth as a final authority on any specific term or definition. Insurance terminology is subject to a never-ending development and refinement process, which causes definitions and usages to change over time. **If you are involved in a dispute over an insurance policy's language or construction, consult with a regulatory agency or an attorney familiar with insurance in your state or region before taking any action.**

The Silver Lake Editors welcome any feedback. Please call us at 1.888.663.3091 during regular business hours, Pacific time. Or, if you prefer, you can fax us at 1.323.663.3084. Finally, you can e-mail us at TheEditors@silverlakepub.com.

James Walsh, Publisher
Los Angeles, California

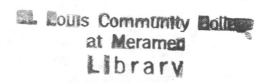

Before You Begin...

The dictionary is divided into sections, in alphabetical sequence. Abbreviations and acronyms (if any) are included in each section, as well as an alphabetical presentation of terms. Each term is set in bold type. To help you gain a quick reference point, definitions are immediately followed by one or more icons for general categories of insurance. The abbreviations for the reference categories used in this dictionary are:

 = **Annuities**

 = **Automobile**

 = **Aviation**

 = **Crime**

 = **Estate Planning**

 = **General**

 = **Health**

 = **Inland Marine**

 = **Legal**

 = **Liability**

 = **Life**

 = **Ocean Marine**

 = **Pension & Profit Sharing**

 = **Property**

 = **Reinsurance**

 = **Surety**

 = **Workers' Compensation**

"A" (or Judgment) Rates. Rates that are not backed up by loss experience statistics. They are based on the judgment of the underwriter on an individual risk basis.

A&H, A&S. Accident and Health Insurance, Accident and Sickness Insurance. Once commonly used as generic designations for the entire field now called health insurance. See Health Insurance.

AAI. See Alliance of American Insurers.

AAIS. See American Association of Insurance Services.

AB. ACAS. Associate of the Casualty Actuarial Society. See Fellow of the Casualty Actuarial Society.

Abandonment. Relinquishing ownership of lost or damaged property by the insured to the insurance company so that a total loss may be claimed. This is prohibited in most types of property insurance.

Abandonment Clause or Condition. A clause that prohibits the abandonment of partially damaged property to the insurer in order to claim a total loss. The company may choose to acquire damaged property which can be sold for salvage and choose to pay a total loss, but the insured cannot insist that the insurer take possession of any property.

Absolute Assignment. Assignment by a policy-owner of all control of and rights in the policy to a third party.

Absolute Beneficiary. See Irrevocable Beneficiary.

Absolute Liability. A liability that arises from extremely dangerous operations, such as the use of explosives (e.g., a contractor would almost certainly be liable for damages caused by vibrations of the earth following an explosive detonation). With absolute liability it is usually not necessary to establish that the operation is dangerous. See also Strict Liability.

Accelerated Benefits. Riders on life insurance policies that allow the policy's death benefits to be used to offset expenses incurred in a convalescent or nursing home facility. Any living benefits paid by the insurance company reduce the remaining death benefit. The government does not currently consider accelerated benefits to be taxable income, and the policyowner can get between 50 and 95 percent of the policy's face value. See Living Needs Benefits.

Accelerated Endowment. A dividend option allowing dividend accumulations to be applied to convert a life insurance policy into an endowment, or to shorten the endowment term.

Accelerated Option. A provision whereby an insured may use accumulated policy dividends and the cash value of a life insurance contract to pay up the policy or to mature it as an endowment.

Acceptance. Insurance acceptance occurs when an applicant for insurance receives the policy from the company and, in the case of general insurance, pays the premium. In life insurance, since the initial premium is often submitted with the application, issuance of the policy constitutes acceptance.

Acceptance of the Risk. Once all the underwriting information has been reviewed, an insurance company makes a decision about the acceptance of the risk. Most applicants are classified as standard risks. Occasionally, an applicant for disability income will be classified as a substandard risk.

Access. The availability of medical care to a patient. This can be determined by location, transportation, type of medical services in the area, etc.

Accident and Health Insurance (A&H). An older name for health insurance. See Health Insurance.

Accident and Sickness Insurance (A&S). An older name for health insurance. See Health Insurance.

Accident Frequency. The rate of the occurrence of accidents, often expressed in terms of the number of accidents over a period of time. It is one method used for measuring the effectiveness of loss prevention services. Contrast with Accident Severity.

Accident Insurance. Insurance against loss by accidental bodily injury to the insured.

Accident Only Insurance. Insurance that provides coverage for injury from accident, and excludes sickness. Benefits may be paid for all or any of the following: death, disability, dismemberment or hospital and medical expenses.

Accident Prevention. See Loss Prevention Service.

Accident Severity. A measure of the severity or seriousness of losses, rather than the number of losses. It is measured in terms of time lost from work rather than the number of individual accidents. It is another way of measuring the effectiveness of loss prevention services. Contrast with Accident Frequency.

Accident Year Experience. Measures premiums and losses relating to accidents which occurred during a 12-month period.

Accident. An unintended and unforeseen event, which occurs suddenly and at a definite place, resulting in bodily injury. An accident is also any injury caused by accidental means—the cause was accidental versus intentional. If the cause is accidental, then benefits are payable. If it is intentional, then the claim would be denied. See also Occurrence and Accidental Bodily Injury.

Accidental Bodily Injury. An injury to the body (the result of an accident), of external origin, unintentional and unforeseen by the injured person. Contrast with Accidental Means.

Accidental Death and Dismemberment (AD&D). A policy or a provision in a disability income policy which pays either a specified amount or a multiple of the weekly disability benefit if the insured dies, loses his or her sight, or loses two limbs as the result of an accident. A lesser amount is payable for the loss of one eye, arm, leg, hand or foot. Although technically a health insurance product, AD&D coverage is frequently provided as part of an individual or group life insurance contract.

Accidental Death Benefit. An extra benefit which generally equals the face of the contract or principal sum, payable in addition to other benefits in the event of death as the result of an accident. See also Double Indemnity and Multiple Indemnity.

Accidental Death Insurance. A form that provides payment if the death of the insured results from an accident. Often combined with dismemberment insurance in a form called accidental death and dismemberment.

Accidental Means. Unexpected or undesigned cause of an accidental bodily injury. The mishap itself must be accidental, not just the resulting injury, (e.g., a person chopping wood: If the axe slipped out of his hand and cut his foot, it would have been accidental means. However, if his finger got in the way of the axe, it would not have been).

Accommodation Line. Business accepted from an agent or broker which would normally be rejected according to strict underwriting standards but which is accepted because of the overall profitability of the agent's or customer's other business, (e.g., an insurer might accept coverage on property that would not normally meet its underwriting standards, if the other lines of insurance which it carries for the customer were profitable.

Account Current. A monthly financial statement provided to an agent by an insurer showing premiums written, cancelations endorsements and commissions.

Account Premium Modification Plan. A rating plan for fire, property damage and time element coverages. The maximum credit or surcharge is 25 percent, and it is available to risks which develop a three-year premium of at least $5,000.

Accounts Receivable Insurance. Insurance against loss that occurs when an insured is unable to collect outstanding accounts because of damage to or destruction of the accounts receivable records by a peril covered in the policy.

Accredited Service. All service, by an employee, recognized under a pension plan as being allowable or creditable in calculating the benefits due.

Accrete. A Medicare term which means the process of adding new members to a health plan.

Accrued Benefit. The amount of retirement benefit accumulated by a participating employee.

Accrued Liability. The amount of money needed to offset accumulated benefits under a retirement plan. Accrued liability equals the difference between the present value of the future benefits and the present value of future contributions.

Accumulated Actuarial Benefit. The sum of benefits assigned to credited service before a specified date, and which is determined pursuant to the actuarial valuation method in use.

Accumulated Earnings Tax. A tax penalty imposed on corporate earnings that are retained by the corporation for non-business related needs.

Accumulated Plan Benefit. That portion of a retirement benefit that is attributable pursuant to the plan to the participant's period of credited service before a specified date.

Accumulation at Interest. A dividend option where interest is paid on accumulated dividends and compounded annually at a guaranteed minimum interest rate.

Accumulation Period. The period of time, prior to retirement, during which an annuitant is making payments or investments in an annuity. Such payments will accumulate on a tax deferred basis.

Accumulation Units. These are issued to owners of variable annuities during the accumulation period, as evidence of the annuitant's participation in the separate account.

Accumulation Value. A term used in universal life policies to describe the total of all premiums paid and interest credited to the account before deductions for any expenses, loans or surrenders.

Accumulations (or Accumulation Benefits). Percentage additions to policy benefits when the contract is continuously renewed.

Acquired Immunodeficiency Syndrome (AIDS). An infectious and incurable disease, commonly referred to as AIDS, which is caused by the human immunodeficiency virus, or HIV.

Acquired Locations. Locations acquired after inception of the coverage and during the coverage period.

Acquisition Cost. Expenses incurred by an insurer or reinsurance company that are directly related to putting a business on the books (acquiring a customer), including clerical work, medical examiners fees, inspection costs, etc. The largest portion of this cost is usually the agent's or sales representative's commission or bonus.

Act of God. An event arising out of natural causes (with no human intervention) which could not have been prevented by reasonable care or foresight (e.g., flood, lightning and earthquake).

Action. A lawsuit involving the right of one party to recover from another person in a court of law.

Active Malfunction. When a product, instead of bringing a benefit to the user, actually damages the user's property (e.g., if a bug killer, which is intended to protect a crop, damages the crop instead).

Actively-at-Work. Most group health insurance policies state that if an employee is not actively at work when the policy goes into effect, the coverage will not begin until the employee does return to work.

Activities of Daily Living (ADL). Everyday living functions and activities performed by individuals without assistance, including moving about, dressing, attending to personal hygiene and eating.

Activities of Daily Living (ADL) Standards. Standards used to assess the ability of a person to live independently, measured by the ability to perform unaided such activities as eating, bathing, toiletry, dressing and walking. Sometimes used to measure or define eligibility for long-term care.

Actual Cash Value (ACV). An amount equal to the replacement cost of lost or damaged property at the time of loss, less depreciation. With regard to buildings, there is a tendency for the ACV to closely parallel the market value of the property. If there is a covered loss to the insured dwelling, the insurance company will pay either the depreciated value of the damaged dwelling at the time of loss or the cost of repairing the property with like construction, but only up to the policy's limit of liability. ACV also refers to the maximum limit of auto insurance coverage. The insurer will usually only pay the ACV or the cost to repair or replace the damaged or stolen property, whichever is less. Depreciation and the condition of the vehicle are also considered in determining the ACV. See also Market Value.

Actual Charge. The actual amount charged by a physician for medical services rendered.

Actual Total Loss. See Total Loss.

Actuarial. Having to do with insurance mathematics or actuaries—people hired by insurance companies to create formulas and tables that calculate the present value of future payments and risks related to those payments.

Actuarial Equivalence. Two different series of payments or values are in actuarial equivalence when they have an equal actuarial present value under a given set of actuarial assumptions. See Actuarial Present Value.

Actuarial Experience Gain or Loss. The effect on an actuarial value of deviations between the past events that would have occurred according to the actuarial assumptions and those which actually occurred.

Actuarial Present Value. The single amount as of a given evaluation date that results from applying actuarial assumptions to an amount or series of amounts payable or receivable at various times; with the amount(s) adjusted to reflect expected changes from the valuation date to the date of expected payment or receipt by reason of expected salary changes, cost of living adjustments, etc.; and adjusted to reflect the time value of money (through discounts for interest) and the probability of payment (by means of decrements such as for death, disability, withdrawal or retirement) between the valuation date and the expected date of payment or receipt.

Actuarial Valuation Method. A procedure, using actuarial assumptions, for measuring the expected value of benefits and assigning such value to time periods. Also called actuarial analysis.

Actuarially Sound. When the amount of money in a pension fund, and the current level of contributions to the fund, are sufficient to meet the liabilities that have already accrued and that are accruing on a current basis.

Actuary. A specialist trained in mathematics, statistics and accounting who is responsible for rate, reserve and dividend calculations as well as other statistical studies.

Acute Care. Skilled, medically necessary care provided by medical and nursing personnel in order to restore a person to good health.

AD&D. See Accidental Death and Dismemberment Insurance.

Added Expense. Extra expenses incurred relative to a disabling injury or sickness, including additional medication, doctor's bills, the need for prosthetic appliances, such as braces, and possible hospital bills that are not fully covered by hospitalization insurance.

Additional Coverages. Limited amounts of coverage for specific types of losses or expenses that are provided in addition to the major coverages (e.g., personal liability coverage provides three kinds of insurance in addition to the stated limits of liability: claim expenses, first aid to others and damage to the property of others).

Additional Drug Benefit List. Prescription drugs listed as commonly prescribed by physicians for patients' long-term use. Subject to review and change by the health plan involved. Also called drug maintenance list.

Additional Indemnity Riders. These riders provide additional amounts of indemnity for short periods of time, such as six or 12 months. The primary purpose of these riders is to supplement or coordinate with other disability benefits, such as Social Security or group disability benefits.

Additional Insured. A person other than the named insured who is protected under the terms of the contract. Usually, additional insureds are added by endorsement or referred to in the wording of the definition of "insured" in the policy. See Named Insured.

Additional Living Expense Insurance. A contract to reimburse the insured for increased living costs when loss of property forces the insured to maintain temporary residence elsewhere, including the costs for a hotel or motel, for restaurant meals or for using a laundromat. The term extra expense insurance refers to additional expenses incurred by businesses. See also Loss of Use.

Additional Living Expenses. Any necessary increase in living expenses—such as rent for alternative housing—incurred so that the household can maintain its normal standard of living.

Additional Monthly Benefit (AMB) Rider. A rider added to a disability income policy to provide additional benefits during the first year of a claim while the insured is waiting for Social Security benefits to begin. Also used to complement other disability income sources, such as short-term group disability benefits provided through the employer. Also called a Social Security Rider.

Additional Premium. When endorsements are added to a policy, there is almost always an additional premium (cost) charged. See Premium.

Additur. A situation where the court increases a previous jury award. Compare to Remittitur.

Adhesion. A characteristic of a unilateral contract that is offered on a "take it or leave it" basis. Most insurance policies are contracts of "adhesion," because the terms are drawn up by the insurer and the insured simply "adheres" to the policy provisions. For this reason ambiguous provisions are often interpreted by courts in favor of the insured. Contrast with Manuscript Policy.

Adjustable Life. A form of life insurance that allows changes on the policy face amount, the amount of premium, period of protection and the length of the premium payment period. See also Flexible Premium Adjustable Life Insurance Policy.

Adjustable Premium. The right of an insurer to change the premium rate on classes of insureds, or blocks of business at the time of policy renewal.

Adjusted Community Rating (ACR). Community rating adjusted by factors specific to a particular group. Also known as factored rating.

Adjusted Gross Estate. In the calculation of federal estate taxes, it is equal to the gross estate less specific deductions.

Adjusted Net Worth. The capital, surplus and voluntary reserves of an insurer, plus an estimated value for business on the books and unrealized capital gains, less the potential income tax on such gains.

Adjuster. A representative of the insurer who seeks to determine the extent of the firm's liability for loss when a claim is submitted. Same as Claim Representative.

Adjuster, Average. See Average Adjuster.

Adjuster, Independent. See Independent Adjuster.

Adjuster, Public. See Public Adjuster.

Adjustment Bureau. A firm organized to provide adjustment services to insurers not wishing to create their own claims division.

ADL. See Activities of Daily Living Standards.

Administration Bond. A bond furnished by the executor or administrator of an estate. It guarantees that the estate will be settled in accordance with the terms of the will, or, if there is no will, in accordance with the law. It guarantees the fidelity of the executor or administrator.

Administrative Services Only. Services provided by an insurer, such as providing claim forms and processing claims, when the insurer is not the party funding the loss payments. See also Self Funded Plan.

Administrator. A person appointed by a court as a fiduciary to settle the financial affairs and the estate of a deceased person. Compare to Executor.

Admiralty Liability. All laws relating to liability resulting from any kind of maritime activity. This includes common law and statutory law, such as the Jones' Act and the Seamen's Remedies.

Admiralty Proceeding. A type of proceeding involving questions of maritime suit. Any insurance claims involving ocean marine insurance would generally be settled by an admiralty court.

Admissions/1,000. The number of hospital admissions for each 1,000 members of the health plan.

Admits. The number of admissions to a hospital (including outpatient and inpatient facilities).

Admitted (or Allowed) Assets. Assets whose values are permitted by state law to be included in the annual statement of the insurer.

Admitted Company. An insurance company authorized and licensed to do business in a given state.

Admitted Liability. Coverage for guests in an aircraft. In the event of an accident, with this coverage guests can recover without having to go through a determination as to whether or not the insured was liable. It is written with a limit per seat in the aircraft.

Adult Day Care. An optional group program for functionally impaired adults, designed to meet health, social and functional needs in a setting away from home. Available under LTC insurance.

Advance Funding. Periodically setting aside a predetermined sum of money to fund future retirement benefits of a pension plan.

Advance Payment. Premiums paid in advance of the current policy period, including the amount tendered with an application for life insurance.

Advance Premium. See Deposit Premium.

Adverse Selection. The tendency of poorer than average risks to buy and maintain insurance. Adverse selection occurs when insureds select only those coverages that are most likely to have losses.

Adverse Underwriting Decision. Any decision involving individually underwritten coverages resulting in termination of existing insurance, declination of an application or writing the coverage only at higher rates. For property and casualty insurance, it also includes placing the coverage with a residual market mechanism or unauthorized insurer.

Advertising Injury. Injury arising out of libel or slander, violation of the right to privacy, misappropriation of advertising ideas or infringement of copyright, title or slogan committed in the course of advertising goods, products or services. Contrast with Personal Injury.

Affiant. The person who executes an affidavit.

Affidavit. A written or printed declaration or statement of fact, made voluntarily and confirmed by the oath or affirmation of the party making it, and taken before an officer having authority to administer such oath.

Affiliated Companies. Insurers linked together through common stock ownership or through interlocking directorates.

Affirmed. When an appellate court declares that a judgment, decree or order is valid and right, and must stand as rendered in the lower court.

After Charge. A charge often included in fire rates for commercial buildings. It is usually added for conditions that can be corrected by an insured, such as failure to have the proper fire extinguishers.

Aftercare. Individualized patient services required after hospitalization or rehabilitation.

Age Change. The date on which a person's age, for insurance purposes, changes. In most life policies this is the date midway between the insured's natural birth dates. Health insurers frequently use the age of the previous birth date for rate determinations. On the date of age change, a person's age may change to that of the last birth date, the nearer birth date or the next birth date, depending upon the way in which the rating structure has been established by that particular insurer.

Age Limits. The ages below which or above which an insurer will not write certain forms of insurance or above which it will not continue a policy presently in force.

Age/Sex Factor. Compares the age and sex risk of medical costs of one group relative to another. An age/sex factor above 1.00 indicates higher than average risk of medical costs due to that factor. Conversely, a factor below 1.00 indicates a lower than average risk. This measurement is used in underwriting.

Age/Sex Rates (ASR). Separate rates are established for each grouping of age and sex categories. Preferred over single and family rating because the rates and premiums automatically reflect changes in age and sex content of the group. Also called table rates.

Agency Company. An insurance company that produces business through an agency network. Contrast with Direct Writer.

Agency Contract (or Agreement). A document that establishes the legal relationship between an agent and an insurer.

Agency Plant. The total force of agents representing an insurer.

Agency System. See Independent Agency System.

Agency. (1) An insurance sales office which is directed by a general agent, manager, independent agent or company manager. (2) When one person acts on behalf of another person, an agency is created with the first person being the agent and the second person being the principal. The principal generally can be held responsible for acts of its agents.

Agent. One who solicits, negotiates or effects contracts of insurance on behalf of an insurer. The agent's right to exercise various functions, authority and obligations, and the obligations of the insurer to the agent are subject to the agency contract with the insurer, to statutory law and to common law.

Agent's Appointment. Official authorization from an insurance company granting an agent the authority to act as its agent. In most states, agents must be appointed by at least one insurer in addition to being licensed by the state.

Agent's Authority. The authority and power granted to an agent by the agency contract. The agent also has additional power under the legal concept of apparent agency. See Presumption of Agency.

Agent's Balance. A periodic statement of the sums due and owed to an agent under contract.

Agent's Commission. What an insurance company pays its agents for placing insurance. Commission is usually a percentage of the premium for the policy. See also Commission.

Agent, General. See General Agent.

Agent, Independent. See Independent Agent.

Agent's License. A certificate of authority from the state which permits the agent to conduct business.

Agent, Policywriting. See Policywriting Agent.

Agent's Qualification Laws. Education, experience and other requirements imposed by the state upon persons desiring to be licensed as agents.

Agent, Recording. See Recording Agent.

Agent, Special. See Special Agent.

Agent, State. See State Agent.

Aggregate Excess of Loss Reinsurance. A form of excess of loss reinsurance that indemnifies the ceding company against the amount by which its losses incurred during a specific period, usually 12 months, exceed either: a predetermined dollar amount; or a percentage of the company's premiums (loss ratio) for that period. Commonly referred to as stop loss reinsurance or excess of loss ratio reinsurance.

Aggregate Funding Method. Accumulating money for a pension plan by actuarially determining the present value of all future benefit payments, deducting whatever funds may be on hand with the trustee or insurance company and distributing the balance as a cost over the future.

Aggregate Indemnity. A maximum dollar amount that may be collected by the claimant for any disability, for any period of disability or under the policy as a whole.

Aggregate Limit. Usually refers to liability insurance and indicates the amount of coverage that the insured has under the contract for a specific period of time, usually the contract period, no matter how many separate accidents may occur.

Aggregate Products Liability Limit. Indicates the amount of money that the insurer will pay during the term of a policy for all products liability claims that it covers.

Agreed Amount Clause. Under this clause, the insured and the insurer agree that the amount of insurance carried will automatically satisfy the co-insurance clause. This eliminates the necessity of determining whether or not the amount carried is equal to the stated percentage of the actual cash value indicated in the coinsurance clause.

Agreement. One element of a legal contract. When an offer made by one party has been accepted by the other, with mutual understanding by both, an agreement exists.

AIA. See American Insurance Association.

AIDS Related Complex (ARC). A variety of symptoms and opportunistic infections and conditions which frequently manifest themselves in patients suffering from AIDS, or acquired immunodeficiency syndrome, which is caused by the human immunodeficiency virus.

AIDS. See Acquired Immunodeficiency Syndrome.

Alcoholic Beverage Control Laws. See Dram Shop Laws.

Alcoholic Beverage Liability Insurance. See Dram Shop Liability Insurance.

Aleatory Contract. A contract in which the number of dollars to be given up by each party is not equal. Insurance contracts are of this type, as the policyholder pays a premium and may collect nothing from the insurer or may collect a great deal more than the amount of the premium if a loss occurs.

Alien Insurer. An insurer formed under the laws of a country other than the U.S. A U.S. company selling in other countries is also an alien insurer.

Alienated. Property to which an insured no longer owns or holds title. Generally, a public liability policy covers the insured's liability for premises alienated by him or her.

All or Nothing Rider. A rider to a health insurance policy that provides additional benefits in the event no benefits are payable under Social Security.

All Risk Insurance. Special coverage forms. See Open Peril. Contrast with Named Perils.

Alliance of American Insurers (AAI). An association of insurance companies working together in the following areas of common interest: 1) government affairs affecting insurance; 2) education of the employees of member companies; 3) loss prevention; and 4) other insurance activities.

Allied Health Personnel. Health personnel who perform duties which would otherwise have to be performed by physicians, optometrists, dentists, podiatrists, nurses and chiropractors. Also called paramedical personnel.

Allied Lines. Various insurance coverages for additional types of losses, and against loss by additional perils, which are closely associated with and usually sold with fire insurance. Includes coverage against loss by perils other than fire, coverage for sprinkler leakage damage and business interruption coverage. The fire insurance field consists of coverages for "fire and allied lines."

Allocated Benefits. Payments authorized for specific purposes with a maximum specified for each. In hospital policies, for instance, there may be scheduled benefits for X-rays, drugs, dressings, etc.

Allocated Funds. Qualified plan funds which are identified in the name of specific plan participants.

Allocation Formula. In a profit-sharing trust, the formula under which the employer's contributions are credited to the employees.

Allowable Charge. The lesser of the actual charge, the customary charge and the prevailing charge. It is the amount on which Medicare will base its Part B payment. The Medicare allowable amount is basically Medicare's version of reasonable and customary charges (e.g., if a doctor charges a Medicare patient $600 for certain services, Medicare may only approve a portion of the benefits.)

Allowable Costs. Charges which qualify as covered expenses.

Allowed Assets. See Admitted Assets.

Alternative Delivery Systems. Systems which cover health care costs, other than on the usual fee-for-service basis. Includes HMOs, IPAs, PPOs.

Alzheimer's Disease. A progressive, irreversible disease characterized by degeneration of the brain cells and severe loss of memory causing the individual to become dysfunctional and dependent upon others for basic living needs.

Ambiguity. Terms or words in an insurance policy which make the meaning unclear or which can be interpreted in more than one way. The general rule of law is that any ambiguity in the policy is construed against the insurer and in favor of the insured. This is because the contract is one of adhesion; that is, the insured must adhere to what the insurer has written. If the insurer does not make its contract clear, it is responsible.

Ambulatory Care. Outpatient treatment that does not require hospitalization.

Ambulatory Setting. Surgery centers, clinics or other outpatient facilities which provide health care on an outpatient basis.

Amendment. A formal document that corrects or revises an insurance master policy. See also Endorsement and Rider.

American Academy of Actuaries. A society concerned with the development of education and standards in the actuarial field. Members may use the designation MAAA (Member, American Academy of Actuaries).

American Agency System. See Independent Agency System.

American Association of Insurance Services (AAIS). An association of insurance companies performing various technical functions for its members and subscribers. Licensed to operate in all states, the District of Columbia and the Commonwealth of Puerto Rico, AAIS offers program services, files rates, rules and forms on behalf of member and subscriber companies, acts as an official statistical agent and offers a variety of professional services for its member companies.

American College. An educational institution within the life insurance business. It confers the Chartered Life Underwriter designation and is concerned with continuing agents' training and with research and publication in areas related to the life insurance business. It also sponsors specialty life insurance courses and offers a college degree in financial services. Formerly known as the American College of Life Underwriters (ACLU).

American Council of Life Insurance, Inc. An association made up of several previously independent insurance groups that is concerned with legislative matters, intercompany communications and the exchange of information.

American Experience Table of Mortality. A statement of expected mortality rates based upon data accumulated in 1868 from a large number of insured persons. Widely used by life insurers until the 1950s to establish rates.

American Institute for Chartered Property and Casualty Underwriters, Inc. An insurance educational organization that establishes insurance standards and fosters educational work. Properly qualified individuals who pass a series of examinations given by this body receive the designation Chartered Property and Casualty Underwriter (CPCU).

American Insurance Association (AIA). The informational, educational, technical and legislative organization of the capital stock insurance companies in the property and liability fields. See Capital Stock.

American Lloyd's. See Lloyd's Association.

American Risk and Insurance Association. An association of insurance educators and others interested in insurance study and research.

Amortization. A method of spreading a fixed sum, together with accumulating interest, over a period of years.

Amortized Value. The value of bonds purchased by an insurance company that are eligible for amortization. For example, if a 10-year bond were purchased at $50 more than its face value, that $50 would be "amortized" or spread over the 10-year period. Each year the bonds would be valued at $5 less than the year before.

Amount at Risk. The difference between the face amount of a whole life insurance contract and the cash value which it has built up. The net amount at risk declines throughout the life of the contract, while the policy reserve increases along with the cash value. It is the amount the insurer would have to draw from its own funds rather than the policy reserve were the contract to become a death claim.

Amount Subject. The maximum amount which underwriters estimate can possibly be lost under the most unfavorable circumstances in any given loss, such as a fire or tornado. Contrast with Probable Maximum Loss.

Ancillary Benefits. Benefits for miscellaneous hospital charges.

Ancillary. Additional services (other than room and board charges) such as x-rays, anesthesia, lab work, etc. Fees charged for ancillary care such as x-rays and lab work. This term may also be used to describe the charge made by a pharmacy for prescriptions which exceed the health insurance plan's maximum allowable cost (MAC).

Anniversary. See Policy Anniversary.

Annual (or Yearly) Renewable Term (ART). (1) term life insurance that may be renewed annually without evidence of insurability until a stated age. (2) A form of life, and sometimes health, reinsurance in which the reinsurer assumes only the mortality risk, which is usually calculated as the face amount of reinsurance minus the terminal reserve.

Annual Additions. The total of employer contributions, voluntary employee contributions and forfeited additions of terminated participants that equal the total annual contribution to a qualified retirement plan.

Annual Payment Annuity. An annuity which was purchased by the payment of annual premiums for a specified period of time.

Annual Report. The insurer's published statement to its stockholders (or policyholders in the case of a mutual insurance company), reviewing pertinent financial information about the year's activities.

Annual Return/Report (Form 5500). A required annual report reflecting the pension plan's operation for the year; to be submitted to the IRS and the DOL.

Annual Statement. A report to the state insurance department of the year's financial results. Reports insurer's income and expenses as well as its assets and liabilities.

Annuitant. The person who is covered by an annuity and who triggers payments of a policy. The owner of the contract may or may not be the annuitant, but the annuitant is usually the intended recipient of the annuity payments.

Annuity. (1) An amount of money payable yearly, or by extension, at other regular intervals. (2) An agreement by an insurer to make periodic payments that continue during the lifetime of the annuitant(s) or for a specified period. Protects against the risk of living too long. (Sometimes referred to as upside down life insurance. There are two principal types of annuities: fixed and variable.

Annuity Certain. An annuity that pays income for a fixed number of years regardless of whether the insured lives or dies. If it pays for life after the certain period, it is called an "annuity certain and for life thereafter."

Annuity Due. An annuity that pays benefits at the beginning of the benefit period rather than at the end.

Annuity Option. A method of liquidating and distributing an annuity's principal and interest so that it lasts for the lifetime of the annuitant.

Annuity Payment. See Endowment.

Annuity Period. The period of time, usually at retirement, when the annuitant begins to receive annuity payments or benefits.

Annuity with Period Certain. An annuity that pays throughout the life of the insured, but also guarantees to pay income for a specific number of years regardless of whether the insured lives or dies. If the insured is living at the end of the time specified in the policy, benefits continue beyond the guaranteed period until the death of the insured.

Answer. A statement made by the defendant and filed with a court to respond to a complaint or action brought against the defendant. It states why the defendant should not be held liable.

Anti-Coercion Law. A provision usually contained in a section of the state code entitled "Unfair Trade Practices" or a similar name, declaring the use of coercion an unfair practice and, hence, a violation of the state law.

Anti-Selection. See Adverse Selection.

Apartment Flat. A multi-story building subdivided into one-story units, with each unit usually having one owner. Residents share a common entrance. Commonly bought as a condominium or cooperative.

App. A trade expression for the insurance application. See Application.

Apparent Agency. See Presumption of Agency.

Apparent Authority. Authority of an agent that is created when the agent oversteps actual authority, and when inaction by the insurer does nothing to counter the public impression that such authority exists.

Appeal. The right of a party who has received an adverse decision to take the case to a higher court for review.

Appellant. The person appealing to the higher court.

Appellate. Refers to courts that hear appeals for review of decisions rendered by a lower court.

Appellee. The respondent, or the person against whom the appellant is making an appeal.

Application. A form on which the prospective insured states facts requested by the insurer on the basis of which, together with information from other sources, the insurer decides whether to accept the risk, modify the coverage offered or decline the risk. See App.

Appointment. See Agent's Appointment.

Apportionment. The method of dividing a loss among insurers in the same proportions as their participation when two or more companies cover the same loss.

Appraisal. An evaluation of property made to ascertain either the appropriate amount of insurance to write or the amount of loss to pay. If the parties involved disagree on the value of the property or the amount of loss, either may ask for an appraisal of the loss. In this event, each party selects a competent and impartial appraiser. The two appraisers select an umpire. If they cannot agree, selection may be made by a judge of a court having jurisdiction. The appraisers state separately the value of the property and amount of loss. If they fail to agree, they submit their differences to the umpire. A decision agreed to by any two is binding.

Approved. The condition which exists when the person or object to be insured meets the underwriting standards of the insurer.

Approved Charge. Amounts paid under Medicare as the maximum fee for a covered service.

Approved Health Care Facility or Program. A facility or program that is approved by a health care plan as described in the contract.

Approved Pension Plan. A pension plan qualifying for tax exemptions under provisions of the Internal Revenue Code.

Approved Roof. A term used in building construction that indicates a roof made of fire-resistive materials, such as tile or asphalt shingles.

Appurtenant Structures. Buildings on the same premises as the main building insured under a property insurance policy. Most dwelling policies cover appurtenant structures under most circumstances.

Arbitration. Negotiation by impartial persons when the insured and the insurance company cannot agree on settling a claim. Disagreement might concern whether an insured is legally entitled to recover damages or might concern the amount of recovery. Both parties must agree to arbitration. If so agreed, each party selects an arbitrator. The two arbitrators select a third. Each party pays the cost of its own arbitrator and splits the cost of the third arbitrator. If they cannot agree within 30 days, either may request that selection be made by a judge of a court having jurisdiction.

Arbitration Clause/Provision. The provision in a property insurance contract which states that if the insurer and insured cannot agree on an appropriate claim settlement, each will appoint an appraiser, and these will select a neutral umpire. A decision by any two of the three prescribes a settlement and binds both parties to it.

ARC. See AIDS Related Complex.

ARIA. See American Risk and Insurance Association.

ARM. See Associate in Risk Management.

Armstrong Investigation. A study authorized by the New York state legislature in 1905 which reviewed the operations and practices of life insurers operating in the state. Numerous changes in policy forms and investment practices came from the study and were eventually reflected in other state codes.

Arson. The willful and deliberate burning of property.

ASO. See Administrative Services Only.

Assailing Thieves. Those other than the crew using force or violence to steal a ship or its cargo. Such action is an insured peril under an Ocean Marine contract.

Assessed Value. The value of real estate or personal property as determined by a governmental unit, such as a city, for the purpose of determining taxes.

Assessment Company, Society or Insurer. An insurer who retains the right to assess policyholders additional amounts if premiums are insufficient for operations. In some cases, an assessment insurer may not charge a stipulated premium at all but will merely assess participants in the plan a pro rata share of each claim filed plus expenses.

Asset Share Value. The value of a book of business to an insurer, assuming that the business has been in force long enough to show true mortality rates. This value must be known by the insurer in order to make rates and to sell the business. If assets share values do not grow properly, either the rates have been too low or expenses too high.

Assets. The items on the balance sheet of the insurer which show the book value of property owned. Under state regulations, not all property or other resources can be admitted in the statement of the insurer. See also Nonadmitted Assets.

Assigned Risk. A risk that is not ordinarily acceptable to insurers and that is, therefore, assigned to insurers participating in an assigned risk pool or plan. Each participating company agrees to accept its share of these risks. Assigned-risk programs are most often associated with auto insurance, and apply to any state-run program that helps high-risk property owners find insurance. See Fair Access to Insurance Requirements.

Assigned Risk Plan. A cooperative enterprise that all insurance companies doing business in the state must join. The plan constructs a policy (again, usually expensive and limited) for people whose driving records or location disqualify them from standard coverage. It then forces the participating insurance companies to take a number of assigned risk policies.

Assignee. A person to whom policy rights are assigned in whole or in part by the original policyowner.

Assignment. (1) An authorization to pay Medicare benefits directly to the provider. Medicare payments may be assigned to participating providers only. (2) The transfer of the ownership rights of a life insurance policy from one person to another. Also refers to the document that effects the transfer. (3) Transfer by the policyowner of legal rights or interest in the policy contract to a third party. Most policies cannot be assigned without the permission of the insurer.

Assignment of Benefits. A method where the person receiving the medical benefits assigns the payment of those benefits to a physician or hospital.

Associate in Risk Management. A professional designation granted by the American Institute for Property and Casualty Underwriters to those who have completed a series of examinations.

Association. See Pool and Syndicate.

Association Group Coverage. Technically, group insurance issued to an association rather than to an employer or a union. If the association offers a guaranteed-issue plan, then there is no medical underwriting, as all members are guaranteed a policy. However, most association plans require some medical underwriting, or what is sometimes referred to as simplified or progressive underwriting.

Association of Life Insurance Counsel. An organization of life company attorneys that seeks to increase knowledge in areas of the law affecting life insurance.

Assume. To accept from another insurer all or part of the risk of an insured loss.

Assumed Interest Rate (AIR). An assumed value assigned to the annuitant's account during the annuity period. It is an estimated return for the separate account. Monthly annuity payments are based on the AIR in relation to the actual rate of return experienced by the separate account of a variable annuity.

Assumed Liability. See Contractual Liability.

Assumption Certificate. A statement of coverage by the reinsurer that guarantees payment to a party not in privity with the reinsurance contract. Same as cut-through clause.

Assumption. An amount accepted by the reinsurer.

Assumption of Risk. One of the common law defenses available to an individual. For instance, one person riding with another in a vehicle has generally "assumed the risk" and, therefore, has no action against the driver of the vehicle should an accident occur. This common law concept has been modified by recent case law and by statute in some jurisdictions.

Assurance. Same as Insurance.

Assured. Same as Insured.

Assurer. Same as Insurer.

Atomic Energy Reinsurance. See Mutual Atomic Energy Reinsurance Pool.

Attached Structures. The standard homeowners policy covers not only the house but also structures attached to it—such as an attached garage, breezeway, patio, etc. This coverage also extends to building materials and supplies used to expand the house, build a facility like a pool or make repairs to the existing structure. This material is covered in the event of a fire, etc.

Attachment. A court order allowing one person to take something of value belonging to another into custody for a particular purpose. For example: An insured accidentally drives his car into the wall of someone else's garage. The garage owner has the right to attach the insured's car (take it into custody) as a way of guaranteeing that the insured will pay for repairing the damage. An attachment ensures that something of value is available to settle the claim if the individual is held liable.

Attained Age. The age an insured has reached on a given date.

Attending Physician's Statement (APS). A source of medical information used when underwriting a life or health insurance policy; usually obtained from the proposed insured's doctor. This report provides detailed information about an insured's medical history or current physical condition.

Attested Will. A formal will that is produced (hand-written, typed, etc.), signed by the testator and witnessed.

Attorney-in-Fact. The individual who manages a reciprocal insurance exchange and to whom each subscriber gives authority to exchange insurance on the subscriber's behalf with other subscribers. See also Reciprocal Insurance Exchange.

Attractive Nuisance. The law states that an individual owes no duty of care to a trespasser upon that individual's property. However, the law states that a special duty of care is required of a person with respect to conditions that attract children. Attractive nuisances includes swimming pools, jungle gyms, etc.

Audit. A survey of the insured's payroll records to determine the premium that should be paid for the coverage furnished. Used in workers' compensation and general liability policies.

Audit Bureau. A central office or bureau to which agents and companies send certain daily reports and endorsements for auditing before transmittal to the insurer.

Authorization. The amount of insurance an underwriter agrees to accept on a risk of a given class on specific property. It is given for the guidance and information of agents.

Authorized Insurer. An insurer authorized by the state to transact business in that state for specific types of insurance.

Automatic Cover. Coverage given automatically by a policy, usually for a specified period and limited amount, to cover increasing values and newly acquired and changing interests.

Automatic Increase in Insurance Endorsement. See Inflation Guard Coverage.

Automatic Premium Loan. A provision in a life policy authorizing the insurer to use the loan value to pay any premiums still due at the end of the grace period.

Automatic Reinstatement Clause. A stipulation in a property insurance policy which states that after a partial loss covered by the policy has been paid, the original limit of the policy will be automatically reinstated. Same as Loss Clause.

Automatic Reinsurance. (1) This form of reinsurance, also known as treaty reinsurance, is one whereby an insurer must cede that portion of a risk that is above the limit established by contract, and the reinsurer must accept all risks ceded to it. (2) Reinsurance of specified types of risks which is automatically ceded and accepted within the terms of the contract, called a treaty, without consideration of each one individually. The reinsurance takes effect as soon as the original contract is in force. Same as Obligatory Reinsurance. Contrast with Facultative Reinsurance.

Automobile Fleet. Refers to a number of automobiles under the same ownership. For insurance purposes a fleet usually consists of five or more self-propelled units and generally qualifies for certain premium reductions and rating plans.

Automobile Insurance Plans. A name used to identify assigned risk plans. See Assigned Risk.

Automobile Insurance. Insurance that protects the insured against losses involving automobiles. Different coverages can be purchased depending on the needs and wants of the insured (e.g., the liability coverages of bodily injury liability, property damage liability and medical payments, and the physical damage coverages of collision and comprehensive).

Automobile Use Classifications. An insured's needs and the insurance company's risk analysis coincide in the question of how an insured uses his vehicles. The insurance company's primary rating factors include use classifications. These include "pleasure use," "business use," "farm use" and "driving to work." If a car is used only for pleasure (this is sometimes called occasional use), premiums are lower than if the car is driven every day to work. Cars claimed for business use tend to be more expensive to insure.

Average Adjuster. One whose primary work is the adjusting of ocean marine losses.

Average Benefit Test. A coverage or discrimination test for a qualified plan that states that at least 50 percent of the lower paid employees must benefit from the plan and the average benefit provided must be at least 70 percent of the benefit provided for the higher-paid employees.

Average Clause. A clause providing that similar items in one location or several locations that are insured by a policy shall be covered in the proportion that the value of each bears to the value of all. Also known as the average distribution clause. See also Pro Rata Distribution Clause.

Average Cost Per Claim. The total cost of administrative and/or medical services divided by the number of units of exposure such as costs divided by number of admissions or by number of outpatient claims, etc.

Average Earnings Clause. See Relation of Earning to Insurance Provision.

Average Indexed Monthly Earnings (AIME). A wage indexing formula based on earnings listed in the records of the Social Security Administration; used to compute Social Security benefits for retirement, survivors benefits and disability income benefits.

Average Length of Stay (ALOS). The total number of patient days divided by the number of admissions and discharges during a specified period of time. This gives the average number of days in the hospital for each person admitted.

Average Rate. A rate for a policy established by multiplying the rate for each location by the value at that location and dividing the sum of the results by the total value.

Average Weekly Wage. A term generally used in workers' compensation laws that is the basis for determining weekly benefits under such laws.

Aviation Accident Insurance. Insurance that protects individuals as passengers or pilots, usually on scheduled aircraft, or that covers the flight travel of the employees of a company under a master policy.

Aviation Hazard. The extra hazard of death or injury resulting from participation in aeronautics, usually as other than a fare-paying passenger in licensed aircraft. This generally requires an extra premium rating or waiver of certain benefits or coverage.

Aviation Insurance. Insurance that protects an insured against losses connected with the use of an airplane. Coverage depends upon the needs and desires of the insured and can include the liability coverages of bodily injury, property damage, passenger bodily injury and medical payments, as well as physical damage or hull coverage. Hull coverage can be written to provide either broad or limited coverage. Coverage can also be written for airports, aircraft dealers, airlines and hangarkeepers' liability.

Avocation Questionnaire. A form that an insured must fill out if he or she is engaged in a hazardous hobby. Provides more specific information concerning the hobby.

Avoidance of Risk. Taking steps to remove a hazard, engage in an alternative activity or otherwise end a specific exposure. One of the four major risk management techniques. See Risk Management.

B

Backdating. A procedure for making the effective date of a policy earlier than the application date. Often used to make the age at issue lower than it actually was in order to get a lower premium. State laws often limit (to six months) the time to which policies can be backdated.

Bad Faith. Lawsuits or regulatory complaints relating to delays or denials usually allege bad faith on the part of the insurer. This is one of the heaviest clubs a policyholder can wield to strike back at an insurance company. One way an insurance company can act in bad faith is by investigating a claim with an eye toward not providing coverage.

Bail Bond. A bond that guarantees that a person released from legal confinement will appear as required in court, or the penalty of the bond will be forfeited to the court. In insurance policies, bail bond fees are covered under an auto policy.

Bailee. A person or concern having possession of personal property entrusted to that person by the owner (e.g., a laundry that has custody of customers' clothing for washing or dry cleaning). Bailees must exercise the same care with the property of others as they would with their own property.

Bailees Customer Insurance. Insurance purchased by a bailee to protect the personal property of customers against loss caused by specific perils (e.g., a carpet cleaner who buys coverage to protect customers against loss or damage to their carpets while in the store's care.

Bailees Liability Coverage. Coverage that meets the needs of a bailee's liability. The bailee's legal responsibility is to exercise care appropriate to the circumstances of the bailment. (Most bailees want to carry enough insurance to make good any loss to property in their custody whether or not they are legally liable.)

Bailment. The personal property of one person being held by another with the intent of its being returned to the original owner (e.g., cars in a garage for repairs).

Bailor. A person who owns property that is entrusted to another (e.g., the owner of a fur coat who has entrusted it to a furrier for storage).

Balance Sheet. A listing of the assets, liabilities and surplus of a company or individual as of a specific date.

Bank Loan Plan. See Financed Insurance.

Bankers Blanket Bond. Insurance purchased by banks to pay for losses due to the dishonesty of employees as well as losses caused by people other than employees due to burglary, robbery, larceny, theft, forgery and mysterious disappearance.

Barratry. A fraudulent breach of duty on the part of a master of a ship causing loss to the owner of the ship or the owner of the cargo.

Base Capitation. The total amount which covers the cost of health care per person, minus any mental health or substance abuse services, pharmacy and administrative charges.

Base Premium. See Subject Premium.

Base Rate. The cost of a given unit of insurance for each specific type of auto coverage, such as bodily injury and property damage liability. For example, a base rate might be $300 for $100,000 of liability coverage. A driver with a poor driving record must be charged an increased amount to reflect the poor record. This increased amount is computed by multiplying the base rate by a rating factor. See also Rating Process.

Basic Auto Policy. Once used to insure commercial vehicles, motorcycles, motorscooters and a variety of substandard risks. This policy had broad eligibility rules, but the scope of coverage was narrower than modern auto policies. Most automobile risks today are insured by business or personal auto policies, with appropriate endorsements.

Basic Coverage Form. A commercial or personal lines property form that provides basic coverages. These forms generally provide the most limited coverage, which is surpassed by broad forms and special forms.

Basic Extended Reporting Period. An automatic "tail" for reporting claims after expiration of a "claims-made" liability policy. It is provided without charge and consists of two parts: a mini-tail covers claims made within 60 days after the end of the policy; a midi-tail covers claims made within five years after the end of the policy period arising out of occurrences reported not later than 60 days after the end of the policy. See also Tail.

Basic Form Rates. Under the latest commercial lines program, Basic Form Rates are arrived at by adding Group I and Group II rates together. See Group I Rates and Group II Rates.

Basic Hospital Expense Insurance. Hospital coverage providing benefits for room and board and miscellaneous hospital expenses for a specified number of days during hospital confinement.

Basic Limit. Usually refers to liability policies and indicates the lowest amount for which a policy can be written. This amount is either prescribed by law or company policy.

Basic Limits of Liability. Minimum amounts of insurance. This usually refers to bodily injury and property damage limits that are either the lowest amounts which can be written at the published or manual rates, the minimum amount of insurance an insurer is willing to underwrite or the minimum amount of insurance required by law (e.g., auto insurance financial responsibility laws).

Basic Medical Expense Insurance. Basic medical coverage for doctor visits, diagnostic x-rays, lab tests and emergency treatments. Usually written without deductibles and coinsurance provisions, but benefits are limited to specified dollar amounts. Contrast with Major Medical Insurance.

Basic Premium. A fixed cost charged in a retrospective rating plan. It is a percentage of the standard premium and gives the insurer the money needed for administrative expenses and the agent's commission plus an insurance charge. See also Retrospective Rating.

Basic Rate. The manual rate from which discounts are taken or to which charges are added to reflect the individual circumstances of a risk.

Bed Days/1,000. The number of inpatient hospital days per 1,000 members of a health plan.

Below Market Loan. A demand loan with interest paid below the federal rate; typically, part of an executive loan program provided by an employer.

Bench Error. A loss that occurs in the production process (e.g., if production workers mistakenly use the wrong ingredients in a chemical formula). Bench errors are covered by products insurance.

Beneficiary. A person who may become eligible to receive or is receiving benefits under an insurance policy other than a participant. There may be one or more designated beneficiaries, including primary beneficiaries who are entitled to the proceeds if they are living, and contingent beneficiaries who are entitled to the proceeds if there is no surviving primary beneficiary when an insured dies. See also Irrevocable Beneficiary, Revocable Beneficiary, Primary Beneficiary, Secondary Beneficiary and Contingent Beneficiary.

Benefit. The amount paid to a participant of a retirement plan or to the participant's beneficiary at retirement, death or termination of service.

Benefit, Flat Dollar. A monthly benefit given to all employees regardless of length of service or standard of living. (Everyone receives the same amount.)

Benefit, Flat Percentage. A monthly pension benefit determined by a fixed percentage of compensation. Although recognizing the employee's standard of living, it still ignores length of service.

Benefit Levels. The maximum amount a person is entitled to receive for a particular service or services under a contract with a health plan or insurer.

Benefits of Survivorship. See Survivorship Benefits.

Benefit Package. A description of the services an insurer or health plan offers to those covered under the terms of a health insurance contract.

Benefit Period (BP). The period during which a Medicare beneficiary is eligible for Part A benefits. A benefit period is 90 days and begins the day the patient is admitted to a hospital and ends when the individual has not been hospitalized for a period of 60 consecutive days.

Benefits. The financial reimbursement and other services provided to insureds by insurers under the terms of an insurance contract (e.g., the benefits listed under a life or health policy or benefits as prescribed by a workers' compensation law).

Benefit Stacking. Adding the uninsured motorists limits from insurance on several different cars to apply to a single claim.

Betterment. See Improvements and Betterments Insurance.

BI. (1) Bodily Injury Liability. (2) Business Interruption Insurance and Business Income Coverage Form. This is what these letters most often refer to in the property field.

Bid Bond. A bond filed with a bid for a construction or other project that guarantees that if the contractor has the low bid and is awarded the job, the required performance bond will be furnished.

Billed Claims. The amounts submitted by a health care provider for services provided to a covered individual.

Binder. An agreement executed by an agent or insurer (usually the latter) putting insurance into force before the contract is written or premium is paid. Not used in life insurance. See Cover Note.

Binding Receipt. See Conditional Binding Receipt.

Birth Rate. The number of births related to the total population in a given group during a period of time. (Usually expressed as births per 100,000 people in one year.)

Birthday Rule. A method of determining which parent's medical coverage is primary for dependent children: the parent whose birthday falls earliest in the year usually has the primary plan.

Blackout Period. The period of time during which a surviving spouse no longer receives survivors benefits (after the youngest child is no longer eligible) and before he or she is eligible for retirement benefits.

Blanket Bond. A fidelity bond that covers losses caused by the dishonesty of all employees as opposed to a bond that specifically identifies only certain employees to be covered. See also Blanket Position Bond and Commercial Blanket Bond, and contrast with Name Position Bond and Name Schedule Bond.

Blanket Contract. See Blanket Insurance.

Blanket Crime Policy. A policy that once provided a package of coverages for employee dishonesty, loss of money and securities inside and outside the premises, depositor's forgery, loss of money orders and loss due to counterfeit paper currency. It has been replaced by modern commercial crime coverage.

Blanket Fidelity Bond. See Blanket Bond.

Blanket Honesty Bond. See Commercial Blanket Bond.

Blanket Insurance. (1) Health insurance that covers all of a class of persons not individually identified in the contract. (2) Property insurance that covers, in a single contract, either multiple types of property at a single location or one or more types of property at multiple locations.

Blanket Medical Expense. A policy or provision in a health insurance contract that pays all medical costs, including hospitalization, drugs and treatments, without limitation on any item except possibly for a maximum aggregate benefit under the policy. It is often written with an initial deductible amount.

Blanket Position Bond. A Blanket Fidelity Bond where the amount of coverage applies separately to each position covered. Contrast with Commercial Blanket Bond (offers a single amount of coverage for any one loss, regardless of the number of employees involved). See also Blanket Bond.

Blasting and Explosion Exclusion. Exclusion of liability for damages from blasting or explosions. An additional rate is charged.

Block Policy. An open perils (all risk) policy that derives its name from the French term *en bloc* meaning "all together." It provides coverage on stock, property being transported or in bailment and on the premises of others.

Blowout and Cratering. Accidents that can arise from drilling operations. Generally includes damage to property above the surface of the earth arising out of blowout or cratering of any well. Usually added by endorsement for an additional premium.

Blue Cross. Blue Cross plans are hospital expense prepayment plans designed primarily to provide benefits for hospitalization coverage, with certain restrictions on the type of accommodations.

Blue Plan. A generic designation for those companies, usually writing a service rather than a reimbursement contract, who are authorized to use the designation Blue Cross or Blue Shield and the insignia of either.

Blue Shield. Blue Shield plans are prepayment plans offered by service organizations covering medical and surgical expenses.

Board Certified. A physician or other professional certified as a specialist in a particular medical area.

Board Eligible. A professional or physician who is eligible to become certified as a specialist.

Bobtailing. Using the truck/tractor after unloading the trailer and not driving for trucking purposes.

Bodily Injury. Coverage for bodily harm, sickness or disease. Includes the costs of required care, loss of services or death resulting from an injury.

Bodily Injury Liability (BI). A legal liability that may arise as a result of the injury or death of another person. This coverage pays the other person's medical and rehabilitation expenses and any damages for which they may sue.

Boiler and Machinery Coverage. Insurance against the sudden and accidental breakdown of boilers, machinery, and electrical equipment. Coverage is provided on: 1) damage to the equipment; 2) expediting expenses; 3) property damage to the property of others; 4) supplementary payments; and 5) additional objects. Coverage can be extended to cover consequential losses and loss from business interruption.

Bond. A three-party contract guaranteeing that if one person, the principal, fails to perform as specified or proves to be dishonest, the person to whom the duty is owed, the obligee, will be financially protected by the issuer of the bond, the surety.

Bond, Contract. See Contract Bond.

Bond, Court. See Court Bond.

Bond, Fidelity. See Fidelity Bond.

Bond, Fiduciary. See Fiduciary Bond.

Bond, Forgery. See Forgery Bond.

Bond, Maintenance. See Maintenance Bond.

Bond, Performance. See Contract Bond.

Bond, Permit. See Permit Bond.

Bond, Public Official. See Public Official Bond.

Bond, Surety. See Suretyship.

Book of Business. A total of all insurance accounts written by a company or agent, including: an insurer's book of automobile business; an agent's overall book of business; an agent's book of business with each insurer; etc.

Book Value. The value of assets as shown in the official accounting records of the company.

Bordereau. (1) A written report of individual cessions, usually detailed to show such items as reinsurance premiums or reinsurance losses with respect to specific risks. (2) A memorandum containing information concerning documents that accompany it. Used extensively in passing reinsurance from one insurer to another under a reinsurance agreement and by property and liability general agents for passing information to various insurers on coverages written.

Borderline Risk. An insurance prospect of doubtful quality from an underwriting point of view.

Boston Plan. A plan where insurers agree that they will not reject property coverage on residential buildings in a slum area. Insurers agree to accept the coverage until there has been an inspection and the owner has had an opportunity to correct any faults. Boston was the first city to originate such a plan. Other cities have followed, including New York, Oakland, Cleveland and Buffalo.

Bottomry. A contract of insurance by which a ship or its cargo is pledged as collateral for a loan required to support a maritime venture. If the ship or cargo is lost, the loan is canceled and the borrower would not have to repay the loan.

Boycott. A trade practice that occurs when someone refuses to have business dealings with another until he or she complies with certain conditions or concessions.

Branch Manager. An executive who manages a branch office for an insurer or an agency. See also Regional Office.

Branch Office. See Regional Office.

Breach of the Duty to Act. When a tortfeasor does not act in a reasonably prudent manner toward another. See Negligence.

Brick Construction. A building with at least 75 percent of the exterior walls made of some type of masonry construction (e.g., brick, stone or hollow masonry tile, poured concrete or reinforced concrete, or hollow masonry block).

Brick Veneer Construction. A building with outside walls constructed of wood and a facing of a single layer of brick.

Brief. A statement—prepared by an attorney to be filed with a court—that highlights the principal issues of a case.

Broad Form. Policies that provide insurance for multiple types of perils over and above the usual basic perils, or additional coverages beyond standard coverages.

Broad Form Nuclear Energy Liability Exclusion Endorsement. A form attached to every general liability coverage part that excludes coverage for any loss resulting from the hazardous properties of nuclear material related to the operations of a nuclear facility.

Broad Form Personal Theft Policy. Theft coverage on personal property at private residences, usually on an open perils (all risk) basis. A limited form of the Broad Form Personal Theft policy is known as the Personal Theft policy.

Broad Form Property Damage Endorsement. An endorsement to a general liability policy that deletes the exclusion referring to property in the care, custody or control of the insured and replaces it with a less restrictive exclusion.

Broad Form Storekeepers Insurance. Coverage for small storekeepers that includes several specific crime perils on the same basis as a storekeepers burglary and robbery policy, plus open perils (all risk) protection on money and securities, depositors' forgery and a small limit on employee dishonesty. See Storekeepers Burglary and Robbery Insurance.

Broad Theft Coverage Endorsement. A form attached to a dwelling policy that provides theft coverage for a named insured who is an owner occupant. Provides coverage for loss by theft, including attempted theft, and vandalism and malicious mischief as a result of theft or attempted theft.

Broker. One who represents an insured in the solicitation, negotiation or procurement of contracts of insurance, and who may render services incidental to those functions. A broker may also be an agent of the insurer for certain purposes such as delivery of the policy or collection of the premium.

Brokerage. (1) The fee or commission received by a broker. (2) Insurance placed by brokers contrasted with that placed by agents.

Broker of Record. A broker who has been designated to handle certain insurance contracts for the policyholder.

Brokerage Business. Business offered to an insurer by a broker. Also called excess or surplus business.

Brokerage Department. A department of an insurer whose purpose is to deal with brokers in the placing of insurance.

Broker-Agent. One acting as an agent of one or more insurers and as a broker in dealing with one or more other insurers.

Builder's Risk Coverage Form. A commercial property coverage form specifically designed for buildings in the course of construction.

Building Additions and Alterations. Coverage for improvements to a rental property (apartment or house) that have not been reimbursed by the landlord. Falls under renters insurance. Also called leasehold improvement insurance.

Building and Personal Property Coverage Form. A commercial property coverage form designed to insure most types of commercial property (buildings, contents or both). It is the most frequently used commercial property form, and has replaced the General Property form, Special Building form, Special Personal Property form and others.

Building Code. Municipal or other governmental ordinances regulating the type of construction of buildings within its jurisdiction.

Building Code Upgrade Coverage. Also known as ordinance or law coverage, provides up to

$10,000 of coverage for the additional costs required to bring a damaged dwelling up to current building code requirements. Without this coverage, a policy would pay only the amount needed to repair or replace the damaged dwelling to restore it to the condition it was in prior to the loss, and would not cover any additional costs due to changes required by current building codes.

Bullion. Refers to precious metals, such as gold, in the form of ingots or bars.

Bumbershoot Policy. A liability policy (similar to the umbrella policy) that includes coverage related to ocean marine risks. Includes general liability coverage, protection and indemnity, as well as liability coverage under the Longshoremen's and Harbor Workers' Act. Collision coverage can be provided and general average and salvage charges can be included. Provides coverage for shipyards.

Bureau, Rating. See Rating Bureau.

Burglary. Breaking and entering into the premises of another with felonious intent. Visible marks or damage at the point of entry or exit are needed to confirm the burglary.

Burglary Insurance. Insurance against loss caused by burglars. In personal lines, burglary insurance is provided by homeowners policies and theft endorsements that are added to dwelling policies. In commercial lines, a variety of commercial crime coverage forms include burglary insurance.

Burning Cost Ratio. See Pure Loss Cost Ratio.

Burning Ratio. The ratio of losses suffered to the amount of insurance in effect.

Business. (1) Any trade, profession or occupation. (2) In property, liability and health lines, it usually refers to the volume of premiums. (3) The face amount of life insurance written.

Business Activities. Any agreement, contract, transaction or other interaction that advances a person's occupation. See Business Liability.

Business Auto Coverage Form. The latest commercial automobile insurance coverage form, which may be written as a monoline policy or as part of a commercial package. This form has largely replaced the business auto policy.

Business Auto Policy. A policy that provides liability and physical damage coverages on commercial vehicles. In most jurisdictions, this has been replaced by the business auto coverage form.

Business Income Coverage Form. A commercial property form providing coverage for "indirect losses" resulting from property damage, such as loss of business income and extra expenses incurred. (Replaced earlier business interruption and extra expense forms.)

Business Insurance. (1) Insurance for businesses or commercial establishments. (2) Life and health policies written for business purposes, such as key employee, sole proprietorship, partnership and corporation.

Business Interruption Insurance. A time element coverage that pays for loss of earnings when operations are curtailed or suspended because of property loss due to an insured peril. Now referred to as business income insurance. See Business Income Coverage Form.

Business Interruption Insurance, Contingent. Coverage for business income from dependent properties. See Business Income Coverage Form and Dependent Properties.

Business Liability. Liability coverages provided by the businessowners liability coverage form. It includes liability for bodily injury, property damage, personal injury, advertising injury and fire damage.

Business Overhead Expense (BOE) Policy. A disability income policy which indemnifies the business (not the businessowner) for certain overhead expenses incurred when the businessowner is totally disabled. Often has an elimination period of 30 to 90 days and a benefit period of one or two years.

Business Personal Property. Traditionally known as contents, this includes furniture, fixtures, equipment, machinery, merchandise, materials and any other personal property owned by the insured and used in the insured's business.

Business Risk Exclusion. Also known as the (product) failure to perform exclusion. In products insurance, no coverage is provided for a product that does not meet the level of performance, quality, fitness or durability warranted or represented by the insured.

Coverage is provided, however, if liability results from a bench error or an active malfunction.

Businessowner Policies (BOP). A package policy that provides broad property and liability coverage in a single contract and is designed for small and medium-sized mercantile, office or apartment risks.

"Buy-Back" Deductible. A deductible that may be eliminated for an additional premium in order to provide "first-dollar" coverage—coverage that doesn't have a deductible.

Buyers Guide. A consumer publication that describes the type of coverage offered, and provides general information to help an applicant for life or health insurance compare different policies to reach a decision about whether the proposed coverage is appropriate. Also called a shoppers guide.

Buy-Sell Agreement. (1) An agreement among part owners of a business that says that under stated conditions (i.e., disability or death), the person withdrawing from the business or the person's heirs are legally obligated to sell their interest to the remaining part-owners, and the remaining part-owners are legally obligated to buy at a price fixed in the agreement; (2) a similar agreement between an owner or part-owner of a business and a nonowner, such as a key employee.

Bypass Trust. Also referred to as the B trust; a trust which contains estate assets that will bypass the surviving spouse and pass directly to other family members.

C

Cafeteria Plans. An employee benefit that provides a series of flexible health care benefits from which an employee may choose, including a cash only option. ☤

Calendar Year. January 1 through December 31 of the same year. Many deductible amount provisions are on a calendar year basis under major medical plans. Also, benefits under basic hospital surgical and medical plans are usually stated as so much for each calendar year. ☤

Calendar Year Experience. Measures the premiums and losses entered on accounting records during the 12-month calendar. 🏢

Cancelable. A contract of insurance that may be terminated by the insurer or insured at any time. Practically every form of insurance is cancelable, except life insurance and those health insurance policies designated as a "guaranteed renewable" or "noncancelable and guaranteed renewable." Some states also regulate when, or if, auto policies can be canceled. See Renewability. 🏢

Cancelation. Termination of a contract of insurance by voluntary act of the insurer or insured in accordance with the provisions in the contract or by mutual agreement. In most states, the reasons for which an insurance company is permitted to cancel a policy are limited—if the policy has been in effect for at least 60 days or is a renewal policy. 🏢

Cancelation Changes Endorsement. An endorsement that must be attached to every commercial property coverage part, unless it is in conflict with state law or is replaced by a special state endorsement that affects the cancelation clause of the common policy conditions.

Cancelation, Flat. See Flat Cancelation.

Cancelation, Pro Rata. See Pro Rata Cancelation.

Cancelation, Short-Rate. See Short Rate Cancelation.

Capacity. The largest amount of insurance or reinsurance available from a company. In a broader sense, it refers to the largest amount of insurance or reinsurance available in the marketplace.

Capital Stock Insurer. See Stock Insurer.

Capital Stock. The shares of ownership in a corporation.

Capital Sum. The maximum lump sum payable in the event of accidental death or dismemberment. See Principal Sum.

Capital Transaction. The sale of a capital asset, such as stock, which results in the transaction being taxed as ordinary income and not as a dividend.

Capitation (CAP). A rate paid, usually monthly, to a health care provider. In return, the provider agrees to deliver the health services agreed upon to any covered person.

Captive Agent. One who sells insurance for only one company as opposed to one who represents several. See also Exclusive Agency System.

Captive Insurer. A legally recognized insurance company organized and owned by a corporation or firm whose purpose is to use the captive to write its own insurance at rates lower than those of other insurers. Usually, it is a nonadmitted insurer that has the right, under special circumstances, to reinsure with an admitted insurer.

Care, Custody and Control. Most liability insurance policies exclude coverage for damage to property in the care, custody or control of the insured. In some cases this type of coverage can be purchased through certain forms of inland marine insurance, like installation floaters, and in other cases this exclusion can be made less restrictive by adding a broad form property damage endorsement.

Cargo Insurance. A policy covering cargo transported by a carrier.

Carpenter Cover. See Spread Loss Reinsurance.

Carrier Replacement. This refers to a situation where one carrier replaces one or more carriers.

Carrier. (1) Sometimes refers to the insurer. The term "insurer" is preferred because of the possible confusion of "carrier" with transportation. (2) Usually a commercial insurer contracted by the Department of Health and Human Services to process Medicare Part B claims payments. See also Insurer.

Carryover Provision. In major medical policies, allowing an insured who has submitted no claims during the year to apply any medical expenses incurred in the last three months of the year toward the new calendar year's deductible.

CAS. See Casualty Actuarial Society.

Case Management. The assessment of a person's long-term care needs and the appropriate recommendations for care, monitoring and follow-up as to the extent and quality of services to be provided.

Case Manager. A person, usually an experienced professional, who coordinates the services necessary under the case management approach.

Case Mix. The number of cases requiring different needs and uses of hospital resources.

Cash Flow Plans. Premium payment schemes that allow an insured to retain a large part of the premium and pay it out over a time period such as a year.

Cash Flow Underwriting. The use of rating and premium collection techniques by insurance companies to maximize interest earnings on premiums.

Cash Refund Annuity. An annuity contract which provides that if at the death of the annuitant installments paid out have not totaled the amount of the premium paid for the annuity, the difference will be paid to a designated beneficiary in a lump sum.

Cash Surrender Value. The amount of cash due an insured who surrenders cash value life insurance. Such surrender, with consequent termination of all insurance benefits, is often called "cashing out" or "cashing in" a policy. See Nonforfeiture Values.

Cash Value. (1) See Actual Cash Value. (2) See Cash Surrender Value.

Casualty Actuarial Society (CAS). A professional society for actuaries in areas of insurance work other than life insurance. This society grants the designation of Associate and Fellow of the Casualty Actuarial Society (ACAS and FCAS).

Casualty Insurance. Insurance that is primarily concerned with the legal liability for losses caused by injury to persons or damage to the property of others. Includes such diverse forms as plate glass insurance, crime insurance, boiler and machinery insurance and aviation insurance. Many casualty insurers also write surety bonds. Casualty insurers write forms of insurance not considered property forms. Contrast with Property Insurance.

Catastrophe Hazard/Loss. The hazard of large loss by reason of occurrence of a peril to which a very large number of insureds are subject (e.g., widespread loss due to a hurricane or tornado).

Catastrophe Models. Models used by insurance companies as a basis to estimate homeowner losses. (The models were originally developed by Applied Insurance Research (AIR) of Boston.)

Catastrophe Policy. An older name for major medical. See Major Medical.

Catastrophe Reinsurance. Excess of loss reinsurance which, subject to a specified limit, indemnifies the ceding company against an amount of loss in excess of a specified amount as the result of an accumulation of losses resulting from a catastrophic event or a series of catastrophic events.

Caused Accidents. An incident in which an innocent victim is made an unwitting participant in an actual accident to obtain insurance money, such as a sideswiping (law enforcement people call this scam swoop and squat").

Causes of Loss. Under the latest commercial property, inland marine and crime coverage forms, this term replaces the earlier term "perils" insured against.

Causes of Loss Forms. Commercial property forms stating the perils insured against, additional coverages provided, and exclusions that apply. There are four causes of loss forms—basic, broad, special and earthquake.

Caveat Emptor. Let the buyer beware.

CCRCs. See Continuing Care Retirement Communities (CCRCs).

Cease and Desist Order. An order of the state Insurance Commissioner or of a court requiring that a company/person stop engaging in a particular act or practice, usually involving insurance trade practices.

Cede. (1) The act of buying reinsurance. (2) To transfer to a reinsurer all or part of the insurance or reinsurance written by a ceding company.

Ceding Company. An insurer that cedes all or part of the insurance or reinsurance it has written to another insurer. A company that has placed reinsurance, distinguished from the company that accepts it.

Certificate. See Certificate of Insurance or Participation.

Certificate of Authority (COA). (1) A certificate issued by the state that licenses the operation of an HMO (Health Maintenance Organization). (2) A certificate showing the powers that an insurer grants to its agents. (3) A certificate issued by a state department of insurance showing the power of an insurer to write contracts of insurance in that state.

Certificate of Convenience. A temporary license or permit empowering a person to act as an agent even though not fully licensed according to the law. Usually this certificate is granted to an agent who is studying for a licensing examination. It may also be issued to the administrator or executor of the estate of an insurance agent, who must have the authority of an agent to settle the estate, or to someone acting for an agent during a disability or an absence such as military duty.

Certificate of Insurance. (1) A statement of the coverage and general provisions of a master contract in group insurance that is issued to individuals covered in the group. (2) A form that verifies that a policy has been written and states the coverage in general, often used as proof of insurance in loan transactions and for other legal requirements.

Certificate of Need (CON). A certificate issued by a governmental body, certifying that the proposed facility will meet the needs of those for whom it is intended. May include constructing a new health facility, offering a new or different health service or acquiring new medical equipment.

Certificate of Reinsurance. A short-form documentation of a reinsurance transaction.

Certiorari. A writ issued by a higher court to a lower court asking the lower court to forward the record of a particular case in question.

Cession. The unit of insurance transferred to a reinsurer by a ceding company. It also refers to the process of ceding insurance to a reinsurer.

Cestui Que Vie. The person whose life measures the duration of a trust, gift, estate or insurance contract. In life and health insurance it is the person on whose life or health the policy is written (e.g., the insured, policyholder or policyowner).

CGL. See Commercial General Liability Coverage Part.

Change Endorsement. When adding an endorsement after a policy is in effect, in most cases a change endorsement must be issued. The endorsement lists the policy number and effective date of the change, and acts something like a cover letter, by providing information about an endorsement.

Change of Beneficiary. A mandatory provision that says the policyholder (usually the insured) has the right to name or change a beneficiary. Since a disability income policy may include an accidental death benefit, this provision is relevant—whether the policy comes from a health insurance company or a life insurance company. The only time when this is not the case is if the beneficiary was designated as an irrevocable beneficiary.

Change of Occupation Provision. (1) A provision in a health insurance policy that allows the insurer to adjust policy benefits if the insured has changed to a more hazardous occupation. (2) A provision that provides a method for handling disability income claims if the insured has changed occupations since the initial application. This provision allows the insurer to adjust benefits or premiums to reflect the change in occupation. If this provision is not in the policy, then no changes can be made.

Chapter 7. Also called liquidation, this is the most common type of bankruptcy proceeding. It involves the appointment of a trustee who collects the non-exempt property of the debtor, sells it and then distributes the proceeds to the creditors.

Charter. (1) To rent or lease a ship or boat. (2) Usually the same as articles of incorporation. This is the grant of rights from a state or federal government, such as the right to incorporate and transact business.

Chartered Life Underwriter (CLU). A designation granted by the American College of Life Underwriters upon successful completion of a series of examinations. This is a popular professional designation among people who sell life insurance.

Chartered Property and Casualty Underwriter (CPCU). A designation granted by the American Institute of Property and Casualty Underwriters upon successful completion of a series of examinations.

Chattel. Personal property items.

Chattel Mortgage. A mortgage where the collateral is personal property, rather than land or buildings.

Chemical Dependency Services. The services required in the treatment and diagnosis of chemical dependency, alcoholism and drug dependency.

Chemical Equivalents. Drugs that contain identical amounts of the same ingredients.

Christian Science Organization. A religious organization that is certified by the First Church of Christian Scientists. The organization may also be Medicare-certified as a hospital or skilled nursing facility.

Churning. An illegal practice where insurance agents unnecessarily replace existing life insurance for the purpose of earning additional (higher) first year commissions.

Civil Commotion. An uprising of a large number of people, usually resulting in damage to property. Generally describes one of the extended coverage perils in the extended coverage endorsement.

Civilian Health and Medical Program of the Uniformed Services (CHAMPUS). Part of the Uniformed Services Health Benefits Program that supplements medical care available for families of active, deceased and retired military personnel.

Claim. A demand made by the insured, or the insured's beneficiary, for payment of the benefits provided by the contract.

Claim Expense. The expense of adjusting a claim, such as investigation and attorneys' fees. It does not include the cost of the claim itself. Other expenses incurred by the company, such as witness fees and any trial costs assessed against the insured are also covered.

Claim Report. A report filed by an agent setting forth the facts of a claim. Same as loss report.

Claim Representative. See Adjuster.

Claimant. The person making a demand for payment of benefits.

Claims Payment Provision. A provision that identifies to whom benefits will be paid. This, of course, is the insured person, or loss payee. It is possible that policy benefits may be paid to a third party, such as a doctor or hospital, if the insured person executes a proper assignment form.

Claims Reserve. Amounts set aside to meet costs of claims incurred but not yet finally settled (e.g., a workers' compensation case where benefits are payable for several years. At any given point in time, the reserve would be the funds kept based on the estimate of what the claim will cost when finally settled).

Claims Tail. Claims that take place after the end of a policy period create an exposure known as a claims tail. Coverage is automatically built into the insuring agreements of occurrence forms.

Claims-Made Coverage. A policy providing liability coverage only if a written claim is made during the policy period or any applicable extended reporting period. For example, a claim made in the current year could be charged against the current policy even if the injury or loss occurred many years in the past. If the policy has a retroactive date, an occurrence prior to that date is not covered. Contrast with Occurrence Coverage.

Class (or Classification). A group of insureds having the same general characteristics who are grouped together for rating purposes. Class rates apply to dwellings and apartments, since they usually have the same general characteristics and are exposed to the same perils.

Class Action Suit. A legal device allowing a group of individuals with a claim against a company or an individual to join together as plaintiffs in a single suit.

Class Rate. A rate for risks of similar hazard. Class rates, for example, apply to dwellings.

Classified Insurance. Life or health insurance on risks which do not meet the standards for the regular manual rate. See also Substandard.

Clause. A section of a policy contract or endorsement dealing with a particular subject (e.g., a subrogation clause deals with the rights of the insurer in the event of payment of a loss under the contract).

Cleanup Fund. Policies whose express purpose is to pay final expenses of death.

Clear Space Clause. A clause requiring that insured property, such as stacks of lumber, be stored at some particular distance from each other or from other property.

Clerical Error. A provision in a group health insurance policy that provides if there is an error or omission in the administration of a group policy, the coverage is considered to be what it would be if there had been no error or omission.

Close Corporation. A corporate form of business controled and operated by a small, close group of persons such as family members. The corporation's stock is not sold to outsiders.

Closed Panel. A situation where covered insureds must select one primary care physician—the only one allowed to refer the patient to other health care providers within the plan. Also called closed access or gatekeeper model.

CLU. See Chartered Life Underwriter.

Cluster or Patio Homes. A group of houses similar in every way to single-family homes, except that the residents share ownership and maintenance of the land in the development—often a golf course or other recreation facility.

COB. Coordination of Benefits. See Nonduplication of Benefits.

COBRA. See Consolidated Omnibus Budget Reconciliation Act of 1986.

Codicil. A change or amendment to a will.

Coding. A method of putting information into a numerical form for statistical use. Most information on policies is coded and then put into reports.

Coercion. An unfair trade practice that occurs when someone in the insurance business applies a physical or mental force to persuade another to transact insurance.

Cognitive Impairment. A deficiency in the ability to think, perceive, reason or remember resulting in loss of the ability to take care of one's daily living needs.

Coinsurance Clause. (1) A provision stating that the insured and the insurer will share all losses covered by the policy in a proportion agreed upon in advance. See also Percentage Participation. (2) A clause under which the insured shares in losses to the extent that he or she is underinsured at the time of loss. The insurer grants a reduced rate to the insured providing the insured carries insurance 80, 90 or 100 percent to value. If, at the time of loss, the insured carries less coverage than required, the loss must be shared. For example, if an insured has a building worth $100,000 and carries an 80 percent coinsurance clause, it means that the insured agrees to carry at least $80,000 of insurance. If the insurance carried is just $60,000, then any loss under the policy would be paid for on the basis of the comparison of $60,000 (amount carried) divided by $80,000 (amount agreed upon in advance) times the amount of the loss. Thus, in the event of a $10,000 loss the insured would only receive 75 percent of a loss or $7,500.

Cold Lead Advertising. An illegal method of marketing insurance policies (often associated with Medicare supplement policies) that fails to disclose in a conspicuous manner the solicitation of insurance or other similar coverage, and that further contact will be made by an insurance agent, other producer or insurer.

Collapse. Literally, to cave in or give way. Several court decisions have interpreted collapse as the "loss of structural integrity." See Blasting and Explosion Exclusion.

Collateral Assignment. Assignment of a life insurance policy or its value as security for a loan. In the event of default, the creditor would receive proceeds or values only to the extent of the creditor's interest.

Collateral Source. A rule allowing a plaintiff to recover damages even if the plaintiff has already recovered damages from a source other than the defendant.

Collateral Split Dollar. A split dollar plan in which the employee controls the policy and pledges it as collateral for a series of employer loans to pay the premiums.

Collection Book. The debit agent's record book showing the amount collected on each policy, the week of the collection and the policy period for which the premium has been paid.

Collection Commission. A percentage of premiums collected that is paid to an agent as the commission on collections of debit life insurance premiums.

Collection Fee. An industrial life insurance agent's fee. Serves as compensation for making policy premium collections for which no commission is paid.

College Retirement Equities Fund (CREF). An organization affiliated with the Teachers Insurance Annuity Association that sells a variable annuity to college and university personnel.

Collegia. Groups of associations in ancient Rome that were influential historically in the development of life insurance and pensions. (The forerunners of mutual benefit societies or friendly societies.)

Collision, Convertible. See Convertible Collision Insurance.

Collision Damage Waiver (CDW). A waiver offered by rental companies (also called loss damage waiver) that releases an insured from responsibility for damage to the rental car, provided the insured complies with the rental contract terms. CDW often duplicates coverage an insured already has.

Collision Insurance. Auto insurance that covers loss (direct or accidental) to the insured's own vehicle caused by its collision with another vehicle or object or its upset. It does not cover bodily injury or property damage liability arising out of the collision.

Collusion. An agreement, usually secret, between two or more persons to defraud or deprive another or others of their property or rights.

Combination Annuity. A contract that combines both the guarantees of a fixed annuity and the non-guarantees and investment risk of a variable annuity.

Combination Business Interruption Extra Expense Insurance. A policy with both business interruption and extra expense coverages in a single contract. See Business Income Coverage Form.

Combination. An agent, agency or insurer that sells both industrial life and ordinary life policies.

Combination Crime Coverage Plan. Under the latest commercial lines program, two combination crime coverage plans are available. When written with a separate limits option, any combination of a variety of coverages may be included at different limits (coverage is similar to the earlier comprehensive dishonesty, disappearance and destruction (3-D) policy). When written with a single limit, major coverages are mandatory, optional coverages may be included, but one limit applies to all coverages purchased (coverage is similar to the earlier blanket crime policy).

Combination Plan. The combining of life insurance contracts with a fund called a side fund or auxiliary fund in order to increase the amount of money available for a pension or annuity at some future date.

Combination Plan Reinsurance. Combined reinsurance that provides that in consideration of a premium, which is a fixed percentage of the ceding company's subject premium on the business covered, the reinsurer will indemnify the ceding company for the amount of loss of each risk in excess of a specified retention and subject to a specified limit and, after deducting the excess recoveries on each risk, the reinsurer will indemnify the ceding company against a fixed quota share percent of all remaining losses.

Combination Policy. A policy made up of the contracts of two or more insurers in which each provides a different kind of insurance. Once used in auto insurance when state law limited casualty companies to the writing of liability insurance and fire insurance companies to physical damage insurance, combination policies are rarely written today.

Combined Annuity Mortality Table. A mortality table published in 1928 for use in determining rates for group annuities.

Combined Ratio. The sum of an expense ratio and a loss ratio. An underwriting profit occurs when the combined ratio is under 100 percent and an underwriting loss occurs when the combined ratio is over 100 percent.

Combined Single Limit (CSL). The maximum amount that the insurance company must pay for all damages arising out of a single accident. The

CSL is a single limit of protection for both bodily injury and/or property damage, contrasted with split limits, where specific limits apply to bodily injury and property damage separately.

Commercial Blanket Bond. A bond that covers the insured against the dishonesty of all regular employees. A single amount of coverage applies to any one loss, regardless of the number of employees involved in the loss. See also Blanket Bond, and contrast with Blanket Position Bond.

Commercial Carrier Regulations. Special regulations that apply to commercial carriers of both passengers and cargo because of the risk of common carrier accidents. State and federal laws have created minimum financial responsibility requirements for commercial carriers that may be met by purchasing insurance or obtaining a surety bond guaranteeing payment in amounts which at least equal the minimum limits. In some cases, full or partial self-insurance is permitted, if the carrier provides the necessary financial data to demonstrate the ability to fully or partially self-insure.

Commercial General Liability (CGL) Policy. General liability coverage that is written as a monoline policy or as part of a commercial package. The latest forms include all sublines, provide very broad coverage, and two variations are available—occurrence or claims-made coverage.

Commercial Lines. Insurance for businesses, professionals and commercial establishments. See also Business Insurance. Contrast with Personal Lines.

Commercial Package Policy (CPP). A commercial lines policy that contains more than one of the following coverage parts: commercial property, commercial general liability, commercial inland marine, commercial crime, boiler and machinery insurance, commercial auto insurance and farm coverage. In the late 1980s, ISO introduced a modular approach for constructing commercial property insurance policies. Instead of just updating old policies, ISO developed a series of specialized forms, with each form fulfilling a specific policy function. The right combination of forms would create a complete, custom-made policy.

Commercial Policy. Policies that do not guarantee renewability.

Commercial Property Coverage. Property coverage that is written as a monoline policy or part of a commercial package.

Commingling. An illegal practice that occurs when an agent mixes personal funds with the insured's or insurer's funds.

Commission. (1) An allowance made by the reinsurer to the original insurer for part of the original insurer's acquisition and other costs. It may also include a profit factor. (2) That portion of the premium paid to the agent as compensation for services. See also First Year Commission, Renewal Commission, Level Commission System, Unlevel Commission System, Contingent Commission and Graded Commission.

Commission of Authority. A document outlining the powers delegated to an agent by an insurer.

Commissioner of Insurance. The head of most state insurance departments. In some states, the title Director or Superintendent of Insurance is used.

Commissioners' Disability Table. A morbidity table approved by the National Association of Insurance Commissioners for use in setting legal minimums for disability income insurance policy reserves.

Commissioners' Industrial Extended Term Mortality Table. An industrial mortality table approved by the NAIC for evaluation and computation of extended term insurance in industrial policies, where additional mortality margins are deemed necessary. This is a companion table to the CSI.

Commissioners' Standard Industrial Mortality Table. An industrial mortality table approved by the NAIC as a standard for evaluation and for computation of nonforfeiture values for Industrial policies.

Commissioners' Standard Ordinary (CSO) A mortality table approved by the NAIC as a standard for evaluation and for computation of nonforfeiture values for ordinary life policies.

Commissioners' Values. An annual list of securities published by the NAIC. The values are to be used in recording security values on insurance company balance sheets.

Common Accident. An accident in which two or more persons are injured.

Common Carrier. An individual or organization that offers its services to the public for carrying persons or property from one place to another for payment. A common carrier cannot refuse to carry goods for one customer as opposed to another.

Common Disaster. A situation in which an insured and the beneficiary appear to die simultaneously with no clear evidence of who died first.

Common Disaster Clause. A clause sometimes added to a life insurance policy that provides a means for the insurer to distribute the proceeds of the policy in the event of a common disaster.

Common Law. The unwritten law developed primarily from judicial case decisions based on custom and precedent. It was developed in England and constitutes the basis for the legal systems of most of the states in the U.S.

Common Law Defenses. Pleas that can defeat an injured worker's suit for injuries against the employer in the absence of a workers' compensation law or employers liability legislation. The three defenses are contributory negligence, assumption of risk and fellow servant rule.

Common Law Liability. Responsibility based on common law for injury or damage to another's person or property that rests on an individual because of the person's actions or negligence. This is opposed to liability based on statutory law.

Common Policy Conditions. Under the latest commercial lines program, a form including six common conditions that apply to all coverage parts attached to a commercial policy.

Common Policy Declarations. A declaration page that is part of every commercial policy. It shows information applicable to the entire policy (policy number, insurer, insured, total premium, forms attached, etc.). Each individual coverage part may also have its own declarations page.

Common Stock. A security that provides an ownership or equity position in a company. Shareholders may receive dividends if declared by the board of directors.

Community Property. Common or statutory law that holds that husband and wife are each entitled to half of the total earnings and property of both parties to the marriage. It is applicable in Arizona, California, Idaho, Louisiana, Nevada, New Mexico, Texas and Washington state.

Community Rating. Under this rating system, the charge for insurance to all insureds depends on the medical and hospital costs in the community or area to be covered. Individual characteristics of the insureds are not considered at all.

Commutation. The exchange of one thing for another. In insurance it is usually the exchange of installment benefits for a lump sum.

Commutation Clause. A clause that provides for estimation, payment and complete discharge of all future obligations for reinsurance loss or losses incurred, regardless of the continuing nature of certain losses. Often found in Lloyd's treaties.

Commutation Rights. The right of a beneficiary to receive in one sum the unpaid payments remaining under an installment option that was selected for the settlement of the proceeds or values of a life insurance policy.

Commute. To determine as of a given date the single sum that is the equivalent of a series of sums due at various future dates, with allowances for interest that would have been earned on the unpaid portion of the series of payments.

Commuted Value. The amount of a single sum payment as determined under the definition of commute.

Comparative Negligence. In some states the negligence of both parties to an accident is established in proportion to the degree of their contribution to the accident. Several states have comparative negligence laws, and each one varies somewhat from the others. This is in contrast to contributory negligence, which is a general common law rule. See Contributory Negligence.

Compensation Related Loan. A below market loan between an employer and employee.

Compensatory Damages. Compensation for the loss incurred. These may include specific damages (the documentable, actual expenses incurred by the injured party, such as medical bills, wages lost and property replacement), and general damages (monetary awards for more subjective, less quantifiable aspects of the loss, such as pain and suffering or loss of consortium). However, this does not include punitive damages.

Competency. One of the elements that must be present in order to have a legal contract. It relates to the fitness or ability of either of the parties to the contract. See also Incompetent.

Competitive Medical Plan (CMP). Refers to permission given by the federal government that allows an organization to write a Medicare risk contract.

Competitive State Fund. A fund established by a state to write workers' compensation insurance in competition with private insurers.

Completed Operations Insurance. Insurance issued particularly to various types of contractors. It covers a contractor's liability for accidents arising out of jobs or operations that have been completed. See Products and Completed Operations Insurance.

Completion Bond. A bond issued to a mortgagee. It guarantees that the construction for which the mortgagor has borrowed money will be completed and serve as collateral for the mortgage upon completion.

Composite Rate. (1) One rate for all members of the group regardless of their status as single or members of a family. (2) A single rate with a single basis of premium, e.g., payroll or sales. For this single rate the insured is covered for a variety of hazards, such as premises and operations, completed operations, products liability and automobile. Its primary value is to make it simpler for the policy's premium to be computed. (AU

Composition Roof. A roof of either asbestos or asphalt shingles. Often used in connection with construction factors used in determining the rate for property insurance.

Comprehensive or Blanket Coverage. The traditional name for physical damage coverage for losses by fire, theft, vandalism, falling objects and various other perils. Personal auto policies now call this "other than collision" coverage. Commercial forms continue to call it "comprehensive" coverage.

Comprehensive General Liability. A policy covering a variety of general liability exposures, including premises and operations (OL&T or M&C), completed operations, products liability and owners and contractors protective. Contractual liability and broad form coverages may be added. In most jurisdictions, the comprehensive general liability policy has been replaced by the newer commercial general liability (CGL) forms. See also Commercial General Liability.

Comprehensive Glass Insurance Policy. Protection against loss by breakage of glass from almost any peril. Fire is usually excluded (it is covered under any basic property policy), and war is excluded. This policy has largely been replaced by a new commercial form. See Glass Coverage Form.

Comprehensive Major Medical. A plan of insurance with a low deductible, high maximum benefits and a coinsurance feature. It is a combination of basic coverage and major medical coverage which has virtually replaced separate hospital, surgical and medical policies with each having its own deductible requirements. Also see Major Medical Insurance.

Comprehensive Personal Liability. Protects individuals and families from liability for nearly all types of accidents caused by them in their personal lives as opposed to business lives. Most commonly provided by a homeowners policy.

Comprehensive Policy. In automobile and liability insurance, this is an open perils (all risk) coverage with certain named exclusions.

Comprehensive "3-D" Policy. See Dishonesty, Disappearance and Destruction Policy.

Compromise and Release Agreement. A settlement practice where an injured worker agrees to a compromised liability amount (usually a lump sum) in exchange for releasing the employer from further liability.

Compulsory Insurance. Any form of insurance required by law. For example, some states have compulsory automobile insurance laws, some have compulsory disability benefits laws, etc.

Computation Base Years. The total of the computation elapsed years less the five lowest earnings years for Social Security tax purposes.

Computation Elapsed Years. The total number of years since 1950 or attainment of age 21, if later, up to age 62, during which Social Security taxes have been paid.

Computer Fraud. Fraudulent theft or transfer of money, securities or other property resulting from the use of any computerized equipment or systems.

Computer Fraud Coverage Form. A commercial crime coverage form that protects against loss of money, securities and property other than money and securities resulting from computer fraud.

Concealment. The failure to disclose a material fact. See Material Fact.

Concurrent Causation. Two or more perils acting concurrently (at the same time or in sequence) to cause a loss.

Concurrent Insurance. Two or more policies with the same conditions and coverages that cover the same interest in the same property. If an insured has two or more property policies, the policies should be concurrent (similar) or the property will not be insured properly in the event of a loss.

Concurrent Review. A case management technique that allows insurers to monitor an insured's hospital stay and to know in advance if there are any changes in the expected period of confinement and the planned release date.

Conditional Binding Receipt. A binding receipt that provides that if a premium accompanies an application, the coverage will be in force from the date of application or medical examination, if any, whichever is later, provided the insurer would have issued the coverage on the basis of the facts revealed on the application, medical examination and other usual sources of underwriting information. A life and health insurance policy without a conditional binding receipt is not effective until it is delivered to the insured and the premium is paid.

Conditional Sales Floater. A policy that covers property that has been sold on an installment or conditional sales basis. It covers the interest of the seller.

Conditional Vesting. A form of vesting in a contributory pension plan where entitlement to a vested benefit is conditional upon nonwithdrawal of the participant's contribution. See also Vesting.

Conditionally Renewable. A contract that provides that the insured may renew it to a stated date or an advanced age, subject to the right of the insurer to decline renewal only under conditions stated in the contract.

Conditions. Provisions of an insurance policy that state either the rights and duties of the insured or the rights and duties of the insurer. Typical conditions have to do with such things as duties in the event of loss, cancelation provisions and the right of the insurer to inspect the property.

Condominium. Townhouses, manor homes or—most often—apartment flats.

Condominium Association Coverage Form. A commercial property form that covers the joint insurance needs of members of a condo association who collectively own commercial property.

Condominium Unit Owners Coverage Form. A commercial property form designed to cover the individual needs of commercial (not residential) condominium unit-owners.

Confining. A form of disability or sickness that confines the insured indoors, usually at home or in a hospital. Many policies state that coverage is afforded only if the insured is confined.

Consent Order. A disciplinary action in which the party at fault (usually an insurance company or agent) agrees to discontinue a particular practice (usually an unfair trade or claims practice) through a written agreement with the Insurance Department. Consent orders (also known as consent decrees) may or may not involve a fine.

Consequential Loss (or Damage). (1) An indirect loss arising out of the policyholder's inability to use the property over a period of time, as opposed to a direct loss that happens almost instantaneously. Business interruption, extra expense, rents insurance and leasehold interest are the most common coverages under this category of loss. (2) A loss not directly caused by a peril insured against, such as spoilage of frozen foods caused by fire damage to refrigeration equipment. See also Indirect Loss, and contrast with Direct Loss.

Conservation. The insurance company's efforts to prevent current policies from lapsing.

Conservator. Someone appointed to manage an insurer deemed by law or court action to be in danger of failure.

Consideration. For a contract to be binding each party to the contract must give what is known as consideration or the exchange of values on which a contract is based. In an insurance contract, the insured person makes a premium payment (consideration now) and promises to comply with the provisions of the policy (consideration future). In return, the insurance company promises to pay in accordance with the terms of the contract.

Consignee. The person to whom materials or goods are delivered for resale. The consignee pays the owner after the goods have been sold.

Consolidated Omnibus Budget Reconciliation Act (COBRA) of 1986. Legislation providing for a continuation of group health benefits under the group plan for a period of time when benefits would otherwise terminate. Continuation rights apply to enrolled persons and their dependents in companies with 20 or more employees. Coverage may be continued for up to 18 months if the insured terminates employment or is no longer eligible. Coverage may be continued for up to 36 months in nearly all other cases, such as loss of dependent eligibility because of death of the enrolled person, divorce or attainment of the limiting age.

Consortium. Companionship of a spouse. If a spouse is injured through the fault of another, part of the damages could include the value of the spouse's services or companionship that was lost due to the accident.

Conspiracy. A combination of two or more persons that by concerted action seek to accomplish an unlawful purpose or to accomplish a lawful purpose by unlawful means.

Construction Bond. A bond that protects the owner of a building or other structure under construction if the contractor cannot complete the job. If the contractor defaults, the insurer is obligated to see that the work is completed.

Constructive Delivery. Intentionally relinquishing control over a policy and turning it over to someone acting for the policyowner, such as when an insurer mails the policy to its own agent for delivery to the insured. Legally, an insurance policy is considered delivered when mailed or turned over to the policyowner or someone acting on his or her behalf.

Constructive Performance. A situation in which an act has not actually been completed but conduct has gone so far as to show intent to complete the act.

Constructive Total Loss. A partial loss of sufficient degree to make the cost of repairing the damaged property more than the property is worth (e.g., an old automobile might suffer damage that can be repaired, but the cost of repairs would be more than the actual cash value of the car).

Consumer Credit Insurance Association (CCIA). A trade association for insurers of credit insurance in the areas of life and health.

Consumer Protection Act. A law that protects a policyholder from the misconduct, misrepresentation or "sharp" trade practices of insurers, brokers and agents.

Consumer Report. A report ordered on an insured or applicant under which information about the person's credit, character, reputation, personal characteristics or lifestyle is obtained primarily through institutional sources.

Contents. (1) In relation to car theft, it is the contents of a vehicle or personal effects.

Contents Coverage. Coverage for business personal property. Includes more than building contents because it applies to property located in or on the described building, or within 100 feet of the described premises while in a vehicle or out in the open.

Contents Rate. The fire insurance rate on the contents of a building rather than on the building itself.

Contestable Clause. A provision in a policy setting forth the conditions under which or the period of time during which the insurer may contest or void the policy. After that time has lapsed, normally two years, a policy cannot be contested.

Contingency Reserve. A reserve in an insurer's annual statement, in addition to the legal requirements, to provide for unexpected contingencies or losses.

Contingency Surplus. See Contingency Reserve.

Contingent Annuitant. A person(s) named to receive annuity benefits if the primary annuitant is deceased at the time benefits become payable.

Contingent Annuity. An annuity in which payment of benefits is contingent upon the occurrence of an uncertain event, such as death of a person not an annuitant (e.g., an annuity purchased to pay benefits to a wife if her husband dies.)

Contingent Beneficiary. The person(s) entitled to receive policy benefits if the primary beneficiary is deceased when the benefits become payable.

Contingent Business Interruption Insurance. Coverage for the loss of earnings of an insured because of a loss to a business that is a major supplier or customer. Also known as business income from dependent properties. See Business Income Coverage Form and Dependent Properties.

Contingent (or Profit) Commission. An allowance payable to the ceding insurer, in addition to the normal ceding commission, based on the net profit derived from a reinsurance treaty.

Contingent Fund. A reserve to cover possible liabilities resulting from an unusual happening.

Contingent Interest. An interest in personal property that is dependent upon a future event.

Contingent Liability. A liability imposed due to accidents caused by persons other than employees for whose acts an individual, partnership or corporation may be responsible. For example, an insured who hires an independent contractor can, in some cases, be held liable for negligence.

Contingent Trust. A revocable living trust that only becomes operational upon a specified occurrence or contingency.

Contingent Vesting. In pensions, a form of vesting where entitlement to a vested interest is conditional upon circumstances surrounding the employee's termination of service or conduct after termination. See also Vesting.

Continuation. Allows terminated employees to continue group health insurance coverage under certain conditions.

Continuing Care Retirement Communities (CCRCs). Residential communities that provide residents with easy access to health care.

Continuing Education Requirement. State-level requirement that insurance licensees periodically complete a minimum number of hours of insurance-related education to be eligible for license renewal.

Continuous Premium Whole Life Policy. A whole life policy that stretches the premium payments over the insured's lifetime (to age 100). Also known as straight life. Compare with Limited Payment Whole Life and Single Premium Whole Life.

Contract. (1) An agreement entered into by two or more persons under which one or more of them agree, for a consideration, to do or refrain from doing acts in accordance with the wishes of the other party(s). (2) In insurance, the agreement by which an insurer agrees, for a consideration, to provide benefits, reimburse losses or provide services for an insured. (3) An agreement under which an agency or agent does business with an insurer.

Contract Bond. A guarantee of the faithful performance of a construction contract and the payment of all relevant material and labor bills. See also Performance Bond and Payment Bond.

Contract Carrier. A transportation company that carries, for payment, the goods of certain customers only, as contrasted with a common carrier who carries goods for the public in general.

Contract of Adhesion. A contract that one party must accept or reject *in toto*, without bargaining over the wording. An insurance contract, for example, is developed by the insurer, and the insured must accept it as it is.

Contract of Insurance. A contract under which an insurer agrees to indemnify an insured for losses, provide other benefits or render services to or on behalf of the insured. It is often called an insurance policy, but the policy is merely evidence of the agreement.

Contractual (or Assumed) Liability Insurance. Protects the insured in the event of a loss for which the insured has assumed liability, express or implied, under a written contract. For example, under most construction agreements with a municipality, the contractor agrees to "hold the municipality harmless" for any accidents arising out of the job. Contractual liability insurance would thus protect the contractor from any loss for which the municipality would be liable in connection with the construction.

Contract Year. The period of time from the effective date to the expiration date of the contract.

Contributing Location. A location upon which the insured depends as a source of materials or services. One type of dependent properties for which business income coverage may be written.

Contribution. (1) The share of a loss payable by an insurer when contracts with two or more insurers cover the same loss. See also Apportionment. (2) The insurer's share of a loss under a coinsurance or similar provision. (3) The amount of the premium for group insurance or a pension plan paid by the employee.

Contribution Clause. See Coinsurance Clause. Both are similar in effect, but contribution clause is identified mostly with business interruption forms.

Contribution Formula. As used under a qualified profit-sharing trust or money-purchase plan, the formula that spells out when and in what amounts the employer will make contributions to the trust.

Contributory. An plan of employee coverage in which the employee pays at least a potion of the premium.

Contributory Negligence. If an injured party fails to exercise proper care and in some way contributes to his or her injury, the doctrine of contributory negligence will probably negate or defeat the claim, even though the other party is also negligent. Contrast with Comparative Negligence.

Contributory Retirement Plan. A plan in which the participant pays part of the cost of purchasing the annuity or building up the fund from which benefits are paid.

Control. Authority given to an agent or broker by a policyowner to place the insurance where the agent or broker sees it.

Control Provision. A policy provision found most frequently in juvenile contracts, providing that ownership control is to be exercised for a stated or indefinite duration by a person other than the one whose life is insured.

Controled Business. The amount of insurance countersigned, issued or sold by a producer covering the life, property or interests of that producer, members of the producer's immediate family or the producer's employer or employees. Many states limit the amount of controled business that may be written, and if the premium or commissions on controled business exceed a given percentage (usually 50 percent) of all business, the producer's license may be suspended, revoked or not renewed.

Controled Insurance. (1) An insurance account that an agent or broker controls by influencing the buyer, as contrasted with controling it by actual agreement. See Control and Control Provision.

Convention (or Statement) Blank. The uniform annual financial statement required by all U.S. insurance jurisdictions as prescribed by the NAIC. It must be filed annually in an insurer's home state and every state in which it is licensed to do business. Nearly all insurance accounting practices are geared to it.

Convention Values. Values assigned to insurers' assets in the convention blank.

Conversion. (1) Wrongful use of property by one in lawful possession of it. (2) Change of one policy form to another, usually without evidence of insurability. Usually refers to life or health insurance contracts.

Conversion Fund (Supplemental). A fund used with ordinary life or limited payment life insurance to augment the cash value at retirement to provide monthly retirement income.

Conversion Privilege. The right of an individual to convert a group health or life policy to an individual policy should the individual cease to be a member of the group.

Convertible. A policy that may be changed to another form by contractual provision and without evidence of insurability. Most term policies convert to permanent insurance.

Convertible Collision Insurance. Automobile collision insurance with a deductible that, after claims exceeding the deductible have been paid, converts to full coverage for all losses thereafter.

Cooperative. Ownership in the form of a corporation. Owners buy a share of stock in the corporation, which gives them the privilege of occupancy. Cooperatives can be more restrictive on who moves in. Taxes are paid on the building rather than on each unit.

Cooperative Insurance. Insurance issued by a mutual association such as a fraternal society, an employee association, an industrial association or a trade union.

Coordination of Benefits (COB). A group policy provision that helps determine the primary carrier in situations where an insured is covered by more than one policy. This provision prevents an insured from receiving claims overpayments. See Non-duplication of Benefits.

Copay. An arrangement where the covered person pays a specified amount for various services and the health care provider pays the remainder. The covered person usually must pay his or her share when the service is rendered. Similar to coinsurance, except that coinsurance is usually a percentage of certain charges where the copayment is a dollar amount.

Copayment(s). See Copay.

Copay Provision. Often used with major medical policies. This provision states what percentage of a claim the company will pay and what percentage the insured will pay (e.g., an 80 percent copay provision would provide that the insurer pay 80 percent of claims and the insured pay 20 percent).

Corridor. In universal life insurance, it is necessary to maintain a certain level of pure insurance protection in excess of the accumulation value in order to qualify as life insurance for income tax purposes. This portion of the pure insurance protection is a corridor.

Corridor Deductible. A major medical provision that provides for a deductible, or "corridor," that applies after full payment of basic hospital and medical expenses up to a stated amount, and before additional expenses are shared on a coinsurance basis. For example, a policy might pay 100 percent of the first $2,000 of expenses, followed by a $500 corridor deductible paid by the insured, followed by a sharing of additional expenses on the basis of 80 percent payable by the insurer and 20 percent payable by the insured.

Cosmetic Procedures. Procedures that improve appearance, but are not medically necessary.

Cost Basis. Money that has already been taxed; used in reference to taxation of investment dollars.

Cost Contract. An agreement between a provider and the Health Care Financing Administration to provide health services to covered persons based on reasonable costs for service.

Cost of Insurance. The amount a policyowner pays to an insurer, minus what he or she gets back from the insurer. This expression is used when determining the true cost of permanent forms of life insurance to a policyowner. It considers the fact that premiums are paid in but also that an actual cash value is being built up, which is the portion that the insured will get back from the insurance.

Cost of Insurance Charge. Another term for the charge for the pure insurance protection element of a life insurance contract. See Mortality Charge.

Cost of Living Benefit. An optional disability benefit where the monthly benefit is increased annually after the insured is on claim for 12 months.

Cost-of-Living Rider. Adjusts policy benefits in relation to the change in the economic climate. The majority of such riders are tied to changes in the Consumer Price Index (CPI).

Cost Sharing. A situation where covered persons pay a portion of the health costs such as deductibles, coinsurance or copayment amounts.

Co-Surety. One of a group of sureties directly participating in a bond with obligations joint and several.

Countersignature Law. Refers to state laws requiring that any insurance contract in a state be countersigned by a representative of the insurer located in that state.

Countersignature. The signature of a licensed agent or representative on a policy.

Countrywide Rates. For each major division of the commercial lines manual, a section called "countrywide rates" contains rates and minimum premiums. State rates are used for coverages for which there are no countrywide rates, or to modify countrywide rates.

Countrywide Rules. For each major division of the Commercial Lines Manual, a section called "Countrywide Rules" contains rules and rating factors applicable to coverages in that division.

Coupon Policy. A life insurance policy, usually 20-pay life or some other limited payment period, with attached coupons that may be cashed in for a specified amount at the time of the payment of each annual premium.

Court Bond. Any bond required of a litigant to enable him or her to pursue a remedy in court.

Cover. (1) A contract of insurance. (2) To effect insurance, that is, to "cover" an insured, for instance, for automobile insurance effective as of a given time. (3) To include within the coverage of a contract of insurance. For example, one could "cover" additional buildings under a property insurance contract.

Cover Note. Similar to a binder, but binders are usually issued by companies and delivered to agents. A cover note is usually written by an agent, and it informs the insured that coverage is in effect. See also Binder. In reinsurance, a cover note is a statement issued by an intermediary or broker indicating that coverage has been effected.

Coverage. The scope of protection provided by an insurance policy. The policy spells out many agreements, but perhaps most important, it specifies the type of losses that will be reimbursed by the insurance company.

Coverage Part. Any one of the individual commercial coverage parts that may be attached to a commercial policy. Under the latest commercial lines program, a coverage part may be issued as a monoline policy or may be combined with others as part of a package policy.

Coverage Trigger. A mechanism that determines whether a policy covers a particular claim for loss. For example, the difference between the coverage triggers of liability "occurrence" forms and "claims made" forms is that loss must occur during the policy period in the first case and the claim must be made during the policy period in the second case.

Covered Expenses. Health care expenses incurred by an insured or covered person that qualify for reimbursement under the terms of a policy contract.

Covered Loss. Illness, injury, death, property loss, legal liability, or any other situation or loss that is covered under a policy.

Covered Person. An insured person under a contract of insurance.

CPCU. See Chartered Property and Casualty Underwriter.

Crash Coverage. Optional coverage under an aviation policy that provides coverage for damage to an airplane caused by a crash, and is usually referred to as Hull coverage or physical damage coverage.

Crash Involvement Rate. The rate of accidents per million vehicle miles traveled. This rate is based on various age groups.

Credentialing. Approving a provider based on certain criteria to provide or participate in a health plan.

Credit Card Forgery Insurance. Protects the insured against losses caused by forgery in the use of credit cards or the alteration of them or of any other written instruments connected with them.

Credit Carried Forward. The transfer of credit or profit from one accounting period to another under a spread loss or other form of long-term reinsurance.

Credit Carryover. Each year an employer is allowed to contribute 15 percent of payroll towards a profit-sharing plan and deduct it from taxable income. If the contribution is less than 15 percent in a particular year, the unused percentage can be made up in succeeding years. However, deductible contributions are limited to a total amount not greater than 25 percent of the participants' payroll: 15 percent for the current year's contribution plus 10 percent for credit carryover.

Credit Health Insurance. A group disability income insurance contract whereby a creditor is protected in the event of the total disability of a debtor. The policy pays benefits equal to the monthly installment of the debtor.

Credit Insurance. Insurance on a debtor in favor of a creditor to pay off the balance due on a loan in the event of the death or disability of the debtor. Liability insurance for abnormal loss from bad debts. The coverage is limited to the total amount of indebtedness.

Credit Life Insurance. A group life insurance contract whereby a creditor is protected in the event of death of the insured prior to the indebtedness being paid in full.

Credit Report. A confidential report made by an independent individual or organization that has investigated the reputation and record of an applicant for insurance. See Consumer Report.

Creditor. The person to whom a debt is owed. See also Debtor.

CREF. See College Retirement Equities Fund.

Crime. A public wrong, a violation of criminal law. See also Tort.

Criticism. A correction suggested by a rating or auditing bureau to an insurer.

Cromie Rule. A method or guide used to apportion losses under policies which are nonconcurrent, that is, not identical as to coverage provided.

Crop Insurance. Protection against damage to growing crops by such perils as hail, windstorm and fire. Traditionally, crop-hail coverage was the most common coverage sold. In recent years, premiums for broad multi-peril crop insurance (MPCI) have exceeded those for crop-hail business.

Cross Purchase. Business life insurance where each party to a mutual agreement (usually to buy out a disabled or deceased co-owner) insures each of the other parties.

Cross Purchase Agreement. A binding buy-sell agreement usually used with a partnership where each partner agrees to purchase the business interest of a deceased or disabled partner.

Crude Death (or Mortality) Rate. The ratio of total deaths to total population during any given period. See also Mortality Rate.

Crummey Privilege. The annual withdrawal privilege offered by a trust to trust beneficiaries in order for the trust property to remain qualified for the gift tax exclusion.

CSI 1961. See Commissioner's Standard Industrial Mortality Table, 1961.

CSO. See Commissioners' Standard Ordinary.

Cumulative Liability. (1) The liability of a surety bonding company for the accumulation of loss under its own bond and under a bond that it replaced before a loss under the replaced bond was discovered. (2) The accumulation of the liability of a reinsurer that has been assumed under several policies from several ceding companies covering different lines of insurance, all of which are involved in a common event or disaster.

Current Disbursement. The funding and disbursement of pension benefits as they become due. Also known as "pay-as-you-go." In the long run, this is the most costly method of funding pension plans.

Current Future Service. The amount of pension payable for each year of future participation in the pension plan.

Current Guarantee. A guaranteed interest that reflects current interest rates and is guaranteed at the beginning of each calendar year. The policy also has a minimum guaranteed interest rate (3 or 4 percent) that is paid even if the current rate falls below the policy's guaranteed rate.

Current Ratio. The ratio of current assets to current liabilities. Bond underwriters like this ratio to be 2 to 1 on the balance sheets of contractors for whom they are considering contract bonds.

Current Service Benefit. The portion of a participant's pension benefit that relates to credited service in a contemporary period, usually 12 months.

Current Service Cost. The cost in a pension plan to make provision for annuity credits earned by employees in the current year.

Current Value. The fair market value of a security or other property as determined by the trustees or a named beneficiary, according to the terms of the plan.

Currently Insured Status. A provision of old age, survivors, disability and health insurance. The requirements for being "currently insured" are less than those for being "fully insured," and the former entitles a worker's dependents to survivor benefits in the event of the worker's death. See Fully Insured.

Custodial Care. Care that is provided for the purpose of meeting personal needs, such as walking, bathing, dressing, eating and other essential activities of daily living. Also known as personal care. It may be administered by licensed practical nurses, by non-medical personal, such as volunteer workers, therapists and, in some cases, other family members. The most common type of long-term care, it can be provided in a variety of settings—ranging from a nursing home to the patient's own home. See also Activities of Daily Living.

Custodian. Under commercial crime insurance coverages, the named insured or any of the insured's partners or employees while having care and custody of insured property inside the insured's premises, but it does not include any person while acting as a watchperson or a janitor.

Custom House Bonds. Bonds required by U.S. customs in connection with the payment of duties or the production of bills of lading.

Customary Charge. Used to determine Medicare benefit amounts, the average fee charged for a particular medical service in the geographical area in the preceding year. See also Allowable Charge and Prevailing Charge.

Cut Rate. A term used when insurance companies charge premiums below a normal or average rate.

Cut-Off. The termination provision of a reinsurance contract stating that the reinsurer shall not be liable for loss as a result of occurrences taking place after the date of termination.

Cut-Through Clause. See Assumption Certificate.

D

D&B. See Dun and Bradstreet, Inc.

DA. See Deposit Administration.

Daily Reports (DR). (1) An abbreviated statement of pertinent policy information with copies for the insurer, the agent and others. It is usually the top page of a policy. (2) Monthly reports compiled on the last day of each month must show actual values at the end of each day during the month.

Damages. The amount required to pay for a loss. When someone is held liable for injury or property damage to another, that person must compensate the injured parties. See also Compensatory Damages and Punitive Damages.

Damage to Property of Others. Damage caused by an insured person to the property of others.

Damage to Your Auto Coverage. Physical damage coverage provided under an auto policy. The insurance company will "pay for direct and accidental loss to a covered auto, or any non-owned auto, including its equipment, minus any applicable deductible." Includes collision and other than collision coverage.

Data Processing Coverage. Protection for loss due to the breakdown of data processing system, including coverage for the additional expense of putting the system back into operation.

Date of Issue. The date (stated in a policy) as the date the contract was issued by the insurer. This is not necessarily the effective date of the policy.

Date of Service. The date that the health service was provided.

DBL. See Disability Benefits Law.

Death Benefit. The amount stated in a policy as payable upon the death of the person whose life is being insured (*cesti que vie*). See Principal Sum.

Death Benefit Only (DBO) Plan. A plan that defers part of an employee's salary and pays upon the contingency of death.

Death Rate. See Mortality Rate.

Debit. (1) The amount of premium charged or debited to an agent to be collected. (2) The book of business represented by such premiums. (3) The territory where most of the insureds are located. (4) The total number of individual or home service insureds assigned to a given agent for collection of weekly or monthly premiums and for servicing, commonly referred to as "people in my debit."

Debit Agent. An agent who works on the debit system.

Debit Life Insurance. See Industrial Life Insurance.

Debit System. The system of collecting insurance premiums weekly or monthly by an agent.

Debris Removal Clause. A provision included in a property policy that provides indemnification for expenditures incurred in the removal of debris produced by the occurrence of an insured peril. These costs are included in the claim amount as long as there is sufficient coverage to pay for the damaged property plus debris removal. If combined loss exceeds the policy limit, then an additional amount of coverage equal to 5 percent of the limit of liability is made available for debris removal.

Debtor. One who owes a legal obligation or money to another. See also Creditor.

Debts and Restrictions. Mortgages, liens and other encumbrances on real estate property, including margin loans on capital investments and liquidation costs or penalties on accessible pension funds.

Decedent. The deceased.

Declaration. (1) A term used in insurance other than life or health to denote that portion of the contract that lists such information as the name and address of the insured, the property insured, its location and description, the policy period, the amount of insurance coverage, applicable premiums and supplemental representations by the insured. (2) A formal written statement in which an individual avows under oath certain facts as personally known to him or her specifying of the facts constituting the plaintiff's cause of action against the defendant.

Declarations Page. Typically the first page of an insurance application. This page includes specific details relating to coverage: the names of the people covered by the policy; the dates it's in effect; and the vehicles, boats, etc. covered. Also included are details on everything from policy limits and premiums due to any specific additions or exclusions based on personal circumstances. Also called the declarations sheet, dec sheet or dec page.

Declination. Rejection of an application for insurance by the insurer.

Decreasing Term. Life insurance that provides a death benefit that declines throughout the term of the contract, reaching zero at the end of the term.

Decreasing Term Insurance. Term life insurance where the death benefit decreases but the premium remains level for the policy term. See also Increasing Term Insurance, Level Term Insurance and Term Insurance.

Deductible. The portion of an insured loss to be borne by the insured before the insurance company takes over. Higher deductibles reduce the insurance company's exposure. Small losses that do not exceed the deductible do not require a claim settlement, and large losses that exceed the deductible result in a smaller settlement.

Deductible Carryover Credit. During the last three months of a calendar year, charges incurred for health services can be used to satisfy the deductible for the following calendar year. These credits may be applied whether or not the prior calendar year's deductible had been met.

Deductible, Calendar Year. A deductible that specifies that one deductible needs to be satisfied for a calendar year regardless of the number of claims.

Deductible Clause. A contract provision that sets forth the deductible.

Deductible, Disappearing. See Disappearing Deductible.

Deductible, Franchise. See Franchise Deductible.

Deductible, Per Cause. A deductible that must be satisfied for each separate claim.

"Deep Pockets" Liability. The legal doctrine of joint-and-several liability under which recovery can be sought from any of several codefendants based on ability to pay, rather than the degree of negligence. If A and B are jointly liable for an injury; A was 90 percent negligent and B was 10 percent negligent, but A has no assets; the claimant is permitted to reach into the "deep pockets" of B for the full amount of the award against A and B.

Defamation. (1) An unfair trade practice involving false, maliciously critical or derogatory statements intended to injure a person engaged in the insurance business. (2) Any derogatory statement that injures a person's business or reputation. Defamation can be written (libel) or spoken (slander). See also Libel or Slander.

Defendant. The person being sued in a court action.

Defense Costs. An important part of liability insurance coverage. In some cases, the cost of defense is as much as, or more than, the amount ultimately awarded as damages.

Defensive Insurance. Pays the legal costs of defending against legal charges. Some defensive policies also cover damages incurred as a result of infringement or other specific activities.

Deferred Annuity. An annuity contract that provides for the initiation of payments at some designated future date in contrast to one in which payment begins immediately on purchase.

Deferred Compensation. A qualified or non-qualified plan that allows a key person to defer receipt of current income in accordance with a written agreement with the employer. Deferral is usually until death, disability or retirement.

Deferred Compensation Administrator. A company that provides services under a deferred compensation plan. Services include administration of self-insured plans, compensation planning, salary surveys, retirement planning, etc.

Deferred Group Annuity. A group annuity contract providing for the purchase each year of a paid-up deferred annuity for each person covered in the group. The total amount of the annuity payments starts at a deferred date, usually retirement, and is the sum of the individual paid-up annuities.

Deferred Premium. The unpaid and yet undue premiums on life insurance, paid on other than an annual premium basis.

Deferred Vesting. A form of vesting where rights to vested benefits are acquired by a participant commencing upon a fulfillment of specified requirements, usually, reaching a certain age or number of years of service/membership. See also Vesting.

Deficiency Reserve. A supplemental reserve that life insurers are required to show in their balance sheet if the gross premium charged on a class of insureds is less than the net level premium reserve or modified reserve.

Deficit. Any excess of debits over credits at the end of a given accounting period.

Deficit Carried Forward. The transfer of a debit balance from one accounting period to another.

Defined Benefit Pension Plan. A qualified retirement plan where the employer makes contributions on behalf of all eligible employees in order to provide a specific retirement benefit. The amount of the contribution is not specifically defined, but the amount of the retirement benefit is defined.

Defined Contribution Pension Plan. A type of pension plan under which contributions are fixed as flat amounts or flat percentages of an employee's salary. Benefits consist of whatever amounts the accumulated contributions will produce.

Definitions Page. The page of an insurance policy that identifies who is covered, when and where coverage applies and what is covered (e.g., vehicles, property, etc.).

Deflation. An economic period characterized by falling prices, high unemployment and a generally sluggish or slow economy.

DEFRA. Deficit Reduction Act of 1984.

Degree of Care. A duty owed to others that depends on circumstances. Persons who invite others on their premises, invite children on their premises and sell what might be considered inherently dangerous products are all required to take different degrees of care to prevent harm to others.

Degree of Risk. The amount of uncertainty that exists in a given situation. For instance, if heads is chosen in a coin toss, the degree of risk present is 50 percent, since there is a 50 percent chance any coin toss will come up tails. See also Law of Large Number, Odds and Probability.

Delay Clause. (1) A contract provision that excludes liability as a result of damage or loss of market arising out of delayed voyages. (2) A contract provision permitting the insurer to defer granting a loan on the sole security of the policy for any other purpose than paying premiums on the policy for a stated interval of time, usually six months.

Delayed Payment Clause. In life insurance, a clause deferring payment to the beneficiary for a specified period after the death of the insured with proceeds to be paid to contingent beneficiaries or the estate if the primary beneficiary does not survive the delay. It is one method of handling common-disaster situations, such as the death of the insured and the primary beneficiary occurring in the same accident. The clause usually states that the beneficiary has to survive the death of the insured by a certain period of time in order to collect.

Delivered Business. Contracts issued by an insurer and delivered to an insured but not yet paid for. See also Examined Business, Paid Business and Written Business.

Delivery. The actual placing of a life or health insurance policy in the hands of an insured.

Demand Loan. Any loan with an indefinite maturity.

Demolition Clause. A provision that excludes liability for costs incurred in demolishing undamaged property, often necessitated by building ordinances requiring that structures must be demolished after a certain degree of damage has been sustained.

Demolition Cost Endorsement. Provides coverage for the cost of demolishing any undamaged part of the building and the cost of clearing the site if a covered building is damaged or destroyed by a covered peril. A specific amount of insurance must be purchased, and covered costs will be paid up to but not exceeding the amount stated on the form.

Demolition Insurance. Coverage for the cost of demolition excluded by a demolition clause. It may be endorsed to property insurance for an additional premium. See also Demolition Clause.

Demurrer. A formal statement in a court action which states that even if the other party's facts are true, there is no cause of action.

Dental Insurance. A group health insurance contract that provides payment for certain enumerated dental services.

Dental Plan. Any contractual arrangement for dental services provided or arranged for on a prepaid or postpaid individual or group service basis.

Dental Plan Organization (DPO). A direct provider of dental services compensated on a prepaid or postpaid basis to individuals or groups. An arrangement for providing dental services indirectly through independent contractors or on a fee-for-service basis is not a DPO. A DPO is an arrangement for providing dental services through an agreement with providers or by employing dentists.

Dental Plan, Supplemental. An arrangement where a dentist or group of dentists agree to relieve patients of paying any patient charges or copayments associated with dental insurance or other dental coverage for a predetermined fee. The term also refers to an arrangement that covers less than 50 percent of an enrollee's dental expenses, regardless of whether the enrollee has other coverage.

Department of Health and Human Services. A federal department whose responsibility is primarily dealing with social service functions, such as administration and supervision of the Medicare program.

Dependent. An individual who depends on another for support and maintenance.

Dependent Care Plan. An employee benefit whereby the employee is reimbursed for dependent care expenses or an actual day care program provided by the employer on business premises.

Dependent Coverage. Insurance coverage on the head of a family that extends to his or her dependents, including only the lawful spouse and unmarried children (step, foster and adopted) who are not yet employed on a full-time basis.

Dependent Life Insurance. A life insurance benefit that is part of a group life insurance contract and provides death protection to the eligible dependents of a covered employee.

Dependent Properties. Properties that an insured business does not own, operate or control, but upon which the insured's income depends. Examples include major suppliers or customers. Also known as "contingent" properties.

Deposit. The contributions or payments made to a fund by the employer; or, sometimes by both the employer and employee if there are employee contributions in the plan.

Deposit Administration (DA). A group annuity providing for the accumulation of contributions in an undivided fund out of which annuities are purchased for each covered person in the group for retirement purposes.

Deposit Administration Group Annuity. A group contract providing a deposit fund prior to retirement, with annuities bought from the fund at retirement.

Deposit (or Provisional) Premium. The premium paid at the inception of a contract that provides for future premium adjustments. It is based on an estimate of what the final premium will be. See also Basic Premium.

Deposition. A sworn statement of a witness or other party in a judicial proceeding, usually conducted in an oral question and answer format where attendance is compelled.

Depositor's Forgery Insurance. Protection against the forgery or alteration of things such as checks, drafts and promissory notes purported to have been written by the insured. It is issued to individuals, firms and corporations, but not to banks or building and loan associations. It can be written to cover incoming items, but this is seldom done.

Depository Bond. A form of bond that guarantees to the government that its deposits with banks will not be subject to loss.

Depreciation. A decrease in the value of any type of tangible property over a period of time resulting from use, wear and tear or obsolescence.

Designated Mental Health Provider. The organization hired by a health plan to provide mental health and substance abuse services.

Detoxification. The process an individual goes through when withdrawing from alcohol. Usually is done under guidance of medical personnel.

Deviated Rate. Companies that adhere to rates promulgated by a bureau sometimes offer lower rates than those recommended in certain areas. The company is said to have "deviated" from the bureau rate for that area.

Deviation. (1) Voluntary departure, not brought about by necessity and not resulting from reasonable cause, from the customary, usual course between the port of shipment and the port of destination; or certain fundamental breaches of the carrier's obligations under the contract of carriage. There are conditions where deviation is excused, such as when it is reasonably necessary for the safety of the ship and cargo or for humanitarian reasons, such as rescuing another ship in distress. (2) A rate that varies from the manual rate.

Deviation Clause. An ocean marine clause providing coverage in the event of a deviation en route beyond the insured's control.

Devise. A gift of real property in accordance with a valid will.

Diagnosis. The process of identifying a disease.

Diagnosis Related Groups (DRGs). A method of classifying inpatient hospital services. It is used as a method of determining financing to reimburse various providers for services performed.

DIC. See Difference in Conditions.

Difference in Conditions (DIC). A separate contract that expands or supplements insurance on property written on a named perils basis so as to cover on an open perils (all risk) basis, subject to certain exclusions.

Direct Damage Form. A form that covers actual damage, directly resulting from a covered peril, to covered property.

Direct Loss (or Damage). A loss that is a direct consequence of a particular peril. Fire damage to a refrigerator constitutes a direct loss. Spoiling of food in the refrigerator as a result of the fire damage is an indirect loss. Contrast with Indirect Loss and Consequential Loss.

Direct Repair Programs. Plans that insurance companies began offering in the late 1980s that allow owners to choose a body shop recommended by the insurance firm. The owner also can go to a shop not on the list.

Direct Selling System. A distribution system where an insurer deals directly with its insureds through its own employees. This definition applies typically to property and liability insurance business. Included are mail-order insurance and the sale of insurance from vending machines at airport booths and elsewhere. Contrast with Independent Agency System.

Direct Writer. (1) The insurer that negotiates with the insured as distinguished from the reinsurer. (2) An insurer whose distribution mechanism is either the direct selling system or the exclusive agency system.

Direct Written Premium. The premiums collected, without any allowance for premiums ceded to reinsurers.

Directed Verdict. A verdict for the defendant based on the court's decision that the plaintiff's case has not been proven.

Director of Insurance. A title used in some states for the head of the department of insurance. See also Commissioner of Insurance.

Directors and Officers Liability Insurance. Insurance that protects directors and officers from liability claims arising out of alleged errors in judgment, breaches of duty, and wrongful acts related to their organizational activities.

Disability. A condition that curtails to a lesser or greater degree a person's ability to carry on normal pursuits. A disability may be partial or total, and temporary or permanent.

Disability Benefit. The benefit payable under a disability income policy or a provision of some other policy, such as a life insurance contract.

Disability Benefits Law. A state law requiring an employer to provide disability benefits to covered employees for nonoccupational injuries, in contrast to workers' compensation, which pays for occupational injuries. These laws are currently in effect in New York, New Jersey, Rhode Island, California and Hawaii.

Disability Income Insurance. Also called loss of time insurance, this health insurance provides periodic payments to replace income, actually or presumptively lost, when the insured is unable to work as a result of sickness or injury.

Disability Insurance Training Council, Inc. The educational arm of the National Association of Health Underwriters, the health insurance agents' professional society. It encourages agent educational projects by local health associations, conducts university seminars in advanced health underwriting areas and conducts annual seminars for home office executives in sociological social insurance and demographic trends that may affect future application of policy forms and health insurance.

Disability Insured. A Social Security insured status required to satisfy eligibility for disability income benefits. The status is based on having paid Social Security taxes in 20 of the 40 calendar quarters ending with the quarter in which a disability claim is submitted.

Disability, Long-Term. See Long-Term Disability.

Disability Pension. A pension paid to a disabled worker prior to the time of normal retirement.

Disability, Permanent Partial. See Permanent Partial Disability.

Disability, Permanent Total. See Permanent Total Disability.

Disability, Short-Term. See Short-Term Disability.

Disability, Temporary Partial. See Temporary Partial Disability.

Disability, Temporary Total. See Temporary Total Disability.

Disappearing Deductible. A deductible that gradually disappears as the loss gets larger. If the deductible is $50, the insurer will pay 111 percent of the loss that is in excess of $50. The deductible on losses between $50 and $500 is gradually reduced by this system, and if the loss reaches $500, the full amount is covered.

Discharge Planning. Determining what the patient's medical needs will be after discharge from a hospital or other inpatient treatment facility.

Disclosure Authorization Form. A form authorizing the disclosure of personal information obtained in connection with an insurance transaction. Insurers must give applicants advance notice of their information practices. Among other things, the form must state the kind of information collected and to whom information may be disclosed.

Discount. The difference between an amount due at a future date and its present value at a specified rate of interest.

Discounted (Commuted) Value Table. A table showing the discounted or present value, for several interest rates, of dollars payable at various times in the future.

Discovery Cover. A reinsurance treaty covering losses that are discovered during the term of the treaty regardless of when they were sustained.

Discovery Period. The period of time allowed an insured who has canceled a bond to discover and report to the previous surety a loss that occurred during the term of that bond. Losses so reported are paid by the original surety even though another surety is on the risk at the time of the discovery. The usual discovery period is one year.

Discrimination. Refusal of an insurer to provide comparable insurance or use comparable rates for certain individuals or groups with basic characteristics the same as those to whom the coverage or rates are offered. This is prohibited by law.

Dishonesty, Disappearance and Destruction Policy ("3-D" Policy). A once-popular commercial crime insurance form used to protect money and securities against loss by employee dishonesty, robbery, depositor's forgery and other causes of loss. The 3-D policy was replaced by modern commercial crime coverage forms. See Combination Crime Coverage Plan.

Dismemberment. The loss of, or loss of use of, specified parts of the body resulting from accidental bodily injury.

Dismemberment Benefit. The benefits payable for various types of dismemberment. See also AD&D and Dismemberment and Multiple Indemnity.

Dissent. This occurs when one or more judges disagrees with the majority decision.

Distribution Clause. See Pro Rata Distribution Clause.

Divided Cover. The placing of insurance on a given subject or object with more than one insurer.

Dividend Accumulation. An option in a life insurance policy that allows the policyholder to leave any premium dividends with the insurer to accumulate at compound interest.

Dividend Additions. An option whereby the insured can leave dividends with the insurer, and each dividend is used to buy a single premium life insurance policy for whatever amount it will purchase. Also called paid-up additions.

Dividend Option. Alternative ways in which insureds under participating life policies may elect to receive their policyholder dividends.

Dividend. (1) The return of part of the premium paid for a policy issued on a participating basis by either a mutual or stock insurer. (2) A portion of the surplus paid to a corporation's stockholders.

Divisible Contract Clause. A clause providing that a violation of the conditions of the policy at one insured location will not void coverage at other locations.

DOC. See Drive-Other-Car Endorsement.

Domestic. See Residence Employee.

Domestic Insurer (or Company). An insurer formed under the laws of the state where the insurance is written.

Donee. The recipient of a gift.

Donor. The individual who gives a gift.

Double Dipping. Collecting money twice in an accident (e.g., from the at-fault driver and an insured's no-fault policy, or from a personal health policy and an employer's workers' comp insurance).

Double Indemnity. Payment of twice the basic benefit in the event of loss resulting from specified causes or under specified circumstances. For example, a life insurance contract may provide for twice the basic benefit if death is due to accident. Accident policies may provide double indemnity coverage for death due to an elevator accident. See also Multiple Indemnity.

Double Protection. A form of life insurance combining whole life and an equivalent amount of term, with the term expiring at a stated future date, usually at 65 years of age. For example, an individual may purchase $50,000 worth of life insurance protection, $25,000 of it being term insurance and the other $25,000 whole life. The provision would state that the $25,000 of term insurance ceases when the insured reaches age 65.

Dram Shop Laws. Liquor liability laws that provide that a person serving someone who is intoxicated or contributing to the intoxication of another may be liable for injury or damage caused by the intoxicated person.

Dram Shop Liability Insurance. Insurance that protects the owners of an establishment in which alcoholic beverages are sold against liability arising

132

out of accidents caused by intoxicated customers who have been served/sold alcoholic beverages.

"D" Ratio. A factor used in workers' compensation experience rating plans. It is the ratio of smaller losses (those under $2,000), plus the discounted value of large losses, as compared to the total losses that are expected of an insured in a particular type of business.

Dread (or Specified) Disease Policy. Coverage, usually with a high maximum limit, for all types of medical expenses arising out of diseases named in the contract. Common diseases covered are polio-myelitis, diphtheria, multiple sclerosis, spinal men-ingitis and tetanus. Cancer is sometimes covered or may be added by a rider.

Drive-In Claim Service. A facility maintained by an automobile insurer in which the extent of damage to a claimant's automobile can be determined and, in many cases, a settlement made.

Drive-Other-Car Endorsement (DOC). A coverage that may be added to an auto that protects the individuals named in the endorsement while they are driving cars not owned by the individuals and not named in the policy.

Drop Down Coverages. Coverages provided by a personal umbrella that are not provided by under-lying liability policies, including: personal injury coverage; regularly furnished autos; contractual li-ability; and damage to property of others.

Drug Formulary. A schedule of prescription drugs approved for coverage under a plan and dispensed through participating pharmacies.

Drug Price Review (DPR). A procedure used to determine drug price maximums. It involves determining wholesale drug prices based on the American Druggist Blue Book.

Drug Utilization Review (DUR). A method for evaluating or reviewing the use of drugs to determine the appropriateness of the drug therapy and whether it will be paid for by insurance.

Druggists Liability Insurance. A contract that protects a druggist in case of a suit arising out of filling prescriptions, missed delivery of drugs and other operations normal to a drugstore.

Dual Choice. The federal requirement that employers having 25 or more employees who are within the service area of a federally qualified HMO, who are paying at least minimum wage and offer a health plan to their employees, must offer HMO coverage as well as an indemnity plan.

Dual Life Stock Company. A stock life insurer issuing both participating and nonparticipating policy contracts.

Dun and Bradstreet, Inc. (D&B). A corporation that furnishes insurance companies with financial reports to assist them in the underwriting of prospective policyholders.

Duplicate Coverage Inquiry (DCI). A request to determine whether or not other coverage exists.

Used to apply the coordination of benefits provisions where two or more insurance companies are involved.

Duplication of Benefits. Identical or overlapping coverage exists between two or more insurance companies or service organizations.

Duties After a Loss. A clause that specifies what a person must do in order to recover for losses covered by the policy. Most insurance companies have no duty to provide coverage unless there has been full compliance with the following duties: The insurer must be notified promptly of how, when and where the accident or loss happened. Notice should also include the names and addresses of any injured persons or witnesses.

Duty to Defend. The insurance company has the right and the option to investigate and settle any lawsuit and claim. In the same process, it also accepts a duty to defend an insured person in any related lawsuit or claim—whether the insured is guilty or liable.

Dwelling Coverage/Forms. A policy form designed specifically to cover a dwelling building and the personal property in it plus other additional coverages. Coverage applies to the dwelling, attached structures and materials and supplies on or adjacent to the residence premises for use in the construction, alteration or repair of the dwelling or other structures.

Dynamo Clause. See Electrical Exemption Clause.

E

Earned Income. The money individuals earn as a result of working at some job or occupation for which they are paid a salary. Insurance companies base this number on an insured's salary and other earned income. An insurer typically asks for some kind of proof of income—like an IRS W-2 form or other tax document.

Earned Premium. The amount of the premium that has been "used up" during the term of a policy (i.e., if a one-year policy has been in effect six months, half of the total premium has been earned.)

Earnings Figure. An indexed or adjusted figure, that changes annually due to increases in wages. Thus, in most years, the earnings figure will be higher than the year before—and, consequently, the requirements for a quarter of coverage are higher.

Earnings Insurance. A form of gross earnings business interruption insurance that lacks a coinsurance clause. Designed for small risks, the maximum amount of loss an insured can collect in any 30-day period is established when the policy is written.

Earth Movement. A peril including landslide, mudflow, earth sinking, rising or shifting and earthquake. Usually excluded on homeowners' and commercial property policies. If direct loss by fire, explosion or breakage of glass, storm door or storm window follow earth movement, the policies cover the additional loss, and that loss only.

Earthquake Insurance. Insurance covering damage caused by an earthquake. Homeowners insurance does not automatically cover losses caused by an earthquake—but earthquake coverage for the residence, other structures and personal property may be attached by endorsement. Several earthquake-prone states—most notably California—require insurance companies that write homeowners coverage to also write earthquake coverage.

Easement. An interest in land owned by another that entitles its easement holder to specific uses.

EC. See Extended Coverage.

Economic Risk. A risk experienced by those who invest in securities identified as the uncertainty of the economy.

Educational Assistance Plan. An employee benefit whereby certain educational expenses incurred by the employee are reimbursed on a tax-favorable basis by the employer.

Educational Fund. A fund that provides money for a child's education should the breadwinner of the family die.

Effective Date. The start date of an insurance policy, or the date on which the protection of an insurance policy or bond goes into effect.

Elective Benefits. Lump sum payments that the insured may choose in lieu of periodic payments for certain injuries, such as fractures and dislocations.

Elective Deferral Plan. A qualified plan (401(k) or tax sheltered annuity) whereby participants voluntarily elect to defer amounts of compensation for placement in a retirement plan on a tax favorable basis.

Elective Indemnities. See Elective Benefits.

Electrical (or Electrical Apparatus) Exemption Clause. A clause providing that damage to electrical appliances caused by artificially generated electrical currents is recoverable only if fire ensues and then only for the damage caused by the fire.

Electronic Data Processing (EDP) Coverage. Insurance that covers computer equipment, data systems, information storage media and expenses or income loss related to EDP losses.

Elevator Collision Coverage. Coverage for damage caused by collision of an elevator without regard to fault. Includes damage to personal property, the building and the elevator itself. Liability coverage is usually provided automatically by business liability policies.

Eligibility. Particular people, vehicles and situations are eligible for coverage under a policy for a number of different reasons. The conditions of eligibility are sprinkled throughout the policy and the manual rules that govern how and when a policy may be written.

Eligibility Date. The date that a person is eligible for benefits.

Eligibility Period. (1) The period of time during which potential members of a group life or health program may enroll without providing evidence of insurability. (2) The period of time under a Major Medical policy during which reimbursable expenses may be accrued.

Eligibility Requirements. Requirements imposed for eligibility for coverage, usually in a group insurance or pension plan.

Eligible Dependent. A dependent of an insured person who is eligible for coverage according to the requirements set forth in the contract.

Eligible Employee. An employee who is eligible based on the requirements as indicated in the group contract.

Eligible Expenses. Expenses as defined in the health plan as being eligible for coverage, including specified health services fees or "customary and reasonable charges."

Eligible Person. Similar to eligible employee except it could cover people who are not employees of a specified employer (e.g., members of an association, union, etc.)

Elimination Period. A loosely used term, sometimes designating the probationary period, but most often designating the waiting period in a health insurance policy. See also Probationary Period and Waiting Period.

Embezzlement. Fraudulent use of money or property that has been entrusted to one's care.

Emergency Accident Benefit. A group medical benefit that reimburses the insured for expenses incurred for emergency treatment of accidents.

Emergency. An injury or disease that occurs suddenly and requires treatment within 24 hours.

Emergency Fund. A fund that provides money for the emergency expenses of a deceased's family prior to the final settlement of the estate.

Emergi-Center. See Freestanding Emergency Medical Services Center.

Emotional Distress. See Mental Distress.

Employee Benefit Program. Benefits offered to employees, covering such contingencies as medical expenses, disability, retirement and death, usually paid for wholly or in part by the employer. These benefits are usually insured.

Employee Certificate of Insurance. Evidence of participation in a group insurance plan, consisting of a brief summary of plan benefits. The employee receives this certificate rather than the actual insurance policy.

Employee Contribution. (1) The employee's share of the premium costs. (2) Deduction from employee's pay to apply toward the cost of a retirement plan.

Employee Dishonesty. Any dishonest act by an employee that contributes to a loss for the employer. Fidelity bonds usually protect against such losses.

Employee Dishonesty Coverage Form. A commercial crime coverage form, which is actually a fidelity bond, providing coverage for losses resulting from employee dishonesty. It covers losses of money, securities and property other than money and securities.

Employee Pension Benefit Plan or Pension Plan. Any program established and maintained by an employer or an employee organization that provides retirement benefits to employees or deferred income until employment is terminated.

Employee Retirement Income Security Act of 1974 (ERISA). An act that prescribes federal standards for funding, participation, vesting, termination, disclosure, fiduciary responsibility and tax treatment of private pension plans. ERISA also applies to retirement plans and to "employee welfare benefit plans" (any plan of group medical, surgical, hospital or other health care benefits and group accident, sickness and disability benefit plans).

Employee Stock Ownership Plan (ESOP). A qualified employee plan that provides eligible employees with part ownership in the corporation for which they work. Stock is issued and held in trust for the benefit of the employees.

Employee Welfare Benefit Plan. Any program established or maintained by an employer or an employee organization to provide medical, surgical, or hospital care or benefits in the event of sickness, accident, disability, death or unemployment.

Employees' Trust. One way for a pension or profit-sharing plan to be financed and given effect.

Employer Contribution. The portion of the cost of a health insurance plan borne by the employer.

Employers Liability Coverage. Provides coverage against the common law liability of an employer for injuries to employees as distinguished from the liability imposed by a workers' compensation law. Employers liability applies in situations where a worker does not come under these laws.

Employers Nonownership Liability Insurance. Protects the employer for liability arising from the use by employees of their own cars on company business.

Employment Benefit Plan. Any plan that is both an employee welfare plan and an employee pension plan.

Encounter. Each time a person meets with a health care provider to receive services.

Encumbrance. A claim on property, such as a mortgage, a lien for work and materials or a right of dower. The interest of the property owner is reduced by the amount of the encumbrance.

Endorsement. A written or printed form attached to the policy that alters provisions of the contract. Endorsements and riders serve as addenda—adding coverage or conditions to standard insurance contracts.

Endorsement Extending Period of Indemnity. An endorsement attached to business interruption policies that extends coverage to the period during which a business has reopened for business but has not reached the level of business activity that existed prior to the business interruption loss.

Endorsement Split Dollar. A split dollar plan in which the employer owns and controls a life policy on the life of an employee. The employee's rights to certain policy benefits are protected by an employer endorsement.

Endowment Insurance. Life insurance where the face amount is payable to the insured at the end of the contract period or to a beneficiary if the insured dies before that (e.g., an insured purchasing an endowment payable at age 65. Upon reaching that age, the proceeds would be payable to the insured. If the insured dies prior to that age, the proceeds would be payable to the designated beneficiary as a life insurance benefit).

Engineer (Loss Prevention Engineer or Safety Consultant). The employee of an insurance company who has the responsibility of loss prevention and who assists in the securing of underwriting and rating information.

Enrollee. An eligible individual enrolled in a health plan—does not include an eligible dependent.

Enrolling Unit. An organization (such as an employer) that contracts for participation in a health insurance plan.

Enrollment. The total number of enrollees in a health plan. Also refers to the process of enrolling people in a health plan.

Enrollment Period. The amount of time an employee has to sign up for a contributory health plan.

Entire Contract Clause. A provision in an insurance contract stating that the entire agreement between the insured and the insurer is contained in the contract, including the application if it is attached, declarations, insuring agreements, exclusions, conditions and endorsements.

Entity Agreement. A buy-sell agreement usually used with a partnership in which the partnership agrees to purchase the interest of a deceased or disabled partner.

Entrustment. When an insured person rents or lends property to a non-insured person.

Entry Age. The age when an employee satisfies all the age, service and other eligibility requirements for participation in a pension plan.

Entry Date into Claims-Made. Initial effective date of a "claims-made" liability policy. It determines the extent of maturity for rating purposes. If claims-made coverage is interrupted and reestablished, or if a retroactive date is changed on renewal, the entry date will change.

Environmental Restoration. Restitution for the loss, damage or destruction of natural resources arising out of the accidental discharge or escape of any commodity transported by a motor carrier, including the cost of removal and measures to minimize damage to human health, the natural environment, fish, shellfish and wildlife. Federal regulations require common carriers of hazardous materials to maintain minimum liability coverages for BI, PD and environmental restoration.

Equifax. One of three major credit reporting companies.

Equipment Floater. A form covering various types of equipment (e.g., construction equipment, against specified perils or occasionally on an all-risk basis subject to exclusions).

Equity. The money value of an insurance company that is over and above its liabilities. Liabilities include almost all of its reserves.

ERISA. See Employee Retirement Income Security Act.

ERISA Liability. Liability imposed by law upon officers or other employees operating in a fiduciary capacity for the proper handling of pension funds and other employee benefits. It is excluded from most general liability policies. See Employee Retirement Income Security Act (ERISA).

Errors and Omissions Clause. A clause usually found in an obligatory reinsurance treaty that provides that if an error or an omission takes place in describing a risk that falls within the automatic reinsurance coverage of the treaty, it shall not invalidate the liability of the reinsurer for the risk.

Errors and Omissions Insurance. (1) Insurance that indemnifies an insured for a loss sustained because of an error/oversight on his or her part (e.g., an insurer purchases this coverage to protect itself against losses from such things as failing to issue a policy). (2) Coverage for losses resulting from financial institutions failing to effect coverage.

Estate Plan. A plan for the disposition of one's property at death, including the handling of property in the event of the incompetency or total disability of the estate owner. A will is part of an estate plan.

Estate Planning. The process of accumulation, conservation, distribution and administration of an estate in order to minimize the impact of taxation and estate shrinkage.

Estate Tax. A tax payable to the federal government. The amount is based on the value of the estate of the decedent.

Estimated Premium. A provisional premium that is adjusted at the end of the year (e.g., in workers' comp insurance an estimated premium is based on estimated payrolls for the coming year. At the end of the year, final payrolls are determined and the final premium is computed).

Estoppel. The legal principle whereby a person loses the right to deny that a certain condition exists by virtue of having acted in such a way as to persuade others that the condition does exist (e.g., if an insurer allows an insured to violate a condition of the policy, the insurer cannot at a later date void the policy because the condition was violated. The insurer has acted in such a way as to lead the insured to believe that the violation did not void the coverage).

Evidence Clause. A clause that requires the insured to cooperate in the investigation of a claim by producing records and submitting to examinations. This helps the adjuster establish the validity of a claim. In a health policy, this clause requires the insured to submit to physical examinations.

Evidence of Coverage. See Certificate of Insurance.

Evidence of Insurability. Any information concerning health status required to satisfy underwriting standards, such as a medical examination or physician's statement.

Ex Gratia Payment. Latin for "from favor." A payment by an insurer to an insured for which there is no liability under the contract. In some cases, an insurer may feel there has been a mistake or a misunderstanding, and may pay a claim even though it does not appear to be liable.

Examination. An examination of an insurance company by the state insurance department.

Examiner. (1) An employee assigned by the state insurance department to audit insurers' records. (2) A physician appointed by the medical director of a life or health insurer to examine applicants.

Excepted Period. See Probationary Period.

Exception. A provision in an insurance policy that eliminates coverage. See also Exclusion.

Excess Coverage/Insurance. Coverage in excess of one or more primary coverages that does not pay a loss until the loss amount exceeds a certain sum. If an accident is covered by more than one policy, the second policy is said to be excess.

Excess Interest. Interest credited to an insured's contract in excess of the amount guaranteed by the terms of the contract.

Excess Limit. (1) That limit provided in a policy that is in excess of the basic limit. See Basic Limit. (2) A limit provided in a separate policy with another insurer that is in excess of the limit provided in the basic policy.

Excess Line Broker. A person licensed to place insurance not available in his or her state through insurers not licensed to do business in the state. A person licensed to deal with nonadmitted insurers.

Excess Loss Premium Factor. Used in connection with retrospective rating plans, this factor compensates the insurer for the fact that the insured has elected to limit the effects of any one large loss under the retrospective rating formula (e.g., the insured elects a loss limitation of $50,000, which mean that would be the maximum amount of any one loss that would go into the retrospective calculation).

Excess of Loss Ratio Reinsurance. See Aggregate Excess of Loss Reinsurance.

Excess of Loss Reinsurance. (1) Reinsurance which, subject to a specified limit, indemnifies the ceding company against the amount of loss in excess of the specified retention. It includes various types of reinsurance, such as catastrophe, per risk, per account and aggregate excess of loss. Contrast with Pro Rata Reinsurance. (2) Reinsurance which indemnifies the ceding company for that portion of the loss resulting from a single occurrence, however defined, that exceeds a predetermined amount, which is referred to as a first loss retention or deductible.

Excess Per Risk Reinsurance. A form of excess of loss reinsurance which, subject to a specified limit, indemnifies the ceding company against the amount of loss in excess of a specified retention with respect to each risk involved in each occurrence.

Excess Plan. A retirement plan designed around the benefits of Social Security.

Excluded Period. See Probationary Period.

Exclusion. A contractual provision in an insurance policy that denies coverage for certain perils, persons, property or locations. Most exclusions exist simply to remove coverage for above-average risks which are not anticipated in average rates and premiums. In some cases, the coverage is available for an additional charge. Common policy exclusions include: war and acts of war, self-inflicted injury and aviation. Other exclusions limit the insurer's exposure to events that may have been caused intentionally or events that dramatically increase the chance of loss. See also Exception.

Exclusion Ratio. The relationship or ratio of the total investment in the contract (cost basis) to the total expected return from an annuity (calculated based on average life expectancy tables); used to calculate the percentage of each annuity payment which is considered to be a return of cost basis.

Exclusive Agency System. An insurance distribution system that allows agents to sell and service insurance contracts that limit representation to one insurer and reserve to the insurer the ownership, use and control of policy records and expiration date. See also Captive Agent and Direct Writer, and contrast with Independent Agency System.

Exclusive Provider Organization (EPO). A preferred provider organization where individual members use particular preferred providers rather than choosing from a variety of preferred providers. In an EPO, a primary physician monitors care and makes referrals to a network of providers.

Exculpatory. The portion of a contract or agreement that relieves one party to the agreement of the consequences of his or her own acts.

Executor. The person or entity specified by will who is responsible for the probating of an individual's will and the settlement of an estate.

Exemplary Damages. See Punitive Damages.

Exhibitions Insurance. A policy for people who display their products through public exhibitions. Usually written on an all-risk basis with certain specified exclusions.

Expectation of Life. The average number of years of life remaining for persons of a given age according to a particular mortality table. Also called life expectancy.

Expected Claims. Estimated claims for a person/group for a contract year based on actuarial data.

Expected Morbidity. The expected incidence of sickness or injury within a given group during a given period of time as shown on a morbidity table.

Expected Mortality. The expected incidence of death within a given group during a given period of time as shown on a mortality table.

Expediting Expenses. Expenses incurred in order to speed up repair or replacement to reduce the amount of loss by a peril covered in a policy. Most commonly used in connection with business interruption and boiler and machinery insurance. Expediting expenses are generally covered if they reduce the amount of the loss that the insurer would otherwise have to pay.

Expense. (1) The cost of conducting an insurance operation aside from the amount paid for losses. (2) A policy's share of the company's operating costs, fees for medical examinations and inspection reports, underwriting, printing costs, commissions, advertising, agency expenses, premium taxes, salaries, rent, etc. Such costs are important in determining dividends and premium rates.

Expense Allowance. A compensation paid to an insurance agent in excess of prescribed commissions.

Expense Constant. A flat charge added to the premium of small accounts where the premium is so low that the cost of issuing and servicing the policy cannot be recovered. Most often used with workers' compensation policies.

Expense Guarantee. One of the guarantees of all annuities; that is, the guarantee that expenses, the cost of doing business, will not increase or exceed a certain percentage of the annuity contributions.

Expense Incurred Basis. Some long-term care policies are issued on an expense incurred basis, which means the contracts reimburse a proportion of the actual expenses incurred. These benefits function much like some forms of hospital and medical insurance because the insurance pays only a percentage of the costs (usually 50 to 80 percent), and the insured is responsible for the remainder—a requirement known as coinsurance.

Expense Incurred. See Incurred Expense.

Expense Loading. The amount added to the rate during the ratemaking process to cover expenses.

Expense Ratio. The percentage of the premium dollar devoted to paying the expenses of an insurer, other than losses.

Expense Reimbursement Allowance. See Expense Allowance.

Expense Reserve. A liability for incurred but unpaid expenses.

Experian. One of three major credit reporting companies.

Experience. (1) The loss record of an insured, an agent, a territory, a type of insurance written, etc. (2) A statistical compilation relating losses to premiums.

Experience Modification. The increase or decrease in premiums resulting from the application of an experience rating plan, usually expressed as a percentage. See Experience Rating.

Experience, Policy Year. See Policy Year Experience.

Experience Rating. A method of adjusting the premium for a risk based on past loss experience for that risk compared to loss experience for an average risk. See also Prospective Rating and Retrospective Rating.

Experience Refund. In life reinsurance, a predetermined percentage of the net reinsurance profit that the reinsurer returns to the ceding company as a form of profit sharing at year's end.

Experienced Mortality or Morbidity. The actual mortality or morbidity experienced in a group of insureds as compared to the expected mortality or morbidity.

Experimental or Unproven Procedures. Any health care services, supplies, procedures, therapies or devices that the health plan determines regarding coverage for a particular case to be either (1) not proven by scientific evidence to be effective, or

(2) not accepted by health care professionals as being effective.

Expiration Card. A way of recording the date that
a policy terminates. It reminds the agent or sales
representative of a policy coming up for renewal.

Expiration Date. The date indicated as the end of
the coverage period. If a policy is not renewed by
this date, premiums and coverage are terminated.
However, expiration is not absolute—it does not
affect payments for loss of use. If a loss occurs just
before the expiration date and continues for two
months after this date, the loss is fully covered.

Expiration File. A record kept by agents or insurers of the dates that policies they have written or
are servicing expire.

Expiration Notice. Notification to the insured of
the impending termination of the insurance contract.

Expiry. The termination of a term life insurance
policy at the end of its period of coverage.

Explanation of Benefits (EOB). The statement sent
to a participant in a health plan listing services,
amounts paid by the plan and total amount billed
to the patient.

Explanation of Medicare Benefits. A notice which
is sent to the Medicare patient providing information about how the claim is to be paid.

Explosion, Collapse and Underground Damage (XCU). See XCU.

Explosion Insurance. Insurance against loss of property due to explosion but not including explosion of steam boilers, pipes and certain pressure instruments. Most commonly written as part of the extended coverage endorsement.

Exports. Materials and goods shipped to other countries.

Exposure. (1) The state of being subject to the possibility of loss. (2) The extent of risk as measured by payroll, gate receipts, area or other standards. (3) The possibility of loss to a risk being caused by its surroundings. This is used in property insurance rating. (4) Surroundings producing a loss to the insured property. (An example of definitions (3) and (4): an insured building suffering loss because a dynamite factory next to it exploded.)

Exposure Units. (1) Individuals or property which may be subject to loss or damage on which a monetary value may be placed. When these exposure units have similar characteristics they meet the requirement of insurability as homogeneous exposure units. (2) Also refers to the premium base, in the sense that the exposure units times the rate equals the premium (e.g., in workers' compensation, each $100 of payroll is an exposure unit.)

Express Authority. Authority of an agent that is specifically granted by the insurer in the agency contract or agreement.

Extended Care Facility. A facility such as a nursing home that is licensed to provide 24-hour nursing care in accordance with state and local laws. Three levels of care may be provided—skilled, intermediate, custodial or any combination.

Extended Coverage (EC). A common extension of property insurance beyond coverage for fire and lightning that includes coverage for loss by the perils of windstorm, hail, explosion, riot and riot attending a strike, aircraft damage, vehicle damage and smoke damage. At one time EC was added by endorsement. In recent years it has been included on many forms as either an optional coverage or as part of the minimum coverages provided.

Extended Death Benefit. A group policy provision that pays the life benefit when: 1) the insured is totally and continuously disabled at the time the policyholder stops paying premium until the insured's death; and 2) the insured dies within one year of the date the premium payments stopped, or prior to age 65.

Extended Non-Owner Liability. An endorsement attached to a personal auto policy to provide broader liability coverage only for specifically named individuals. When attached, it covers non-owned autos furnished for the regular use of an insured, use of vehicles to carry persons or property for a fee and broader coverage for business use of vehicles.

Extended Period of Indemnity. A business income coverage that continues coverage for income losses for a period of time after operations have resumed.

Extended Reporting Period (ERP). A period allowing claims after expiration of a "claims-made" liability policy. Also known as a "tail." See also Basic ERP, Supplemental ERP, Mini Tail, Midi Tail, Maxi Tail.

Extended Term Insurance. A provision in most policies that provides the option of continuing the existing amount of insurance as term insurance for as long a period of time as the contract's cash value will purchase. This is one of the nonforfeiture options available to the insured in case a premium is not paid within the grace period. See also Nonforfeiture Values.

Extended Wait. A form of reinsurance whereby after the ceding insurer has paid monthly benefits to the claimant for a given number of months under a disability insurance contract, further benefits are paid by the reinsurer.

Extension of Benefits. A condition that allows coverage to continue beyond the expiration date of the policy in the case of employees who are not actively at work or dependents who are hospitalized on that date. The extension applies only if the employee or dependent is disabled as of that date and continues only until the employee returns to work or the dependent leaves the hospital.

Extortion. The surrender of property away from an insured's premises as a result of a threat to do bodily harm to an insured, employee or to a relative or invitee of either, who is or allegedly is being held captive.

Extortion Coverage Form. A commercial crime coverage form that protects against loss of money, securities and property other than money and securities, resulting from extortion.

Extra Expense Coverage Form. A commercial property form designed to cover extra expenses incurred by a business so it can remain in operation following a property loss. See Extra Expense Insurance.

Extra Expense Insurance. A form that provides reimbursement for the extra expenses reasonably incurred to continue the operation of a business when the described property has been damaged by a peril covered by the contract. It is normally used by businesses where continuity of operation, regardless of cost, is a necessity as, for example, any business that would permanently lose customers if there were any suspension of operations.

Extra Percentage Tables. Mortality or morbidity tables showing the extra premium for certain impaired health conditions. Usually this premium is shown as a percentage of the standard premium. A form of substandard rating.

Extra Premium. An added premium charge for extra hazardous exposures that is levied because the normal rate does not take these into account.

Extra Premium Removal. Removal of an extra premium when the cause for it ceases to exist.

Extraordinary Medical Benefits. This coverage pays when an insured's medical and rehabilitation expenses exceed the limits in his or her policy. It provides $1 million of coverage.

F

Face. The first page of a life insurance policy.

Face Amount. The amount of insurance provided by the terms of an insurance contract, usually found on the face of the policy. In a life insurance policy, the death benefit.

Facility-of-Payment Clause. A contract provision found in industrial life policies that permits the insurer to pay a portion of the proceeds of the policy to any relative or person who has possession of the policy and who appears equitably entitled to such payment. This provision facilitates payment when doubt exists as to who the beneficiary is and to save legal expenses in the settling of an estate.

Factored Rating. See Adjusted Community Rating.

Factory Mutuals. Member insurers of the Factory Mutual System, a group of mutual coinsurers formed to provide member insurers with insurance and engineering services.

Facultative Certificate of Reinsurance. A document formalizing a facultative reinsurance policy.

Facultative (or Specific) Reinsurance. Reinsurance by offer and acceptance of individual risks, wherein the reinsurer retains the "faculty" to accept or reject each risk offered by the ceding company. Contrast with Treaty Reinsurance.

Fair Access to Insurance Requirements (FAIR Plans). State run pools that offer insurance to those in high-risk areas who cannot obtain insurance through normal channels. Includes coverages for fire and allied perils, with considerably high limits, after inspection of the premises. By law, any insurer that buys riot reinsurance must participate in a HUD-approved FAIR plan. See also Assigned-Risk.

Fair Credit Reporting Act. Public Law 91-508 requires that an applicant be advised if a consumer report is requested and told the scope of the possible investigation. Should the request for insurance be declined because of information in the report, the applicant must be given the name and address of the reporting agency.

FAIR Plan. See Fair Access to Insurance Requirements.

Fair Rental Value Coverage. Insurance that pays the loss of rental value, minus expenses which do not continue, when property rented to others or held for rental is damaged by a covered peril. Fair rental value coverage applies only when the residence insured is the principal residence.

Fallen Building Clause. A provision in property policies specifying that if a material part of an insured building collapses from causes other than fire or explosion, the fire coverage becomes void.

False Arrest Claims. Damage to a person's reputation when a suspected wrongdoer has been arrested without proper cause. False detention or imprisonment restrict a person's freedom of movement, and can also lead to a claim for damages.

Family Automobile Policy. A package policy that provides protection against legal liability for bodily injury and property damage to others, injury to the insured and other occupants of the vehicle and damage to the vehicle itself. It has largely been replaced by the modern personal auto policy.

Family Dependent. A person entitled to coverage because he or she is: 1) the enrollee's spouse; 2) a single dependent child of either the enrollee or the enrollee's spouse (including stepchildren or legally adopted children); or 3) a resident of the enrollee's home.

Family Expense Policy. Coverage for medical expenses of all members of a family.

Family Income Policy. A policy that pays an income up to some future date designated in the policy to the beneficiary after the death of the insured. The period of payment is measured from the date of inception, and at the end of the income period the face amount of the policy is paid to the beneficiary. If the insured lives beyond the income period, only the face amount is payable in the event of the insured's death.

Family Maintenance Policy. A policy that pays an income to the beneficiary starting after the death of the insured and continuing for a stated period of time. At the end of the income period, the face amount of the policy is paid to the beneficiary.

Family Maximum Benefit. A benefit that is approximately 20 percent greater than the benefit equal to the primary insurance amount (PIA).

Family Members. Persons who reside in the same household as the insured and are related to a named insured by blood, marriage or adoption, or are wards or foster children. Family members also include a student temporarily living away at school.

Family Policy. A policy typically consisting of whole life insurance for the head of the household with smaller amounts of term insurance on other family members.

Family Protection Endorsement. See Uninsured Motorists Endorsement.

Farm Coverage Part. A coverage part available under the commercial package policy. Coverages may be included for farm property, agricultural equipment, livestock and farm liability.

Farm Liability Coverage Form. A commercial liability form attached to a farm coverage part to provide coverage for bodily injury, property damage, personal injury, advertising injury and medical payments for farm exposures.

Farm Personal Property. Scheduled or unscheduled classes of farm property that are covered by the farm property coverage form, including grain, feed, supplies, livestock, farm machines and farm vehicles. Contrast with Household Personal Property.

Farm Property Coverage Form. A farm coverage form that covers residential dwellings, other private structures, household personal property, farm personal property and other farm structures.

Farmers Comprehensive Personal Liability. Similar to the comprehensive personal liability policy but adapted to cover farm hazards, such as damage caused by grazing animals.

Farmowners-Ranchowners Policy. A package policy providing property coverage on farm dwelling buildings and contents, as well as barns, stables and other farm outbuildings. Liability coverage is also included. It is similar to a homeowners policy adapted to cover farm properties.

FAS. See Free Along Side.

FASB. See Financial Accounting Standards Board.

Faultiness. Faulty planning, construction or maintenance that causes a loss. The standard homeowners policy will most likely not cover these losses.

FC&S. See Free-of-Capture-and-Seizure Clause.

FC&S Bulletins. Fire, Casualty and Surety Bulletins. A service, published by the National Underwriter Company, explaining coverages, forms, underwriting and rating procedures for the various property, casualty and surety lines of insurance.

FCAS. See Fellow of the Casualty Actuarial Society.

FCII. Fellow of the Chartered Insurance Institute, whose designation is gained by the completion of examinations and other requisites.

FDIC. See Federal Deposit Insurance Corporation.

Federal Crime Insurance Program. A federally administered program where pooling companies write crime insurance for those unable to secure it in the open market. Available for residential and commercial risks in various states.

Federal Crop Insurance Corporation. An agency within the U.S. Department of Agriculture that provides insurance on growing crops.

Federal Deposit Insurance Corporation (FDIC). An agency of the federal government that insures bank deposits up to a stated maximum.

Federal Emergency Management Agency (FEMA). A government agency that provides disaster relief during emergencies, such as floods, fire, earthquakes, etc.

Federal Employees Compensation Act. Provides workers' compensation benefits to civilian federal government employees. The government administers and operates the system, as well as provides the benefits; no private insurance is involved.

Federal Employers Liability Act (FELA). Passed by Congress in 1908 before there were workers' compensation statutes and benefits, this Act covers railroad workers only. It puts injured workers in a favorable position in terms of liability claims, allowing them to sue the employer for negligence. Because railroad workers and their unions were unwilling to trade their favorable positions for statutory benefits, they remain exempt from compensation laws in many states. Cases are decided on the issue of employer liability.

Federal Estate Tax. A federal tax imposed on the deceased's estate that includes the total assets comprising a person's estate at death.

Federal Insurance Administration. A government office, part of HUD, that oversees FAIR plans, federal crime plans and the flood program.

Federal Insurance Contributions Act (FICA). See FICA.

Federal Officials Bond. Reimburses the government for loss resulting from the dishonest acts of its employees or their lack of faithful performance.

Federal Qualification. Approval of any HMO made by the Health Care Financing Administration after conducting an evaluation of methods of doing business, documents, contracts facilities and systems.

Fee Maximum. The maximum amount available to a provider for specific health care services under a contract.

Fee Schedule. A list of maximum fees for providers who are on a fee-for-service basis.

Fee Simple. Complete ownership of property with the unconditional right to dispose of it. Compare with Joint Tenancy and Tenancy in Common.

Fee-for-Service Equivalency. The difference between the amount a provider receives from a reimbursement system, such as capitation (a flat charge per month, for instance), compared to fee-for-service reimbursement.

Fee-for-Service Reimbursement. A health care system where physicians and other providers receive payment based on their billed charge for each service provided.

FEGLI. Federal Employees Group Life Insurance.

Fellow of the Casualty Actuarial Society (FCAS). A designation gained by the completion of a series of examinations and other requirements.

Fellow of the Society of Actuaries (FSA). A designation which is gained by the completion of a series of examinations, as well as other experience requirements.

Fellow Servant Rule. A common law defense used by employers before the passage of compensation laws. It held that if an employee was injured due to the carelessness of a fellow employee, the right of action was against the fellow worker and not against the employer. Gradually, the class of "fellow servants" was narrowed, to exclude managers and supervisors—the negligence of a "boss" would no longer release the employer.

Fellow, Life Management Institute (FLMI). See Life Office Management Association.

FEMA. See Federal Emergency Management Agency.

FICA. Federal Insurance Contributions Act. A law imposing a payroll tax to assist in funding Social Security benefits.

Fictitious Groups. Groups formed primarily for the purpose of buying insurance. Under law, such groups may not be underwritten.

Fidelity Bond. Reimburses employers for loss due to the dishonest acts of a covered employee.

Fiduciary. A person holding the funds or property of another in a position of trust, and who is obligated to act in a prudent and ethical manner (e.g., an attorney, bank trustee, the executor of an estate, etc.).

Fiduciary Bond. A bond guaranteeing the faithful performance of a fiduciary.

Field. (1) See Field Force. (2) A type or line of insurance (e.g., life insurance). (3) An area or territory covered by an agent, agency or insurer.

Field Force. The agents and supervisory personnel of insurers who operate away from the home office in the branch offices and general agencies of the company.

Field Representative. See Special Agent.

Field Underwriting. The initial screening of prospective buyers of health insurance, performed by
sales personnel "in the field." May also include quot-
ing of premium rates.

File-and-Use Rating Laws. State laws pertaining
to insurance rates which permit insurers to adopt
new rates without the prior approval of the insurance department. Usually, insurers submit new rates
along with supporting statistical evidence, but this
is not necessary in all cases.

Financed Insurance. Payment of insurance premiums, in whole or in part, with funds derived from
borrowing, usually from the cash value of the policy.
Also known as minimum deposit insurance.

Financed Premium. Paying insurance premiums with
funds borrowed outside the contract itself.

Financial Accounting Standards Board (FASB).
A non-governmental group that sets standards for
generally accepted accounting principles.

Financial Guarantee Bond. A guarantee that others will pay sums of money due (e.g., a sales tax
bond guarantees the state that the merchant will
pay sales taxes on time and in full).

Financial Responsibility Clause. A clause that says
a policy conforms to the financial responsibility laws
of any state in which the insured is operating the
insured vehicle.

Financial Responsibility Law/Requirements. Laws
that mandate that the insured furnish evidence of
ability to pay for losses, which most often takes the

form of an insurance policy with certain minimum limits of coverage.

Financial Statement. The disclosure of the financial results of a firm's operations, including the balance sheet, profit and loss statement and associated information.

Fine Arts Floater. Covers fine arts, such as antiques, leaded glass and other works of art, usually on an open perils (all risk) basis.

Fine Print. A reference to imaginary small type in a policy contract that contains exclusions, reductions, exemptions and limitations of coverage. Most state laws specify the minimum type size that can be used in a policy, and provide that exclusions cannot be printed in type smaller than that used for the benefits.

Fire. Combustion that is rapid enough to produce a flame or glow. Property insurance only covers "hostile" fires, or those that have escaped their intended limits or were not started intentionally. Fires in their proper contained area are called "friendly fires" and are not covered under most basic property insurance policies.

Fire Damage Limit. A general liability limit that applies only to the coverage for fire legal liability.

Fire Department Service Clause. A provision in a fire insurance policy that indemnifies the insured for charges incurred due to action by a fire department to save the insured's property.

Fire Legal Liability. Protects the insured against liability incurred when the insured's negligent actions result in the destruction of property that is in the insured's care, custody or control.

Fire Maps. A visual record of the distribution of fire insurance written by all reporting insurers placed on sectional maps. The maps show the distribution of the covered properties in a given area and make it possible to avoid catastrophic losses.

Fire Mark. An insignia, generally metal, once placed on buildings insured by the insurer represented by the mark. Since insurers had their own fire brigades, they had to check the mark on a building to determine whether they should extinguish the fire.

Fire Marshal. A public official responsible for the prevention and investigation of fires. This service is usually financed by a tax on the premiums of property insurers.

Fire Resistive Construction. A building with exterior walls, floors and roof constructed of masonry or other fire-resistive materials.

Fire Wall. A structure (wall) designed to seal off fires within a building.

Fireproof. Buildings that cannot be damaged by fire. However, the term is a misnomer, since no building is completely undamageable by fire, and it is gradually being replaced by the words "fire resistive."

First Aid to Others. An insured is authorized by the insurance company to incur expenses for first aid to an injured third party when there is bodily injury covered by the policy. Expenses for first aid to an insured person are not covered.

First Loss Insurance. (1) An insurance policy that pays a loss before others covering the same risk. (2) A contract written in such an amount as to cover only an insured's expected loss during the policy period with no other insurance in existence.

First Loss Retention (or Deductible). See Excess of Loss Reinsurance.

"First" Named Insured. The first person named as an insured on a commercial policy. These forms require an insurer to notify the first named insured rather than notifying all named insureds.

First Offer Plan. A provision in a buy-sell agreement specifying that an offer to sell common stock must first be made to current stockholders.

First Party. In terms of liability, this means the insurance policyholder is at fault in an accident. First party liabilities—or, damage an insured does to himself and his own property—are relatively easy for insurance companies to calculate and control. See also Third Party.

First Party Insurance. Coverage for the insured's own property or person. Contrast with Third Party Insurance.

First Surplus Reinsurance. The first amount allocated to reinsurance in excess of the original insurer's net retention. See also Surplus Reinsurance and Lines.

First Surplus Treaty. A contract whereby the reinsurer shares the risk with the ceding company on a pro rata basis. The reinsurer pays a proportion of each loss.

First Year. Refers to various matters during the first year a policy is in force, such as first year premiums and first year claims.

First Year Commission. The commission paid to an insurance agent on the first year's premium as compensation for a newly sold policy.

Fiscal Intermediary. A commercial insurer contracted by the Department of Health and Human Services to process and administer Part A Medicare claims.

501(c)(9) Trust. A voluntary employee beneficiary association. This is used by some companies to administer benefits.

Five Year Income Averaging. A tax device for lump sum distributions from a qualified plan that enables the individual to pay a lesser amount of income tax on the distribution.

Fixed-Amount Installments. A settlement option that pays a fixed, periodic (annual, semiannual, quarterly, monthly) benefit of a predetermined amount until the proceeds (principal) and interest are exhausted. Also called the amount option and the principal and interest to exhaustion option.

Fixed Annuity. An annuity that provides the annuitant with a fixed payment during the period of the annuity. Fixed annuity payments are considered part of the insurance company's general account assets (the conservative investment portfolio, not the stock market portfolio).

Fixed Base Liability. The liability coverage needed by fixed base operators, i.e., those who operate commercial enterprises and operate out of one airport (e.g., aircraft dealers, charterers and instructors).

Fixed Benefit Retirement Plan. A plan providing retirement benefits only on a fixed amount or at a fixed percentage—such as 1 percent of monthly salary times the number of years of credited employment; or 25 percent of the employee's average pay over the last few years prior to retirement.

Fixed Benefit. A benefit with a dollar amount that does not vary.

Fixed Dollar Annuity. Guarantees a fixed, minimum dollar payout during each payout period.

Fixed-Period Installment Option. A settlement option whereby the proceeds are guaranteed to be paid in equal installments for a specified period of time. Proceeds are retained by the insurance company and paid in equal installments over a specified period of months or years. Payments are comprised of both principal and interest. The payments also are established without regard to the length of life of the primary beneficiary. If the beneficiary dies, payments are continued to a second beneficiary. Also called installments certain or time option.

Fixed Period Option. An option for paying the proceeds of a life insurance policy to beneficiaries whereby the insured chooses the dollar amount of the benefit payment. This fixed amount is paid periodically until the entire proceeds are exhausted. Interest, at a minimum guaranteed rate, is added to the proceeds annually.

Flat. Without interest or service charges. See also Flat Cancelation.

Flat Cancelation. A policy that is canceled on its effective date. Usually under a flat cancelation no premium charge is made.

Flat Commission. A standard scale commission paid to agents regardless of the type of exposure or type of policy. Contrast with Graded Commission.

Flat Deductible. A deductible which is not one of the disappearing or franchise type. A specific amount deducted from each loss or claim.

Flat Maternity Benefit. A stipulated benefit in a hospital reimbursement policy that is paid for maternity confinement, regardless of the actual cost of the confinement.

Flat Rate. A reinsurance premium rate based on the entire premium income received by the ceding company from business ceded to the reinsurer, as distinguished from a rate applicable only to the excess limits premium.

Fleet (or Group) of Companies. A number of insurance organizations under common ownership and often common management.

Fleet Policy. An insurance contract that applies to a number of vehicles. Usually five or more self-propelled vehicles constitute a fleet.

Flesch Test. A method for determining the degree of ease or difficulty for reading material. This method counts not only the number of words in a sentence, but also the number of syllables in each word. It has come into popular use because of state laws requiring that contracts of insurance be easily understandable by someone at the eighth grade level.

Flexible Benefit Plan. A program that allows employees to tailor benefits to meet their own specific needs.

Flexible Premium Adjustable Life Insurance Policy. Another term for universal life policies.

Flexible Premium Annuity. An annuity that allows the contract holder to vary the amount of the premium payment, or stop payments and resume payments at will. A flexible premium annuity is used to fund IRA and Keogh retirement plans because it allows the amount of premium to change as wages change.

Flexible Premium Policy. A life insurance policy that allows the policyholder to vary the amount or timing of premium payments.

Flexible Premium Variable Life. A whole life contract and a security that features flexible premium payments, nonguaranteed cash values and either a minimum guaranteed death benefit or no guaranteed death benefit. Policy values are dependent on the performance of a separate account.

Flexible Spending Account (FSA). A salary reduction cafeteria plan whereby employee funds are used to provide various types of health care benefits.

FLMI. Fellow of the Life Management Institute. See Life Office Management Association.

Floater. An endorsement that applies to movable property, whatever its location, if it is within the territorial limits imposed by the contract. Coverage "floats" with the property.

Flood. A general and temporary condition of partial or complete inundation of normally dry land areas from: overflow of inland/tidal waters; unusual accumulation and runoff of surface waters from any source; or abnormal, flood-related erosion and undermining of shorelines. Flood also means inundation from mud flows caused by accumulations of water on or under the ground, as long as the mud flow and not a landslide is the proximate cause of loss.

Flood Insurance. Reimburses property owners for loss due to the defined peril of flood. Often sold in connection with a government insurance plan.

Floor Plan Insurance. Coverage for merchandise held for sale by a retailer that has been used as collateral for a loan. The lending institution, in effect, is insuring its collateral the merchandise "on the floor" of the retailer.

FOB. See Free On Board.

Following Form. A fire or other form written exactly under the same terms and coverages as other insurance on the same property.

Foreign Insurer. An insurer domiciled in a state other than the one in which the insured's insurance is written.

Forfeitures. Non-vested remainders in pension plans left by terminated employees. Forfeitures must be used to reduce employer contributions in subsequent years. In profit-sharing plans, forfeitures may be allocated among remaining participants.

Forgery. The false and fraudulent making or altering of a written instrument.

Forgery Bond. See Depositor's Forgery Insurance.

Forgery or Alteration Coverage Form. A commercial crime coverage form that protects the insured against losses resulting from forgery or alteration of outgoing checks, drafts, promissory notes and similar instruments drawn against the insured's accounts.

Form. (1) An insurance policy, sometimes called a form, is the written statement of a contract of insurance. (2) An insurance document which, when attached to a policy, makes it complete (e.g., a standard fire policy would have to have a business interruption form attached to it to make up a business interruption policy. (3) Any rider or endorsement, such as a deductible endorsement form.

Formal Plan. A retirement plan set forth in writing whereby contractual and legally enforceable rights pass on to the participating employees.

Formula. How the amount of pension to be received, or contribution to be made under a retirement plan is determined.

Formulary. See Drug Formulary.

Fortuitous Event. See Accident.

Foundation Exclusion Clause. A provision in a fire insurance policy which provides that the value of the foundation is not to be included when determining the value of property at the time of a loss.

Foundering. A term that refers to a ship that is sinking.

401(h) Trust. Governed by IRS Codes, these accounts have limited use for tax-free funding of post retirement benefits. An employer's 401(h) contribution is limited to no more than 25 percent of total contributions to all retiree benefits, including pension benefits. Since the health liabilities for most employers are so large, a 401(h) could provide only incidental funding.

401(k) Plan. A qualified elective deferral plan where employee contributions are made by means of a salary reduction agreement, with or without matching employer contributions.

403(b). A section of the Internal Revenue Code authorizing tax sheltered annuities as qualified pension plans for employees of nonprofit organizations.

FPA. See Free of Particular Average.

Fractional Premium. A proportionate amount of the annual premium, such as semiannual, quarterly, etc.

Frame. A type of construction. A frame building is primarily made with wood frames and joists.

Franchise Clause. See Franchise Deductible.

Franchise Deductible. A deductible that originated with marine insurance. It states that no claim is payable unless it exceeds a stated amount or a stated percentage of the amount of insurance. Once the claim exceeds that amount or percentage, the entire amount of the claim is payable.

Franchise Insurance. A plan for covering groups of persons with individual policies having uniform provisions, although they may differ in benefits. Individual contracts are issued to each person with individual underwriting. It is usually applied to groups too small to qualify for true group coverage, and the solicitation of cases usually takes place among a workforce with employer consent. In life insurance, it is sometimes called wholesale insurance. Contrast with True Group Insurance.

Fraternal Insurance. Insurance offered to a special group of people, namely, members of a lodge or a fraternal order. It may be written on an assessment basis or on a legal reserve basis.

Fraud. Deceit, trickery or misrepresentation with the intent to induce another to part with something of value or surrender a legal right.

Fraudulent Delivery. In connection with transportation floaters, when a shipper surrenders goods to someone posing as an agent for the carrier, it is held that the goods did not come into the custody of the carrier. If the carrier delivers goods to someone posing as an agent for the receiver, it is held that no valid delivery is made, and the carrier is liable for the loss.

Free Alongside (FAS). A marine shipping agreement which requires the seller to place the goods alongside a named vessel or a designated dock. The seller is responsible for insuring goods up to the time they are alongside.

Free Look Period. A period of time (usually 10, 20 or 30 days) during which a policyholder may examine a newly issued individual policy of life or health insurance, and surrender it in exchange for a full refund of premium if not satisfied for any reason.

Free of Particular Average (FPA). A contract provision that excuses the insurer from liability for losses below a certain percentage or fixed amount. Similar to a deductible.

Free on Board (FOB). The term has special significance in marine insurance, where it is vital to determine when title passes from the seller to the buyer. If the materials are shipped FOB point of destination, the seller is liable for damage caused during the course of transportation. If the material is shipped FOB point of departure, then the buyer becomes liable for it.

Free-of-Capture-and-Seizure Clause. An insurance contract provision that excludes losses due to war, capture and seizure.

Free-Standing Emergency Medical Service Center. A facility whose primary purpose is to provide care for emergency medical conditions. Also called emergi-center or surgi-center.

Free-Standing Outpatient Surgical Center. A facility that only provides outpatient surgical services. Also called surgi-center.

Freight. A charge for the transportation of goods.

Frequency. The number of times a service is provided over a given time period.

Friendly Fire. See Fire.

Fringe Benefits. See Employee Benefit Program.

Fronting. When the ceding company retains a very small part of a risk and reinsures the large majority of it with one or more reinsurers.

FSA. See Fellow of the Society of Actuaries.

Full Coverage. Insurance that provides for the payment of all insured losses in full. For example, some health insurance policies provide for full coverage without a deductible, participation or a coinsurance clause.

Full Preliminary Term Reserve Valuation. A method for determining reserves on life insurance contracts, whereby no reserve is required for the first year of a contract's life, with an appropriate adjustment in subsequent years' reserves to make up the difference. This method of valuation makes it possible for an insured to have more funds available for the high first-year expenses incurred in the writing of life insurance.

Full Reporting Clause. A clause that requires an insured to report values periodically. The clause provides for a penalty to the insured if true values are not reported.

Fully Insured Plan. A qualified plan whereby contributions are made to an insurer and benefits and plan administration are provided by the insurance company in behalf of plan participants.

Fully Insured Status. A provision of OASDHI that sets forth the qualifications for eligibility for retirement benefits under the Social Security system. For most people, this means having worked 40 calendar quarters (usually 10 years) at covered employment, though there are some exceptions. Contrast with Currently Insured Status. See also Social Security Disability Income Benefits.

Fully Paid Policy. A limited payment life insurance contract on which all required payments have been made. For instance, a 20-pay life policy would be fully paid after the insured has paid premiums for 20 years.

Functional Valuation Endorsements. Endorsements that allow property to be replaced with less costly property that is functionally equivalent to the damaged or destroyed property; that is, similar property that performs the same function when replacement with identical property is impossible or unnecessary.

Fund. (1) Money and investments held in trust in order to pay pension benefits. (2) To accumulate money necessary to pay pension benefits; to pay into the fund each year enough to cover the pension plan's obligations for that year.

Funded. Having sufficient funds to meet future liabilities. Often used with a pension plan's outstanding claims account.

Funded Deferred Compensation Plan. A compensation plan in which the employer actually sets aside a sum of money or other assets into an account or trust as security for the employer's promise to deliver the deferred benefits at a later date. The employee usually is named as the beneficiary of this trust, cash or property. This plan ties the employee to the company and the employer except for retirement, death or disability. If the employee leaves for any other reason, the deferred amounts are forfeited.

Funding, Advance. See Advance Funding. Predetermined sums set aside to provide for the payment of future retirement benefits.

Funding, Disbursement. Also known as the "pay-as-you-go" method, this type of funding requires no funds to be set aside to provide retirement benefits. All benefits paid to retired employees are paid from the company's gross income and are deducted as a normal business expense.

Funding, Terminal. See Terminal Funding. Funding that requires no funds to be set aside for retirement benefits, however, as each employee retires, an immediate lifetime annuity is purchased for him or her.

Funding Level. The dollar amount required to purchase a particular medical care program. Usually measured by the premium rate for an insured program, or an amount assessed for expected claim loss and related fees under a self-funded program.

Funding Medium/Funding Vehicle. The arrangement through which funding methods operate (e.g., trust agreement; custodial account; deposit administration contract; or group annuity contract).

Funding Method. (1) The agreed means by which an employer pays for health coverage. (2) How money is accumulated for future payment of pension benefits.

Funeral Benefit. Coverage under an auto policy that pays if the insured or a family member dies in an auto accident.

Fur and Jewelry Floater. Usually an open perils (all risk) form that applies to the furs and jewelry scheduled in the policy whatever their location.

Furriers Customers Insurance. An inland marine form purchased by a furrier to protect furs in storage belonging to customers.

Future Increase Option (FIO). An option that allows the insured to increase disability income benefits at predetermined times, specified in the policy, without evidence of insurability. Normally, the rider is not available past age 40, although some insurers may offer it up to age 50.

Future Interest. Generally means the future interest and enjoyment of personal property provided for an individual by means of a gift.

G

GA. See General Agent.

GAAP. See Generally Accepted Accounting Principles.

GAB. See General Adjustment Bureau, Inc.

Gain and Loss Exhibit. The portion of the convention blank that represents an analysis of gains, losses and surplus during an accounting period.

Gambling. A situation where there is a chance of either loss or gain. It is the opposite of insurance, which either eliminates or reduces risk of loss.

GAMC. See General Agents and Managers Conference.

Garage Coverage Form. A commercial auto insurance coverage form used to insure automobile dealers, repair shops, service stations and garage risks. Garage liability, garagekeepers coverage and physical damage coverages may be included.

Garage Keepers Legal Liability Insurance. Coverage that protects a garage keeper against liability for damage to vehicles in the keeper's care, custody or control caused by specific perils.

Garage Liability Insurance. Protects garage owners or automobile dealers for liabilities arising out of their business operations.

Gatekeeper Model. Under this model of HMO and PPO organizations, the primary care physician (the gatekeeper) is the initial contact for the patient for medical care and for referrals. Also called a closed access or closed panel.

Gender Rule. A method of determining which parent's medical coverage will be primary for dependent children; the father's coverage is often considered primary and pays first.

General Account. An investment portfolio used by the insurer for investment of premium income. This portfolio generally consists of safe, conservative, guaranteed investments, such as real estate and mortgages.

General Adjustment Bureau, Inc. (GAB). An independent company that adjusts claims of all types for insurance companies. GAB also provides training programs for adjusters.

General Agency System. The marketing of life insurance through general agents.

General Agent (GA). An individual appointed by a life or health insurer to administer its business in a given territory. General agents are responsible for building their own agency and service force and are compensated on a commission basis, with possibly some additional expense allowances.

General Agents and Managers Conference (GAMC). An association of insurance general agents and managers affiliated with the National Association of Life Underwriters.

General Aggregate Limit. A commercial general liability limit that applies to all damages paid for bodily injury, property damage, personal injury, advertising injury and medical expenses, except damages included in the products-completed operations hazard.

General Agreement. A brief statement stating that all of the remaining provisions of the contract (the policy terms) apply. The reason that the general agreement is so brief is that each coverage section contains a much more detailed insuring agreement.

General and Insurance Expense. See General Operating Expense.

General Average. A partial loss incurred to save the total venture from destruction. Any such losses are prorated among all parties to the venture, including the parties whose interests first suffered such loss (e.g., throwing cargo overboard in order to save a ship from a particular peril).

General Cover Form. An older term for reporting form policy. See Reporting Form.

General Exclusions. Exclusions that eliminate coverage for war risks, nuclear risks, floods and other types of water damage.

General Liability Insurance. A form of insurance designed to protect owners and operators of businesses from a wide variety of liability exposures, including liability arising out of accidents resulting from the premises or the operations of an insured, products sold by the insured, operations completed by the insured and contractual liability.

General LTC Rider. A long-term care rider that is attached to a life insurance policy but stands alone or is independent of the life policy. Any LTC benefits paid do not reduce life insurance benefits.

General Operating Expense. The expense of an insurer other than commissions and taxes. Also called general and insurance expense.

General Partnership. A business enterprise owned and operated by two or more persons for the purpose of generating business income and profits.

General Power of Appointment. A donee is given the authority to pass on a property interest to whomever he or she pleases.

General Property Form. A form that covers the property of commercial risks from whatever perils are specified in the contract.

Generally Accepted Accounting Principles (GAAP). These principles have substantial authoritative support for use in the insurance business. They are intended to produce financial results consistent with those of other industries and to assure consistency in financial reporting. Contrast with Statutory Accounting Principles.

Generation Skipping Transfer. A transfer of property due to death or by gift, to a person who is two or more generations below the grantor.

Generic Drug. A drug that is exactly the same as a brand name drug and that is allowed to be produced after the brand name drug's patent has expired. It is also called a "generic equivalent."

Generic Equivalence. See Generic Drug.

Geographical Limitation. A contractual provision that specifically names geographical areas outside of which the insurance is not effective. Also called territorial limitation.

GI Insurance. See United States Government Life Insurance.

Gift. A sale, exchange or transfer of property without adequate consideration.

Gift Tax. Federal and state tax on gifts made by one person to another.

Glass Coverage Form. A commercial property form that insures plate glass, lettering, frames and ornamentation. It replaced earlier commercial glass insurance forms.

Good Driver Discount. A system that entitles good drivers (as defined by driving safety record, number of miles driven annually, number of years driving experience, etc.) to discounts on auto insurance rates and premiums. See also Safe Driver Plan.

Good Student Discount. A discount granted to students with high scholastic ratings. This discount offered offers up to as much as 25 percent off premiums.

Goodwill. An intangible business asset. The value of a business that is built up through the reputation of the business concern and its owners.

Governing Classification. The classification assigned to the operations of an insured that carries the largest amount of payroll. If a company has several different operations in one plant, the one that employs most workers will usually be ruled the governing classification.

Grace Period. A prescribed period, usually 30 to 31 days from the premium due date, when an insurance contract is in force and the premium may be paid. The grace period simply allows the policyholder additional time to pay a premium after the due date.

Graded Commission. A compensation scale for agents that provides for varying commission rates depending upon the class, type or volume of insurance written. Contrast with Flat Commission.

Graded Death Benefits. A provision in life insurance contracts for death benefits that, in the early years of the contract, are less than the face amount of the policy but that increase with the passage of time. Most commonly found in juvenile policies issued at or near age zero.

Graded Premium. A modified life insurance policy for which the initial premium is low, and then increases over a period of time (usually five years), after which it becomes a level premium.

Grading Schedule for Cities and Towns. A schedule prepared by the National Board of Fire Underwriters to determine which of ten grades to assign to a city for fire rating purposes, based on such factors of fire protection as water supply.

Graduated Life Table. A mortality table in which the experience has been smoothed out by formula. See also Experience.

Grantee. The buyer of real estate.

Grantor. The seller of real estate.

Grantor Retained Annuity Trust (GRAT). A trust in which the grantor substitutes retention of a right to payment of a fixed income in exchange for a fixed period of time.

Grantor Retained Interest Trust (GRIT). An irrevocable trust whereby the grantor of the trust property (e.g., a personal residence) receives an income for a fixed period of time.

Grantor Retained Unitrust Trust (GRUT). A trust in which a grantor substitutes retention of a right to a fixed percentage of the trust value in exchange for a fixed period of time.

Grievance Procedure. A procedure that allows a member of a health plan or a provider of benefits to express complaints and seek remedies.

Gross Earnings. An accounting term that is arrived at by subtracting the cost of goods sold from the total sales. Traditionally, the term was used primarily in business interruption insurance to determine how much insurance a policyholder should carry. The latest business income insurance forms have dropped this term.

Gross Earnings Form. A form once used widely in business interruption insurance. Coverage was written on either the gross earnings form or the earnings form. Business income coverage forms no longer refer to gross earnings.

Gross Line. The total limit accepted by an insurer on an individual risk, including the amount to be reinsured.

Gross Negligence. Willful and wanton negligence or misconduct. See also Negligence.

Gross Premium. (1) The premium for participating life insurance. If an insured elects to use dividends to pay premiums, this becomes the net premium when dividends are subtracted from it. Contrast with net premium. (2) The net premium plus operating expenses, commissions and other expenses.

Ground Coverage. Similar to collision and comprehensive coverage in an automobile policy. This insurance covers a plane's hull from specific perils when the plane is on the ground. There are different forms of ground coverage: "Not in Flight" covers the plane on the ground only but includes taxiing. "Not in Motion" covers the plane on the ground and not in motion.

Group. Coverage of a number of individuals under one contract. The most common group is employees of the same employer.

Group Annuity. A retirement plan for a group of persons (usually employees of a single employer) funded by a single annuity contract which is written on a group basis.

Group Certificate. The document provided to each member of a group plan that shows the benefits provided under the group contract issued to the employer or other insured.

Group Contract. A contract of insurance made with an employer or other entity that covers a group of persons identified by reference to their relationship to the entity buying the contract. Generally covers employees of a common employer, members of a trade association or trusteeship, members of a welfare or employee benefit association, members of a labor union or members of a professional or other association not formed only for the purpose of obtaining insurance.

Group Credit Insurance. Insurance on the life or health of debtors of a creditor, payable for reduction or extinguishment of the debts in case of the disability or death of the debtor.

Group Deposit Administration Contract. A funding contract for a qualified plan whereby contributions are accounted for on an unallocated basis for the benefit of all plan participants.

Group Disability Benefits. Coverage for a group of individuals for loss of compensation due to accident or sickness. These work-related benefits are available from a qualified plan, a salary continuation plan, employee stock plans, workers' compensation, etc. Group disability benefits are of short duration—a year or less—and cover only a percentage of lost income.

Group Health Insurance. The same as group life insurance but with the application to health insurance coverages. See Group Life Insurance.

Group I Rates. Under the latest commercial lines program, this term replaces the term "fire rates" for property coverages.

Group II Rates. Under the latest commercial lines program, this term replaces the term "extended coverage rates" for property coverages.

Group Life Insurance. Life insurance provided for members of a group. It is most often issued to a group of employees but may be issued to any group provided it is not formed for the purpose of buying insurance. The cost is lower than for individual policies because administrative expenses per life are decreased, there are certain tax advantages and measures taken against adverse selection are effective. See also franchise insurance, true group and master policy.

Group Model HMO. A health plan where a group of physicians is reimbursed for services they provide at a negotiated rate. The HMO also contracts with hospitals for the care of the patients of the physicians who belong to the group.

Group of Companies. See Fleet of Companies.

Group Ordinary Life Insurance. Level premium ordinary life insurance issued on a group basis.

Group Permanent Insurance. (1) A form of life insurance whereby members of a group are provided one of several plans of permanent life insurance on a group basis instead of the more usual plan of term life insurance. (2) A retirement plan that combines life insurance with retirement benefits. It uses the level premium method under a group contract.

Group Property and Liability Insurance. The same as group life insurance but applied to property and liability coverages. See Group Life Insurance.

Group Renewable Term Insurance. Yearly renewable term insurance on a group basis; often called group life insurance.

Group Retirement Income Insurance. Level premium retirement income insurance issued on a group basis.

Guaranteed Cash Value. In whole life insurance, the policy's cash value increases over the life of the policy until at the insured's age 100 the cash value is equal to the policy's face amount.

Guaranteed Continuable. See Guaranteed Renewable.

Guaranteed Cost. A premium charged on a prospective basis, fixed or adjustable, or on a specified rating basis, but never on the basis of loss experience. In other words, the cost is guaranteed to the extent that it will not be adjusted based on the loss experience of the insured during the period of coverage.

Guaranteed Insurability. An option in life and health insurance contracts that permits the insured to buy additional prescribed amounts of insurance at prescribed future time intervals without evidence of insurability.

Guaranteed Interest. Interest that is guaranteed to be paid on a fixed annuity investment contract. There are two types of guaranteed interest: current and minimum.

Guaranteed Period. Also known as a period certain, this means that payments of a life insurance policy to the beneficiaries will be guaranteed for a specified period of time.

Guaranteed Renewable. A contract that the insured has the right to continue in force by the timely payment of premiums for a substantial period of time as set forth in the contract. During that period of time, the insurer has no right to make any change in any provision of the contract other than a change in the premium rate for all insureds in the same class. Contrast with Noncancelable, from which Guaranteed Renewable should be distinguished.

Guaranteed Replacement Cost. The surest way to arrange full coverage. This policy pays up to 50 percent more than the face value of the policy to rebuild a home. (A few companies offer unlimited coverage.)

Guaranteed Standard Issue (GSI). An underwriting term used to describe the fact that a group insurance contract was issued without reference to any medical underwriting. All group participants are covered regardless of health history.

Guarantor. One who guarantees or promises to back up another's actions or debts. It is used in surety bonds, usually the surety company is the guarantor.

Guaranty Funds. Funds created by state law from contributions by insurers operating in the state which are used to make good any unpaid claims or otherwise to make money available to insolvent companies. Each state has a different plan. See Insurance Guaranty Act.

Guardian. A person appointed by the court to take care of affairs of another (e.g., a guardian to take care of the affairs of a minor or a mentally incompetent).

Guertin Laws. The valuation and nonforfeiture laws which have been standard in all states since 1947, named for Alfred Guertin, then actuary of the New Jersey Insurance Department and head of the NAIC committee which developed the model bill for these laws. See also Nonforfeiture Values.

Guest Law. Some states have legislation that restricts the rights of a guest to collect from the driver of an automobile he is riding in on the grounds of ordinary negligence. Usually such cases require proof of willful and wanton negligence on the part of the driver before the guest can collect. See also Assumption of Risk.

Guest Property Coverage. Commercial crime coverage for hotels, motels, inns and other lodging facilities to protect the property of guests against loss or damage. Includes coverage for guests' property while it is in a safe deposit box on the insured's premises, or for an insured's legal liability for loss or damage to guests' property while in the insured's premises or in the insured's possession.

Guideline Premium. A universal life insurance term used to describe the maximum premium that may be paid while still qualifying as life insurance under the federal Internal Revenue Code.

Guiding Principles. Rules established by major property and liability trade associations for the adjustment of losses, particularly with respect to how losses should be apportioned between insurance companies under certain circumstances.

Hail Insurance. Insurance against loss of crops caused by hail.

Hangarkeepers Legal Liability Insurance. Protection against liability for damage or injury to others arising out of the ownership, maintenance or use of the premises for an aircraft hanger.

Hazard. A specific situation that increases the probability of the occurrence of loss arising from a peril, or that influences the extent of the loss (e.g., slippery floors, unsanitary conditions, shingled roofs, congested traffic, unguarded premises, uninspected boilers, etc.).

Hazard, Legal. See Legal Hazard.

Hazard, Moral. See Moral Hazard.

Hazard, Morale. See Morale Hazard.

Hazard, Physical. See Physical Hazard.

Hazardous Avocation. A pricing factor related to occupational risk. Includes such hobbies as skin diving, scuba diving, sky diving and auto racing. Insurance companies ask insureds to inform them of any such high-risk hobbies when considering applications for disability income.

HCFA. See Health Care Financing Administration.

HCFA 1500. A form used by providers of health services to bill their fees to health carriers. It was developed by the government agency known as the Health Care Financing Administration.

Head Office. See Home Office. The term "head office" is primarily used in British insurance operations, whereas "home office" is used for American operations.

Health Benefits Package. The coverages offered by a health plan to an individual or group.

Health Care Financing Administration (HCFA). Part of the Department of Health and Human Services, responsible for administration of the Medicare and Medicaid programs. The HCFA establishes standards for medical providers which must be complied with if the provider is to meet certification requirements.

Health History. A form used by underwriters to assist in evaluating groups or individuals to determine whether they are acceptable risks.

Health Insurance. Insurance against loss by sickness or bodily injury. The generic form for those forms of insurance that provide lump sum or periodic payments in the event of loss occasioned by bodily injury, sickness or disease and medical expense. The term health insurance replaces such terms as accident insurance, sickness insurance, medical expense insurance, accidental death insurance and dismemberment insurance. The form is sometimes called accident and health, accident and sickness, accident or disability income insurance.

HHS

Health Insurance Association of America (HIAA). An association supported by life and health insurers to provide the research, public relations, education and legislative base for the promotion of voluntary private health insurance.

Health Maintenance Organization (HMO). A prepaid medical service plan that provides services to plan members. Medical providers contract with the HMO to provide medical services to plan members. Members must use contracted providers. The emphasis is on preventive medicine, and it is an alternative to employee benefit plans. Employers of more than 25 persons are required to offer the alternative of HMO to employees, but not if the cost exceeds that of present employee benefit plans.

Health Plan. Any plan that covers health care services such as HMOs, insured plans, preferred provider organizations, etc.

Health Service Agreement (HSA). An agreement between employer and the health plan that outlines a description of benefits, enrollment procedures, eligibility standards, etc.

Health Services. Benefits covered under a health contract.

Hearsay. Testimony based on what someone else has said or told a witness.

HHS. The U.S. Department of Health and Human Services, which administers the OASDHI, Medicare and Public Assistance programs.

HIAA. See Health Insurance Association of America.

High Pressure Tactics. An illegal method of marketing insurance policies (often associated with Medicare supplement policies) employing tactics that induce the purchase or recommend the purchase of coverage through force, fright, explicit or implied threat or undue pressure.

Highly Protected Risk (HPR). Property risks which meet the standards required for lower rates. Risks of this type are usually protected by sprinklers and have better-than-average construction and occupancy. It is often used in connection with the factory mutuals, factory insurance association and improved risk mutuals.

HIQA. Health Insurance Quality Award. An award granted annually by the International Association of Health Underwriters or the National Association of Life Underwriters for high persistency of health insurance policies written by agents. See also Persistency.

Hired Automobile. Autos the insured leases, hires, rents or borrows, but not autos owned by employees or members of their households.

HIV. See Human Immunodeficiency Virus.

HMO. See Health Maintenance Organization.

HO-1 The Basic Homeowners Form. Covers the dwelling, other structures on premises and personal property against 11 named perils—mostly having to do with fire and water damage.

HO-2 The Broad Homeowners Form. Insures the dwelling, other structures and personal property against loss by all basic form perils plus six additional perils.

HO-3 The Special Homeowners Form. Insures personal property against loss by the same broad form perils included on HO-2 and insures the dwelling and other structures against "risk of direct physical loss" except to the extent that exclusions and limitations apply. HO-3 has a number of exclusions. Also called the all-risk form.

HO-4 Tenant Broad Form. This policy and HO-6 both insure personal property against all of the perils found on the broad form. Also called the renters form.

HO-6 Condo Unit Owner Form. Provides coverage for stated perils and also applies to the limited dwelling coverage for alterations and other owned building items.

HO-8 Modified Homeowners Form. Special coverage for older homes.

Hold Harmless Agreement. A contractual arrangement whereby one party assumes the liability inherent in a situation, thereby relieving the other party of responsibility. Typically found in contracts like leases, sidetrack agreements and easements (e.g., a typical lease may provide that the lessee must "hold harmless" the lessor for any liability from accidents arising out of the premises). The effect: the lessee must provide a defense for the lessor, and if any judgment is rendered against the lessor, the lessee would have to pay.

Hold-Up. A form of robbery. See Robbery.

Holographic Will. A valid will that is completely handwritten and signed by the testator.

Home Health Agency. A certified facility approved by a health plan to provide services under contract.

Home Health Care. Care received at home as part-time skilled nursing care, speech therapy, physical or occupational therapy, part-time services of home health aides or help from homemakers or choreworkers.

Home Health Services. Health care services provided by a licensed home health agency in the patient's home. It is a covered expense under Part A of Medicare.

Home Office. Generally the corporate headquarters of insurers and the location where the chief officers of the organization are housed.

Home Office Life Underwriters Association. An organization offering a course of study for home office life underwriters.

Home Service Insurance. A variation in the industrial life concept, home service life insurance policies are usually modest in size, ranging from $10,000 to $15,000 in face value, and are typically sold on a monthly debit plan (automatic bank draft) or payments by mail.

Homeowners Insurance Policy. A property and liability insurance contract that provides insurance against any of the property and liability perils to which a homeowner or renter is exposed. It covers the average residential and personal exposures that most individuals and families encounter.

Honesty Clause. See Full Reporting Clause.

Honorable Undertaking. Reinsurance contracts state that: "This agreement is considered by the parties hereto as an honorable undertaking, the purpose of which is not to be defeated by a strict or narrow interaction of the language thereof."

Hospice. An organization that provides pain relief, symptom management and supportive services for the terminally ill and their families. Hospice care is covered under Part A of Medicare.

Hospice Care. An optional benefit available under LTC insurance.

Hospital Affiliation. A contract whereby one or more hospitals agrees to provide benefits to members of a specific health plan.

Hospital Alliances. A group of hospitals that work together to share common services and reduce health costs. By grouping together, they are better able to compete with other alliances or chains.

Hospital Benefits. Benefits payable for hospital room and board, plus miscellaneous charges resulting from hospitalization.

Hospital Confinement Rider. An optional disability income rider that waives the elimination period when an insured is hospitalized as an inpatient.

Hospital Expense Insurance. See Hospitalization Insurance.

Hospital Income Insurance. Insurance that provides a stated weekly or monthly payment while the insured is hospitalized, regardless of expenses incurred and regardless of whether or not other insurance is in force. The insured can use the weekly or monthly benefit as he chooses, for hospital or other expenses.

Hospital Indemnity. Coverage that pays based on daily, weekly or monthly limits regardless of the amount of actual hospital expenses.

Hospital Insurance. Also identified as Part A of Medicare, this provides inpatient hospital care, skilled nursing care home health and hospice care subject to a benefit period deductible and copayments for certain services.

Hospital Tax. A Social Security tax of 1.45 percent on an unlimited amount of income, paid by both the employee and employer to prepay for Part A of Medicare.

Hospitalization Expense Policy. A policy that covers daily hospital room and board charges and also covers miscellaneous hospital expenses (such as x-ray, etc.). It often covers emergency treatment charges or includes a surgical benefit.

Hospitalization Insurance. Insurance that provides reimbursement within contractual limits for hospital and specific related expenses arising from hospitalization caused by injury or sickness.

Host Liability. Liability for the damages a guest caused after an insured allowed him to consume alcohol—and engage in various other activities—and then leave. Some states have laws that mandate a host's liability, much like a restaurateur's or a bartender's liability. In at least 21 states, statutory liability extends to noncommercial servers. In 10 other states, similar liability has been established by common law.

Hostile Fire. See Fire.

House Confinement. A provision in some health insurance contracts that requires an insured to be confined to the house in order to be eligible for benefits. This provision is most commonly found in policies providing loss of income benefits.

Household Personal Property. Household goods, furniture and personal belongings of residents of a farm dwelling. The Farm Property Coverage Form uses the term "household" to distinguish it from the separate coverage for "farm" property. Contrast with Farm Personal Property.

Housekeeping. The general care, cleanliness and maintenance of an insured's property. It is an important underwriting consideration in many forms of insurance, such as workers' compensation and property.

HPR. See Highly Protected Risk.

HR-10 Plan. See Keogh Act Plan.

HR-10. A qualified retirement plan for the self-employed. Also known as a Keogh Plan.

HUD. United States Department of Housing and Urban Development.

Hull Policy. A contract that provides indemnification for damage sustained to or loss of an insured vessel or airplane.

Hull Syndicates. A group of companies that agree to share or prorate insurance on oceangoing vessels or aircraft. Coverage on the ship or plane itself is called hull insurance.

Human Immunodeficiency Virus. The virus, known as HIV, which causes acquired immunodeficiency syndrome, an infectious and incurable disease commonly referred to as AIDS.

Human Life Value. A method of determining life insurance needs by considering a person's income, expenses, remaining years of earning capacity and depreciation in the value of the dollar over time.

IASA. Insurance Accounting Statistical Association.

IASS. Insurance Accounting and Statistical Society.

IBNR. See Incurred But Not Reported.

ICA. International Claim Association.

ICC. Interstate Commerce Commission.

ICEDS. Insurance Company Education Directors Society.

ICPI. Insurance Crime Prevention Institute.

Identification Card. A card given to an insured that identifies him or her as being eligible for benefits.

Identification of Benefits. A provision that says the cost of putting a disabled insured in touch with and in the care of relatives will be reimbursed, usually up to a maximum amount.

"If" Clauses. Clauses that terminate coverage "if" certain conditions are created or discovered (e.g., the concealment or misrepresentation provision, which states that if this is discovered, the coverage is void). Contrast with "While" Clauses.

IHOU. Institute of Home Office Underwriters.

IIA. See Insurance Institute of America, Inc.

IIAA. See Independent Insurance Agents of America.

IIC. Independent Insurance Conference or Insurance Institute of Canada.

III. See Insurance Information Institute.

IIS. See International Insurance Seminars, Inc.

Illegal Occupation Provision. A health insurance policy provision that voids liability if the loss results from the insured's committing or attempting to commit a felony or from the insured's engaging in an illegal occupation.

Illness. A loss sustained due to sickness or disease usually due to an organic cause.

Immature Policies. Claims-made coverage that has not been in effect, on an uninterrupted basis, for at least five years. For rating purposes, a discount applies to manual rates for immature policies.

Immediate Annuity. An annuity that commences payment to the annuitant at the end of the first prescribed payment period. If an insured buys an immediate annuity with monthly payments, he will start receiving benefits at the end of the first month after the purchase.

Immediate Vesting. A term used in pension or retirement plans, indicating that an employee's right to benefits begin as soon as he enters the plan. See also Vesting.

Impaired Insurer. An insurer that is in financial difficulty to the point where its ability to meet financial obligations or regulatory requirements is in question.

Impaired Property. Tangible property that cannot be used or has become less useful because it incorporates the insured's product or work, which is defective or inadequate, or because the insured has failed to fulfill a contractual obligation.

Impaired Risk. A risk, or subject of insurance, with insurable qualifications below the standard of risks on which the premium for the coverage was based (e.g., a life insurance prospect with heart disease). See also Substandard Risk and Standard Risk.

Impairment of Capital. When the surplus account of a stock insurer has been exhausted such that it must invade the capital account (amounts contributed by stockholders) to meet liabilities. Some jurisdictions allow a percentage invasion of capital; some do not.

Impeach. Evidence that tends to detract from the credibility of the witness.

Implied Authority. Authority of an agent that the public may reasonably believe the agent has. If the authority to collect and remit premiums is not expressly granted in the agency contract, but the agent does so on a regular basis and the insurer accepts, the agent has implied authority to do so.

Implied Coinsurance. After determining rebuilding costs, an insured must determine how much insurance he needs. If an insured is insured for less than 80 percent, the insurance company makes two estimates and pays the larger. This significant risk is called implied coinsurance.

Implied Seaworthiness. The assumption that a sea vessel, its equipment and its crew are in good condition and prepared to make the voyage.

Implied Warranty. In certain cases the law says that one has given a warranty to another even though the warranty is not in writing (e.g., in sales, a seller implies that the product is fit for the purpose it purports to serve).

Import. Goods or services purchased from another country and brought into one's own country.

Improvements and Betterments. Additions or changes made by a lessee at his own cost to a building that he occupies, which enhance its value. These become part of the realty and require special insurance consideration.

Imputed. When actions of one party, usually the agent, are deemed to be actions of the other party, usually the principal.

In Kind. An expression relating to the insurer's right in many property contracts to replace damaged objects with new or equivalent (in kind) material, rather than to pay a cash benefit.

In-Area Services. Services provided within the authorized service area as designated by a plan.

Incentive Stock Option (ISO) Plans. A stock plan whereby executives are granted options to purchase company stock without incurring a tax liability.

Inchmaree Clause. Reimburses an insured in the event of a loss due to the negligence of the master or crew of a vessel.

Incidental Locations. Locations other than those described, reported and acquired, where the value of insured property is $25,000 or less.

Incidents of Ownership. Various rights that may be exercised under the policy contract by the policyowner, including: 1) the right to cash in the policy; 2) to receive a loan on the cash value of the policy; and 3) to change the beneficiary.

Income Continuation Benefit. See Lost Wages.

Income Loss. Coverage for the amount of an insured's take-home pay when injuries from an accident keep him from working.

Income Policy. A life insurance contract that provides income on a monthly basis instead of a lump sum.

Incompetent. A person who cannot manage his or her own affairs. Children and legally insane people are often considered incompetent.

Incontestable Clause. A clause that states an insured's statements in his application cannot be contested by the insurer after the policy has been in effect for a given time (two or three years). For example, in life policies, if an insured lied about the condition of his health at the time the policy was taken out, that lie could not be used to contest payment under the policy if death occurred after the time limit stated in the incontestable clause.

Increased Cost of Construction Insurance. Covers the additional cost of reconstructing a damaged or destroyed building where ordinances require rebuilding with more expensive materials, services or techniques.

Increased Hazard. Property insurance policies suspend coverage when the hazard in a risk goes beyond that contemplated when the policy was written (e.g., if an insured commences manufacturing dynamite in his home, the hazard is extremely increased, and coverage could be denied by the insurer if there were a loss).

Increasing Premium Term. Term life insurance that provides a growing amount of insurance.

Increasing Term Insurance. A term life insurance policy where the death benefit increases but the premium remains level for the policy term. See also Decreasing Term Insurance, Level Term Insurance and Term Insurance.

Incurred But Not Reported. Losses that have occurred during a stated period, usually a calendar year, but have not yet been reported to the insurer as of the date under consideration (e.g., insurance company statements prepared after the end of the calendar year would have to include an estimate of losses that occurred during that year but have not yet been reported).

Incurred Expense. Expenses not yet paid. Includes paid expenses in some accounting systems.

Incurred Loss Ratio. The percentage of losses incurred to premiums earned.

Incurred Losses. The losses occurring within a fixed period, whether or not adjusted or paid during the same period (e.g., in workers' compensation claims, losses occur during a given policy period but benefits may continue for many years. The estimated value of the total claim would be an incurred loss for the policy period during which the loss occurred).

Indemnification. Payment in money or replacement of the property. Stolen property may be returned and payment made for any damage, or the company may keep the property and pay an agreed or appraised amount in money.

Indemnify. To restore the victim of a loss to the same position as before the loss occurred, either by payment, repair or replacement.

Indemnitor. An entity/person who enters an agreement with a surety to hold the surety harmless from loss incurred as a result of issuing a contract bond to an applicant who falls just short of acceptability. If the principal defaults, the indemnitor, rather than the surety, assumes the obligation.

Indemnity Basis. Most long-term care policies are issued on an indemnity basis, which means the contracts provide a daily maximum benefit, such as $100 per day, for each day of confinement in a nursing home or other long-term care facility. If the policy also includes benefits for home care, the daily limit for home care expenses typically is 50 percent of the daily nursing home benefit amount.

Indemnity Bond. A bond that indemnifies an obligee against loss that may arise as the result of failure to perform on the part of the principal.

Independent Adjuster. Adjusters who work as independent contractors, hiring out to insurance companies, etc., for the investigation and settlement of claims. They represent the interests of insurance companies. Contrast with Public Adjuster.

Independent Agency System. An insurance distribution system within which independent contractors, known as agents, sell and service property liability insurance solely on a commission or fee basis under contract with one or more insurers that recognize the agent's ownership use, and control of policy records and expiration data.

Independent Agent. An agent operating as an independent contractor under the independent agency system. They sell policies from several companies for a commission, attempting to find the lowest price available.

Independent Contractor. One who agrees to perform according to a contract and who is not an employee.

Independent Contractors Insurance. See Owners and Contractors Protective Liability Policy.

Independent Insurance Agents of America (IIAA). An association of independent insurance agents historically known to represent stock insurance companies more than mutual companies. Members are also members of their state associations.

Index Bureau Experience. A measure of losses relating to claims reported through a claim office during a 12-month period.

Indexing Year. The second year prior to attainment of age 62, death or disability, whichever occurs first, used to adjust wages to allow for inflation when calculating Social Security benefits.

Indigent. The state of being with no assets at risk.

Indirect Loss (or Damage). Loss resulting from a peril but not caused directly and immediately by that peril (e.g., loss of property due to fire is a direct loss, while the loss of rental income due to the fire would be an indirect loss). See also Consequential Loss.

Individual Account Plan. A defined contribution plan or profit sharing plan that provides an individual account for each participant and whose benefits are based solely upon the amount contributed to a participant's account and any income, expenses, gains and losses, as well as forfeitures that may be allocated to the remaining participant's account.

Individual Contract. A contract made with an individual that covers that individual and perhaps specified members of his family for benefits as described in the policy.

Individual Contract Pension Trust. A pension plan under which a trust holds title to individual insur-

ance or annuity contracts for employees covered by
the plan.

Individual Life Insurance. (1) A life insurance contract that covers usually one insured. (2) The term
used to distinguish this type of life insurance from
group life insurance.

**Individual Practice Association (IPA) Model
HMO.** An individual practice association contracted
to provide health care services. The IPAs contract
with individual physicians or groups of physicians
for their services.

Individual Retirement Account (IRA). A qualified retirement plan established by ERISA for anyone under age 70 1/2 with earned income, allowing them to set aside up to $2,000 per year on a tax
favorable basis for retirement purposes.

**Individual Risk Premium Modification Rating
Plan.** A plan that modifies the premium on large package policies by considering such factors as reduced
expenses for handling costs (expense modification) and
special characteristics of the risk not contemplated
by the basic rate (risk modification).

Industrial Life Insurance. One of the major classes
of insurance. It is generally sold in amounts of less
than $1,000 by agents who service insureds on deb-
its. Premiums are collected weekly or monthly at
the address of the insured. See also Debit.

Industrial Risk Insurers. A consortium of major
stock property and casualty insurers that write large,
highly protected risks.

Inevitable Accident. See Accident.

Inflation Factor. A premium loading to provide for future increases in medical costs and loss payments resulting from inflation.

Inflation Guard Coverage. Coverage that provides for automatic periodic increases in the amount of insurance on buildings to keep an appropriate "limit to value" considering the effect of inflation on building replacement costs. An endorsement is usually used to add this coverage to a homeowners policy. On the latest commercial property forms, inflation guard coverage is an option that may be activated by an entry in the declarations.

Inflation Protection. Provisions in a health insurance policy that increase benefit levels to account for anticipated increases in the cost of services.

Inflation. An economic period characterized by rising prices, low unemployment, an expanding economy and erosion of consumer's purchasing power due to the higher cost of living.

In-Force Business. Life or health insurance for which premiums are being paid or for which premiums have been fully paid. It refers to the total face amount of a life insurer's portfolio of business. In health insurance it refers to the total premium volume of an insurer's portfolio of business.

Informal Plan. A retirement system whereby the employer has no legal obligation and the employee has no legal rights. These plans have no standard of benefits to be paid, and have no special method of funding.

Inherent Explosion. An explosion caused by a condition existing in and natural to an insured's premises (e.g., a dust explosion in a grain elevator).

Inherent Vice. A fault in property that leads to its self-destruction. Insurance contracts usually exclude such damage.

Initial Eligibility Period. The time period during which prospective members can apply for coverage without providing evidence of insurability.

Initial Premium. An amount paid at the inception of an insurance contract, usually subject to adjustment at the end of the policy period.

Injunction. A court order intended to prevent a person from doing something.

Inland Marine Insurance. A branch of the insurance business that developed from the insuring of shipments not involving ocean voyages. These forms borrowed their language from fire, ocean marine, theft and other contracts. Exposures eligible for this protection are described in the nationwide definition of marine insurance and include bridges, tunnels, jewelry and furs.

Innkeepers Legal Liability. Coverage for motel and hotel operators, protecting them against the legal liability they have for the safekeeping of the property of guests. The policy usually has a limit per guest and an aggregate limit per policy year.

Innocent Spouse Doctrine. This doctrine holds that, if one spouse is not involved in and unaware of activity in which the other spouse has engaged and which nullifies an insurance contract, the innocent spouse must remain insured. Some policies state specifically that any misconduct of an insured bars recovery by any other insured. Courts frequently back up the insurance companies in these disputes.

In-Patient. A patient admitted to a hospital or other similar medical facility as a resident patient.

Inside Limits. Limits placed on hospital expense benefits, which modify benefits from the overall maximums listed in the policy. An inside limit when applied to room and board, limits the benefit to not only a maximum amount payable, but also limits the number of days the benefit is paid.

Insolvency Clause. A clause that holds a reinsurer liable for its share of a loss assumed under a treaty even though the primary insurer has become insolvent. See also Strike-Through Clause.

Insolvency Funds. See Guarantee Funds.

Insolvent. When a person's or business's liabilities exceed their assets.

Insolvent Insurer. An insurer that is unable to meet its financial obligations.

Inspection. Independent checking on facts about an applicant, policyholder or claimant, usually by a commercial inspection agency.

Inspection Bureau. An organization created by property and liability insurers to investigate exposures and to establish rates.

Inspection Report. A summary of the physical, financial and moral attributes of an insured or an applicant for insurance on the insured's property. Such reports are prepared by inspection bureaus, specialized organizations and insurers.

Installment Refund Annuity. An annuity that promises to continue the periodic payments after the death of the annuitant, until the combined benefits paid to the annuitant and to the beneficiary have equaled the purchase price of the annuity.

Installment Refund Option. An annuity option that provides for continued payments after the death of the annuitant until the total benefits paid have equalled the purchase price of the annuity.

Installment Sales Floater. See Conditional Sales Floater.

Installment Settlement. Payment of the proceeds of a life insurance policy or its cash value in installments rather than in a lump sum. The term refers to any one of the options in a life insurance policy that has this result.

Installments Certain. A settlement option that guarantees to pay proceeds in equal installments for a specified period of time.

Institute of Life Insurance. Formerly an agency responsible for building the image of life insurance through a variety of programs. It is now a division of the American Council of Life Insurance.

Institutional Property. Property eligible for special treatment under package policies, often properties occupied by sanitariums and educational, religious, charitable, government and non-profit organizations.

Insurability. Acceptability to the insurer of an applicant for insurance.

Insurable Interest. Any interest a person has in a possible subject of insurance, such as a car or home, of such a nature that a certain happening might cause that person financial loss. This condition provides that the company will not pay an amount greater than the insured's interest in the property or the amount of coverage under the policy. If an insured loss occurs—but the company denies the claim because the insured hasn't complied with some condition or requirement—payment would still be made up to its insurable interest. This usually means the balance of whatever an insured owes on the property, be it a mortgage or an auto loan.

Insurable Net Worth. The sum of the equity value an insured has in his house and other property, major personal possessions like jewelry or collectibles and any savings or liquid investments he has.

Insurable Risk. A risk that meets most of the following requisites: 1) The loss must be capable of being defined; 2) It must be accidental; 3) It must be large enough to cause a hardship to the insured; 4) It must belong to a homogeneous group of risks large enough to make losses predictable; 5) It must not be subject to the same loss at the same time as a large number of other risks; 6) The insurance company must be able to determine a reasonable cost for the insurance; and 7) The insurance company must be able to calculate the chance of loss.

Insurance. A formal social device for reducing risk by transferring the risks of several individual entities to an insurer. The insurer agrees, for a consideration, to assume, to a specified extent, the losses suffered by the insured.

Insurance Carrier. See Insurer.

Insurance Commissioner. Head of a state's insurance regulatory agency. Some states use the title of Director or Superintendent.

Insurance Company Education Directors Society (ICEDS). An organization of insurance company educators whose primary purposes are to promote insurance education and exchange information on the subject.

Insurance Company. See Insurer.

Insurance Department. A governmental bureau in each state and the federal government in Canada charged with the administration of insurance laws, including the licensing of agents and insurers and their regulation and examination. In some jurisdictions the department is a division of another state department or bureau.

Insurance Examiner. The representative of a state insurance department assigned to participate in the official audit and examination of an insurer.

Insurance Guaranty Act. The legislation enacted in many states providing for guaranty funds for the policyholders of insolvent insurers. See Guaranty Funds.

Insurance Hall of Fame. An institution honoring those who have made outstanding contributions to insurance thought and practice. Selections are made on an international basis.

Insurance in Force. (1) The face amounts of contracts still to be paid out to insureds. (2) The annual premium payable on current contracts of insurance.

Insurance Information Institute (III). The agency of the property and liability business designed to deal with the public relations programs of various segments of the business.

Insurance Institute of America, Inc. (IIA). An organization that develops programs and conducts national examinations in general insurance, risk management, management, adjusting, underwriting, auditing and loss control.

Insurance Policy. The form that serves as the contract between an insurer and an insured. It sets forth the rights and duties of parties to the contract.

Insurance Regulatory Examiners Society (IRES). An organization made up of the state regulatory examiners who conduct financial and market conduct examinations of insurers, and whose purpose it is to foster educational programs, cooperation and support between state examiners.

Insurance Regulatory Information System (IRIS). Information and early-warning system used by the National Association of Insurance Commissioners to keep track of the financial soundness of insurers.

Insurance Services Office (ISO). An organization of the property and liability insurance business designed to gather statistics, promulgate rates and develop policy forms.

Insurance to Value. Insurance written in an amount approximating the value of the property insured.

Insured. The party to an insurance arrangement whom the insurer agrees to indemnify for losses, provide benefits for or render services to. See also Named Insured.

Insured Contract. A definition that shapes the extent of contractual liability coverage by describing the types of insured contracts. On modern liability forms, "insured contract" includes leases of premises, sidetrack agreements, elevator maintenance agreements, easement agreements and other agreements related to the insured's business.

Insured Location. A sweeping definition that frequently applies to liability coverages. It includes all of the following: the residence premises; that part of any other premises, other structures and grounds, used by the named insured as a residence that is either shown in the declarations or acquired during the policy period; any premises used by the named insured in connection with the residence premises or a newly-acquired premises; any part of a non-owned premises where an insured temporarily resides; vacant land owned by or rented to an insured (but not farm land); individual or family cemetery plots or burial vaults of any insured; and any part of a premises occasionally rented to any insured for other than business use.

Insured, Named. See Named Insured.

Insured Plan. A retirement plan under which some kind of benefits are guaranteed by an insurance carrier. It does not imply that there is an element of life insurance connected with the plan.

Insured Status. In addition to meeting the eligibility requirements of an employee and paying Social Security taxes, eligibility for Social Security benefits is determined by insured status. Insured status is based on an insured's quarters of coverage for Social Security tax purposes. There are basically three forms of insured status, which determine eligibility for certain OASDHI benefits: fully insured; currently insured; and disability insured.

Insurer. The party to an insurance arrangement who agrees to indemnify for losses, provide pecuniary benefits or render services. The term is preferred over carrier and company since it is a functional word applicable without ambiguity to all types of individuals or organizations performing the insurance function.

Insuring Agreement (or Clause). That portion of an insurance contract which defines the scope or extent of the policy's benefits (i.e., the perils insured against, the persons and/or property covered, their locations and the period of the contract).

Intangible Damages. Damages awarded for such things as pain and suffering following an accident (e.g., when an insured damages another car, his liability might be limited to the value of the vehicle. But if he injures a person in that car, causing a permanent disability or pain and suffering, which prevents the person from working, courts can award millions in damages.

Integrated LTC Rider. An LTC rider that is added to a life insurance policy whereby LTC benefits paid will reduce the policy's benefits. LTC benefits are dependent on the life insurance benefits available.

Integrated Plan. A pension plan that builds benefits according to an approved Treasury Department formula.

Intellectual Property. A company's most valuable assets—copyrights, patents, trademarks, trade secrets and brand names.

Intentional Injury. An injury resulting from an act intended to inflict injury. In an accident insurance contract, this type of injury is not covered (because it is not an accident). In general, intentional injuries inflicted on the insured are covered (assuming no collusion).

Intentional Loss. Damage caused intentionally by an insured person. Most policies exclude coverage for this type of loss.

Intentional Torts. May involve infringement of property and privacy rights (e.g., trespassing). Property rights also can be violated by nuisance-type activities, which interrupt the property owner's ability to use the property. Other intentional torts involve personal injury, which include (besides the traditional bodily injury) damage to reputation through untrue statements, be it libel or slander.

Inter Vivos Transfer. Transfer of all or a portion of the assets of a person's estate while that person is still alive. Contrast with Testamentary Transfer.

Inter Vivos Trust. A trust created to take effect during the lifetime of the grantor. Contrast with Testamentary Trust.

Interest. In the calculation of premium, it is the rate of return on the company's investment of premium dollars over the lifetime of the policy. Insurance company investment experience will affect life insurance cost.

Interest Adjusted Cost. A method of determining the cost of life insurance, taking into account the interest that might have been earned on premium money if it had been invested rather than put into premiums.

Interest Only Option. An option for paying the proceeds of a life insurance policy to beneficiaries in which the insurance company holds the entire proceeds and makes period payments of the earned interest only. The interest rate may be flexible but a minimum rate of interest is usually guaranteed.

Interest, Post-Judgment. Money the plaintiff would have earned if the favorable judgment had been paid at the time of the first judgment, before the appeal.

Interest, Pre-Judgment. Money the plaintiff would have earned if the favorable judgment had been paid at the time of injury or damage, before trial.

Interest Rate Risk. A risk faced by investors who invest in bonds characterized by an individual being locked into a lower interest rate when interest rates are generally increasing in the economy.

Interest Sensitive Provision. Provisions in variable and flexible premium policies that guarantee certain interest earnings plus an additional interest percentage should the current interest rate rise above a specified percentage.

Interinsurance Exchange. See Reciprocal Insurance Exchange.

Interline Endorsement. Commercial endorsements that apply, or could apply, to more than one coverage part of a package policy. These were developed to reduce redundancy.

Intermediary. A reinsurance broker who negotiates contracts of reinsurance on behalf of the insured. These transactions normally take place with those reinsurers who recognize brokers and pay them commissions on reinsurance premiums ceded.

Intermediate Care. Medically supervised health care for those who do not require the degree of care and supervision provided by hospitals or skilled nursing homes, but who need daily medical care and other assistance.

Intermediate Care Facility. A facility licensed by the state, which provides nursing care to persons who do not require the degree of care that a hospital or skilled nursing facility provides.

Intermediate Disability. See Temporary Partial Disability and Permanent Partial Disability.

Intermediate Report. A claim report on the condition of a continuing disability.

Internal Explosion. Explosion occurring in a dwelling or other covered structure, excluding breakage of water pipes or loss by explosion of steam boilers or steam pipes. Provides coverage for an explosion where a fire doesn't ensue.

International Association of Health Underwriters. An association of agents and related personnel on the health insurance business.

International Insurance Seminars, Inc. (IIS). An institution that promotes worldwide exchanges of ideas and techniques among people, including academicians and insurance practitioners.

Interrogatories. A procedure for gaining evidence which involves one party submitting questions to the other party in order to gather facts and information to prepare for a trial.

Interstate Carrier. A transportation company that does business across state lines.

Interstate Commerce Commission Endorsement. An endorsement required on all policies issued to interstate motor carriers who haul goods for hire. It guarantees that all losses to cargo will be paid by the insurer, up to specified minimum limits, regardless of the perils specified in a policy. The common carrier, however, agrees to repay the insurer for any loss that is not covered by the policy.

Intervening Cause. A possible defense against negligence. Negligence may be avoided or reduced if it can be shown that an intervening cause broke the uninterrupted chain of events required to establish a proximate cause. Contrast with Proximate Cause.

Intestate. Dying without a will thus permitting the probate court to appoint an administrator to settle the estate.

Intoxicants and Narcotics Provision. A health insurance provision that voids liability if the loss results from the insured's being intoxicated or under the influence of any narcotic unless administered on the advice of a physician.

Intrastate Carrier. A transportation company whose business is confined to one state.

Invalidity. Sickness.

Invasion of Privacy. The publicizing of another's private affairs for which there is no legitimate public purpose, or the invasion into another's private activities that causes shame or humiliation to that person.

Investigative Consumer Report. A report ordered on an insured or applicant under which information about the person's character, reputation or lifestyle is obtained through personal interviews with the person's neighbors, friends, associates or acquaintances. Contrast with Consumer Report.

Investment Company Act of 1940. A federal law that regulates the organization and activities of investment companies and requires the registration of investment companies with the government.

Investment Income. The return received by insurers from their investment portfolios, including interest, dividends and realized capital gains on stocks. Realized capital gains means the profit realized on stocks that have actually been sold for more than their purchase price.

Investment Manager. A fiduciary (other than a trustee or a plan's named fiduciary) who manages, acquires or disposes of a pension plan's assets.

Investment Reserve. An item in the balance sheet of an insurance company that represents a setting aside of assets to compensate for a possible reduction in the market value of securities owned by the company.

Invitee. One who has been expressly or implicitly invited onto the premises of another (e.g., customers entering a store).

Involuntary Unemployment Insurance. Coverage for consumer credit repayment obligations when an insured is involuntarily unemployed due to individual or mass layoff, general strike, termination by employer, unionized labor dispute and lockout. Usually sold to borrowers under a master group policy issued to a creditor (bank, association or other financial institution). Also called job loss insurance. Can be classified as either property/casualty or life/health insurance.

IRA. See Individual Retirement Accounts.

IRIS. See Insurance Regulatory Information System.

Iron Safe Clause. A provision in a property insurance policy that requires the insured to keep records in a safe when they are not used.

Irrevocable Beneficiary. A beneficiary designation that cannot be changed without the beneficiary's consent. See Change of Beneficiary.

Irrevocable Trust. A trust instrument that cannot be revoked by the person who created it. Contrast with Revocable Trust.

ISO. See Insurance Services Office.

Issue and Participation Limits. A question on an application for insurance that requires an insured to indicate the name of the insurer and particulars regarding the additional coverage. Any other coverage will cause the amount requested to be limited to the insurer's underwriting limits.

Issued Business. Contracts actually written by an insurer and paid for but not yet delivered to or accepted by the insured.

Item. (1) A term used to identify a statement in a policy as to what is insured. In a fire policy one might refer to the contents item, meaning the coverage in the policy which applies to the contents. (2) An individual entry, such as a piece of jewelry, listed with its description and valuation on a schedule by a policy showing items covered.

Jettison. The act of throwing overboard part of a vessel's cargo or hull in hopes of saving the ship from sinking.

Jewelers Block Insurance. An open perils (all risk) insurance contract that provides jewelers with coverage on most types of losses to which they are exposed. It covers both owned property and property in their care, custody and control.

Jewelry Floater. An all-risk policy covering listed jewelry. Usually each item is described and insured for a specific amount.

Joint and Several Liability. A legal doctrine permitting recovery from any of several codefendants based on ability to pay, rather than the degree of negligence. See "Deep Pockets" Liability.

Joint and Survivorship Annuity. An annuity payable to the named annuitants during the period of their joint lives, which continue to the survivor when the first annuitant dies.

Joint and Survivorship Option. An option in a life insurance contract that permits the cash value of the policy to be paid out as a joint and survivorship annuity. Under this option, two beneficiaries receive the proceeds of a life insurance policy. When the first beneficiary dies, the second beneficiary (if he or she is still living) continues to receive the proceeds of the policy, in installments, for his or her lifetime (or for a specified period). See also Joint and Survivorship Annuity.

Joint Annuity. An annuity that is paid to the two named persons until the first one dies, at which time the annuity ceases.

Joint Committee on Interpretation and Complaint. A committee formed to rule on what types of insurance can come within the standard definition of marine insurance. See Nationwide Definition of Marine Insurance.

Joint Control. Control of the handling of an estate by both the surety (bonding company) and the fiduciary (administrator, executor, etc.). Funds are kept in joint accounts, and disbursements made only with both signatures.

Joint Insurance. Insurance written on two or more persons with benefits usually payable upon the first death.

Joint Insured. One whose life is insured by a joint insurance contract. See Joint Insurance.

Joint Liability. Liability that rests upon more than one person or corporate entity.

Joint Life and Survivorship Annuity. A contract that provides income to two or more people and continues so long as any one of them survives.

Joint Life Annuity. This policy pays a benefit that continues throughout the joint lifetime of two people but terminates at the first death.

Joint Life Insurance. See Joint Insurance.

Joint Ownership Coverage. An endorsement attached to a standard personal auto policy that insures vehicles normally ineligible under the standard ownership rules.

Joint Tenancy. Ownership of property shared equally by two or more parties under which the survivor assumes complete ownership. Compare with Fee Simple and Tenants in Common.

Joint Underwriting Association (JUA). An unincorporated association of insurance companies formed to provide a particular type of insurance to the public. Those who insure with a JUA pay assessments in addition to their premiums, which provide monies for the operation of the association. They usually set their own rate levels and use whatever coverage forms are deemed proper, subject to approval by state authorities.

Joint Venture. An expression applied most often to construction ventures where several contractors agree to combine together on a construction project rather than act as separate contractors. Under the joint venture agreement, they share profits and losses in some agreed-upon proportion.

Joint-Survivor Option. An annuity option that provides for a guaranteed income to the annuitant and upon death of the annuitant, a continued income to the annuitant's survivor.

Joisted Masonry Construction. A building that has exterior walls constructed of masonry materials, such as adobe, brick, concrete, gypsum block, hollow concrete block, stone, tile, or other similar materials, and a roof and floor constructed of combustible materials. A floor that rests directly on the ground is an exception and may be disregarded.

Jones Act. A federal act that provides for the covering of ships' crews under workers' compensation plans.

JUA. See Joint Underwriting Association.

Judgment or Decree. The formal decision by a judge or court.

Judgment Rates. See "A" Rates.

Judicial Bond. A bond required in civil and criminal court actions.

Jumping Juvenile. A popular name for a life insurance contract written on the life of a child, usually in units of $1,000. When the child reaches a prescribed age, generally 21, the face of the policy is increased automatically without the imposition of either an additional premium charge or a medical examination. Hence the term "jumping" juvenile.

Jurisdiction. Authority of the court to decide cases of a particular type or in a particular area.

Juvenile Insurance. Life insurance written on a child.

K

Keogh Act (HR-10) Plan. A plan under the Self-Employed Individual's Tax Retirement Act that permits a self-employed individual to establish a formal retirement plan and to obtain tax advantages similar to those available in qualified corporate pension plans.

Key Employee Insurance. (1) Insurance on the life or health of a key employee, the loss of whose services would cause an employer financial loss. The policy is owned by and payable to the employer. (2) In health insurance the term is also used to designate salary continuation insurance or a medical benefit plan payable to the key employee, with the employer paying all or part of the premium.

Kidnapping Coverage. Insurance against the hazard of a person being seized outside the insured premises and forced to return and open the premises of a safe, or to give information that enables the criminal to do so. This has frequently been one of the perils covered under a package crime policy. See also Extortion Coverage Form.

Kidnap-Ransom Insurance. This insurance is written primarily for financial institutions and covers named employees for individual or aggregate amounts paid as ransom, with a deductible requiring the insured to participate in about 10 percent of any loss. There are few markets for this coverage and no standardization of rates. See also Extortion Coverage Form.

L

Labor and Material Bond. See Payment Bond.

Lag Coverage. See Endorsement Extending Period of Indemnity.

Land Contract. An instrument used in connection with the sale of real estate. It differs from a mortgage in that title to the land remains with the seller until the buyer has completed the payments, though possession rests with the buyer. This contract is the instrument that conveys the deed of land from one person to another upon full payment of the stated purchase price.

Landlords Protective Liability. Coverage provided to the owner of property who leases the entire premises to another.

Lapse. Termination of a policy because of failure to pay the premium.

Lapse Ratio. The ratio of the number of life insurance contracts lapsed within a given period to the number in force at the beginning of that period.

Lapsed Policy. A policy allowed to expire because of nonpayment of premiums.

Larceny. The unlawful taking of a person's personal property without his consent and with intent to deprive him of ownership or use. It is a broader term than burglary or robbery, largely synonymous with theft.

Large Claim Pooling. A system designed to help stabilize premium fluctuations in smaller groups. Large claims (those over a stated amount) are charged to a pool contributed to by many small groups who belong and share in that pool. The smaller the group, the lower the pooling level. Larger groups will have a larger pooling level.

Laser Beam Endorsement. An endorsement to a "claims made" liability form used to exclude specific accidents, products, work or locations.

Last Clear Chance. A doctrine that liability may attach to a person who, immediately before an accident, had a last clear chance to avoid it and did not.

Last In, First Out. See LIFO.

Latent Defect. A defect not immediately apparent.

Law of Large Numbers (LLN). This law states that the larger the number of exposures considered, the more closely the losses reported will match the underlying probability of loss. Under the LLN, the insurer knows from experience approximately how many policies will suffer a loss and how severe most of those losses will be. While actual experience may differ from expectation, pooling a large number of policies allows the company to be fairly accurate with its prediction. The simplest example of this law is the flipping of a coin. The more times the coin is flipped, the closer it will come to actually reaching the underlying probability of 50 percent heads and 50 percent tails. See also Degree of Risk, Odds and Probability.

Leader Location. A location that attracts customers to the insured's business. One of the four types of dependent properties for which business income coverage may be written.

Lease. Contract whereby the property owner/user (lessor) agrees to let another party (lessee) use the property for a consideration (money or rent).

Leasehold. An agreement that gives a person the right to use and occupy property.

Leasehold Interest Coverage Form. Commercial property coverage form that insures an insured tenant's interest in a favorable lease under which the rent paid is less than the rental value of alternative premises. It pays the difference between rent paid and the rental value for the remainder of the lease if the lease is canceled because of property damage caused by a peril insured against.

Leasehold Interest Insurance. A form of property insurance that provides protection against the loss of a favorable lease should it be terminated as a result of damage to the property by a peril covered by the contract. A leasehold value is determined by finding the difference between the rental value of the property at current rates and the rent payable under the terms of the lease. This amount is multiplied times the remaining term of the lease.

Leasing Companies. Lessors in a similar position to lending companies, in that they have an insurable interest in autos they have leased to their customers. Since the leasing company remains the legal owner of the leased vehicle, it is possible for that company to become legally liable for injury or damage involving the leased vehicle. For these reasons, leasing companies usually require that they be included as additional insureds on the policies of people leasing vehicles.

Ledger Cost. The net cost of a life insurance contract, calculated by subtracting the cash value of the contract at the end of a given year from the premiums paid, less all dividends.

Legacy. A gift of personal property in accordance with the provisions of a will.

Legal Expense Insurance. Group coverage that provides members with legal services paid for on a schedule basis. Similar to dental insurance.

Legal Hazard. Increased likelihood that a loss will occur because of court actions.

Legal Liability. Liability under the law as opposed to liability arising from contracts or agreements. It is most often used to refer to a person's liability if he should negligently injure another party.

Legal Reserve. The minimum reserves required to be established for a life insurance contract under the laws of the jurisdiction within which an insurer operates.

Legal Reserve Life Insurance Company. A life insurer that maintains the reserves required by the jurisdiction within which it operates.

Legend Drug. A drug that has on its label "Caution: Federal law prohibits dispensing without a prescription."

Legislated Coverages. Coverages provided through programs legislated by federal or state law (e.g., FAIR Plans, the Flood Insurance Program and assigned risk pools).

Legislative Risk. A risk faced by investors whereby changes in tax laws can result in adverse effects on the individual's investment results.

Length of Stay (LOS). The total number of days a participant stays in a facility such as a hospital.

Lessee. The person to whom a lease is granted. Commonly called the "tenant."

Lessee's Safe Deposit Box Coverage Form. Commercial crime coverage that protects against loss of property other than money while it is in the insured's safe deposit box inside a depository premises.

Lessor. The person granting a lease. Also known as the "landlord."

Level Annual Premium Funding Method. A method of accumulating money for payment of future pensions under which the level annual charge is payable each year until retirement so that the benefit is fully funded.

Level Commission System. A system of commissions in which the first year and all renewal commissions are the same percentage of the premium.

Level Death Benefit Option. Under universal life insurance, the level death benefit option provides the greater of: 1) the face amount of the policy at the time of death; or 2) a stipulated percentage of the accumulation value.

Level Premium Insurance. Insurance with premiums that remain the same throughout the life of the contract. Most whole life insurance works this way. The amount of a level premium is higher than needed for the protection afforded in the early years of the contract but less than needed in the later years. It levels off the cost of insurance so as not to have it increase each year until it becomes too expensive. See also Net Level Premium.

Level Term Insurance. (1) A term life insurance policy where the death benefit and premium remain level for the policy term. See also Decreasing Term Insurance, Increasing Term Insurance and Term Insurance. (2) A term policy where the face value remains the same from the effective date until the expiration date. See also Term Insurance.

Liabilities. Money owed or expected to be owed. Insurance company financial statements, for instance, show assets and liabilities.

Liability. See Legal Liability.

Liability Insurance. Insurance that pays and renders service on behalf of an insured for loss arising out of his responsibility to others imposed by law or assumed by contract.

Liability Limit. The maximum amount the liability insurance company pays for any one occurrence (an accident or an exposure to substantially the same conditions over a period of time which causes an injury). This limit is the same regardless of the number of insureds, claims made or persons injured. See Per Person Limit.

Liable. Being legally responsible for damages suffered by a third party.

Libel. (1) The defaming of another by writings, pictures or other publication injurious to the person's reputation. See also Defamation and Slander. (2) In maritime law it means legal action brought against the owner of another ship.

Libel Insurance. A form of liability insurance that protects the insured against legal liability for libelous statements he may write.

Liberalization Clause. A clause in property insurance contracts that provides: if policy or endorsement forms are broadened by legislation or rulings from rating authorities and no additional premium is required (e.g., if it drops a policy exclusion), then all existing similar policies are assumed to include the broadened coverage. This eliminates the need of the insurance company to endorse all existing policies when coverage is expanded without a change in premium.

License. A certification of authority for an agent or insurer to operate, given by the appropriate jurisdiction.

License and Permit Bonds. Bonds often required by jurisdictions to be posted by persons performing certain services, such as security dealers and plumbers. It provides indemnification in the event that the licensee fails to conform to pertinent regulations of the jurisdiction.

Licensee. (1) One who is licensed. (2) A person who uses or enters the property of another for his own interests. The owner of the property must use ordinary care not to injure a licensee (e.g., a person using another's land for a shortcut, as long as he had the permission of the owner). See Degree of Care.

Lien. A claim against property, which then serves as security for the payment of that claim.

Lien Plan. (1) A plan for issuing coverage on substandard risks under which a standard premium is paid; less than the full face amount of the policy is payable if death occurs within a certain period of years. These are rarely used and are illegal in some states. (2) A plan under which an impairment of the insurer's assets if offset by pro rata liens against policies to be deducted from the face amount when paid as a claim.

Life Annuity. A contract providing a stated income for life, payable annually or more frequently. (AN)

Life Conservation. The administration of efforts to preserve human life through research, legislation and appeals to society.

Life Estate. Ownership of land for an individual's lifetime.

Life Expectancy. The average number of years remaining for a person of a given age to live as referenced on a mortality or annuity table.

Life Expectancy Term Insurance. Term life insurance that provides protection for a person's "expectation of life." This becomes the term of the policy, as opposed to ordinary term policies that are for a given number of years or to a stated age, such as 65.

Life Income Option. An option for paying the proceeds of a life insurance policy to beneficiaries under which equal installments are paid as long as the beneficiary lives, even if the principal has been exhausted. Proceeds are retained by the insurer and paid in equal installments (monthly, quarterly, semiannually or annually). However, this option provides no refund when the beneficiary dies—even if only one installment has been paid. It is frequently elected as the form of payment for a death benefit to a surviving spouse, or for payment of cash values to an insured who lives to retirement age.

Life Income with Period Certain Option. Guaranteed payments for a specified period of time. Under this option, the benefits are guaranteed for a certain period (usually five, 10 or 20 years). If the beneficiary dies before the end of the period, benefits will continue to be paid to another person for the remainder of the period. If the original recipient lives beyond the period certain, the benefit payments continue for as long as he lives.

Life Insurance (Generic). A contractual system of risk sharing under which contributions are accumulated and redistributed to meet the economic consequences of the uncertain duration of life.

Life Insurance, Ordinary. See Ordinary Life Policy.

Life Insurance (Narrow). An agreement that guarantees the payment of a stated amount of monetary benefits upon the death of the insured, or under other circumstances specified in the contract, such as total disability.

Life Insurance Cost Surrender Index. The guaranteed cash surrender value of a life insurance policy is often required to be calculated into an index for presentation to prospective life insurance buyers. Such an index determines the guaranteed cash surrender value, if any, available at the end of the 10th and 20th policy years according to the accumulation of the annual cash dividends at 5 percent interest compounded annually to the end of a selected period, if the policy is a participating policy.

Life Insurance, Straight. See Ordinary Life Policy.

Life Insurance Trust. A type of life insurance policy where a trust company is named as the beneficiary and distributes the proceeds of the policy under the terms of the trust agreement.

Life Insurance, Whole Life. See Whole Life Insurance.

Life Insurers Conference. An organization that provides for the exchange of information on management problems among the member insurers.

Life Office Management Association (LOMA). An organization serving a large proportion of the life insurance business by providing educational programs relating to administrative and technical procedures within the industry. It confers the designation of Fellow, Life Management Institute (FLMI) upon those who complete a prescribed course of study.

Life Paid Up at Age. A form of limited payment life insurance that provides protection for the whole of life but with payment of premiums to stop at a particular age, thus paying up the policy. A common form would be Life Paid Up at Age 65.

Life Underwriter. Usually, a life insurance agent. It can be more narrowly defined as a risk appraiser. See also Risk Appraiser.

Life Underwriting Training Council (LUTC). An organization that prepares and administers training programs for life insurance agents.

Life with Period Certain. An annuity option that provides a lifetime income to the annuitant plus an extra guarantee of income for a specified period of time such as 5 or 10 years. The period certain provides income to the annuitant or the annuitant's survivor.

Lifetime Benefit. An optional benefit that provides lifetime disability income benefits—usually if the disability commences prior to a certain age. Otherwise, benefits may be restricted.

Lifetime Policy. (1) A policy guaranteed renewable or noncancelable to age 65 or some later date. (2) A policy paying disability benefits for life.

LIFO. Last in, first out. A method of keeping inventory records for accounting purposes where the last item purchased is the first item used.

Limit, Aggregate. See Aggregate Limit.

Limit, Basic. See Basic Limit.

Limit, Excess. See Excess Limit.

Limit of Liability. The maximum amount of insurance or upper limit that the insurance company is legally obligated to pay if a covered loss occurs.

Limit of Liability Rule. A prescribed procedure for allocating property insurance losses among insurers that provide protection on a given piece of property. It is called the "pro rata liability rule" in a standard fire policy.

Limit, Standard. See Basic Limit.

Limitations. Exceptions to coverage and limitations of coverage in an insurance contract (e.g., a limit of liability in an auto policy, policies covering only certain described vehicles or, in the case of general liability insurance, certain described premises).

Limited Agent. An agent authorized to transact only a limited form of insurance, such as travel-accident or credit insurance. In many states, limited agents are exempt from licensing examination and education requirements.

Limited Health Insurance. Special policies that provide limited coverage for specific injuries or illnesses, such as travel-accident, hospital income and specified disease coverage.

Limited Partnership. An association of two or more persons who operate and manage a business for profit; at least one the partners does not work in the business but does have some management voice and financial investment. The limited partner has limited liability.

Limited Payment Life. A life insurance contract providing protection for the whole of life with premiums paid for an indicated number of years. See also Life Paid Up At Age.

Limited Payment Whole Life. A whole life policy that allows the policyholder to pay the entire premium in a shorter period of time (such as a 20 year period or to age 65). Compare with Continuous Premium Whole Life and Single Premium Whole Life.

Limited Policies. (1) Health insurance contracts, such as those offered by newspapers to their customers, with low limits and somewhat restricted forms. (2) Policies paid only upon the occurrence of certain contingencies, such as cancer, in contrast to policies covering all contingencies other than those excluded.

Limited Pollution Liability Coverage Form. Commercial form providing pollution liability coverage on a "claims made" basis, but not providing any coverage for clean-up costs.

Limited Theft Coverage Endorsement. This form may be attached to a dwelling policy to provide theft coverage for a named insured who is not an owner occupant.

Limits. (1) Ages below or above which the insurer will not issue a policy or above which it will not continue a policy presently in force. (2) The maximum benefit payable for a given situation or occurrence (e.g., a limit of $50,000 on the contents of a home, or a $40,000 per accident limit for property damage liability). See also Limit of Liability.

LIMRA International. An organization that, through research, seeks solutions to the problems of administering the agency costs of a life insurer.

Line. A colloquial term with several meanings. It may describe a particular type of insurance, such as the liability "line," or the various types of insurance written for a property owner (e.g., carrying all "lines" of the XYZ Company). It also describes the amount of insurance on a given property (e.g., a $250,000 "line" on buildings of the XYZ Company).

Line Card. A record kept by a property insurer of the insurance sold to an insured.

Line of Business. The general classification of business as utilized in the insurance industry (e.g., fire, allied lines and homeowners).

Lines. The amount a reinsurer accepts, usually in multiples of a net retention, under a surplus policy. If a policy specifies a retention of $10,000, and a risk is written for $50,000, 4 lines ($40,000) would be reinsured. See also Surplus Reinsurance.

Line Sheet. A schedule showing the limits of liability to be written by an insurer for different classes of risks. It is also used by a ceding company to define the limits of liability it will assume on various exposures.

Line Slip. A document that describes a risk to be insured. Underwriters subscribe to it by indicating what percentage of the risk they are willing to take.

Liquidated Damages. Damages that are agreed to either by the court or by the parties to a suit or action. These damages are often negotiated or calculated to represent a present value of monies that would otherwise be paid in the future.

Liquidation of Insurer. Action undertaken by a state insurance department to dissolve an impaired or insolvent insurer that cannot be restored to sound financial standing.

Liquidity. The ability of an insurer to convert its assets into cash to pay claims if necessary.

Liquor Control Laws. See Dram Shop Laws.

Liquor Liability Insurance. See Dram Shop Liability Insurance.

Litigant. One who is engaged in a lawsuit.

Litigation. Settling disputes about coverage or the amount of a claim in court.

Litigation Bond. See Court Bond.

Livery Use. Use of a vehicle for hire to carry persons. This is usually excluded in automobile insurance contracts unless otherwise stated.

Livestock Coverage Form. A commercial property form that may be attached to a farm coverage part to insure livestock. This form replaced various inland marine forms that were commonly used to insure farm property and livestock.

Livestock Insurance. A named perils contract that provides a prescribed lump sum payment to an insured upon the death of any animal covered by the policy.

Livestock Mortality Insurance. The equivalent of life insurance for livestock.

Livestock Transit Insurance. Insurance against accidents causing death or crippling on shipments of livestock while in transit by rail, truck or other similar means of transportation.

Living Benefits Rider. A rider attached to a life insurance policy that provides LTC benefits or benefits for the terminally ill. The benefits provided are derived from the available life insurance benefits.

Living Need Benefits. A combination of life insurance and long-term care insurance that allows life insurance benefits to generate long-term care benefits. Up to a certain percentage of the life insurance policy's death benefit may be used in advance to offset nursing home or medical expenses, reducing the face amount of the life policy.

Living Needs Clause. A clause that combines life insurance and LTC benefits, drawing on the life insurance benefits to generate LTC benefits. Also called an accelerated benefit.

Living Trust. A trust created by a person during his lifetime. Also called an inter vivos trust.

Lloyd's. Generally refers to Lloyd's of London, England, an institution where individual underwriters accept or reject the risks offered to them. The Lloyd's Corporation provides the support facility for their activities.

Lloyd's Association. A group of individuals who band together to assume risks are sometimes called a Lloyd's association. They are organized along the same lines as, though not connected with, Lloyd's of London. Each person is responsible only for the share of the risk that he assumes. There are a limited number of these associations in the U.S.

Lloyd's Broker. A person who has the authority to negotiate insurance contracts with the underwriters on the floor at Lloyd's. See also Lloyd's.

Lloyd's Syndicate. A consortium of individual Lloyd's underwriters. Usually one person acts for the syndicate in accepting or rejecting risks.

Lloyd's Underwriter. An individual who underwrites risks through the facility of Lloyd's of London. These individuals are liable only for their own assumptions of risk and not those assumed by others in the same syndicate or in the overall Lloyd's organization.

Loading. The amount added to the pure insurance cost to cover the operations cost of an insurer, the possibility that losses will be greater than statistically expected and fluctuating interest rates on the insurer's investments. The "pure" insurance cost is that portion of the premium estimated to be necessary for losses.

Loan Value. A term that refers to the amount of money an insured can borrow using the cash value of his life insurance policy as security.

Local Agent. An agent representing companies in a sales and service capacity as an independent contractor on a commission basis. A local agent usually has a small territory, and agent powers are limited by contract.

LOMA. See Life Office Management Association.

Longshoremen's and Harbor Workers' Act. A federal act that stipulates compensation levels for injured longshoremen and harbor workers.

Long-Term Care (LTC). Care provided for persons with chronic diseases or disabilities.

Long-Term Care (LTC) Insurance. A policy that reimburses daily health and social service expenses incurred when an insured is confined to a convalescent or nursing home facility. Often marketed as a rider to a life insurance policy, this coverage pays for the care of persons with chronic diseases or disabilities, and may include a wide range of health and social services provided under the supervision of medical professionals.

Long-Term Care Facility. Usually a state licensed facility that provides skilled nursing services, intermediate care and custodial care.

Long-Term Care Riders. In recent years, some insurers have begun to offer long-term care coverage in the form of riders attached to life insurance policies or annuity contracts—and even in connection with some other policy forms, such as disability income insurance. Life insurance LTC riders provide benefits very similar to those found in LTC policies.

Long-Term Disability Insurance. A group/individual policy that provides coverage for longer than a short term, often until the insured reaches age 65 in the case of illness and for life in the case of accident. See also Short-Term Disability Insurance.

Loss. (1) The amount of reduction in the value of an insured's property caused by an insured peril. (2) The amount sought through an insured's claim. (3) The amount paid on behalf of an insured under an insurance contract.

Loss Adjustment Expense. The cost of adjusting losses, excluding the amount of the loss itself.

Loss and Expense Data. Insurance rates are based on broad averages of loss and expense data and include components for expected losses and expenses. Individual companies have generally been permitted to deviate from published rates based on individual company differences in experience and expense factors.

Loss Assessment Charge. An insured's share of a loss assessment for property damage or liability, which is charged by a corporation or association of property owners. Homeowners policies provide some coverage for loss assessments charged against the insured as owner or tenant of a residence.

Loss Clause. See Automatic Reinstatement Clause.

Loss Constant. A flat amount included in the premium for small workers' compensation policies, for dwellings in some jurisdictions and for some prescribed inland marine insurance lines. The loss constant offsets the greater-than-average loss experience that most small risks have when compared to all other risks in a given classification.

Loss Control. Any combination of actions taken to reduce the frequency or severity of losses (e.g., installing locks, burglar alarms or sprinklers).

Loss Conversion Factor. A factor applied to the losses in the formula to give the insurer the funds needed to handle the investigation of claims (used in a retrospective rating plan).

Loss Cost Multiplier. A multiplier insurers use to account for individual company expenses, underwriting profit and contingencies, in order to arrive at final rates.

Loss Costs. In 1989, ISO began a transition from providing advisory base rates to providing only prospective loss costs, made up of claims payments and loss adjustment expenses. Each insurer develops its own rating factors to reflect its own underwriting expense and profit/contingencies.

Loss Development. The difference between the amount of losses initially estimated by the insurer and the amount reported in an evaluation at a later date.

Loss Development Factor. This was a development under retrospective rating plans to consider the effect of inflation on losses that take a long time to settle. It gives the insurer additional money to allow for the subsequent development of losses and to reimburse for claims that are late in being reported. See also IBNR.

Loss Expectancy. An underwriter's estimate of the maximum loss suffered on an exposure being considered, with focus on the expected level of loss prevention activities on the part of the insured.

Loss Frequency. The number of times a loss occurs over a specific period of time.

Loss Limitation. Another term used in retrospective rating formulas, designed to limit the effect of catastrophic losses that would otherwise be considered in full when figuring the final retrospective premium.

Loss Loading. A factor applied to the pure loss cost to produce a reinsurance rate or premium.

Loss of Future Earnings. Claims that seek money for income that might have been earned in the future. People hurt while in someone else's car, or their own car and even the families of people killed in car accidents often make these claims. In most cases, courts allow coverage for lost wages only during a period of recuperation from injuries suffered in an accident. It is not an indefinite benefit.

Loss of Income Insurance. Insurance paying loss of income benefits.

Loss of Market. The inability to sell a product to prospective buyers. This is considered a normal business risk and not covered except in some cases such as meats, where spoilage can result in loss of market. However, if spoilage is the result of a storm at sea or a derailing, coverage can be purchased for an additional premium.

Loss of Time Insurance. See Loss of Income Insurance.

Loss of Use Insurance. Coverage for the loss of use of property if it cannot be used because of a peril covered by the policy. If a covered loss makes the residence premises uninhabitable, this covers—at the insured's option—either additional living expenses related to maintaining the normal standard of living of the household or the fair rental value of the part of the residence where the insured lives. (If a part of a residence rented to others is uninhabitable, coverage is offered for loss of fair rental value.) See Additional Living Expenses.

Loss Payable Clause. A provision in property insurance contracts authorizing payment to persons other than the insured to the extent that they have an insurable interest in the property. This clause may be used when there is a lien or loan on the property, and it protects the lender.

Loss Payee. The party to whom money or insurance proceeds is to be paid in the event of loss, such as the lienholder on an automobile or the mortgagee on real property.

Loss Payment. A condition that specifies the rights and obligations of the insurance company after a covered loss occurs. The insurer has the option of paying the value of lost or damaged property, paying the cost of repairing or replacing lost or damaged property or of repairing, rebuilding or replacing property with property of like kind and quality. It may also take possession of any part of the property at an agreed or appraised value. An insurer must give notice of its intent within 30 days after receiving a sworn statement of loss.

Loss Prevention Engineer. See Engineer.

Loss Prevention Service. Engineering and inspection by an insurance company or independent organization with the aim of removing or reducing dangerous conditions in order to prevent losses.

Loss Ratio. The losses divided by the premiums paid. The numerator (losses) can be losses incurred or losses paid, and the denominator (premium) can be earned premiums or written premiums, depending on how the loss ratio is going to be used.

Loss Report. See Claim Report.

Loss Reserve. The estimated liability for unpaid insurance claims or losses that have occurred as of a given evaluation date, including losses incurred but not reported (IBNR), losses due but not yet paid and amount not yet due. The above refers to a loss reserve in an insurer's financial statement. As to individual claims, the loss reserve is the estimate of what will ultimately be paid out on that case.

Loss Severity. The amount of a loss expressed in financial terms.

Losses Incurred. The total losses, whether paid or not, sustained by an insurer in a given period.

Losses Outstanding. A summary statement prepared by property, life and liability insurers showing claims not yet settled.

Losses Paid. A summary of claims paid.

Loss-of-Income Benefits. Benefits paid for inability to work for remuneration because of disability resulting from accidental bodily injury or sickness. The loss of income may be real or presumptive.

Lost Instrument Bond. When the owner of a stock certificate loses it, the insurer of the certificate will not issue a duplicate until the owner furnishes an indemnity bond guaranteeing that if he finds the original he will give it to the surety company.

Lost Policy Release. A statement signed by an insured releasing the insurer from all liability for a lost or mislaid contract of insurance (usually signed after a replacement policy has been issued).

Lost-or-Not-Lost Clause. (1) A provision in an ocean marine contract that assures coverage whether the property is in existence at the time the contract is written or has been destroyed. (2) Coverage of a ship at sea "afloat or sunk."

LTC. See Long Term Care insurance.

Lump Sum. A method for paying the proceeds of a life insurance policy whereby the beneficiary receives the entire proceeds of a policy at once rather than in installments.

LUTC. See Life Underwriting Training Council.

M

M&C. See Manufacturers and Contractors Liability Insurance.

Machinery Breakdown Insurance. See Boiler and Machinery Insurance.

Maintenance Bond. A bond guaranteeing against defects in workmanship or materials for a stated time after the acceptance of completed work.

Maintenance, Care and Wages. An admiralty law provision for coverage for injured seamen. Maintenance refers to providing food, shelter and rehabilitation. Care refers to the medical treatment necessary for recovery. Wages, of course, refers to the usual seaman's wages, which must be paid even during an illness or after an accident.

Major Hospitalization Policy. The same as major medical insurance, except that it applies to expenses incurred only when the insured is hospitalized. See also Major Medical Insurance.

Major Medical Insurance. Health insurance that provides benefits up to a high limit for most medical expenses incurred, subject to a large deductible. Such contracts may contain limits on specific types of charges, like room and board, and a percentage participation clause sometimes called a coinsurance clause. These policies usually pay covered expenses whether an individual is in or out of the hospital.

Malicious Mischief. Purposely damaging the rights or property of another. See also V&MM.

Malinger. To feign a disability in order to continue collecting benefits longer than actually necessary.

Maloney Act. A 1938 amendment to the Securities Exchange Act of 1934. The Maloney Act established the National Association of Security Dealers (NASD) as a self regulatory organization (SRO) for those involved in the sale of securities.

Malpractice. Professional misconduct or lack of ordinary skill in a professional act which renders the practitioner liable for damages.

Malpractice Insurance. Insurance on a professional practitioner that: 1) defends suits instituted against the insured professional for malpractice; or 2) pays any damages set by a court, subject to policy limits.

Managed Care. A system of health care that delivers quality, cost effective health care through monitoring and recommending utilization of services and cost of services.

Managed Health Care Plan. A plan that involves financing, managing and delivery of health care. Typically, it involves a group of providers who share the financial risk of the plan or who have an incentive to deliver cost effective and quality service.

Management Expense. A charge deducted in a contingent commission formula to cover the reinsurer's overhead expenses.

Manager. Head of an agency that is operated as a branch office, as opposed to being operated as a general agency. The manager is a salaried employee, usually with an incentive bonus based on the agency's volume.

Mandated Benefits. Benefits required by state or federal law.

Mandated Providers. Providers of medical care whose services must be included by state or federal law.

Mandatory Arbitration. See Arbitration.

Mandatory Provisions. All disability policies contain a group of mandatory provisions required by all states in any life or health insurance contract. In addition, there are some provisions that are common to most disability income policies.

Mandatory Retirement. A provision in a pension plan stating that the member must retire at a specific age even if he or she does not wish to do so.

Mandatory Valuation Reserve. A reserve required by state law to offset any declines in the valuation of securities listed as admitted assets.

Manor House. A four-unit building (two units downstairs, two upstairs) with one entrance and a four-car garage. Commonly bought as a condo.

Manual. A book giving rates, classifications and underwriting rules for a line of insurance (e.g., the Automobile Manual gives such information for automobile insurance).

Manual Excess. The premium for an amount of insurance in excess of the basic limit of liability. This premium is determined by referring to a table of rate factors which are multiplied by the manual rate in order to arrive at a premium for the higher limit selected.

Manual Rates. (1) The published rate for some unit of insurance. (2) Rates based on average claims data for a large number of groups. These rates are then adjusted for specific groups based on that group's characteristics, such as the type of industry, changes in benefits from the standard, etc.

Manufacturers and Contractors Liability Insurance (M&C). Premises and operations liability insurance that covers manufacturing or contracting risks. The basis of premiums for this coverage is the payroll.

Manufacturers Output Policy. Coverage for the personal property of a manufacturer on an open perils (all risk) basis. Coverage is usually restricted to property away from the premises.

Manufacturer's Selling Price Clause. Values unsold finished goods at the price at which they could have been sold at the time of a loss.

Manufacturing Location. A location that manufactures products for delivery to the insured's customers under a sales contract. One of the four types of dependent properties for which business income coverage may be written.

Manuscript Endorsement. Any endorsement not promulgated on a standard ISO form, changing any conditions, agreements, exclusions or warranties of the insurance contract.

Manuscript Policy. A policy written for specific coverages or conditions not provided in a standard policy. It is often prepared by a large brokerage house for a large account and must conform to state laws.

Map. A geographical map used by a property insurance underwriter to locate the area and character of a risk. Maps also track the number of insureds in a particular area so that an insurer does not subject itself to a possible catastrophic loss.

Map Clerk. A junior underwriter who enters such essential data as policy numbers, amounts of coverage, and property covered on maps to determine its liability or exposure in a given area.

Marine Definition. See Nationwide Definition of Marine Insurance.

Marine Insurance. Insurance primarily concerned with means of transportation and goods in transit. Marine used alone refers to ocean transportation, and inland marine refers to transportation and goods in transit by land. See also Inland Marine Insurance and Ocean Marine Insurance.

Marital Deduction. An unlimited amount of qualifying property that can be passed or transferred upon the death of one spouse to the surviving spouse.

Marital Deduction Trust. An arrangement whereby the surviving spouse is provided with full use of the family's wealth while minimizing the impact of federal estate taxes.

Market Assistance Plan (MAP). A plan promulgated by the Department of Insurance to assist buyers in obtaining certain types of insurance when they are limited in availability.

Market Conduct. Compliance with state laws regulating the sales and marketing, underwriting and issuance of insurance products. Proper market conduct means conducting insurance business fairly and responsibly.

Market Conduct Examination. When state insurance department investigators examine the business practices and operations of an insurer and its agents in order to determine their authority to conduct insurance business in the state.

Market Risk. A risk experienced by those who invest in securities; the risk of possible loss of investment since there are no guarantees associated with such investments.

Market Value. The price for which something would sell, especially the value of certain types of assets, such as stocks and bonds. It is based on what they would sell for under current market conditions. See also Actual Cash Value.

Market Value Clause. A provision in certain property insurance forms that obligates an insurer to pay the established market price of destroyed or damaged stock rather than its cost to the insured, as is usually provided in the standard fire policy. Coverage is only available to manufacturers with finished products, not to wholesalers or retailers.

Marketing Representative. See Special Agent.

Masonry Noncombustible Construction. A building with exterior walls constructed of masonry materials, such as adobe, brick, concrete, gypsum block, hollow concrete block, stone, tile, etc., with floors and roof constructed of metal or other noncombustible materials.

Mass Merchandising. A technique whereby a group of people, usually employees or members of a union or trade association, insure with one company. Premiums are collected and remitted to the insurer in a lump sum.

Master Contract. In group insurance, the master contract is given to the employer. Individuals insured under the plan receive certificates to evidence their coverage under the plan.

Master Deed or Bylaws. A document that creates a common property (i.e., condominiums, etc.) and its association. It defines homeowners' undivided shares in the common property, membership and voting rights in the association and covenants and restrictions on the use of units and common property. It also defines the governing regulations dealing with routine operational, administrative and management matters of the property.

Master Policy. (1) The policy contract issued to an employer or other entity authorized by state law for a group insurance plan. See also Certificate of Insurance. (2) A property insurance policy issued to an insured who can issue certificates of coverage to cover the property of others.

Master. The captain of a ship.

Master-Servant Rule. A rule that says all employers are obligated to protect the public from the acts of their employees. Courts hold employers liable for torts committed by employees in the course of their employment.

Material Fact. A fact that is so important that its disclosure would change the decision of an insurance company, either with respect to writing coverage, settling a loss or determining a premium. Usually, the misrepresentation of a material fact voids a policy.

Mature. A policy matures when its face amount becomes payable. This could occur upon the death of the insured, or in some forms of insurance such as endowments, as of a specified date.

Mature Policies. Uninterrupted claims-made coverage continuously in effect for at least five years, and no longer eligible for rating credits given on immature policies.

Maturity Date. The date that the face amount of a life insurance policy becomes payable by reason of death or endowment.

Maturity Value. The amount payable to a living insured at the end of an endowment period or to the owner of a whole life policy if he lives past a certain age.

Maxi Tail or Full Tail. Unlimited extended reporting period allowing for claims to be made after expiration of a "claims-made" liability policy. See also Supplemental Extended Reporting Period.

Maximum Allowable Costs (MAC) List. A list of prescriptions that bases reimbursement on the cost of the generic product.

Maximum Disability Policy. Noncancelable disability income insurance that limits an insurer's liability for any one claim but not the aggregate amount of all claims. For one claim there is a maximum amount payable, but there could be any number of separate claims for different disabilities.

Maximum Foreseeable Loss. See Amount Subject.

Maximum Out-of-Pocket Costs. The most a member will pay for copayments, coinsurance, deductibles, etc.

Maximum Possible Loss. See Amount Subject.

Maximum Retrospective Premium. The most an insured is required to pay under a retrospective rating plan, regardless of the amount of losses incurred. See Retrospective Rating.

McCarran-Ferguson Act. See Public Law 15.

MDO. See Monthly Debit Ordinary.

MDRT. See Million Dollar Round Table.

Mediation. An informal means of settling a dispute that involves a third-party mediator who meets both parties to the dispute and encourages them to agree on a settlement.

Medicaid. A medical benefits program administered by states and subsidized by the federal government. Under this plan, various medical expenses are paid to those who qualify. Also called Title XIX Benefits.

Medical Application. An application consisting of information gained from a physical exam performed by a doctor instead of a simple medical profile.

Medical Benefits. Coverage that pays reasonable medical expenses incurred by an insured, members of the insured's family and passengers for bodily injuries sustained while riding in the insured's car. It pays medical bills for an insured and others covered on the policy, regardless of who was at fault. Coverage also applies while riding in another vehicle or if injured as a pedestrian by a vehicle.

Medical Care Insurance. See Medical Expense Insurance.

Medical Examination. The examination of an applicant for insurance or a claimant by a physician who acts in the capacity of the insurer's agent.

Medical Examiner. The physician who examines an applicant or claimant on behalf of the insurer and as an agent of the insurer.

Medical Expense Insurance. Health insurance that provides benefits for medical, surgical and hospital expenses. This term is used to include coverage under the terms hospital-surgical expense insurance and medical care insurance.

Medical Expense Reimbursement Plan (MERP). A plan which provides for corporate reimbursement of specific health care expenses to employees.

Medical Information Bureau (MIB). A data pool service that stores coded information on the health histories of persons who have applied for insurance from subscribing companies in the past. Most life and health insurers subscribe to this bureau to get more complete underwriting information.

Medical Loss Ratio. Total health benefits divided by total premium.

Medical Payments Insurance. A form of optional coverage under automobile and other public liability policies that provides for the payment of medical and similar expenses without regard for liability. See Medical Benefits, also Personal Injury Protection.

Medical Profile. Record of an insured's past medical history and current physical condition. Most disability insurance companies request this information. They also will ask an insured to take a physical exam (usually at the company's expense).

Medical Savings Account (MSA). An employer-funded account linked to a high deductible medical indemnity plan. Usually, the employer raises the plan deductible (usually by 300 to 400 percent) and in turn returns a portion of the premium savings to employees as contributions to the medical

savings account. Employees can use the contributions to pay for health care expenses throughout
the year, and at the end of the year may withdraw
whatever remains in the account as cash. ⚕

Medical Supplies. Any items that are essential in
carrying out the treatment of a patient's illness or
injury. ⚕

Medically Necessary. A service or treatment that
is absolutely necessary in treating a patient and
which could adversely affect the patient's condition
if it were omitted. ⚕

Medicare. The federal government plan for paying
certain hospital and medical expenses for persons
qualifying under the plan, usually those over 65.
The hospital benefits are Part A, and the medical
expense portion is Part B. Part A is compulsory social insurance; Part B is voluntary government-sub-
sidized, government-operated insurance. ⚕

Medicare Beneficiary. Anyone entitled to Medicare benefits based on the designation by the Social
Security Administration. ⚕

Medicare Select Policy. A Medicare supplement
policy or certificate that contains restricted network
provisions conditioning the payment of benefits on
the use of network providers. ⚕

Medicare Supplement Insurance. Insurance coverage sold on an individual or group basis that helps
to fill the gaps in the protection provided by the
Medicare program. Medicare supplements cannot
duplicate any benefits provided by Medicare, but
may pay part or all of Medicare's deductibles and

copayments, and may cover some services and expenses not covered by Medicare.

Member. (1) An employee who is qualified for coverage under a pension plan. Also called a "participant." (2) Anyone covered under a health plan (enrollee or eligible dependent).

Member Certificate. Another term for certificate of coverage.

Member Month. The total number of participants who are members for each month.

Members Per Year. The total number of member months divided by 12.

Mental (or Emotional) Distress. Usually not covered if a claimant was a bystander to an accident, but covered if he was physically involved.

Mental Health Provider. Individuals who are qualified to provide mental health services in accordance with the state or federal law which applies. Includes psychiatrists, social workers and psychologists.

Mental Health Services and Supplies. Items required for treatment of mental illness, including substance abuse and alcoholism.

Mercantile Open Stock Policy. A crime insurance form used by retail establishments to cover merchandise, furniture and equipment after hours while the insured business is closed. It covered losses by burglary or robbery of a watchperson. It has been replaced by modern commercial crime coverage forms.

Mercantile Risk. A retail or wholesale risk as contrasted with a service risk, manufacturing risk or a habitational risk.

Mercantile Robbery and Safe Burglary Policy. A crime insurance form used by retail establishments to insure money and securities. It has been replaced by modern commercial crime coverage forms.

Merchant Marine Act. Also known as the Jones Act. A law that permits an injured seaman to sue his employer for damages and to have a jury trial. Insurance is provided under the employers liability section of a standard workers' comp policy, but when the exposure exists the insurance company usually requires attachment of the maritime coverage endorsement, which actually limits the insurance and adds a few exclusions to the policy.

Merit Rating. A rating plan used in several forms of insurance but most commonly in personal auto. It is a method whereby the insured's premium varies up or down depending on the insured's own past loss record.

MERP. See Medical Expense Reimbursement Plan.

Messenger. Under commercial crime insurance coverages, the named insured or any of the insured's partners or employees while having care and custody of property outside the insured's premises.

Messenger Robbery Insurance. Coverage on money and other property in the possession of persons who are away from the premises (e.g., an employee taking a deposit to the bank).

MIB. See Medical Information Bureau.

Midi Tail. Automatic five-year extended reporting period allowing for the making of claims after expiration of a "claims-made" liability policy, but only applies to claims arising from occurrences that were reported no later than 60 days after the end of the policy. See also Extended Reporting Period.

Mill (or Slow-Burning) Construction. Construction meeting certain high specifications and standards. Factories and warehouses, constructed to meet these specifications qualify for reduced fire insurance rates.

Million Dollar Round Table (MDRT). An association of life insurance agents who qualify by selling $1 million worth or more of life insurance coverage. The policies must meet certain qualification standards, and applicants must be members of the National Association of Life Underwriters.

Mini Tail. Automatic 60-day extended reporting period allowing for the making of claims after expiration of a "claims-made" liability policy. See also Extended Reporting Period.

Minimum Amount Policy. A life insurance policy that is sold only with a minimum face amount. It can have a lower rate than other inexpensive coverages because certain insurance company expenses, like those of policy writing, do not increase proportionately with the face amount of the policy sold.

Minimum Compensation Level. The amount of compensation an employee must earn before being eligible to participate in a pension or profit sharing plan.

Minimum Deposit Insurance. See Financed Insurance and Minimum Deposit Policy.

Minimum Deposit Policy. A cash value life insurance policy having a first-year loan value that is available to borrow against immediately upon payment of the first-year premium.

Minimum Guarantee. Guaranteed interest that is the predetermined lowest rate.

Minimum Premium. (1) The smallest amount of premium for which an insurer will issue coverage under a given policy. (2) A cost plus arrangement whereby the employer pays the insurer only a portion of the premium which is to be used for administration costs. The remainder is placed in a "bank account" which is then used by the insurer to pay claims.

Minimum Rate. A rate for low hazard risks.

Minimum Retained Limit. The greater of the deductible shown in the Declarations or the actual amount of underlying insurance available to the insured.

Minimum Retrospective Premium. Used in a retrospective rating plan, the lowest amount the insured can pay under the plan, regardless of the losses incurred.

Miscellaneous Benefits. Benefits provided by a group medical policy that cover most inpatient medical expenses except room and board charges and surgical fees.

Miscellaneous Dwelling Endorsement. An endorsement attached to an insured's policy that modifies some of the policy provisions, particularly provisions concerning the amount of insurance and the premium.

Miscellaneous Endorsements. Endorsements that increase coverage limits for specified property, limit coverage for specified property or portions of the premises and exclude coverage for specified persons, premises or types of property.

Miscellaneous Expenses. Ancillary expenses, usually hospital charges other than daily room and board (e.g., x-rays, drugs and lab fees). The total amount of such charges that are reimbursed is limited in most basic hospitalization policies.

Miscellaneous Type Vehicle Endorsement. An endorsement that insures types of vehicles that are not normally eligible for personal auto coverage under a standard policy—like cars not designed for road travel and recreational vehicles. The endorsement changes the policy definition of the covered auto to include miscellaneous type vehicles, and states the type of miscellaneous vehicle in the schedule or Declarations. Also covers any miscellaneous type vehicle acquired during the policy period.

Misrepresentation. The use of oral or written statements that do not truly reflect the facts either by an insured on an application for insurance or by an insurer concerning the terms or benefits of an insurance policy. These situations usually involve issues—like reasonable reliance and bad faith refusal to pay, and can be grounds for nullification of the policy—or damages in excess of policy limits.

Misstatement of Age. (1) Providing the wrong age on an application for life and health insurance or for a beneficiary who is to receive benefits on a basis involving his or her life contingency. (2) A provision in most life and health policies setting forth the action to be taken if a misstatement of age is discovered after the policy is issued. This is one of the uniform provisions for individual health insurance policies.

Mixed Insurer (or Company). An insurance company that splits ownership among stockholders and policyowners. The term also indicates an insurer issuing both life and health insurance policies. It is often erroneously used to describe an insurer offering both participating (dividend paying) and nonparticipating plans.

MLIRB. Multi-Line Insurance Rating Bureau.

Mobile Agricultural Machinery and Equipment Coverage Form. A commercial property form specifically designed to insure farm machinery and equipment when it is the only exposure, or when the coverage must be written separately. Similar coverage may also be included in the farm property coverage form.

Mobile Equipment. Land vehicles, including attached machinery and apparatus, whether or not self-propelled, and: 1) not subject to motor vehicle registration; 2) used exclusively on the insured's premises; 3) principally for use off public roads; or

4) designed or maintained to provide mobility for permanently attached equipment such as cranes, loaders, pumps, generators or welding equipment.

Mobile Home Endorsement/Policy. A homeowners policy written on a mobile home that is permanently situated. Alters certain policy provisions as necessary to provide mobile home coverage. Mobile homes may also be covered with separate, stand-alone insurance policies designed particularly for that use.

Mode of Premium Payment. The method of premium payment (mode) elected by the policyowner. Modes generally available are monthly, quarterly, semiannually and annually.

Model Year. The auto manufacturer's model year. Auto manufacturers usually start selling their new models in the fall of the previous year—for example, 1994 models are often introduced in the fall of 1993. It is the model year and not the year of purchase that appears in the Declarations.

Modified. (1) Under a modified coinsurance provision in life reinsurance, the ceding insurer retains and maintains the entire reserve, with the annual increase in reserve being transferred to the ceding insurer by the reinsurer at the end of the year. (2) Under preliminary term insurance, a modified reserving system permits at least part, if not all, of the first year's net premium on a life insurance policy to be used to meet first-year acquisition costs and claim expenses and requires that part of the renewal loading be added to the policy reserve accumulation. (3) Any premium that is altered from the regular premium for similar life policies, such as the premium for a modified life policy.

Modified Adjusted Gross Income. A worker's adjusted gross income plus tax exempt interest received during a tax year.

Modified Community Rating. A method of determining rates for medical services based on data from a given geographic area.

Modified Endowment Contract. An endowment contract where the amount payable upon survival of the endowment period is greater than the face amount and the amount payable at death is the greater of the face amount or cash value. Modified endowment contracts are subject to taxation and subsequent penalties.

Modified Fee-for-Service. A situation where reimbursement is made based on the actual fees subject to maximums for each procedure.

Modified Fire-Resistive Construction. A building with exterior walls, floors and roof constructed of masonry or fire-resistive materials.

Modified Life Policy. An ordinary life contract under which the premiums are modified so as to be lower than normal for the first three to five years and higher than normal after that. A special case: a level term policy, under which no part of the premium goes towards savings, that automatically converts to a whole life policy at a designated time.

Money and Securities Broad Form. A once popular crime insurance form used by businesses to protect money and securities against many types of losses that has been replaced by modern commercial crime coverage forms. See Theft, Disappearance and Destruction Coverage Form.

Money Purchase Plan. A pension or retirement plan. A plan where a specified amount of money is used periodically to purchase an annuity for each employee covered by the plan. The total of these annuities is then paid to the employee at retirement.

Money-Purchase Benefit Formula. A pension plan under which contributions of both the employer and the employee are fixed as flat amounts or flat percentages of the employee's salary. See Defined Contribution Pension Plan.

Monoline Policy. Any insurance coverage written as a single line policy. Contrast with Multiple Line or Package Policy.

Monopolistic State Fund. The state-operated company in those states having laws that require all businesses to buy workers' compensation insurance from the state. Private insurers cannot compete in these states.

Monthly Administration Fee. In universal life insurance, an administrative fee is charged each month to cover administrative expenses.

Monthly Debit Ordinary (MDO). Ordinary insurance policies whose premiums are collected at the door monthly in the same fashion as industrial policies.

Moral Hazard. A condition of morals or habits that increases the probability of loss from a peril (e.g., an individual who previously burned his or her own property to collect the insurance). Some insurance professionals use the terms moral and morale hazard interchangeably. See Morale Hazard.

Morale Hazard. Hazard arising out of an insured's indifference to loss because of the existence of insurance (e.g., the attitude, "It's insured, so why worry.") If an insurer concludes that a person poses a morale hazard risk, it may add a surcharge to the disability premium or—more likely—will decline the application. See Moral Hazard.

Morbidity. The relative incidence of disease.

Morbidity Rate. The ratio of the incidence of sickness to the number of well persons in a given group of people over a given period of time. It may be the incidence of the number of new cases in the given time or the total number of cases of a given disease or disorder.

Morbidity Table. A table showing the incidence of sickness at specified ages in the same fashion that a mortality table shows the incidence of death at specified ages.

Mortality Charge. The charge for the element of pure insurance protection in a life insurance policy.

Mortality Cost. A factor considered in life insurance premium rates. Insurers have an idea of the probability that any person will die at any particular age; this is the information shown on a mortality table. The pure mortality cost is the face amount of the policy multiplied by the probability that it will have to be paid out as a claim.

Mortality, Experienced. See Experienced Mortality.

Mortality Guarantee. The provision that guarantees an annuitant income for life regardless of changes in the mortality of the population.

Mortality Rate. The number of deaths in a group of people, usually expressed as deaths per thousand. It can be the rate for the total population, called the crude mortality rate, or it can be refined by factors such as age groupings or causes of deaths. Same as Death Rate.

Mortality Savings. The remainder, if any, after subtracting experienced mortality from expected mortality.

Mortality Table. A table showing the incidence of death at specified ages. It shows the number of persons in each age group that die, expressed in terms of deaths per thousand, and based on the deaths in a population of a million persons. Insurance companies use these tables to determine the life expectancy of insureds and possible insureds.

Mortgage. Interest in real property conveyed to mortgagee as security for the loan of money by the mortgagee to the mortgagor, often the money being used by the mortgagor for the purchase of the real property from its seller (also known as a purchase money mortgage).

Mortgage (or Mortgagee) Clause. A provision attached to a fire or other direct damage policy that covers mortgaged property, specifying that the loss reimbursement shall be paid to the mortgagee as the mortgagee's interest may appear, that the mortgagee's rights of recovery shall not be defeated by any act or neglect of the insured, and giving the mortgagee other rights, privileges and duties.

Mortgagee. The creditor to whom a mortgage is given and who lends money on the security of the value of the property mortgaged.

Mortgage Holders Errors and Omissions Coverage Form. A commercial property form that protects the interests of mortgage holders from losses resulting from errors and omissions.

Mortgage Insurance. In life and health insurance, a policy covering a mortgagor. The benefits are usually intended (1) to pay off the balance due on a mortgage upon the death of the insured, or (2) to meet the payments on a mortgage as they fall due in the case of the insured's death or disability. Also called Mortgage Redemption Insurance.

Mortgagor. The debtor who receives money and in turn grants a mortgage on his or her property as security for a loan.

Mortgage Redemption Insurance. (1) See Mortgage Insurance. (2) A monthly reducing term policy used for mortgage insurance.

Motor Carrier Act of 1980. The act requires minimum liability coverage for carriers of certain hazardous substances. In addition to the direct injury and damage that can be caused by a collision involving a commercial carrier, hazardous substances pose a special threat.

Motor Truck Cargo Policy (Carrier's Form). Indemnifies truckers, for loss or damage resulting from legal liability as a carrier while transporting the property of others. It does not insure against any loss for which the trucker is not legally liable. Statutory law requires a trucker to carry a minimum amount of coverage.

Motor Truck Cargo Policy (Owner's Form). Insures the owner of a truck against loss to his or her own property while being transported. It pays for the loss or damage of cargo for the perils insured against, regardless of the legal liability.

Motor Vehicle Record (MVR). Record of a driver's accidents and/or traffic violations.

MPIC. Multiple Peril Insurance Conference.

Multi-Disciplinary. Treatment which involves care provided by a wide range of specialists.

Multiemployer Plan. A plan to which more than one employer contributes, or a plan mandated by a collective bargaining agreement.

Multi-Peril Crop Insurance (MPCI). Crop insurance usually providing coverage against crop losses by adverse weather (hail, wind, etc.), fire, flood, insects, etc.

Multi-Peril Policies. Policies that cover a number of perils, such as fire, burglary and liability, in a single contract.

Multiple Employer Trust (MET). A trust consisting of multiple small employers in the same industry, that is formed for the purpose of purchasing group health insurance or establishing a self-funded plan at a lower cost than any available to the employers individually.

Multiple Employer Welfare Arrangements (MEWA). Employer funds and trusts providing health care benefits to individuals.

Multiple Funding. Providing retirement benefits through the use of a separate fund in addition to insurance cash values.

Multiple Indemnity. A provision that some or all of the benefits under a policy will be increased by a stated multiple, such as 100 or 200 percent, in the event that a peril occurs in a specified way (e.g., double indemnity on life insurance for accidental death).

Multiple Line Law. A law passed by states that allows an insurance company to write both property and casualty insurance. Prior to these laws, it was common for a state to allow some companies to write only property insurance and other companies to write only casualty insurance, depending on which type of insurance the company applied for in its license.

Multiple Line Policy. A policy that includes several different coverages such as property, liability and crime. Any personal or commercial package policy.

Multiple Location Policy. Protection of property in more than one location that is owned or controled by one person.

Multiple Location Rating Plan. See Premium and Dispersion Credit Plan.

Multiple Option Plan. Under this plan, employees can optionally choose from an HMO, PPO or a major medical plan.

Multiple Protection Insurance. A combination of term and whole life insurance that pays some multiple of the face during the period of the term policy, becoming a regular whole life policy after the term policy expires. The multiple protection period is thus the period during which both the term and the whole life coverages are in effect.

Mutual Atomic Energy Reinsurance Pool. A group of mutual insurance companies that reinsure liability policies written on private nuclear energy reactors. Most insurers exclude this coverage. See also Radioactive Contamination Insurance.

Mutual Benefit Association. An organization offering benefits to members on a plan under which no fixed premiums are paid in advance but assessments are levied on members to meet specific losses as they occur. See also Assessment Company, Society or Insurer.

Mutual Fund. An investment company that raises money by selling its own stock to the public. It then invests the proceeds in other securities and the value of its own stock fluctuates with its experience with the securities in its portfolio. Mutual funds are of two types: 1) open-end, in which capitalization is not fixed and more shares may be sold at any time; and 2) closed-end, in which capitalization is fixed and only the number of shares originally authorized may be sold.

Mutual Insurer. An incorporated insurer without incorporated capital owned by its policyholders. Although mutual insurers do distribute their earnings to their policyholders in the form of dividends, the term should not be used in a sense that makes it synonymous with participating. In most jurisdictions, a mutual insurer is free to issue nonparticipating insurance if it chooses and a stock insurer is free to issue participating insurance. Contrast with Stock Insurer.

Mutual Insurer Policy. Insurance issued by a mutual insurer.

Mutual Investment Trust. See Mutual Fund.

Mutualization. The process of converting a stock insurer to a mutual insurer, accomplished by having the insurer buy stock and retire it.

MVRs. See Motor Vehicle Record.

Mysterious Disappearance. A disappearance of property that cannot be explained. Crime insurance policies use this term to give very broad coverage as opposed to policies which narrow definitions to specific perils such as robbery and burglary.

N

NAIB. See National Association of Insurance Brokers, Inc.

NAIC. See National Association of Insurance Commissioners.

NAII. See National Association of Independent Insurers.

NAIW. National Association of Insurance Women.

NALC. See National Association of Life Companies.

Name Position Bond. A fidelity bond that covers losses caused by the dishonesty of employees holding positions specifically named in the bond. Contrast with Name Schedule Bond and Blanket Bond.

Name Schedule Bond. A fidelity bond that covers losses caused by the dishonesty of employees specifically named in the bond. Contrast with Name Position and Blanket Bond.

Named Insured. Any person, firm, corporation or any member thereof, specifically designated by name as the insured(s) in a policy. Others may be protected as insureds even though their names do not appear on the policy (e.g., automobile policies where, under the definition of insured, protection is extended to cover other drivers using the car with the permission of the named insured).

Named Non-Owner Policy. An automobile policy issued to someone who does not own a vehicle, but who drives borrowed or rented autos.

Named Perils. Perils specifically covered on property insured. Contrast with Open Perils (All Risk) Insurance.

NAMIC. See National Association Of Mutual Insurance Companies.

NAPIA. National Association of Professional Insurance Agents.

NASD. See National Association of Securities Dealers.

National Association of Independent Insurers (NAII). An association comprised of fire, casualty and surety insurers that do not belong to large rating bureaus. It distributes considerable information about legislation and litigation.

National Association of Insurance Brokers, Inc. (NAIB). A voluntary association of insurance brokers that exchange information and make recommendations to state legislatures.

National Association of Insurance Commissioners (NAIC). An association of state insurance commissioners formed for the purpose of exchanging information and for developing uniformity in the regulatory practices of the states through drafting model legislation and regulations. The NAIC has no official power to enforce compliance with its recommendations.

National Association of Life Companies (NALC). A voluntary association of smaller and newer companies for exchange of information and ideas.

National Association of Life Underwriters (NALU). An association of life insurance agents, the activities of which center on the welfare and education of agents and legislation affecting agents.

National Association of Mutual Insurance Companies (NAMIC). A voluntary intercompany organization of mutual property and liability insurers formed for the exchange of information and discussion.

National Association of Securities Dealers (NASD). A voluntary association of brokers and securities dealers handling over-the-counter securities. It serves a quasi-official function in the regulation of licensing and also acts as a bureau that formulates rates, rating plans and policy wording for about half of the states. Many other states subscribe to the various services it provides. It is supported by the insurance companies that belong to it.

National Auto Theft Bureau. An organization engaged in the prevention and reduction of motor vehicle fire and theft losses.

National Council on Compensation Insurance (NCCI). An association of insurers selling compensation coverage and operating as a rating organization. NCCI collects statistics, develops rates and policy forms and makes state filings for its members.

National Crop Insurance Association. A sister organization to the Crop Hail Insurance Actuarial Association (CHIAA). In 1989, these two organizations were consolidated to become National Crop Insurance Services (NCIS).

National Crop Insurance Services (NCIS). A voluntary, nonprofit organization made up of more than 140 member companies that compiles research and statistics in order to develop crop insurance rates and forms.

National Drug Code (NDC). A system for identifying drugs.

National Flood Insurance Program (NFIP). Federal program providing flood insurance for fixed property. Under a "dual" program, coverage may be written directly by the NFIP or by private carriers who may be reimbursed by the NFIP.

National Fraternal Congress of America. A federation of fraternal benefit societies.

National Health Insurance. Any system of socialized insurance benefits covering all or nearly all of the citizens of a country, established by its federal law, administered by its federal government and supported or subsidized by taxation.

National Insurance Association, Inc. An intercompany association of insurers formed to exchange information and ideas on common problems unique to the black community.

National Safety Council. A nonprofit organization chartered by Congress in 1913 to disseminate safety education material. It is made up of approximately 12,000 industry members nationwide.

National Service Life Insurance (NSLI). Life insurance made available by the federal government for members of the United States armed forces from 1940 to 1951.

Nationwide Definition of Marine Insurance. A statement recommended by the National Association of Insurance Commissioners indicating the types of insurance written under ocean or inland marine policies. Most states use this definition, subject to some individual exceptions. See also Ocean Marine and Inland Marine Insurance.

Natural Death. Death by means other than accident or homicide.

Natural Premium. The pure mortality cost of life insurance for one year at any given age. See also Pure Premium.

NCCI. See National Council on Compensation Insurance.

Negligence. Failure to use that degree of care which an ordinary person of reasonable prudence would use under the given or similar circumstances. A person may be negligent by acts of omission or commission or both. In order for negligence to exist, four elements must be present: 1) duty to act; 2) breach of the duty to act; 3) occurrence of injury or damage; and 4) negligence as the proximate cause of the injury or damage. If any of these elements is absent, negligence does not exist, and the tortfeasor will not be held liable due to negligence.

Negligence, Comparative. See Comparative Negligence.

Negligence, Contributory. See Contributory Negligence.

Negligence, Gross. See Gross Negligence.

Negligence, Presumed. See *Res Ipsa Loquitur*.

Net Amount at Risk. The differences between the face amount of a policy and the reserve or cash value that has been built up under that policy.

Net Cost. Premiums paid minus cash value and any policy dividends paid as of the date the calculation is being made. In the life business, it is common to draw up net cost comparisons at the end of 10 and 20 years.

Net Increase. The increase in the total amount of business an insurer has to force over a given period of time. It is figured as the total of new policies issued plus those renewed less policies lapsed and canceled.

Net Interest Earned. The average interest earned by an insurer on its investments after investment expense but before federal income taxes.

Net Level Premium. The pure mortality cost of a life insurance policy from its inception to its maturity date, divided by the number of years the policy is to be in force. See Level Premium Insurance.

Net Level Premium Reserve. The reserve needed by an insurer to cover net level policies that are in their later years. Loosely speaking, the level premium system of paying for a long-term life or health policy involves overpayment in the early years and underpayment in the later years.

Net Line. The amount of coverage retained by the ceding company on an individual risk in a surplus reinsurance treaty. It also refers to the maximum amount of loss on a particular risk to which an insurer will expose itself without reinsurance. See also Lines and Retention.

Net Loss. The amount of loss sustained by an insurer after giving effect to all applicable reinsurance, salvage and subrogation recoveries.

Net Premium. (1) The amount of premium minus the agent's commission. (2) The premium necessary to cover only anticipated losses, before covering other expenses. (3) The original premium minus dividends paid or anticipated in participating life insurance when the insured elects to use dividends toward payment of the premiums. Contrast with Gross Premium.

Net Quick Assets. The difference between allowable current assets and changeable current liabilities. This figure is referred to as the working capital. A contractor must have adequate working capital in order to be bonded.

Net Rate. (1) See Net Premium for the definition applicable to participating life insurance policies. (2) In a nonparticipating policy, the book rate.

Net Retained Line. See Net Line.

Net Retention. The amount of insurance that a ceding company keeps for its own account and does not reinsure.

Net Worth. The amount by which assets exceed liabilities. It is of concern to bond indemnifiers in determining the size of a job a contractor can handle.

Network Model HMO. Under this model, an HMO contracts with several physician groups. Physicians may share in savings, but may provide care for other than HMO members.

New for Old. Replacing old damaged parts or equipment with new ones rather than repairing them.

New York Standard Fire Policy (SFP). The basic fire insurance contract that was used in nearly every state. It provided coverage against loss by fire, lightning and removal, and established policy provisions that became the foundation for property insurance contracts. EC and VMM coverage could be added by endorsement. In recent years, the standard fire policy has become obsolete, except in a few states where its use is still required by law.

Newly Acquired Autos. Any automobile purchased after the effective date but before the end of the term of an automobile policy. Newly acquired autos receive some automatic coverage but the insured must notify the insurance company of the acquisition within 30 days.

Newspaper Policy. A form of limited health insurance often sold by newspapers to build or conserve circulation.

NFIA. National Flood Insurers Association.

NFPA. National Fire Protection Association.

No Benefit to Bailee. A provision in an inland marine form that states that any insurance a person has on property in the possession of a bailee will not be for the direct or indirect benefit of any carrier or other bailee for hire. A bailee is someone who has been entrusted with someone else's property, usually for the purpose of service, repair or storage (e.g., dry cleaners, television repair shops, garages and public parking lots).

NOC. Not Otherwise Classified. A term used in the classification section of liability or workers' comp rating manuals. If a listing is followed by an NOC, it means to use this classification if an insured cannot be classified more specifically.

No-Fault Insurance. Many states have passed laws permitting the individual automobile accident victim to collect directly from his or her own insurance company for medical and hospital expenses regardless of who was at fault in the accident.

Nominal Damages. A small amount of money awarded to a plaintiff to verify his or her legal rights, even though no actual damages have been proven.

Nonadmitted Assets. Assets that do not qualify under state law for insurance statement purposes (e.g., furniture, fixtures, agents' debit balances and accounts receivable that are over 90 days old).

Nonadmitted Insurer. An insurer not licensed to do business in the jurisdiction in question. Also called unauthorized or unlicensed insurer.

Nonadmitted Reinsurance. Reinsurance for which no credit is given in a ceding company's annual statement because the reinsurer is not licensed or authorized to transact that particular line of business in the jurisdiction in question.

Nonassessable Policy. A policy for which the policyowner pays a set premium. No additional premiums or amounts can be assessed. These are issued primarily by stock insurers, but are also issued by mutual insurers who qualify to do so by meeting certain standards under state laws.

Nonassignable. A policy that cannot be assigned to a third party. Most policies are nonassignable unless approval is given by the insurer.

Noncancelable ("Non-Can") Contract. A contract of health insurance that the insured has a right to continue in force by payment of premiums, as set forth in the contract, for a substantial period of time, also as set forth in the contract. During that period, the insurer has no right to make any change to the contract. The NAIC recommends that the term "noncancelable" not be used to designate any form that is not renewable to at least age 50 or for at least five years if issued after age 44. Note that this is in contrast to guaranteed renewable, on which the premium may be increased by classes. The premium for noncancelable policies must remain as stated in the policy at the time of issue. Contrast with Guaranteed Renewable.

Nonconcurrency. When a number of insurance policies intended to cover the same property against the same hazards are not identical as to the extent of coverage. Nonconcurrency usually results in an insured not being fully covered for a loss. Modern forms have minimized this problem.

Nonconfining Sickness. Sickness that does not confine the insured indoors.

Noncontributory Retirement Plan. A retirement plan funded entirely by the employer.

Noncontributory. A plan, usually group, for which the employer pays the entire premium and the employee contributes no part of the premium.

Noncupative Will. An oral will given in the presence of witnesses usually at the time when the testator is very near death.

Non-Disabling Injury. An injury that does not qualify the insured for total or partial disability benefits. Disability income policies may contain a provision for a small benefit in the case of such an injury, including medical costs of up to 25 to 50 percent of one month's disability benefit payment.

Non-Disabling Injury Rider. An optional disability income policy rider that does not pay a disability benefit but rather provides for the payment of medical expenses incurred due to injury that does not result in total disability.

Nonduplication of Benefits. A provision in some health policies specifying that benefits will not be paid for amounts reimbursed by others. In group insurance, it is called coordination of benefits.

Non-Earned Income. Group disability income insurance, interest income, dividends, rental income, deferred compensation and residual commissions, royalties and other miscellaneous income.

Nonforfeitable Benefit. A benefit payable under a pension plan that unconditionally belongs to a participant of the plan.

Nonforfeiture Provisions. Protects the contract holder from total forfeiture or loss of benefits if he stops making the required periodic payments and surrender charges, or penalties for cashing in the annuity before the pay out period.

Nonforfeiture Values. Those values in a life insurance policy that by law the policyowner cannot forfeit even if he ceases to pay the premiums. These benefits are the cash surrender value, the loan value, the paid-up insurance value and the extended term insurance value. The insured may choose one of these nonforfeiture options, but even if he fails to do so, the one specified in the contract for such a case automatically goes into effect.

Noninsurable Risk. A risk that cannot be measured actuarially or in which the chance of loss is so high that insurance cannot be written against it.

Noninsurance. Making no financial preparation for meeting losses.

Nonmedical (Non-Med) Contract. Life or health insurance underwritten on the basis of an insured's statement of health with no medical examination required.

Nonoccupational Insurance. See Unemployment Compensation Disability Insurance.

Non-Occupational Policy. A policy or provision of a policy which excludes accidents occurring on the job, when such employment is covered by workers' compensation. Policies make these distinctions because occupational disabilities normally are covered through workers' compensation or similar statutory plans. Most often, group disability income contracts will specify occupational or non-occupational coverage. See Occupational Coverage.

Nonowned Auto. (1) Any auto, pickup, van or trailer that is operated by or in the custody of, but is not owned by or furnished for the regular use of, the named insured or a family member (includes temporary substitute vehicles—borrowed or rented). (2) Any autos not owned, leased, hired or borrowed that are used in connection with the business.

Nonparticipating (Non-Par) Contracts. Insurance contracts on which no policy dividends are paid because there is no contractual provision for the policyowner to participate in the surplus. Contrast with Participating.

Non-Participating Physician. One who is not approved by Medicare for direct payment and may charge more for services. See Participating Physician.

Nonparticipating Provider. (1) A provider who has not signed a contract with a health plan. (2) A medical or health care provider who is not certified to participate in the Medicare program.

Nonparticipating Provider Indemnity Benefits. Coverage where services provided by nonparticipating providers are reimbursed under an indemnity basis.

Nonprofit Insurers. Insurers organized under special state laws, usually exempting them from some taxes imposed on regular insurers, to supply medical expense reimbursement insurance, usually on a service basis (e.g., "Blue Cross and Blue Shield).

Nonproportional Reinsurance. See Aggregate Excess of Loss Reinsurance.

Non-Qualified Plan. A benefit plan, such as a retirement plan, that may be discriminatory, need not be filed with the IRS and does not provide a current tax deduction for contributions. The employer can choose which employees will participate in this program; any investment income on contributions made to the plan is not tax-deferred (for the employer); the employer does not enjoy a current tax deduction on contributions; and the plan must be in writing and communicated to the employee(s). See Qualified Deferred Compensation Plan.

Nonrenewal/Cancelation. Termination of insurance coverage at an expiration or anniversary date. This action may be taken by an insurer who refuses to renew, or by an insured who rejects a renewal offer.

Nonresident Agent. An agent licensed in a state in which he does not live.

Nonvalued Policy. A policy that is not valued; that is, when the policy is written, the amount to be paid in the event of a loss is not stated. Most property policies are nonvalued.

Noon Clause. A provision that says insurance coverage starts at noon, standard time, at the location of the insured's property. Most property policies have been changed so that the effective time is 12:01 a.m., thus the noon clause is rare.

"Normal" Retirement. Retirement at an age specified by the pension plan as being the standard age for retirement. See Mandatory Retirement.

Normal Retirement Benefit. An employee's early retirement benefit from a plan, or the benefit payable at the time of his or her normal retirement age, whichever is greater. The value of the benefits are determined without regard to medical and/or disability benefits.

Not Otherwise Classified. See NOC.

Not Taken. Policies applied for and issued but rejected by the proposed owner and not paid for.

Notice of Cancelation. Written notice by an insurer of intent to cancel insurance, or written notice by an insured requesting cancelation.

Notice of Claim. Also known as notice of loss. Notice to an insurer that a loss has occurred. This is a condition of most policies, and it is frequently required within a given time and in a particular manner. Typically an insured has 20 days to notify the insurer of a claim. Notification may take the form of a written communication or a telephone call to the insurance company or agent. If an insured is seriously injured and unable to notify the insurer within 20 days (e.g., due to being in a coma), then notification may occur later.

Notice of Loss. Notice to an insurer that a loss has occurred. Notice of loss is a condition of most policies, and it is frequently required within a given time and in a particular manner.

Notice to Company. Written notice to an insurer of the occurrence of an event.

NPD. No Payroll Division.

NSLI. See National Service Life Insurance.

Nuclear Energy Contamination. See Mutual Atomic Energy Reinsurance Pool and Radioactive Contamination Insurance.

Nuisance Value. An amount that an insurance company pays to settle a claim not because it is a valid claim but because the company considers it worth that amount to dispose of it.

Numerical Rating. An underwriting method of determining the extra rate to be charged for a substandard insured. "Standard" is rated 100. Various impairments are assigned various numerical values. The sum of 100 plus the values of the ratings of the impairments indicates the table to use in determining the rate of the policy.

Nurse Fees. A provision in a medical expense reimbursement policy calling for reimbursement for the fees of nurses other than those employed by the hospital.

Nursing Home. A licensed facility that provides general nursing care to those who are chronically ill or unable to take care of necessary daily living needs. Also called a long-term care facility.

O

OAA. Old Age Assistance, a form of public assistance. See Public Assistance.

OASDHI. See Old Age, Survivors, Disability and Health Insurance.

Object. In boiler and machinery insurance, the name of the vessel insured; the object of insurance.

Obligatory Reinsurance. See Automatic Reinsurance.

Obligee. Broadly, anyone in whose favor an obligation runs. This term is used most frequently in surety bonds where it refers to the person, firm or corporation protected by the bond. The obligee under a bond is similar to the insured under an insurance policy. In the case of a construction bond, the person for whom the building is being built is the obligee.

Obligor. Commonly called the principal. One bound by an obligation. In the case of a construction bond, the contractor is the principal.

OBRA. See Omnibus Budget Reconciliation Act.

Occasional Use. See Automobile Use Classifications.

Occupancy. The type or character of use of the property in question. The type of occupancy has a bearing on its desirability and also effects the rate for the policy.

Occupational Accident. An accident arising out of or occurring in the course of one's employment and caused by hazards inherent in or related to it.

Occupational Classification. A critical underwriting factor for disability insurance. Most insurance companies group jobs according to the degree of injury risk they pose. These groups are typically identified as classes 1, 2, 3 and 4 (or A, B, C and D). Class 1 occupations are the least hazardous and class 4 occupations are the most hazardous. Other forms of income insurance—particularly workers' comp—also use occupational classifications.

Occupational Coverage. 24-hour-a-day disability income protection. The insured person is covered under the terms of the policy whether the sickness or injury occurs on the job or off the job. Some policies may be identified as non-occupational. Usually, individual policies provide occupational coverage in combination with workers' comp benefits. See Non-Occupational Coverage.

Occupational Disease. Impairment of health caused by continued exposure to conditions inherent in an occupation or a disease caused by or resulting from the nature of an employment. State compensation laws cover this type of loss.

Occupational Hazard. A condition in an occupation that increases the risk of accident, sickness or death.

Occupational Manual. A book listing occupational classifications for various types of work.

Occupational Safety and Health Act (OSHA). A federal statute that establishes safety and health standards on a nationwide basis. The Act is enforced by Labor Department safety inspectors and also provides for the recordkeeping of statistics relevant to work injuries and illnesses.

Occupying. Includes most situations involving any injury as a result of the use or maintenance of an automobile, including entering or alighting from or getting on or off a vehicle. This includes such things as jumping from the bed of a pickup truck and injuring an ankle or slipping off a curb while getting into an automobile.

Occurrence. An event that results in an insured loss. In some lines of insurance, such as liability, it is distinguished from accident in that the loss does not have to be sudden and fortuitous and can result from continuous or repeated exposure that results in bodily injury or property damage neither expected nor intended by the insured. A situation must be deemed an occurrence before insurance applies.

Occurrence Coverage. A policy form providing liability coverage only for injury or damage that occurs during the policy period, regardless of when the claim is actually made (e.g., a claim made in the current policy year could be charged against a prior policy period, or may not be covered, if it arises from an occurrence prior to the effective date). Contrast with Claims-Made Coverage.

Ocean Marine Insurance. A general term used to indicate all types of insurance associated with coverage on vessels and their cargoes.

Odds. The probable frequency of incidence of a given occurrence in a statistical sample. It is expressed as a ratio to the probable number of nonoccurrences or as a decimal fraction of the total occurrences. For example, a probability of .25 equals odds of three to one against. A probability of .75 equals odds of three to one for. See also Probability, Law of Large Numbers and Degree of Risk.

Off Premises. A clause in a property insurance contract extending coverage away from the premises listed in the policy. Coverage away from the premises is usually restricted to a percentage of the total coverage on the premises (e.g., 10 percent).

Offer. The terms of a contract proposed by one party to another. In property and casualty insurance, submitting an application to the company is usually considered an offer. In life insurance, the application plus the initial premium constitutes an offer.

Offeree. One to whom an offer is made.

Offeror. One who makes an offer.

Office Burglary and Robbery Policy. A special policy designed for offices. It usually consists of several crime coverages on office equipment and supplies which are purchased as a package. There is relatively low limit for each coverage and very little flexibility in that the policyholder must buy the complete package.

Office Visit. Services provided in the physician's office.

Officers and Directors Liability Insurance. A type of insurance that protects the officers and directors of a corporation against damages resulting from negligent or wrongful acts that may harm the corporation or its stockholders.

Offset Rider. A rider in a health insurance policy designed to reduce the benefit by a portion of the Social Security benefits received.

OL&T. See Owners, Landlords and Tenants Liability Insurance.

Old Age, Survivors, Disability and Health Insurance. The system of social insurance benefits for the aged, surviving dependents and disabled workers set up by the Social Security Act of 1935, plus amendments and additions. See also Social Insurance and Social Security.

Old Line. A term generally applied to related insurers operating on a legal reserve basis. The term seems to have come into use at the time of the competition between newly acquired or formed insurers and older insurers to indicate the fact that the related companies were "newcomers."

Omnibus Budget Reconciliation Act. A federal law that extends the minimum COBRA continuation of group health care coverage from 18 to 29 months for qualified beneficiaries who are disabled at the time of qualification.

Omnibus Clause. An agreement in most auto liability policies and some others that, by its definition of insured, extends the protection of the policy to others within the definition without the necessity of specifically naming them in the policy (e.g., a policy covering the named insured and "those residing with him or her").

Omnibus Risk. A structure housing a number of tenants engaged in a variety of businesses.

Open Access. Allows a participant to see another participating provider without a referral. Also called Open Panel.

Open Cover. A reinsurance facility under which risks of a specified category are declared and insured.

Open Debit. A life and health insurance debit (territory) currently without an agent.

Open End Investment Company. An investment company managed by professional investment advisors who invest in stocks and bonds on behalf of shareholders. Also known as a mutual fund.

Open Enrollment Period. A period during which members can elect to come under an alternate plan, usually without providing evidence of insurability.

Open Panel. See Open Access.

Open Perils. Insurance against loss of or damage to property arising from any cause except those that are specifically excluded. See All-Risk Insurance. Contrast with Named Perils.

Open Policy. An insurance contract where the terms of the policy are not fixed at the inception nor is an expiration date specified, but limits of liability are set forth for the protection it offers. No deposit premium is required, but monthly reports are made and sent with premiums due at that time, and certificates of insurance are issued to indicate the property covered. Commonly used to cover goods in transit.

Open Rating. A system whereby a state allows an insurer to use rates without prior approval.

Open Stock Burglary Policy. See Mercantile Open Stock Burglary Coverage.

Option. A choice of methods of receiving policy dividends, nonforfeiture values, death benefits or cash values.

Optional Benefits. See Elective Benefits.

Optional Modes of Settlement. The different options from which the beneficiary can choose to receive the proceeds from a life insurance policy.

Optional Policy Benefits. Benefits beyond the basic disability benefits. Their inclusion most often is dependent on an insured's needs and ability to pay the extra premium for these options. The options that appeal to most people include: future increase options, cost of living rider and lifetime accident and sickness benefit. See Elective Benefits.

Optionally Renewable. A contract of health insurance where an insurer reserves the unrestricted right to terminate coverage at any anniversary or, in some cases, at any premium due date. It may not do so in between.

Ordinance or Law Coverage. Coverage for the additional loss caused by the enforcement of laws that regulate building repair or construction. This coverage is added by endorsements and includes debris removal expenses.

Ordinary Agency. A life insurance agency handling only ordinary life. See also Ordinary Life Policy.

Ordinary Construction. A building with floors on wood joists, in which the interior finish usually conceals space where fire can spread, and which has little protection of stair shafts.

Ordinary Life Pension Trust. A pension plan funded by means of a trust that provides death benefits through the purchase of ordinary or whole life insurance contracts for covered employees. The trust pays the insurance premium until the employee reaches retirement age, and accumulates the additional sums necessary to purchase the retirement benefits, using the paid-up value of the life insurance policies.

Ordinary Life Policy. A whole life policy that pays premiums continuously as long as the insured lives. Same as Straight Life Policy. See also Whole Life Insurance.

Ordinary Living Expenses. Typical expenses such as groceries, regular evenings out or ordinary utility bills.

Ordinary Payroll. A business interruption term that means the entire payroll expense for all the employees of an insured except officers, executives, department managers, employees under contract and other important employees. This payroll can be excluded or limited from business interruption forms, reducing the amount of insurance and insured is required to carry.

Ordinary Register. The record book in a combination insurer or agency containing data on the ordinary policies in an agent's account.

OSHA. See Occupational Safety and Health Act.

Other Insurance Clause. A provision found in almost every insurance policy except life and sometimes health stating what is to be done in case any other contract of insurance embraces the same property and/or hazards. See also Nonduplication of Benefits and Apportionment.

Other Insurance. The existence of other contracts covering the same interest and perils. See also Concurrent Insurance.

Other Structures. Structures, such as a garage or storage shed, that are separated from an insured dwelling by a clear space, or are connected only by a fence or utility line. Dwelling and homeowners policies provide coverage for other structures. This coverage is sometimes called "appurtenant structures" coverage.

Other than Collision Coverage. A broad category of coverage that includes many types of loss. The standard policy clearly spells out the losses that are not collision losses: missiles, falling objects, theft, explosion, earthquake, windstorm, hail, water, flood, malicious mischief, vandalism, riot, civil commotion, contact with a bird or animal. Historically, this has been known as comprehensive coverage.

Outage Insurance. Coverage against loss of earnings due to the failure of machinery to operate because of an insured peril causing damage to the premises. Similar to Extra Expense Insurance.

Outcomes Measurement. A method of keeping track of a patient's treatment and the responses to that treatment.

Outline of Coverage. A document presented to applicants for life or health insurance that provides a brief description of proposed coverages, premiums, benefits, limitations and exclusions. It is a summary only and encourages the applicant to read the actual policy or certificate carefully. The outline may also include various disclosures, and inform the applicant of certain rights, such as the right to a "free look"—the right to return the policy and receive a full refund of premium within a stipulated time period if not satisfied.

Out-of-Area (OOA). Treatment given to a member outside of the normal area.

Out-of-Pocket Costs. The amount a covered person must pay out of his or her own pocket (e.g., for coinsurance, deductibles, etc.).

Out-of-Pocket Limit. The maximum coinsurance an individual is required to pay, after which the insurer pays 100 percent of covered expenses up to the policy limit.

Out-of-State Coverage. This means that if an insured drives into a state where no-fault benefits or other types of coverage are required, the policy will automatically provide the minimum amounts and types of coverage. Most personal auto policies restrict the policy territory to the United States, its territories and possessions, Puerto Rico and Canada. If an insured travels outside his home state, the policy will adjust to these laws by automatically increasing the liability limits to conform to that state's laws with respect to a nonresident driving in the state.

Outpatient. A patient who is not a bed patient in the hospital where he or she is receiving treatment.

Outstanding Premiums. Premiums due but not yet collected.

Overage Insurance. Health insurance issued at ages above the usual limit—generally 65.

Overhead Expense Insurance. Coverage for such things as rent, utilities and employee salaries when a business owner becomes disabled. The insurance benefit is generally not a fixed amount, but pays the amount of expenses actually incurred.

Overinsured. The condition that exists when an insured has purchased coverage for more than the actual cash value or replacement cost of a subject of insurance. It is also describes a situation where so much insurance is in force as to constitute a moral or morale hazard, such as having so much disability income insurance in force that it becomes profitable to be disabled.

Overlapping Insurance. Coverage from two or more policies or insurers that duplicates coverage of certain risks. See also Concurrent Insurance.

Overline. (1) The amount of insurance or reinsurance exceeding an insurer's or reinsurer's normal capacity inclusive of any contractual reinsurance coverage. (2) A commitment by an insurer or reinsurer above and beyond normal facilities or capacities.

Overriding Commission. (1) A commission that an agent or broker receives on any business sold in his or her exclusive territory by subagents. Also sometimes called "overwriting" or "overriding." (2) An allowance paid to a ceding company over and above the acquisition cost to allow for overhead expenses, often including a margin for profit.

Over-the-Counter Drugs (OTC). A drug that can be purchased without a prescription.

Owned Autos. Those "autos" an insured owns (and for liability coverage any "trailers" not owned while attached to power units that are owned). This includes those "autos" acquired after the policy begins.

Owned Private Passenger Autos. The private passenger autos an insured owns, including those private passenger autos acquired after the policy begins.

Owner of a Policy. An applicant for insurance agrees to pay the premiums, and has certain ownership rights. Generally, the policy owner has the right to elect or change the beneficiary, to elect settlement options and to assign ownership to another person. The owner of a policy may or may not be the insured person, and may or may not be the beneficiary. The same person cannot be both the insured and the beneficiary, but the insured's estate can.

Owners and Contractors Protective Liability Policy. Protection against losses caused by the negligence of a hired contractor or subcontractor. Also called independent contractors insurance.

Owners, Landlords and Tenants Liability Insurance (OL&T). Coverage against legal liability for bodily injury or property damage caused to others by negligence and arising out of the ownership, maintenance or use of the premises designated in the policy and all operations necessary or incidental to those premises. The OL&T form has largely been replaced by the Commercial General Liability Coverage Form.

Ownership. (1) All rights, benefits and privileges under life insurance policies are controled by their owners. Policy owners may or may not be the insureds. Ownership may be assigned or transferred by written request of the current owner. (2) Under the general eligibility rules, a private passenger auto must be owned or leased by an individual or married couple who live together. However, a personal auto policy may also be issued to cover an auto owned by relatives other than husband and wife, or an auto owned by unrelated individuals who reside together, if a joint ownership endorsement is attached to the policy.

Ownership of Expirations. An agreement by an insurer that certain information regarding the details of a policy, usually a property or liability form, are revealed to no agent or broker other than the originating agent.

Ownership Provision. A provision stating that the policy may be owned by a person other than the insured. This provision is often found in business or juvenile life insurance policies.

P

P&I. See Protection and Indemnity Insurance.

P.S. 58 Charges. An IRS table that identifies the cost of pure death protection. The taxable economic benefit to an employee under a split dollar plan and certain other plans is equal to the P.S. 58 charges less any employee contributions.

Package Policy. Any policy including two or more lines or types of coverages in the same contract. Personal and commercial package policies are very common. In fact, most policies sold are package policies.

Paid Business. Insurance for which the application has been signed, the medical examination completed and the settlement for the premium tendered.

Paid Claims. Amounts paid to providers based on the health plan.

Paid Claims Loss Ratio. Paid claims divided by total premiums.

Paid Losses. The amount paid in losses during a specified period of time, not including estimates of amounts that will be paid in the future for losses that occurred then.

Paid-For. Insurance on which the premium has been paid.

Paid-In Capital. The amount paid for the stock sold by a corporation.

Paid-In Surplus. Surplus paid in by stockholders, as contrasted with surplus earned through the operations of a business.

Paid-Up Additions (or Adds). See Dividend Additions.

Paid-Up Insurance. Insurance on which all premiums are paid but which has not yet matured by either death or endowment (e.g., a limited payment life policy for which the premium-paying period is over).

Pain and Suffering. Non-economic damages or intangible benefits, including not only physical discomfort and distress but also mental and emotional trauma. See Non-Economic Benefits.

Pair and Set Clause. A clause which states that if a part of a pair or set is lost or damaged the measure of the loss shall be a reasonable and fair proportion of the total value of the set, giving consideration to the importance of the article. The insurer is under no obligation to pay for the total loss of a set when one part is lost, damaged or destroyed.

Paper Accidents. An auto case in which no accident occurred but false accident reports were filed to support insurance claims.

Par. Abbreviation for participating. See Participating.

Parasol Policy. Another name for the difference in conditions policy. See Difference in Conditions.

Parcel Post Insurance. Coverage for damage to or loss of parcels while they are in the care of the United States Post Office Department. Packages can be insured by either the post office or by private insurance companies.

Parent Company. The senior company in a group or fleet of insurers. See also Fleet of Companies.

Parol. A legal term referring to oral statements as distinguished from written statements.

Parol Evidence Rule. This rule states that a written instrument or contract cannot be modified by an oral agreement. It is based on the concept that written contracts should contain all of the facts and agreements between the parties and, therefore, prevents contemporaneous oral declarations from being included in the contract.

Partial Disability. A condition in which, as a result of injury or sickness, the insured cannot perform all of the duties of his or her occupation but can perform some. Exact definitions vary from policy to policy. See also Permanent Partial Disability and Temporary Partial Disability.

Partial Hospitalization Services. Additional services provided to mental health or substance abuse patients that provides outpatient treatment as an alternative or follow-up to inpatient treatment.

Partial Loss. A covered loss that does not completely destroy or render worthless the insured property.

Participant. An employee or former employee who is eligible to receive benefits from an employee benefit plan or whose beneficiaries may be eligible to receive benefits from the plan.

Participating (Par). (1) Insurance that pays policy dividends. In other words, it entitles a policyowner to participate in allocations of the insurer's surplus. In life insurance there are several options available for the use of such dividends. (2) Insurance that contributes proportionately with other insurance on the same risk.

Participating Physician. A health care provider approved by Medicare to receive payment directly from the Social Security Administration. See Non-Participating Physician.

Participating Policy. A policy where the policyholders share in dividends (if a dividend is declared).

Participating Provider. A health care provider approved by Medicare to participate in the program and receive benefit payments directly from carriers or fiscal intermediaries.

Participating Reinsurance. See Pro Rata Reinsurance.

Participation. The number of employees enrolled compared to the total number eligible for coverage. Many times, a minimum participation percentage is required.

Particular Average. A partial loss that must be borne entirely by the individual owning any property that is damaged or lost. It is often used synonymously with partial loss. See also Free of Particular Average.

Partnership Entity. A partnership considered as an entity and not in terms of its individual part-owners.

Partnership Insurance. Life or health insurance sold to a partnership, usually for guaranteeing business continuity in case of the death or disability of one of the partners. For example, two partners might buy life insurance on each other so that in the event of one partner's death, the other can use the insurance proceeds to purchase the deceased partner's share of the business from the heirs.

Party Wall. A common wall between two buildings.

Party-in-Interest. The parties to an employee benefit plan, including individuals serving as a fiduciary or counsel, or employees of an employee benefit plan; or any person providing service to the plan; or the employer who establishes the plan; or an employee organization whose members are covered by the plan; or an owner of 50 percent or more of a company that establishes an employee benefit plan.

Past Service Benefit. A term used in pension or retirement insurance policies that refers to credit given an employee for the amount of time the person was employed prior to the effective date of the retirement plan.

Past Service Liability. The monetary value at the start of a pension plan of all annuity credits vested prior to the effective date.

Patent Enforcement Insurance. Coverage for the costs of enforcing a patent against those who infringe. An insurer may or may not cover preexisting infringement.

Paul v. Virginia. The 1869 U.S. Supreme Court decision holding that insurance is not commerce and, hence, not subject to regulation by the government. This was the ruling decision with respect to insurance regulation until the SEUA case in 1944 which reversed that decision but which was later modified by Public Law 15. See also Southeastern Underwriters Association and Public Law 15.

Pay. An abbreviation for payment as in "20-Pay Life policy."

Pay-As-You-Go. See Current Disbursement.

Payee. The person receiving money.

Paymaster Robbery Insurance. Coverage for payroll money against loss by robbery inside or outside the insured's premises. The Simplified Commercial Crime Coverage Forms A through R have replaced this policy.

Payment Bond. A bond furnished by a contractor to guarantee payment for labor and materials used in a particular project or work under contract.

Payor Benefit. A rider or provision often found in juvenile policies that waives the premiums if the person paying the premium, usually one of the parents, becomes disabled or dies while the child is still a minor.

Payroll Audit. An examination of an insured's payroll record by a representative of the insurer to determine the final premium due on a policy for the latest policy year.

Payroll Deduction Insurance. A plan whereby an employer is authorized by an employee to deduct insurance premiums for an individual life insurance policy he has purchased from an insurer. The employer pays the insurer the amount deducted on a periodic basis.

PD. See Physical Damage.

Peak Season Endorsement. An endorsement that provides increased amounts of coverage on inventories during peak seasons, beginning and ending on dates specified in the endorsement. The form protects an insured during seasonal fluctuations in value.

Peer Review. Review of health care provided by a medical staff with training equal to the staff that provided the treatment.

Peer Review Organization (PRO). Groups of physicians who are paid by the federal government to conduct pre-admission, continued stay and services reviews provided to Medicare patients by Medicare approved hospitals.

Penalty. The limit of an insurance company's liability under a Fidelity Bond.

Pension Benefit Guaranty Corporation (Pen Ben). A non-profit corporation within the Department of Labor that insures participants in, and beneficiaries of covered plans against the loss of benefits arising from a premature termination of a retirement plan.

Pension Plan. A risk experienced by those who invest in securities identified as the uncertainty of the economy.

Pension Trust Fund. A fund consisting of money contributed by the employer, and, in some cases, the employee, to provide pension benefits.

Per Capita. Literally "by heads." Distribution among survivors by persons on a share-and-share-alike basis that is often used in beneficiary designations. Contrast with Per Stirpes.

Per Diem Business Interruption. A business interruption policy that provides a stated amount to be paid for each day that the business is interrupted due to an insured peril.

Per Person Limit. The maximum amount payable to one person arising out of one occurrence. However, there is no limit on the number of claims arising out of an occurrence, nor is there an aggregate limit on the amount payable. See Liability Limit.

Per Risk Excess Reinsurance. Reinsurance in which the retention and the cession apply per risk rather than per accident, per event or on an aggregate basis.

Per Stirpes. Literally "by branches." Distribution of property between or among two or more beneficiaries with the provision that if one dies before the insured, the beneficiary's heirs shall have the beneficiary's full share distributed among them. Contrast with Per Capita.

Percent Subject. See Amount Subject.

Percentage Participation. A provision in a health insurance contract that says the insurer will share losses in an agreed proportion with the insured. An example would be an 80-20 participation where the insurer pays 80 percent and the insured pays the other 20 percent of covered losses. Often erroneously referred to as coinsurance.

Percentage Test. A coverage test for a qualified plan that is a formula to determine if a plan benefits at least 70 percent of the lower paid employees.

Performance Bond. A bond guaranteeing the faithful performance of a contract. See also Contract Bond.

Performance Codes. Most rating tables include different secondary factors for standard, intermediate and high performance vehicles, and for sports vehicles. The four most common codes: "i" or intermediate, "h" or high performance, "s" or sports model, and "p" or sports premium model. If a car model doesn't have a specific performance code, it is presumed to be a standard performance model.

Peril. The actual cause of a possible loss. Insurance policies distinguish between covered perils (also called perils insured against) and non-covered perils. Compare to Hazard and Risk.

Perils of the Sea. A term used in most ocean marine contracts. It refers to such perils as collision, sinking, stranding and burning.

Period. See Term.

Period Certain. See Guaranteed Period.

Period of Restoration. The period when business income coverage applies. It begins when the direct physical loss occurs and interrupts business operations, and ends on the date that the damaged property should be repaired, rebuilt or replaced with reasonable speed.

Periodic Payment Deferred Annuity. An annuity that is bought for its series of periodic payments—the benefits are deferred until all payments have been made.

Permanent and Total Disability. Total disability from which the insured does not recover. When used as a definition in a policy (usually a life insurance policy rider), "permanent" is presumed after a stated period of time, commonly six months.

Permanent Life Insurance. A term loosely applied to life insurance policy forms other than group and term, usually cash value life insurance, such as endowments and whole or ordinary life policies.

Permanent Partial Disability. A condition where the injured party's earning capacity is impaired for life, but he is able to work at reduced efficiency.

Permanent Total Disability. A condition where the injured party is not able to work at any gainful employment for the remaining lifetime.

Permit Bond. A bond guaranteeing that a person who has been issued a permit complies with the laws and ordinances regulating the privilege for which the permit was issued. A house movers permit bond is an example.

Persistency. (1) The tendency or likelihood of insurance business not lapsing or being replaced by another insurer's product; an important underwriting factor. (2) The staying quality of insurance policies, i.e., the renewal quality. High persistency means that a high percentage of policies stay in force to the end of the period coverage, while low persistency means that a high percentage of policies lapse for nonpayment of premiums.

Personal Accident Insurance (PAI). (1) Coverage that provides a one-time payment for an insured or a passenger in a case of death or maiming from a car accident. This is generally covered under auto or health policies. (2) Coverage that provides limited accidental-death benefits for the car renter and—often—passengers.

Personal Articles Floater (PAF). Originally an inland marine policy, PAF can be sold as a separate policy or attached to an existing property insurance policy, such as a homeowners form. The PAF lists items to be covered, such as furs and jewelry, with an amount shown for each item. This is usually an open perils (all risk) form. See also Floater.

Personal Assets. Wealth and things of value accumulated and owned by an individual. These would include real estate, cash, investments and other items of value.

Personal Auto Policy. A revised edition of the Family Auto policy, with simplified wording used in the policy provisions. It is the most common auto insurance policy sold today. See Family Auto Policy.

Personal Credit Ratings. In general, this system is becoming an important element of rating auto premiums. Most large insurance companies use personal credit ratings as a secondary factor if a policy applicant meets some pre-determined risk profile.

Personal Effects Coverage. Coverage that provides limited reimbursement to the renter of an automobile for loss of baggage and other personal property during the rental period.

Personal Effects Floater. A policy covering personal effects usually carried by tourists. It can be written on either an open perils (all risk) or specified-peril form. It covers worldwide but excludes coverage at the insured's residence, as it provides travel coverage only.

Personal Injury. Injury other than bodily injury arising out of false arrest or detention, malicious prosecution, wrongful entry or eviction, libel or slander or violation of a person's right to privacy committed other than in the course of advertising, publishing, broadcasting or telecasting. Contrast with Advertising Injury.

Personal Injury Coverage. The typical underlying homeowners policy provides liability coverage for accidental bodily injury (meaning physical injury or death), but not for events involving libel, slander, false arrest and the like. See Drop Down Coverages.

Personal Injury Mills. A scam where lawyers and physicians—some working alone, some working together—submit claims for patients' nonexistent or exaggerated injuries.

Personal Injury Protection (PIP). Coverage for treatment of injuries to a driver and any passengers in the car. Also known as no-fault benefits in states that have enacted mandatory or optional no-fault auto coverages. PIP usually includes benefits for medical expenses, loss of work income, essential services, accidental death and funeral expenses.

Personal Interview. After the insured submits an insurance application, a personal interview usually is performed by the insurance company or an independent third party to verify application information. Specifically, any application data regarding medical history, hobbies and occupational duties may have to be explained, or additional information may need to be gathered through this report.

Personal Liability Supplement. A form that provides personal liability insurance. It may be attached to a dwelling policy or written as a separate policy.

Personal Liability Umbrella Policy (PLUP). Stand-alone insurance that supplements most other liability insurance. An umbrella policy boosts the liability protection on an insured's homeowners, auto and boat or vacation home policies.

Personal Lines. Refers to insurance for individuals and families, such as private passenger automobile insurance and homeowners policies. Contrast with Business Insurance and Commercial Lines.

Personal Property. Any property of an insured other than real property—such as furniture, linens, drapes, clothing, appliances, etc. Homeowners policies protect the personal property of family members, and commercial forms are used to protect the business personal property of an insured. Personal property of guests and residence employees may be covered at the insured's request.

Personal Property Floater. A broad form policy covering all personal property worldwide, including any at the insured's home. Similar coverage is available by endorsement as part of the "Special" homeowners policy form.

Personal Property Items. Items such as clothing, cameras, sporting equipment, tools, etc., carried around in a car. Most people have this coverage under a homeowners insurance policy, but coverage is also available under Personal Property Floaters and other specialized property insurance policy forms.

Personal Property of Others. Property, other than real property, that is not owned by an insured. Liability forms have traditionally excluded coverage for property of others in an insured's care, custody or control. Modern homeowners forms and commercial property forms provide some coverage for property of others.

Personal Surety. An individual, as opposed to an insurance company or other corporate institution, acting as a surety or guarantor.

Personal Theft Policy. See Broad Form Personal Theft Policy.

Personal Umbrella Policy. Provides broad coverage and high limits of coverage that most commonly sold personal liability coverages, known as underlying policies, do not provide. Umbrella liability policies serve two major functions: They provide so-called "high limits of coverage" that protect against catastrophic losses not covered by standard insurance; and they provide broader coverage than underlying policies.

Personalty. Movable personal property items, as opposed to realty, such as land, buildings and mineral rights.

Phantom Vehicle Claim. A claim in which a motorist says he has suffered a loss from a hit-and-run driver who does not exist.

Pharmacy and Therapeutics (P&T) Committee. A panel of physicians—usually from different specialties—who advise the health plan regarding the proper use of prescription drugs.

Physical Damage. (1) Actual damage to property. (2) Damage from such perils as collision, comprehensive, fire and theft or any damage to the vehicle itself. See Damage to Your Auto Coverage.

Physical Exam and Autopsy. A standard health insurance policy provision allowing the insurer to examine the insured when a claim is pending, and in the event of death perform an autopsy where not prohibited by law.

Physical Hazard. Any hazard arising from the material, structural or operational features of the risk itself apart from the persons owning or managing it.

Physical Therapist. A trained medical person who provides rehabilitative services and therapy to help restore bodily functions such as walking, speech, the use of limbs, etc.

Physician Contingency Reserve (PCR). A portion of a claim that is deducted and withheld by the health plan before payment is made to the physician. It serves as an incentive for proper quality and utilization of health care. A portion of this reserve may be returned to the physician or to pay claims where the plan needs additional funds. It is also sometimes called "withhold."

Physicians and Surgeons Equipment Form. A form used to cover equipment, materials, supplies and office furniture of individuals in the medical and dental professions.

Physicians and Surgeons Professional Liability Insurance. Malpractice insurance for physicians and surgeons. See Malpractice.

Physician's Current Procedural Terminology (CPT). This terminology includes medical services and procedures performed by physicians and other providers of health care. The health care industry uses it as a standard for describing services and procedures.

PIA. Professional Insurance Agents. An association of independent agents involved in educational programs, consumer efforts and government and industry affairs pertaining to the insurance industry.

Pilferage. Petty theft, particularly theft of articles in small batches. It's associated with the insuring of cargo under an inland marine insurance form.

PILR. See Property Insurance Loss Register.

Piracy. Unlawful seizure of a ship and/or its cargo on the high seas. Commonly covered by ocean marine contracts.

Place of Service. This designates where the actual health services are being performed, whether it be at a home, hospital, office, clinic, etc.

Plain Language Laws. Mandatory state law that requires policies to be written in everyday language so that they are easily understood. Technical terms with their technical meanings are used only where required by law or substitution would be misleading.

Plaintiff. The party who brings a legal action against another, called the defendant.

Plan, Excess. A retirement plan designed around the benefits of Social Security.

Plan, Formal. A retirement plan set forth in writing under which contractual and legally enforceable rights are granted to the participating employees.

Plan, Funded. All plans under which funds are deposited to provide for retirement benefits.

Plan, Informal. A retirement system under which the employer has no legal obligation and the employee has no legal rights. These plans have no standard of benefits to be paid, and have no special method of funding.

Plan, Insured. A retirement plan under which some kind of benefits are guaranteed by an insurance carrier.

Plan, Offset. A retirement plan in which each employee's standard benefit is reduced by a portion of the Social Security benefits he or she will receive.

Plan, Point-of-Service. This health care plan allows a choice of whether to receive services from a participating or nonparticipating provider.

Plan, Qualified. A retirement plan where contributions by the employer are allowed as a deduction from taxable income, and provides that the deposits for employees' future benefits are not to be considered as taxable income to them in the year in which they are made.

Plan Sponsor. An employer or other entity that establishes or maintains a retirement plan for its employees or members.

Plan, Unfunded. Any pension plan which follows a "pay-as-you-go" method. See Funding, Disbursement.

Plan, Uninsured. Any pension plan that is not funded through insurance products.

Plan, Unqualified. Any pension plan that does not meet the qualifications for special tax advantages as set forth in the IRS Code.

Plan Year. A calendar, policy or fiscal year on which the records of the plan are kept.

Plate Glass Insurance Policy. See Comprehensive Glass Insurance Policy and Glass Coverage Form.

Pluvious Insurance. Another name for Rain Insurance.

PML. See Probable Maximum Loss.

Point-of-Service Plan. A plan that allows an individual to choose whether to receive services from a participating or nonparticipating provider.

Poisson's Law. See Theory of Probability.

Policy. The written statement of a contract effecting insurance, or certificates of a contract, by whatever name called, and including all clauses, riders, endorsements and papers attached to and made a part of the contract.

Policy Anniversary. The anniversary of the date of issue of a policy.

Policy Change Endorsement. An endorsement that makes changes which are not specifically addressed by any preprinted form. This endorsement lists the policy number, effective date, named insured and coverage parts affected.

Policy Conditions. See Conditions.

Policy Date. See Effective Date.

Policy Dividend. The return of a portion of the premium paid on a participating policy. It represents the difference between the gross premium charged and the actual cost assessed against the policy by actuarial formula.

Policy Fee. (1) A one-time charge added to the first premium to help defray acquisition costs, now illegal in many states. (2) A flat, per policy charge that does not change with the size of the policy and thus serves as a form of quantity discount. Also known as quantity discount factor and quantity adjustment fee.

Policy Loan. A loan made by an insurer to a policyowner of a part or all of the cash value of the policy assigned as security for the loan. This is one of the usual nonforfeiture values.

Policy Number. All insurance companies file their policies by policy number rather than by the insured's name. The number is typically found on the Declarations Page.

Policy Period (or Term). The period during which the policy contract affords protection (e.g., six months, one or three years).

Policy Proceeds. The amount actually paid on a life insurance policy at death or when the insured receives payment at surrender or maturity. It includes any dividends left on deposit and the value of any additional insurance purchased with dividends; and it excludes any loans not repaid, plus unpaid interest on those loans.

Policy Reserve. A reserve which exists because of the concept that each policy has a pro rata share of the total reserve established for all policies. See Unearned Premium Reserve.

Policy Summary. A summary of coverages, benefits, limitations, exclusions, cost and terms of a proposed life insurance policy. Cost and benefit information usually includes annual premiums, guaranteed amounts payable at death, guaranteed cash surrender values at the end of various years, life insurance cost indexes, and (if applicable), dividend information. In many jurisdictions, summaries are required to be delivered to applicants in connection with any solicitation or replacement transaction.

Policy Term. See Policy Period.

Policy Year. The period between policy anniversary dates.

Policy Year Experience. The measure of premiums and losses for each 12-month period a policy is in force. Losses occurring during this 12-month period are assigned to the period regardless of when they are actually paid.

Policyholder. (1) The person in actual possession of an insurance policy. (2) Loosely refers to the policyowner and/or insured. See also Insured.

Policyholder's Surplus. The amount over and above liabilities available for an insurer to meet future obligations to its policyholders. In the case of a mutual insurer, it is the whole equity section of the balance sheet. In the case of a stock insurer, the equity section is divided into two parts: stockholder's surplus and policyholder's surplus.

Policyowner. (1) The person who owns an insurance policy and who may or may not be either the policyholder or the insured. (2) Loosely refers to the policyholder and/or the insured. See also Insured.

Policywriting Agent. An agent who has the authority to prepare and effect an insurer's policy.

Pollutant. Any solid, liquid, gaseous or thermal irritant or contaminant, including smoke, vapor, soot, fumes, acids, alkalis, chemicals and waste. Waste includes materials to be recycled, reconditioned or reclaimed.

Pollution Liability Coverage Form. Commercial form providing pollution insurance on a "claims made" basis, and coverage for clean-up costs. Contrast with Limited Pollution Liability Coverage Form.

Pollution Liability Extension Endorsement. An endorsement to general liability insurance that removes part of the pollution exclusion, creating liability coverage for pollution injury or damage.

Pool (Association or Syndicate). An organization of insurers or reinsurers through which particular types of risks are written with the premiums, losses and expenses shared in agreed amounts among the insurers belonging to the pool. A pool is often the entity to write large values, such as those on commercial aircraft.

Pool (Risk Pool). A separate account that includes entries for income and expenses. It is used when a number of groups are put together for the purposes of combining their premium and paying their losses.

Pooling. Reinsurance where every member assumes a share of each risk written by every other member. Provisions may include a maximum limit to be borne by any member. See Quota Share Insurance and Quota Share Reinsurance.

Portfolio Entry. Part of the mechanics of instituting a reinsurance treaty. It may be arranged on varying bases, such as new and renewal business or business in force, any and all of which are referred to as the portfolio entry.

Portfolio Reinsurance. (1) A transfer of the portfolio of an insured via a cession of reinsurance. (2)

Reinsurance where the reinsurer assumes a percentage of the entire book of the ceding company's business either in a particular class or in all classes.

Portfolio Return. Reassumption by a ceding company of a portfolio which has formerly been reinsured.

Portfolio Runoff. Continuing the reinsurance of a portfolio until all ceded premiums are earned.

Position Schedule Bond. See Name Position Bond and Name Schedule Bond.

Postdated Check Plan. A premium-paying arrangement where the policyowner gives the insurer a series of checks, each dated ahead of the date on which premiums fall due for a year or more. The insurer then presents each check on its date.

Postjudgment Interest. Interest that accrues prior to actual payment. If a judgment is rendered against an insured, there usually is a time lapse between the rendering of the judgment and the payment of the damages awarded. The company pays any interest charges that accrue during this time period.

Postmortem Dividend. A policy dividend allotted after the death of an insured. It's also called a mortuary dividend.

Pour Over Trust. A revocable living trust that serves as a receptacle for distributions from employee benefit plans.

Power Interruption Insurance. Indemnifies the insured in the event of loss due to the interruption of power supplied by a public utility and caused by any of the perils insured against.

Power of Agency. See Agent's Authority.

Power of Appointment. The right or authority given by a donor to a donee, allowing the donee to select the ultimate beneficiary of property or gift(s).

Power of Attorney. (1) The authority given to one person or corporation to act for and obligate another to the extent set forth in the agreement creating the power. (2) The authority given to the chief administrator of a reciprocal insurance exchange, who is called an attorney in fact, by each subscriber. See also Attorney in Fact and Reciprocal Insurance Exchange.

Power Plant Insurance. Insures electricity generating plants against loss caused by certain specified perils.

PPO. See Preferred Provider Organization.

Practical Nurse. A licensed individual who provides custodial type care such as help in walking, bathing, feeding, etc. They do not administer medication or perform other medically-related services.

Pre-Admission Authorization. A cost containment feature of many group medical policies whereby the insured must contact the insurer prior to a hospitalization for authorization of admission.

Pre-Admission Certification. Criteria used to determine whether inpatient care is necessary.

Preauthorization Check Plan. A premium-paying arrangement where the policyowner authorizes the insurer to draft money from his or her bank account for monthly payments.

Precedent. In common law, previous cases used to prove the present case are called precedence.

Precertification Authorization. A cost containment technique requiring physicians to submit a treatment plan and an estimated bill prior to providing treatment. This allows the insurer to evaluate the appropriateness of the procedures, and lets the insured and physician know in advance which procedures are covered and at what rate benefits will be paid.

Pre-Disability Income. The average monthly income earned by the insured during the 12 months prior to the onset of total disability.

Preemptive Right. A current stockholder's right to maintain proportionate ownership in a corporation through the exercising of this right to purchase new issues of stock before the general public.

Pre-Existing Condition. A physical condition that existed prior to the effective date of a policy. In many health policies these are not covered until after a stated period of time has elapsed.

Preferred Provider Option. Under these cost-containment plans, repair shops appraise cars and send the estimates to the insurance company via computer. This cuts several days from the typical time it takes to repair a damaged vehicle.

Preferred Provider Organization (PPO). An organization of hospitals and physicians who provide, for a set fee, services to insurance company clients. Providers are listed as preferred and the insured may select from any number of hospitals and physicians. Coverage is 100 percent, with a minimal copayment for each office visit or hospital stay. Contrast with Health Maintenance Organization.

Preferred Risk. Any risk considered to be better than the standard risk on which the premium rate was calculated.

Prejudgment Interest. Additional damages awarded to a plaintiff to compensate for the delay between the time of injury or damage and the time a judgment is made. Because liability claims may take months or years to resolve, this amount is designed to replace the amount of interest the plaintiff would have earned had the damages been awarded at the time of injury or damage.

Prelicensing Education Requirement. Statutory requirement of many states that an applicant for an insurance license must complete a specified education program before being eligible for the license.

Preliminary Term. (1) A reserve system in life insurance where the entire first-year premium is used for acquisition costs. The effect is to reduce the first year's premium, making it more attractive to the prospective buyer. (2) The period of a short-term insurance policy issued to cover a risk to a date which the policyowner wishes to establish as the anniversary date for future premiums.

Premises. The particular location of property or a portion of the property as designated in a policy. Used principally for private residential purposes (some incidental business occupancies, such as a studio or office, are permitted), and contains no more than two family living units (that means single family homes and duplexes are eligible).

Premises and Operations Liability Insurance. Liability coverage for exposures arising out of an insured's premises and business operations. It is one of the two major sublines of general liability. Contrast with Products and Completed Operations Insurance.

Premises Burglary. A burglary that occurs on an insured premises. Various commercial insurance forms distinguish between coverage provided on and off an insured premises. The coverage may be written separately or as part of a broader package of crime coverages.

Premises Theft—Outside Robbery Coverage Form. A commercial crime coverage form that protects against loss of property other than money and security by theft on the premises or robbery outside the premises.

Premium. The price of insurance protection for a specified risk for a specified period of time.

Premium Adjustment Form. A form wherein a deposit premium is charged at the beginning of the policy period, periodic reports of exposures are made by the insured during the policy term or at the end of it, and premiums are adjusted as reports are received or at the end of the policy period.

Premium Advance. See Deposit Premium

Premium and Dispersion Credit Plan. A method of allowing certain credits to commercial property risks with two or more locations. Credits are based on the fact that there are several locations which are dispersed and, therefore, represent a reduced hazard. Efficiency of management in loss prevention, plus expense savings in handling large amounts of insurance under one policy are also considered.

Premium Base. See Subject Premium.

Premium Deposit. See Deposit Premium.

Premium Discount. (1) A discount on premiums paid in advance of one year, which is based on projected interest to be earned. (2) A discount allowed on certain workers' comp and comprehensive general liability policies to allow for the fact that larger premium policies do not require the same percentage of the premium for basic insurer expenses such as policywriting. The discount percentage increases with the size of the premium.

Premium, Earned. See Earned Premium.

Premium Load. A universal life term, also called a "front-end load," meaning the percentage of premium deducted from each premium payment to help cover expenses. Some policies provide for a "no load" feature.

Premium Loan. A loan made by the insurance company to the insured, with the cash value of the policy as security, to pay a premium due.

Premium Notice. A notice from an insurer or agency to a policyowner that a premium will be due on a given date.

Premium, Pure. See Pure Premium.

Premium Rate. The price per unit of insurance (e.g., a property insurance rate of 10 cents per $100 of the value of the property to be insured).

Premium Receipt. The receipt given a policyowner for the payment of a premium.

Premium Receipt Book. The policyowner's record of premium paid, usually used for a weekly payment or monthly debit ordinary policy.

Premium Refund. A special provision allowing a beneficiary to collect the face amount of a policy plus all the premiums paid.

Premium Return. See Return Premium.

Premium, Unearned. See Unearned Premium.

Premiums Written. See Written Premiums.

Prepaid Legal Service Plan. An employee benefit whereby benefits are provided by the employer for certain legal services.

Prepayment of Premiums. Payment of future premiums through paying the present (discount) value of future premiums or having interest paid on the insured's deposit.

Prescription Medication. A drug dispensed only by prescription and approved by the Food and Drug Administration.

Present Interest. Current use and enjoyment of personal property.

Present Value. (1) The amount of money that future amounts receivable are currently worth. A life insurance policy may provide for monthly payments for 10 years. The present value of that money would be less than the total amount of the monthly payments for 10 years because of the amount of interest that a present lump sum could earn during the term that the payments otherwise would have been made. (2) The present amount equivalent to an amount or series of amounts payable or receivable in the future adjusted for the time value of money (through discounts for interest).

Preservation of Property. Limited coverage for property removed from the described premises to protect it from a covered cause of loss. Also known as "removal" coverage. See Removal.

Pressure Vessel. Any vessel or container designed to hold liquids or gases under pressure.

Presumed Negligence. See *Res Ipsa Loquitur.*

Presumption of Agency. A legally binding agency relationship when, in fact, no formal agency agreement is in effect. If an insurer acts to give the appearance of agency, perhaps by furnishing letterhead and applications before a person has been licensed and appointed, an agency relationship exists under the law and the insurer may be legally bound by the acts of a person acting as agent.

Presumptive Disability. A disability involving loss of sight, hearing, speech or any two limbs, which is presumed to be a permanent and total disability. In such cases, the insurer does not require the insured to submit to periodic medical examinations to prove continuing disability.

Pretext Interview. An interview in which the party gathering information refuses to reveal their identity, pretends to be someone else, misrepresents the true purpose of the interview or pretends to represent someone who is not in fact represented. Federal and state laws prohibit pretext interviews in connection with insurance-related consumer reporting. They are permitted only in connection with investigations into suspected material misrepresentation, fraud or criminal activity.

Prevailing Charge. Used to determine Medicare benefit amounts; this usually means the typical charge in the area where the patient lives. See also Allowable Charge and Customary Charge.

Preventive Care. Care such as routine physical examinations and immunizations, that emphasizes preventing illnesses before they occur.

Prima Facie. Literally means "at first view." It refers to evidence that is, according to law, sufficient to establish or prove a point, unless successfully rebutted by other evidence.

Primary Beneficiary. The beneficiary named as first to receive proceeds or benefits from a policy when they become due.

Primary Care. Basic health care provided by doctors who are in the practice of family care, pediatrics and internal medicine.

Primary Care Network (PCN). A group of primary care physicians who provide care to those members of a particular health plan.

Primary Care Physician. Some health insurance plans require members to select and seek treatment from a primary physician who either renders treatment or refers the member to an appropriate specialist within the approved health care network.

Primary Coverage. (1) Insurance coverage which covers from the first dollar, perhaps after a deductible, as distinguished from excess coverage which pays only after some primary coverage has been exhausted. Contrast with Excess Insurance. (2) Coverage that pays expenses first, without considering whether or not there is any other coverage. See also Coordination of Benefits.

Primary Insurance Amount (PIA). A Social Security calculation which serves as the principal element determining the amount of various Social Security benefits.

Primary Insurer. The company that originates business (e.g., the ceding company).

Primary Liability Responsibility. See Supplemental Liability Insurance.

Principal. The individual or corporation whose performance is guaranteed in a suretyship. See also Suretyship.

Principal Sum. The amount payable in one sum in the event of accidental death or dismemberments. When a contract provides benefits for both accidental death and dismemberment, each dismemberment benefit is an amount equal to the principal sum or some fraction thereof. Examples would be half the principal sum for loss of one arm, half the principal sum for the loss of one leg, etc.

Prior Approval Rating Forms. Indicates that an insurer must have rate changes formally approved by the state insurance department before it can use them.

Prior Authorization. A cost containment measure that provides full payment of health benefits only when hospitalization or medical treatment has been approved in advance.

Priority. Retention in some foreign reinsurance markets.

Private Carrier. A transportation company that contracts to carry goods for specific customers as opposed to a common carrier that carries goods for anyone who wishes to use its service.

Private Passenger Automobile. Four-wheeled motor vehicles of the private passenger, station wagon or van type, designed for use on public highways and subject to motor vehicle registration.

Pro Rata. (1) Distribution of the amount of insurance under one policy among several objects or places covered in proportion to their value or the amounts shown. (2) Distribution of liability among several insurers having policies on a risk, usually in the proportion that the amount of coverage in each policy bears to the total amount of coverage in all policies.

Pro Rata Cancelation. Termination of an insurance contract or bond, premium charge being adjusted in proportion to the exact time the protection has been in force. If a policy is canceled, the insurance company has to refund part of whatever premium was already paid. The refund is calculated on a pro rata basis, which means an even distribution of the premium based on the time coverage was in effect. See Short Rate Cancelations.

Pro Rata Distribution Clause. A provision used in writing blanket form policies under certain circumstances to divide the amount of insurance carried in the policy among several subjects of insurance, in the proportion that the value of each subject of insurance bears to the total of all items covered under the policy. Withdrawn from use in most states in 1978.

Pro Rata Liability Clause. Provides that losses will be paid in the proportion that the amount of the policy bears to the entire amount of insurance on all policies covering the loss. This provides for insurance companies to appropriately share in the loss when more than one policy exists yet prevents the insured from collecting in total from several insurance companies and making a profit.

Pro Rata Liability Rule. See Limit of Liability Rule.

Pro Rata Rate. A rate charged for a period of coverage shorter than the normal period (e.g., if an insured had coverage for only one quarter of a year, the premium would be only one quarter of the annual premium).

Pro Rata Reinsurance. All forms of reinsurance in which the reinsurer shares a pro rata portion of the losses and premiums of the ceding company. Also called Share and Participating Reinsurance. Pro Rata Reinsurance includes Quota Share Reinsurance and Surplus Reinsurance. Contrast with Excess of Loss Reinsurance.

Probability. The likelihood or relative frequency of an event expressed in a number between zero and one (e.g., the throw of a die. The probability of throwing five is found by dividing the number of sides that have a five (1) by the total number of sides (6). That is a probability of one-sixth or one divided by six, which is .17). See also Degree of Risk, Law of Large Numbers and Odds.

Probable Maximum Loss (PML). The maximum amount of loss that one would expect under ordinary circumstances, such as fire departments responding, sprinklers working, etc. Contrast with Amount Subject.

Probate. The process of paying debts, taxes, expenses and disposing of property in accordance with a testator's will and state laws.

Probate Bond. A bond required by a probate court to protect the administration of an estate or the assets of one person being cared for by another, such as assets in the hands of an executor or guardian. They fall within the classification of fiduciary bonds.

Probationary Period. A period of time between the effective date of a health insurance policy, and the date coverage begins for all or certain physical conditions.

Proceeds. The amount payable by a policy, usually in reference to the face amount of a life insurance policy, payable at the death of the insured.

Producer. An agent, solicitor or other person who sells insurance.

Product Failure Exclusion. See Business Risk Exclusion.

Product Recall Insurance. Indemnifies the insured for the cost of recalling products known or suspected to be defective.

Products and Completed Operations Insurance. A major general liability subline which provides coverage for an insured against claims arising out of products sold, manufactured, handled or distributed, or operations which are complete. Claims are covered only after a product has been sold and possession relinquished or operations have been completed or abandoned by the named insured. Manufacturers and contractors buy this coverage. Contrast with Premises and Operations Liability.

Professional Corporation. An artificial person or entity, governed by charter, engaged in a business which provides a professional service to the public such as medicine or law.

Professional Insurance Agents Association. A trade association of mutual insurance agents.

Professional Liability Coverage. Protection against legal liability resulting from negligence, errors and omissions, and other aspects of rendering or failing to render professional services. These exposures exist for many businesses, including travel agencies and telephone exchanges. See Malpractice Insurance. See Errors and Omissions Insurance.

Professional Partnership. An association of two or more individuals who operate and manage a business providing a professional service to the public such as medicine or law.

Profit and Loss Statement. Provides an easy-to-read source of how a firm performed over a period of time. Many profit and loss statements are accompanied by sources and uses of funds statement (cash flow statement).

Profit Commission. See Contingent Commission.

Profits and Commissions Insurance. Insurance with which a salesman or a sales agent whose income is tied to profits or commissions can insure against loss of income due to the destruction of property.

Profit-Sharing Plan. A plan whereby some of the profits of a company are set aside for distribution to qualified employees. The plan may provide for immediate distribution, or distribution upon death, disability, termination or attainment of a specific retirement age. Such plans are subject to special tax exemption if they meet the requirements of the Internal Revenue Code.

Progressive Underwriting. When insurance companies are aggressive in determining a person's true risk. Instead of evaluating risk on a by-the-book basis, the insurer pursues questions to determine the cause of any abnormalities in a person's claims history.

Prohibited List. A list of business risks that an insurance company will not insure. Also called the "undesirable list," the "do not solicit list" and other designations.

Prohibited Risk. Any class of business that an insurance company will not insure under any condition.

Promulgate. (1) To develop, publish and put into effect insurance rates or forms. (2) To publish or announce that a statute or rule of court is a legal order or direction enforceable by law, and violation of such is punishable as provided by law.

Proof of Loss. A formal statement made by a policyowner to an insurer regarding a loss. It is intended to give information to the insurer to enable it to determine the extent of its liability. Upon receipt of the claim forms, an insured has 90 days to file proof of loss.

Proof of Loss Form. A form provided to an insured by the insurance company to document loss. This form generally tends to have uniformity with different insurance companies.

Property Coverage Forms. These forms establish the conditions for coverage and describe the types or kinds of property insured (e.g., buildings, contents, extra expense, structures in the course of construction, glass, leasehold interest, etc.). Each coverage form is designed to insure specific types of property or losses.

Property Damage. Injury to or destruction of tangible property and includes loss of use of the property. This coverage is broader than direct damage or destruction by a covered peril, because it also means loss of use.

Property Damage Liability Insurance. Protection against liability for damage to the property of another, including loss of the use of the property, as distinguished from liability for bodily injury to another. It is often written along with bodily injury liability protection. In most states, an insured must buy at least $5,000 worth of coverage. Many standard policies include a higher limit—often $25,000.

Property Insurance. Insurance that indemnifies a person with an interest in physical property for its loss or the loss of its income producing abilities. This definition encompasses all lines of insurance written by property and inland marine insurers and can also include certain kinds of insurance written by casualty insurers (e.g., burglary and plate glass coverages).

Property Insurance Loss Register (PILR). A computerized record of all fire losses over $500 established by the American Insurance Association (AIA). It enables companies to determine undisclosed duplicate insurance coverage and patterns of losses on submitted risks.

Property Other than Money and Securities. Under commercial crime insurance coverages, any tangible property other than money and securities that has intrinsic value, such as merchandise, supplies, raw materials and office equipment.

Proposal Bond. See Bid Bond.

Proration of Benefits. The adjustment of health insurance policy benefits by reason of the existence of other insurance covering the same contingency.

Prospect. A potential buyer of insurance.

Prospecting. The act of looking for prospects or potential insurance buyers.

Prospective Loss Costs. The ISO has begun to develop prospective loss costs for a number of lines of insurance, including auto insurance. Prospective loss costs are based on loss data and loss adjustment expenses, but not the other components of a final rate (such as an insurance company's expenses and profit). See Loss Costs.

Prospective Payment System. A system of Medicare reimbursement for Part A benefits which bases most hospital payments on the patient's diagnosis at the time of hospital admission.

Prospective Rating. A method used in arriving at the rate and premium for a specified future period, based in whole or in part on the loss experience of a prior specified period. See Experience Rating.

Prospective Rating Plan. A plan that uses a formula to determine premiums for a specified period on the basis, in whole or in part, of the loss experience of the previous period.

Prospective Reimbursement. A system where hospitals or other health care providers are paid annually according to a rate of payment that has been established ahead of time.

Prospective Reserve. A life or health insurance reserve estimated to be sufficient to pay future claims when probable future premiums, interest and survivorship benefits are added to it.

Protected Risk. A property risk that falls within the geographical area protected by a fire department.

Protection. (1) A term used interchangeably with "coverage" to denote insurance provided under a policy. (2) The fire-fighting facilities in the area in which a risk is located.

Protection and Indemnity (P&I) Insurance. Protection for a property owner against loss of life, illness or injury to employees, passengers or crew, plus property damage to the cargo, piers, docks, etc., caused by the insured's negligence.

Protection Class. The grading of fire protection, determined by the grading schedule of cities and towns, for a given area. This designation is used for all fire rating except for dwellings, where the dwelling class is used.

Protective Liability Insurance. See Owners and Contractors Protective Liability.

Prototype Plan Defined. A standard retirement plan available from the sponsoring organization to an employer to use without charge.

Provider. Any individual or group of individuals that provide a health care service such as physicians, hospitals, etc.

Provisional Premium. See Deposit Premium.

Provisional Rate. Tentative rates, premiums or commissions that are subject to subsequent adjustment. See Commission and Premium.

Provisions. Statements contained in an insurance policy that explain the benefits, conditions and other features of the insurance contract.

Proximate Cause. The effective cause of loss or damage.

Public Adjuster. An insurance adjuster who represents an insured on a fee basis in claims settlement. Contrast with Independent Adjuster.

Public Assistance. The federal and state system for providing welfare payments to the aged, blind and disabled and to families with dependent children. See also Social Insurance.

Public Employees Dishonesty Coverage. Commercial crime coverage written for public entities to cover losses of money, securities or other property caused by employee dishonesty. Coverage is written on a "per loss" or "per employee" basis.

Public Law 15. A Congressional Act of 1945 exempting insurance from federal anti-trust laws to the extent that it is regulated properly by states. The law passed after the reversal of *Paul v. Virginia* by the Southeastern Underwiters Association decision.

Public Liability Insurance. A general term applied to forms of third party liability insurance with respect to both bodily injury and property damage liability. It protects the insured against suits brought by members of the public.

Public Official Bond. A surety bond whereby the company (surety) guarantees that the principal (public official) will faithfully perform his or her official duties and will account for all funds entrusted to his or her care.

Punitive Damages. Damages awarded over and above compensatory damages to punish a negligent party because of wanton, reckless or malicious acts or omissions. General liability policies cover punitive damages when included with compensatory damages in a lump sum, but it is up to the courts to decide whether or not they are to be awarded. Also known as Compensatory or Exemplary Damages.

Pure Endowment. An endowment payable if the designated person is alive at the end of the endowment period but not payable if the person is not alive at that time. Rarely used today.

Pure Loss Cost Ratio. (1) The ratio of reinsurance losses incurred to the ceding company's subject premium. (2) The ratio of the reinsurance losses incurred and allocated, less expense to the ceding company's gross earned premium.

Pure Mortality Cost. See Mortality Cost.

Pure No-Fault. A system under which virtually all lawsuits related to auto accidents are eliminated. The right to sue and a chance for a damage award are replaced with the right to guaranteed benefits. Lawsuits are retained only to punish convicted drunken drivers and others guilty of criminal conduct. There is no pure no-fault system in the United States.

Pure Premium. The portion of the total premium that is needed to pay expected losses. It does not take into account money needed for other company expenses.

Pure Risk. Uncertainty as to whether a loss will occur. Under a pure risk situation, there is no possibility for gain. Contrast with Speculative Risk.

Pyramiding. (1) An alleged practice of some consumer credit organizations whereby lenders add new credit insurance coverage for consolidation loans without canceling the old, thus producing a situation of overinsurance for the amount of the loan outstanding. (2) Liability insurance where the limits of liability in several policies may apply, and, in effect, "pyramid" into higher amounts of insurance than was originally intended.

Q

"Q" Schedule. A schedule of the business expenses of a life insurer required by the New York State Code to be filed to determine compliance with the state's limitation on total expenses. This limitation sets a cap on commissions.

Quadruple Indemnity. A multiple indemnity form similar to double indemnity and triple indemnity. See also Multiple Indemnity.

Qualification Period (QP). The period of time that an individual must be totally disabled before becoming eligible for residual benefits. The policy's elimination period also must be satisfied.

Qualified Condition Exclusion. A rider that excludes coverage for a specified medical problem for a specified period of time.

Qualified Medicare Beneficiary (QMB). An individual whose income is below the federal poverty guidelines. In these cases, the state is required to pay the Medicare Part B premiums, plus any deductibles or copayments.

Qualified Plan. A retirement plan filed and approved by the IRS that does not discriminate as to participation, and where the contributor (usually the employer) receives a tax deduction for plan contributions, and investment income is tax deferred until paid out.

Qualifying Event. An occurrence (such as death, termination of employment, divorce, etc.) that triggers an insured's protection under COBRA, and continues to pay benefits under a group insurance plan for former employees and their families who would otherwise lose health care coverage.

Qualifying Terminal Interest Property (QTIP). A trust that may contain marital deduction property as determined by the executor at some future time. All trust income goes to the surviving spouse.

Quality Assurance. Activities involving a review of quality of services and the taking of any corrective actions to remove any deficiencies.

Quantity Discount. A premium discount given for the purchase of a policy with a larger face amount. See also Policy Fee.

Quarantine Benefit. A benefit paid for loss of time resulting from the quarantining of an insured by health authorities.

Quarantine Indemnity. See Quarantine Benefit.

Quasi-Contract. A legal doctrine for situations in which there is no specifically drawn contract. It prevents unjust enrichment or injustice by treating the situation as if a contract actually had been in effect.

Quasi-Insurance Institutions. A term sometimes applied to government institutions created to carry out social insurance arrangements that have some, but not all, the characteristics of insurers (e.g., the U.S. Department of Health and Human Services).

Quick Assets. Assets that are quickly convertible into cash.

Quid Pro Quo. Latin for "this for that," or "one thing for another." In insurance it refers to the consideration in an insurance contract that calls for the exchange of values by both parties to the contract in order for it to be a valid contract. See also Consideration.

Quota Share. When more than one policy or insurer must respond to a property loss for a risk according to a percentage or its proportionate share of the total limits applicable. Premiums are usually shared in the same proportion as the limits.

Quota Share Reinsurance. A form of pro rata reinsurance (proportional) where the reinsurer assumes an agreed percentage of each insurance policy being insured and shares all premiums and losses accordingly with the reinsured.

R

Rabbi Trust. An irrevocable trust often used with an informally funded non-qualified deferred compensation plan whereby plan assets are subject to the claims of creditors and thus current taxation to the employee is avoided.

Radioactive Contamination Insurance. Coverage added to a property policy for certain risks where there is neither a nuclear reactor nor nuclear fuel on the premises but which might occasionally be exposed to contamination damage from other material on the insured's premises. Liability losses caused by nuclear reaction and radioactive contamination are excluded from most insurance contracts and are usually covered under policies issued by pools created for this purpose. See also Mutual Atomic Energy Pool.

Radius of Operation. Used to determine rates for automobiles owned by a business. Beyond a certain number of miles in radius (e.g., 50, the rate is increase).

Railroad Protective Liability. Liability coverage written for a railroad on behalf of those who are conducting operations on or adjacent to railroad property.

Railroad Retirement. A system that provides retirement and other benefits, including eligibility for Medicare, for railroad workers.

Railroad Sidetrack Agreement. See Sidetrack Agreement.

Railroad Subrogation Waiver Clause. A provision in a property insurance contract that says the contract shall be valid even though the insured has an agreement with the railroad waiving subrogation against the railroad. Usually used in connection with a railroad sidetrack agreement.

Railroad Travel Policy. Accident insurance sold in railroad stations by ticket agents or by vending machines. See also Travel Accident Insurance.

Rain Insurance. Protection against losses caused by cancelation of an outdoor event due to rain. The policy usually covers loss of income. The rain, hail, snow or sleet usually must exceed a certain amount and must occur during a stated period of time, either before or during the event.

Rate. (1) The cost of a given unit of insurance. For example, in ordinary life insurance, it is the price of $1,000 of the face amount. In disability income insurance, it is usually the price per $10 or per $100 of monthly benefits. In property insurance, it is the rate per $100 of value to be insured. The premium, then, is the rate multiplied by the number of units of insurance purchased. (2) The percent or factor applied to the ceding company's subject premium to produce the reinsurance premium or the percent applied to the reinsurer's premium to produce the commission. See also Premium.

Rate Card. A card issued by an insurer giving rates for various coverages. It is carried by an agent or sales representative for quotation purposes.

Rate Discrimination. The use of different rates for insureds or risks of the same class and general characteristics. Rate discrimination is prohibited by all state insurance laws.

Rate Manual. A manual containing rates for various coverages, information and instructions for field underwriting, insurer's rules for the guidance of agents, and, in the case of life insurance rate manuals, cash amount forfeiture values and dividend scales (if any).

Rate of Natural Increase (or Decrease). The birth rate minus the death rate. If there were no migration, this would equal the rate of population increase (or decrease).

Rated. Coverages issued at a higher rate than standard because of impairment of the insured. Usually used as an adjective in such expressions as "rated risk," "rated policy" and "rated up."

Rated Up. See Rated.

Rating Bureau. A private organization that classifies and promulgates manual rates and in some cases compiles data and measures the hazards of individual risks in terms of rates in geographic areas, the latter being true especially in connection with property insurance.

Rating Class. The rate class into which a risk has been placed. See also Class.

Rating Process. The steps used to determine a premium rate for a particular group based on the amount of risk that group presents. Items that generally go into the rating process include age, sex, type of industry, benefits and administrative costs.

Rating, Experience. See Experience Rating.

Rating, Merit. See Merit Rating.

Rating, Retrospective. See Retrospective Rating.

Rating, Schedule. See Schedule Rating Plan.

Rating. Within the insurance industry, professionals refer to pricing insurance coverage as rating. A rate is the cost for a unit of insurance. See also Base Rate.

Ratio Test. A coverage test for a qualified plan in which a percentage of lower paid employees benefiting from the plan must equal 70 percent of the higher paid employees from the plan.

Readjustment Income. (1) The income needed after the death or disability of a wage earner to allow the family time to adjust to a new, lower standard of spending. (2) The insurance coverage that provides readjustment income.

Realty. Real property such as land, buildings, mineral rights, etc., as opposed to personalty, such as movable personal property items.

Reasonable and Customary Charges. The charge for medical services that refers to the amount approved by the Medicare carrier for payment. Customary charges are those which are most often made by a provider for services rendered in that particular area.

Reassured. The company that purchases reinsurance. See Ceding Company.

Rebate. A portion of the agent's commission returned to an insured or anything else of value given an insured as an inducement to buy. The payment of policy dividends, retroactive rate adjustments and reduced premiums that reflect the savings of direct payment to an agent or home office are not usually considered rebates. In most cases, rebates are illegal, both for the agent or insurer to give and for the insured to receive.

Recapture of Products. See Product Recall Insurance.

Recapture. The action of a ceding company taking back from a reinsurer insurance previously ceded.

Recidivism. How often a patient returns to an inpatient hospital status for the same reason.

Recipient. Anyone designated by Medicaid as eligible to receive benefits.

Recipient Location. A location that accepts the insured's products or services. One type of dependent property for which business income coverage may be written.

Reciprocal Insurance Exchange. An unincorporated group of individuals, called subscribers, who mutually insure one another, each separately assuming his or her share of each risk. Its chief administrator is an attorney in fact.

Reciprocity. A system of placing reinsurance on a reciprocal basis so that a ceding company will give a share of its reinsurance to a reinsurer who is able to offer reinsurance in return.

Recording Agent. A policywriting agent in the property insurance business.

Recruiting. The hiring of insurance agents, or the process of looking for, interviewing and hiring agents. It is also the process of locating and hiring any type of employee.

Recurrent Disability. Disability resulting from the same or a related cause as a prior disability. In a disability income policy, it is similar to a relapse provision. If an insured suffers a relapse (a disability that is related to a prior disability) and if this relapse occurs within six months of return to work, then the second disability is considered a continuation of the initial disability. This works to the insured's advantage, because the elimination period does not have to be satisfied a second time.

Recurring Clause. A health insurance provision defining the duration of a period of time during which the recurrence of a condition is considered a continuation of a prior period of disability or confinement. Also known as a relapse provision.

Red-Lining. Discriminating unfairly against a risk solely because of its location (e.g., refusing to insure a risk because the building is located in a depressed area or location). Also called blackout areas. This practice penalizes people who live in high-crime and high-accident areas.

Reduced Paid-Up Insurance. A form of insurance available as a nonforfeiture option. It provides that the cash value of the policy be used as a single premium to purchase paid-up insurance in whatever amount the cash value will provide, which will be less than the original face amount in most cases. See also Nonforfeiture Values.

Reduction of Risk. Reducing the probability or severity of a possible loss (e.g., installing alarms and sprinkler systems to reduce the risk of fire loss to a building). See also Risk Management.

Reduction. A decrease in the benefits in an insurance policy because of a specified condition (e.g., benefits may be reduced because a disability is caused by a specific condition).

Referral. Occurs when a physician or other health plan provider receives permission to consult another physician or hospital.

Referral Provider. The person or provider to whom a participating provider has referred a member of the plan.

Reformation. Rewriting an insurance policy to add an omitted coverage retroactively. It's an unusual measure, most often happening by court order after a lawsuit.

Refund Annuity. A form of annuity that provides for a cash or installment refund to the beneficiary if the annuitant dies before having drawn benefits equal to the total consideration that he paid on the policy.

Refund Life Annuity. An annuity paying installments as long as the insured lives and installments after death to the beneficiary until the amount paid equals the principle sum of insurance.

Regional Office. A suboffice of a home office that is equipped to handle all lines of business in a particular territory or region. Some companies use the term branch office.

Register. A record of all policies charged to a debit account.

Registered Mail Insurance. Coverage for loss of money and securities sent through the post office by registered mail.

Registered Nurse (RN). A licensed professional with a four-year nursing degree that provides all levels of nursing care including the administration of medication.

Registered Representative. A person who has met the qualifications set by law or regulation to sell securities to the public.

Registered Tonnage. Warships: The weight or displacement. Commercial vessels: The cubic capacity of enclosed space. One ton occupies 100 cubic feet.

Regular Stock Option (RSO) Plan. An executive stock option plan whereby key executives have the right to purchase company stock at a predetermined price. When the option is exercised it is taxable as compensation to the executive.

Regulatory Information Retrieval Service (RIRS). A database developed by the National Association of Insurance Commissioners in conjunction with state insurance departments that lists regulatory actions such as suspensions, revocations, fines, penalties, cease and desist orders, consent orders, etc., against insurance firms and individuals.

Rehabilitation Benefits. Physical and/or vocational rehabilitation benefits provided to an injured person following a work-related injury, and intended to restore the person to a point where gainful employment is possible.

Rehabilitation Clause. Any clause in a health insurance policy, particularly a disability income policy, that is intended to assist the disabled policyholder in vocational rehabilitation.

Rehabilitation of Insurer. Action undertaken by a state insurance department to restore an impaired or insolvent insurer to sound financial standing. Contrast with Liquidation of Insurer.

Rehearing. A second hearing by a court. Its purpose is to call the court's attention to an error or omission in the court's first consideration of the claim.

Reimbursement. Payment of an amount of money upon the occurrence of a loss covered by the policy.

Reinstatement. (1) Restoration of a lapsed policy. (2) Restoration of the original amount of a type of policy that reduces the principal amount by the amount of claims. (3) Putting back into effect a catastrophe reinsurance coverage that has been reduced by the payment of a reinsurance loss as the result of one catastrophe. This is usually effected by the payment of a reinstatement premium.

Reinstatement Endorsement. If an insured suspends insurance for any reason, he or she must notify the insurance company when he or she wants coverage to be restored. In most cases, the insurance company will then calculate any refund due and restore coverage by issuing a reinstatement endorsement.

Reinsurance. Insurance that involves acceptance by an insurer, called the reinsurer, of all or a part of the risk of loss covered by another insurer, called the ceding company. It is a way for an insurer to avoid having to pay for large or catastrophic losses.

Reinsurance Assumed. (1) See Cession. (2) The premium for an assumption of reinsurance.

Reinsurance, Automatic. See Automatic Reinsurance.

Reinsurance Broker. An individual or organization that places reinsurance for the ceding companies who are its customers.

Reinsurance Ceded. See Cession.

Reinsurance Credit. Credit taken on its annual statement by a ceding company for reinsurance premiums ceded and losses recoverable.

Reinsurance, Excess. See Excess of Loss Reinsurance.

Reinsurance, Facultative. See Facultative Reinsurance.

Reinsurance Premium. The consideration paid by a ceding company to a reinsurer for the reinsurance afforded by the reinsurer.

Reinsurance, Pooling. See Pooling.

Reinsurance, Quota Share. See Quota Share Reinsurance.

Reinsurance, Spread Loss. See Spread Loss Reinsurance.

Reinsurance, Stop Loss. See Stop Loss Reinsurance.

Reinsurance, Surplus. See Surplus Reinsurance.

Reinsurer. An insurer that assumes all or a part of the insurance or reinsurance written by another insurer.

Rejection. (1) Refusal by an insurer to underwrite a risk. (2) Refusal or denial of a claim by an insurer.

Relation of Earnings to Insurance. A health insurance provision used in noncancelable and guaranteed renewable contracts that states if when a disability begins the insured's total disability income exceeds his or her earned income, the benefits will be reduced proportionally and premiums for any excess coverage will be refunded. Also known as the average earnings clause, this prevents overinsurance and allows the company to reduce disability benefits based on a person's current average monthly income.

Relative Value Schedule. A surgical schedule that compares the value of one surgical procedure to another and establishes the surgical fee to be paid.

Relative Value Unit. Sometimes used instead of dollar amounts in a surgical schedule, this number is multiplied by a conversion factor to arrive at the surgical benefit to be paid.

Release. (1) To give up, abandon and discharge a claim or an enforceable right of one person against another. (2) The name of the instrument evidencing such an act (e.g., if a claim representative obtains a release from a claimant, this means that the claimant has given up all further rights against the insurance company).

Remainder. The amount of a risk to be reinsured after deducting the amount the ceding company is keeping in its own account.

Remand. Usually used in appellate courts whereby the appellate court refers the case back to the original court for further action.

Remittitur. Process by which an excessive jury verdict is reduced by the court. Contrast with Additur.

Removal. Removing property to protect it from loss. Most personal and commercial property forms cover damage to property at another location when it has been removed from the premises to protect it from loss by a covered peril insured.

Renewable Term. Term insurance that may be renewed for another term without evidence of insurability.

Renewal. (1) The reestablishment of the in-force status of a policy, the term of which has expired or will expire unless it is renewed. (2) The automatic reestablishment of in-force status effected by the payment of another premium.

Renewal Certificate. A short-form certificate used to renew a policy. It refers to the original policy, keeping all of its provisions, but does not restate all of its insuring agreements, exclusions and conditions.

Renewal Commission. A commission paid on premiums subsequent to the first-year commission.

Renewals. (1) The premiums paid for renewed policies. (2) The commissions paid on renewal premiums.

Rent Insurance. See Rental Value Insurance.

Rental Car Replacement. Coverage for a rental car if an insured's vehicle is being repaired because of an accident. Also called Rental Reimbursement Coverage.

Rental Reimbursement Coverage. See Rental Car Replacement.

Rental Value Insurance. Property insurance that provides indemnity for: 1) the loss of the rental value of property when the owner or tenant is deprived of the use of the property because it has been damaged by an insured peril; or 2) the loss by the owner-landlord of the rent that would have been payable by a tenant of the property, under the terms of the lease or by statute, when he is relieved of liability for the payment of rent during a period of untenantability due to an insured peril.

Renters Insurance. Insurance for renters to insure their property against loss by covered perils.

Replacement. A new policy written to take the place of one currently in force.

Replacement Cost. The cost of replacing property without a reduction for depreciation. By this method of determining value, damages for a claim would be the amount needed to replace the property using new materials. Contrast with Actual Cash Value.

Replacement Cost Insurance. Insurance that provides that loss will be paid on a replacement cost basis. If there is a covered loss to the insured dwelling, the insurance company will pay to repair or replace the property with like construction, but only up to the policy's limit of liability. The recovery will be reduced by any deductible the insured has agreed to pay. To be eligible for replacement cost coverage, the dwelling must be insured for at least 80 percent of its replacement cost at the time of loss. This coverage applies only to dwelling buildings and does not apply to personal property. See also Replacement Cost.

Replacement Value. To replace new up to the limits of the policy, less any deductible, with no reduction in the amount due to depreciation (e.g., in most cases, the older a car, the less insurance an insured needs. This is because the replacement value diminishes with age).

Reporting Form. A periodic report to an insurer by an insured that covers the fluctuating values of stocks of merchandise, furniture and fixtures and improvements and betterments. Premiums are adjusted annually, based on the average values insured during the policy period. An insured with fluctuating inventories might use this form.

Representation. A statement made on an application for insurance that the applicant represents as correct to the best of his or her knowledge and belief. See also Warranty.

Representative. An agent or sales representative.

Res Ipsa Loquitur. Literally translated, this means "facts speak for themselves." Under this doctrine, a person is presumed to be negligent if the circumstances of injury are under his complete and exclusive control, and it can be shown that the injury or damage could only have occurred if the individual were negligent.

Rescission. (1) Repudiation of a contract. A party whose consent to a contract was induced by fraud, misrepresentation or duress may repudiate it. A contract may also be repudiated for failure to perform a duty. (2) The termination of an insurance contract by the insurer when material misrepresentation has occurred.

Reserve. (1) An amount representing actual or potential liabilities kept by an insurer to cover debts to policyholders. (2) An amount allocated for a special purpose. Note that a reserve is usually a liability and not an extra fund. On occasion a reserve may be an asset, such as a reserve for taxes not yet due.

Reserve, Unearned Premium. See Unearned Premium Reserve.

Residence Employee (or Domestic). An employee of any insured who performs full- or part-time services related to the maintenance or use of the residence premises, including household or domestic services; or someone who performs similar duties—not related to a business—elsewhere.

Residence Premises. In homeowners insurance, the dwelling, other structures and grounds, or that part of any other building where the named insured lives and which is identified as the residence premises in the policy. In the case of a two-, three- or four-family dwelling, the named insured must reside in at least one of the family units.

Resident Agent. An agent domiciled in the state in which he writes insurance.

Residual Disability. That form of disability which becomes defined as partial disability when an insured has returned to work immediately following a period of total disability.

Residual Disability Income Benefits. A clause that provides for benefits to be paid when the insured can do some but not all of his or her normal duties (e.g., if the insured suffers a disability that causes him or her to lose a third of his or her earning power, the residual disability clause would provide one-third of the benefit that the policy would provide for total disability).

Residual Markets. Various insurance markets outside of the normal agency-company marketing system. Residual markets include government insurance programs, specialty pools (aviation risks and nuclear risks) and shared market mechanisms (assigned risk plans).

Resource Based Relative Value Scale (RBRVS). A classification system that determines how physicians will be compensated for services provided under Medicare benefits.

Respite Care. Normally associated with hospice care, this is a benefit to family members of a patient whereby the family is provided with a break or respite from caring for the patient. The patient is confined to a nursing home for needed care for a short period of time.

Respondeat Superior. Under certain circumstances, a principal is responsible for the wrongful acts of its agents or an employer for those of its employees. Under this doctrine, if an employee negligently injures a customer while in the course of employment, the employer could be held liable.

Restoration of Benefits. A provision in many major medical plans that restores a person's lifetime maximum benefit amount in small increments after a claim has been paid. Usually, only a small amount ($1,000 to $3,000) may be restored annually.

Retained Limit. (1) The total applicable limits of all required underlying policies and any other insurance available to an insured. (2) The self-insured retention if the loss is not covered by any underlying insurance. See Self-Insured Retention.

Retainer Clause. A clause stating how much a company placing reinsurance intends to retain.

Retaliatory Law. A state law that says that agents from another state applying for a license to operate in the state in question will be accorded the same treatment as agents residing in the retaliatory state are given in the foreign state.

Retention. (1) The portion of the premium that is used by the insurance company for administrative costs. (2) The amount of liability retained by the ceding company and not reinsured. Contrast with Cession.

Retention of Risk. Assuming all or part of a risk instead of purchasing insurance or otherwise transferring the risk. See also Risk Management.

Retirement Annuity. An annuity contract that is entered into before a selected retirement age with the consideration paid in installments until that age is reached. It is a form of deferred annuity.

Retirement Income Policy. An adaptation of an endowment at a selected retirement age in which the annuity benefit is a percentage of the face amount of life insurance in force prior to retirement age, usually 10 percent (e.g., for each $1000 of insurance a $10 per month annuity installment is payable). Under this policy, the cash value will exceed the face amount in the later policy years, and if death occurs before the selected retirement age, the death benefit would be the face amount or the cash value, whichever is greater.

Retroactive Conversion. The conversion of a term life insurance policy to a cash value form as of the original date of issue of the term policy, rather than as of the time the conversion is made. In other words, the cash value policy will have already attained the age of the former term policy.

Retroactive Date. Date on a "claims made" liability policy that triggers the beginning period of insurance coverage. A retroactive date is not required. If one is shown on the policy, any claim made during the policy period will not be covered if the loss occurred before the retroactive date.

Retrocession. The transaction whereby a reinsurer cedes all or part of the reinsurance it has assumed to another reinsurer.

Retrocessionaire. The reinsurer of a reinsurer.

Retrospective Premium. Final premium in a retrospective rating plan. See Retrospective Rating.

Retrospective Rate Derivation (RETRO). A rating system whereby the employer becomes responsible for a portion of the group's health care costs. If the costs are less than the portion the employer agrees to assume, the insurance company may be required to refund a portion of the premium.

Retrospective Rating. A plan for which the final premium is not determined until the end of the coverage period and is based on the insured's own loss experience for that same period. It is subject to a maximum and minimum. It is used in various types of insurance, especially workers' compensation and liability, and is usually elected by only very large insureds. See also Basic Premium.

Return Commission. A commission paid back by the agent if a policy is canceled before its normal expiration date. This occurs when the commission was based on the full annual premium, and if the policy is canceled before it is earned, a pro rata portion of the commission must be returned.

Return of Cash Value. A provision or rider on a life insurance policy that states that if death occurs during a certain period of years (often 20), the policy will pay an amount, in addition to the face amount, that is equal to the cash value of the policy as of the date of death. It is a form of increasing term insurance and is used as a sales tool.

Return Premium. (1) A rider on a life insurance policy providing that, in the event of the death of the insured within a specified period of time, the policy will pay, in addition to the face amount, an amount equal to the sum of all premiums paid to date. This is a form of increasing term insurance and is used as a sales tool. (2) A rider or provision in a health insurance policy agreeing to pay a benefit equal to the sum of all the premiums paid, minus claims paid, if claims over a stated period of time do not exceed a fixed percentage of the premiums paid. (3) A portion of the premium returned to a policyowner as a result of cancelation, rate adjustment or a calculation that an advance premium was in excess of the actual premium. See also Pro Rata Rate and Short Rate Premium.

Revenue. See Premium.

Reversionary Annuity (or Insurance). A contract providing annuity benefits only if the annuitant is living upon the death of the insured, such as the wife upon the death of her husband. Although labeled an annuity, this contract is actually a form of life insurance on the life of the person whose death will initiate the benefit.

Revocable Beneficiary. The beneficiary in a life insurance policy in which the owner reserves the right to revoke or change the beneficiary. See Irrevocable Beneficiary.

Revocable Trust. A trust instrument in which the grantor maintains control over the trust assets and can revoke the trust. Contrast with Irrevocable Trust.

RHU. Registered Health Underwriter.

Rider. An attachment to a policy that modifies its conditions by expanding or restricting benefits or excluding certain conditions from coverage. See Waiver and Endorsement.

RIMS. See Risk and Insurance Management Society, Inc.

Riot. A peril covered by the extended coverage (EC) or by direct reference in some policies. It is violent action by two or more people. State laws vary as to how many people it takes to constitute a riot.

Risk. (1) Uncertainty as to the outcome of an event when two or more possibilities exist. See also Pure Risk and Speculative Risk. (2) A person or thing insured. 3) The physical units of property insured or the physical units of property at risk. Contrast with Hazard and Peril.

Risk Analysis. The process of determining what benefits to offer and premium to charge a particular group.

Risk and Insurance Management Society, Inc. (RIMS). An association of risk managers and insurance buyers, organized for educational purposes to promote the risk management concept. RIMS fosters closer relationships among buyers, makes the insurance needs of businesses known and promotes better relations among all interested parties within the insurance industry.

Risk Appraiser. An employee of a life insurer who screens the applications submitted. He may accept or reject an applicant, or propose an alternative policy or premium.

Risk Control Insurance. See Reinsurance.

Risk Management. Management of the pure risks to which a company might be subject. It involves analyzing all exposures to the possibility of loss and determining how to handle these exposures through such practices as avoiding the risk, reducing the risk, retaining the risk or transferring the risk, usually by insurance.

Risk Pool. See Pool.

Risk Premium Insurance. See Yearly Renewable Term.

Risk Profile. The risk an insured poses to an insurance company. Some elements of this profile are based on demographic factors. Other elements are based on lifestyle needs. Age, sex and marital status classifications are what insurers refer to as primary factors figured into premium formulas.

Risk Retention Groups. Liability insurance companies owned by their policyholders. Membership is limited to people in the same business or activity that exposes them to similar liability risks. The purpose is to assume and spread liability exposure to group members and to provide an alternative risk financing mechanism for liability.

Risk, Degree of. See Degree of Risk.

River Marine. The part of ocean marine insurance that addresses itself to the insuring of craft on inland waterways.

Robbery. The felonious taking, either by force or fear of force, of the personal property of another.

Robbery and Safe Burglary Coverage Form. There are two variations of this commercial crime coverage. One (Form D) covers property other than money and securities against inside or outside loss or damage by robbery, and against inside loss or damage by safe burglary. The other (Form Q) covers money and securities against loss by robbery or safe burglary inside the premises, and loss by robbery outside the premises.

Rollover Contribution. A contribution consisting of a distribution from a qualified plan that is deposited (rolled) in another qualified plan to postpone current taxation of the distribution.

Rule Against Perpetuities. A rule that says a trust is not valid unless individual beneficiaries become vested in the trust property within 21 years.

Running Down Clause. An additional coverage that can be added to an ocean marine hull policy to provide protection against liability for damage to another ship caused by collision.

Runoff. A termination provision in a reinsurance contract stipulating that the reinsurer shall remain liable for loss under each reinsured policy in force until its expiration date.

S

SAA. See Surety Association of America.

Sacrifice. Cargo that is thrown overboard to save the rest of the cargo and the ship. See Jettison.

Safe Burglary. The taking of property from a locked safe or vault by a person unlawfully entering the safe or vault as evidenced by visible marks of forced entry upon its exterior, or the complete removal of a safe from the premises.

Safe Depository Coverage. Two commercial crime coverage forms are available for firms other than financial institutions that rent safe deposit boxes to others. One covers an insured's legal liability for loss or damage, while the other covers direct losses regardless of liability. Both cover customers' property on the insured's premises while in a safe deposit box or vault, or while being deposited or removed from such containers.

Safe Driver Incentive Plan. A system that assigns points for traffic violations and certain accidents, and each point adds a percentage surcharge to the rating factor. It is similar to merit rating. Also called a Safe Driver Incentive Plan.

Safety Consultant. See Engineer.

Safety Responsibility Law. See Financial Responsibility Law.

Salary Savings Insurance (Deductions or Allotment). Insurance issued to an individual employee whose employer agrees to deduct the premiums from the insured's paychecks and submit them to the insurer.

Sales Representatives. See Special Agent.

Salvage Corps. An organization whose duties are limited to preventing further damage to property during or after a fire. They are established by property insurance companies.

Salvage. (1) Property taken over by an insurer to reduce its loss. (2) Property recoverable by salvagers under maritime law.

SAP. See Statutory Accounting Principles.

Savings Bank Life Insurance. Life insurance sold by mutual savings banks. Allowed only in a few states, such as New York, Connecticut and Massachusetts.

Schedule. (1) A list of the items covered by an insurance policy with their descriptions and valuations. (2) A list of individual items covered under one policy, such as various buildings and contents. (3) A list of specified amounts payable for surgical procedures, dismemberments, ancillary expenses and the like in hospital and medical reimbursement policies.

Schedule Bond. See Name Schedule Bond and Position Schedule Bond.

Schedule Policy. An insurance contract that lists separate kinds of property, locations or insurance coverages and the amount of insurance applying to each.

Schedule Rating Plan. (1) Applying debits or credits within established ranges for various characteristics of a risk that are either below or above average according to an established schedule of items. (2) Under liability and auto insurance, a plan allowing credits and debits for various good or bad features of a particular commercial risk (e.g., an automobile schedule rating allowing credits for driver training classes or fleet maintenance programs).

Scheduled Personal Property. Property that has been inventoried and listed. See Unscheduled Personal Property.

Scheduled Premium Variable Life Insurance. A whole life policy featuring a fixed, level premium and a minimum guaranteed face amount. The performance of the policy is dependent on the separate account.

Schedule, "Q." See "Q" Schedule.

Seasonal Risk. A risk that is present only during certain parts of the year (e.g., manufacturing concerns such as canners who have seasonal operations and dwellings such as cottages used for vacations).

Seaworthiness, Implied. See Implied Seaworthiness.

SEC Liability. The Federal Securities Act of 1933 and the Federal Securities Exchange Act of 1934 place very stringent obligations on those offering stock issues to the public to disclose full information on the offering. If misrepresentations, intended or not, are made, liability can attach to them.

Second Injury Fund. Special funds set up by each state to pay all or part of the compensation required when a partially disabled employee suffers a subsequent injury. Because the compound effect of two injuries can be greater than the effect of the same two injuries in isolation, employers might be reluctant to hire the handicapped if they had to bear the full burden for a second injury. Second injury funds relieve employers of some of this burden.

Second Residence. A second residence, such as a summer house or a mountain cabin. It must be shown in the policy declarations at the beginning of the policy term. If the additional residence is acquired after the policy's effective date, automatic coverage is provided for the additional residence for the balance of the policy term.

Second Surgical Opinion. A cost containment technique to help patients and insurance companies determine whether a recommended procedure is necessary, or whether an alternative method of treatment could accomplish the same result. Some health policies require a second surgical opinion before specified procedures will be covered, and many policies pay for a second opinion.

Second Surplus Reinsurance. Reinsurance accepted by a second reinsurer in a surplus treaty. It is the amount that exceeds the total of the original insurer's net retention and the full limit of the first surplus treaty. See also Surplus Reinsurance.

Secondary Beneficiary. The second person named to receive benefits upon the death of an insured if the first-named beneficiary is not alive or does not collect all the benefits before his or her own death. See also Contingent Beneficiary.

Secondary Care. Medical services provided by physicians who do not have first contact with patients (e.g., specialists such as urologists, cardiologists, etc.) See also Primary Care and Tertiary Care.

Secondary Coverage. Covers payment for charges not covered by the primary policy or plan. See also Coordination of Benefits.

Secondary Rating Factors. Secondary factors that influence how insurance companies look at an insured as an auto risk. A person's driving record (what insurers call sub-class) is the most important of these factors. Insurance company statistics say that, the more accidents a person has, the more likely he will be involved in another accident. The neighborhood a person lives in is another factor.

Section 125 Plan. A plan that provides flexible benefits. This plan qualifies under the IRS code which allows employee contributions to meet with pre-tax dollars.

Section 302 Stock Redemption. A total stock redemption that qualifies as a capital transaction and not a dividend distribution.

Section 303 Stock Redemption. A partial stock redemption permitted under Section 303 of the IRC for the purpose of providing funds for estate settlement costs.

Secular Trust. An irrevocable trust that provides for current taxation of deferred compensation assets and a degree of security in an informally funded plan.

Securities. Evidences of a debt or of ownership (e.g., stocks, bonds and checks).

Securities Act of 1933. A federal law that requires full and fair disclosure and the use of a prospectus in the sale of securities.

Securities Deposited with Others Coverage Form. A commercial crime coverage form that protects against loss by theft, disappearance or destruction of securities which have been deposited with others, such as a bank, trust company or stock broker.

Securities Exchange Act of 1934. A federal law which requires the registration of companies and agents with the federal government if they are selling securities.

SEGLI. Service Employees Group Life Insurance is issued to members of the armed forces while they are in the service. After separation it is convertible to individual policies from certain private insurers.

Selection. The choosing by an underwriter of risks acceptable to an insurer.

Selection of Risk. (1) See Selection. (2) A phrase used in reinsurance referring to the practice of ceding poorer business to a reinsurer while retaining good risks.

Self-Administered Trusteed Plan. A retirement plan where contributions are paid to a trustee who invests the money, accumulates the earnings and interest and pays benefits to eligible employees.

Self-Employed Person. An individual operating a business or engaged in a profession as a non-incorporated venture. The self-employed person works for himself or herself. This business may be organized as a sole proprietorship or a partnership or the person may operate as an independent contractor. A self-employed person does not meet the Social Security requirements of an employee—but he must still pay Social Security taxes...and therefore can receive benefits.

Self-Funded Plan. Plan of insurance where an employer, which has fairly predictable claim costs, pays the claims rather than an insurance company. See also Administrative Services Only.

Self-Inflicted Injury. An injury to the body of the insured inflicted by himself or herself.

Self-Insurance. Financial preparations to meet pure risks by appropriating sufficient funds in advance to meet estimated losses, including enough to cover possible losses in excess of those estimated. Few organizations are large or dispersed enough to make this a sound alternative to insurance.

Self-Insured Retention (SIR). The portion of a risk or potential loss assumed by an insured. It may be in the form of a deductible, self-insurance or no insurance. Also called a retained limit in some policies.

Self-Reinsurance. The creation of a fund by an insurer to absorb losses beyond its normal retention. It is used in place of buying reinsurance.

Selling Price Clause. See Market Value Clause.

Separate Account. (1) An investment company (usually a unit investment trust) registered with the SEC that owns and holds assets for the benefit of participants in variable contracts. Because of the investment risk, insurers are required to keep their variable contract portfolios separate from their fixed investment portfolios. (2) An account established or maintained by an insurer under which the income, gains and losses of that specific account are credited or charged without consideration of the income and investment results of the other assets of the insurer. Separate accounts are used to fund variable contracts and provide the participant with a hedge against inflation.

Separate Structure. A separate structure on the property (e.g., a garage, shed or guest house) that's usually covered in addition to the face amount.

Service Area. The area, allowed by state agencies or by the certification of authority, in which a health plan can provide services.

Service Benefits. Medical expense benefits provided by service associations whereby benefits are identified in terms of days of coverage instead of monetary values.

Service Plans. Plans of insurance where benefits are the actual services rendered rather than a monetary benefit. See Blue Cross and Blue Shield.

Set-Off Provisions. Provisions that limit one kind of coverage when another has been claimed (e.g., if an insured has valid coverage for automobile medical payments, the damages that can be recovered from the owner or operator of an uninsured motor vehicle shall be reduced for purposes of uninsured motorists coverage by the amounts paid or due to be paid under such automobile medical payments insurance.

Settle. When a liability claim is made against an insured, the insurer has a choice of whether it will settle (pay the damages) or defend.

Settlement. (1) A policy benefit or claim payment. An agreement between both parties to the policy contract as to the amount and method of payment. (2) Conclusion of litigation by the mutual agreement of parties involved prior to final verdict; certain settlements must be court-approved.

Settlement Options. The various methods for the payment of the proceeds or values of a life insurance policy that may be selected in lieu of a lump sum.

Settlement Tables. Tables depicting the dollar amounts per $1,000 of insurance for the option selected. The tables are simply rows of numbers representing periods of time, adjusted ages of insured people and benefit amounts.

SEUA. See Southeastern Underwriters Association.

Severability of Insurance. Each insured, as defined in the policy, has the same rights and obligations that would exist had a separate policy been issued to each insured. However, this severability does not increase the limits of liability under the policy.

Share Reinsurance. See Pro Rata Reinsurance.

Shared Ownership. As a member of a condo association of unit owners, each individual unit owner has shared ownership in the building structure. Disputes over shared liability can result in large legal judgments against individual owners.

Sherman Antitrust Act. An antitrust law from which insurance is exempted to the extent that it is regulated by state law.

Shock Loss. A catastrophic loss so large that it has a material effect on the underwriting results of a company.

Shoppers Guide. A consumer publication that describes the coverage being offered, and provides general information to help an applicant for life or health insurance compare different policies and reach a decision about whether the proposed coverage is appropriate. Also known as Buyers Guide.

Short Rate Cancelation. A cancelation procedure in which the premium returned to the insured is not in direct proportion to the number of days remaining in the policy period. In effect, the insured has paid more for each day of coverage than if the policy had remained in force for the full term. Contrast with Pro Rata Cancelation.

Short Rate Premium. The premium required to issue a policy for a period less than its normal term.

Short-Term Disability Income Policy. A disability income policy with benefits payable for short-term, usually less than two years, as opposed to a long-term disability income policy.

Short-Term Disability Insurance. A group or individual policy usually written to cover disabilities of 13 or 26 weeks duration, though coverage for as long as two years is not uncommon. Contrast with Long-Term Disability Insurance.

Short-Term Policy. A policy written for a period of less time than is normal for that type of policy.

Sick Pay Plan. A formal program for continuing the compensation of key employees—including the business owner and working stockholders. It is usually best funded with disability insurance (individual or group disability policies may be used).

Sickness Insurance. A form of health insurance against loss by illness or disease. It does not include accidental bodily injury.

Sickness. A disease or illness that first manifests itself while the policy is in force. Includes physical illness, disease, pregnancy, but does not include mental illness. See Pre-Existing Conditions.

Sidetrack Agreement. Any agreement between a railroad and a customer who is served by a railroad sidetrack built on the customer's premises. Among other things, it provides that the customer hold the railroad harmless for losses resulting from certain types of accidents.

Sidetrack Insurance. See Sidetrack Agreement.

Simple Probability. See Probability.

Simplified Employee Pension Plan (SEP). A plan where the employer contributes a specific amount into an eligible employee's IRA on behalf of the employee.

Simplified or Progressive Underwriting. Group underwriting may take the form of three or four medical questions asked of the individual. Due to the size of the group membership, relatively minor medical problems may be overlooked and policies issued. Nevertheless, even with simplified underwriting, it is possible for a member to be declined for the insurance.

Sine Qua Non Rule. A rule stating that a person's conduct is not held to be the cause of a loss if the loss would have occurred anyway.

Single Carrier Replacement. A situation where one carrier replaces several other carriers who had been providing services.

Single Interest Policy. Insurance protecting the interest of only one of the parties having an insurable interest in property, such as insurance protecting a mortgagee but not a mortgagor or protecting a seller but not a buyer.

Single Limit. Insurance coverage that is expressed as a single amount of insurance, or a single limit of liability. Contrast with Split Limit.

Single Payment Deferred Straight Life Annuity. An annuity purchased with a single payment that provides a payout for life. Even if an annuity option is elected at the time of purchase, it may (and probably will) be changed at the annuity period to reflect your changing needs.

Single Premium Funding Method. A method of accumulating money for future payment of pension benefits under which the money required to pay for each year's accumulated benefits is paid to an insurance company or paid to the trust fund annually.

Single Premium Policy. A life insurance policy paid for in one single premium in advance rather than in annual premiums over a period of time.

Single Premium Whole Life. A whole life policy that is paid with a single premium payment at the time of purchase. Compare with Continuous Premium Whole Life and Limited Payment Whole Life.

Sinkhole Collapse. The peril of a sudden sinking or collapse of land into underground empty spaces created by the action of water on limestone or similar rock formations. It is covered by the latest commercial property forms. Other forms of earth movement continue to be excluded in most cases.

SIR. See Self-Insured Retention.

Sistership Exclusion. A products insurance exclusion that denies coverage for the withdrawal and recall of products from the market.

Skilled Nursing Care. Daily nursing and rehabilitative care that is performed only by or under the supervision of skilled professional or technical personnel. Skilled care includes administering medication, medical diagnosis and minor surgery.

Skilled Nursing Facility (SNF). A facility designed for treating Medicare eligible people, including rehabilitation and other care such as 24-hour nursing coverage, physical, occupational and speech therapies, etc.

Slander. Oral defamation of someone that is personally injurious to the individual.

Sliding Scale Commission. A commission adjustment under a formula whereby the actual commissions paid by a reinsurer to a ceding insurer vary inversely with the loss ratio, subject to a maximum and minimum.

Slip. A paper submitted by a broker to the underwriters at Lloyd's of London that identifies syndicates accepting the risk and notes the extent of their participation.

Slow-Burning Construction. See Mill Construction.

Small Group Pooling. The combining of several small group businesses into one pool for computing more accurate premium rates for members of the pool.

Smoke Damage. Damage caused by the smoke from a fire in contrast to damage caused by the actual combustion.

SMP. See Special Multi-Peril.

SNF. Skilled Nursing Facility.

Social Health Maintenance Organization (SHMO). A demonstration project funded by the Health and Human Services Department that combines the delivery of acute and long-term care with adult day care services and transportation.

Social Host Liability. See Host Liability.

Social Insurance. Compulsory insurance legislated to provide minimum economic security for large groups of people, particularly those with low incomes. It is primarily concerned with the costs and loss of income resulting from sickness, accidental injury, old age, unemployment and premature death of the head of a family. See also Legislated Coverages and Social Security.

Social Security. (1) The programs provided under the Social Security Act of 1935, plus amendments and addition. Also called Old Age, Survivors, Disability and Health Insurance. (2) Any government program that provides economic security for portions of the public (e.g., Social Insurance, Public Assistance, Family Allowances, Grants-in-Aid, etc.).

Social Security Disability Income Benefits. Eligibility for disability benefits under Social Security requires that a person be both fully insured and disability insured. In addition, the person must be under age 65, the disability must be expected to last for at least 12 months or end in death, and the disability must be a total disability.

Social Security Insurance Supplements. Supplements to disability income policy benefits. They may be added to the policy by a rider.

Social Security Rider. An optional disability income rider that provides an additional benefit depending on the amount of disability benefits payable by Social Security. See also All or Nothing Rider and Offset Rider.

Social Security Tax. A tax paid by workers and employers on wages earned. The taxes support the benefit programs under the Social Security System.

Society of Chartered Property and Casualty Underwriters (CPCU). The society of people who have been awarded the CPCU designation. Its primary purpose is the continuing education of its members. It also encourages insurance research.

Society of Insurance Research. An organization that encourages insurance research and promotes the exchange of ideas and methods of research.

Sole Proprietorship. A business enterprise owned by a person who is its manager and employee.

Sole Proprietorship Insurance. Life and health insurance that handles the business continuity problems of a sole proprietorship (e.g., to enable the heirs of the sole proprietor to bring the value of the business back to the level where it was prior to the death of the owner, etc.).

Sole Representative. The first named insured shown on the information page. This person acts on behalf of all other insured parties to change the policy, receive return premiums and to give or receive notice of cancelation.

Solicitor. An individual appointed and authorized by an agent to solicit and receive applications for insurance as the agent's representative. Solicitors are not usually given the power to bind coverage but are required to be licensed.

Solvency. With regard to insurers, having sufficient assets (capital, surplus, reserves) and the ability to satisfy financial requirements (investments, annual reports, examinations) to be eligible to transact insurance business and meet liabilities.

Sonic Boom. Noise, pressure and shock waves resulting from an aircraft or missile exceeding the speed of sound. Modern commercial property forms and homeowner policies now cover losses by sonic boom.

Southeastern Underwriters Association (SEUA). A property insurance rating organization which was the defendant in the 1944 United States Supreme Court decision declaring insurance to be commerce and thus subject to regulation by federal law. This pronouncement was later modified by Public Law 15. See also Public Law 15.

Special Acceptance. A specific agreement by a reinsurer to accept a risk that would not be automatically included within the terms of a reinsurance contract.

Special Agent. An insurer's representative in a territory that services the insurer's agents and is responsible for the volume and quality of the business written in that territory. In the property and liability fields this person is a special agent or marketing representative, and in the life field he is known as a sales representative.

Special Auto Policy. An auto policy with a single limit of liability applying to bodily injury and property damage and a corresponding limit applying to medical payments. Broad physical damage coverage can be added. See Personal Auto Policy.

Special Building Form. A form that provides open perils (all risk) coverage on commercial buildings, subject to certain exclusions. Largely replaced by the Building and Personal Property Coverage Form.

Special Coverage Form. Any of the commercial or personal lines property forms which provide coverage on an open perils (all risk) type basis. These forms provide the broadest coverage and do not list covered perils, but do include a lengthy list of exclusions. See also Open Peril and Named Peril.

Special Multi-Peril (SMP). A business policy that combines into one contract the coverages normally purchased under several. Property and liability coverages are mandatory, crime and boiler and machinery are optional. Largely replaced by new commercial forms. See Commercial Package Policy.

Special Personal Property Form. A form that provides open perils (all risk) coverage on the personal property (contents) of commercial risks with certain exclusions. Largely replaced by the Building and Personal Property Coverage Form.

Special Power of Appointment. A donee authorized to appoint interest in property to specific individuals to the exclusion of others.

Specialty Coverages. Additional coverages available to the insured (e.g., personal property coverage that includes mysterious disappearance or utility disruption).

Specific Insurance. A policy that describes specifically the property to be covered. This is in contrast to a policy covering on a blanket basis all property at one or more locations without specific definitions. In the case of overlapping coverages, specific insurance is considered the primary one.

Specific Rate. A rate applying to an individual piece of property.

Specific Reinsurance. See Facultative Reinsurance.

Specified Causes of Loss. A commercial automobile physical damage coverage for loss by the specified perils of fire, lightning, explosion, theft, windstorm, hail, earthquake, flood, vandalism, or the sinking, burning, collision or derailment of any conveyance transporting a covered auto. Comprehensive coverage is slightly broader.

Specified Disease Policy. See Dread Disease Policy.

Specified Perils. See Named Perils.

Speculative Risk. Uncertainty as to whether a gain or loss will occur (e.g., a business enterprise where there is a chance that the business will make money or lose it). These risks are not normally insurable. Contrast with Pure Risk.

Spendthrift Clause. A clause in most life insurance policies that prevents the creditors of a beneficiary from claiming any of the benefits before the beneficiary actually receives the money. The purpose of this clause is to keep those to whom he is in debt from taking legal action to require the insurer to pay the proceeds directly to them.

Split Dollar Coverage. (1) An arrangement of disability income insurance in which the employer and employee each pay a portion of the premium. The employer purchases coverage for the sick pay or paid disability leave provided as an employee benefit. The employee pays for disability coverage beyond what the employer provides as a benefit. (2) An arrangement where an employer pays that part of the premium that equals the annual increase in the cash value of a policy, while the employee pays the rest. Under assignment upon the death of the employee, the employer recovers the total of its payments from the proceeds of the policy, with the remainder going to the employee's beneficiary.

Split Dollar Plan. A method of purchasing life insurance whereby the employer and employee jointly purchase the policy, pay premiums and share in the policy's benefits.

Split Life Insurance. A combination of installment annuity and term insurance where the amount of annuity consideration (premium) paid determines the amount of one-year renewable term insurance an annuitant can purchase and place on the life of anyone designated.

Split Limit. Any insurance coverage which is expressed in different amounts for different types of losses. For example, auto liability of 50/100/50 means bodily injury limits of $50,000 per person, $100,000 per accident and a property damage limit of $50,000 per accident. Contrast with Single Limit.

Sponsor Plan. An employer that establishes or maintains a plan for its employees; or an employee organization that establishes or maintains a plan for the employees of the organization; or in the case of a plan established and maintained by two or more employers, the committee, Board of Trustees or relatives of the parties who establish or maintain the plan.

Spousal Impoverishment Act. Protects a portion of the income and assets that a stay-at-home spouse may retain without terminating Medicaid eligibility for a confined spouse.

Spread Loss Reinsurance. (1) The working cover subject to a prospective rating plan. (2) A form of excess reinsurance wherein each year's premium rate is determined by the amount of the ceding insurer's excess losses for a specified number of preceding years. A form of experience rating.

Sprinkler Leakage Insurance. Coverage for damage resulting from the accidental discharge of water from an automatic sprinkler system, as contrasted with discharge because of heat from a fire.

Sprinkler Leakage Legal Liability Insurance. Insurance covering the legal liability of an insured who has a sprinkler leakage loss which damages the property of others, on a floor below or in adjoining premises, for instance.

Stacking of Limits. Applying the limits of more than one policy to an occurrence, loss or claim. In some cases, courts have required a stacking of limits when multiple policies, or multiple policy periods, cover an occurrence.

Staff Model HMO. An HMO where physicians are employed and all premiums are paid to the HMO, which then compensates the physicians on a salary and bonus arrangement.

Staged Accidents. An accident where vehicles with prior damage are brought together and made to appear to have been involved in an accident.

Stamping Bureau. See Audit Bureau.

Standard Annuity Table. The 1937 Standard Annuity Table; a mortality table widely used for annuities.

Standard Class Rate (SCR). This is a rate which is arrived at by using a base rate per participant multiplied by a factor to allow for group demographic information.

Standard Exception. In workers' compensation insurance certain classes of employees are classified separately for rating, rather than being included in the main classification for a risk (e.g., clerical office employees, outside sales representatives, draftsmen, drivers, chauffeurs and their helpers).

Standard Fire Policy. See New York Standard Fire Policy.

Standard Limit. See Basic Limit.

Standard Policy. (1) Coverage which has identical provisions regardless of the issuing insurer. Many common policies are standardized. (2) Insurance issued to a standard risk.

Standard Premium. Most often used in connection with retrospective rating for workers' compensation and general liability insurance. It is the premium of which the basic premium is a percentage and is developed by applying the regular rates to an insured's payroll. See also Retrospective Rating and Basic Premium.

Standard Provisions. (1) Provisions prescribed by state law that must appear in all policies issued in that jurisdiction. (2) Provisions adopted by the NAIC to apply to group life insurance as minimum protection. They are required by law in most states. (3) Formerly, a set of prescribed provisions regulating the operating conditions of a health insurance policy required by law in most jurisdictions between about 1912 and 1950. They are now superseded by uniform provisions for individual accident and health insurance policies which contain an NAIC model bill. These have been enacted in virtually all jurisdictions.

Standard Risk. A risk on par with those on which the rate has been based in the areas of health, physical condition and morals. These risks are part of the standard cost of a policy, and are not subject to rate loadings or restrictions.

Standard Ownership Rules. Under these rules, an eligible vehicle must be owned or leased by an individual or married couple who are residents of the same household. See Joint Ownership Coverage.

State Agent. An outmoded term meaning an agent who has an exclusive territory of one or more states. Also, an obsolete term for special agent. See Special Agent.

State Associations of Insurance Agents. Each state may have one or more associations of insurance agents. These organizations are made up of individual agents who have joined forces to discuss common problems and promote the American agency system.

State Death Taxes. A tax imposed by states on beneficiaries who receive property from a decedent.

State Fund. A fund set up by a state government to finance a mandatory insurance system, such as workers' compensation, nonoccupational disability benefits, or, in Wisconsin, state-offered life insurance. Such a fund may be monopolistic, i.e., purchasers of the type of insurance required must place it in the state fund; or it may be competitive, i.e., an alternative to private insurance if the purchaser desires to use it.

Stated Amount. An agreed amount of insurance shown on the policy, and paid in the event of total loss regardless of the actual value of the property.

Statement Blank. See Convention Blank.

Statement of Policy Information. For universal life policies, this document is prepared at the end of each year giving complete information on all transactions affecting the policy, such as premium paid, current death benefit, interest credited, loans outstanding, monthly charges and cash surrender value.

Statement of Values. Sometimes property is written using a blanket rate and one single limit of liability applying to all locations. In order to determine the blanket or average rate, a rating bureau or company requires an insured to submit a declaration of the amounts of value at each separate location on this form.

Statewide Average Weekly Wage (SAWW). A statistical computation that is periodically updated and is used to determine compensation benefit amounts. Many benefits are set forth as a percentage of the SAWW.

Statute of Fraud. A statute stating that certain contracts must be in writing in order to be enforceable (e.g., any contract involving the sale of real estate).

Statute of Limitations. The time limit set by law during which a person must bring legal action on a case.

Statutory Accounting Principals (SAP). Principals required by statute which must be followed by an insurance company when submitting its financial statement to the state insurance department. Such principles differ from generally accepted accounting principles (GAAP) in some important respects. For one thing, SAP requires that expenses must be recorded immediately and cannot be deferred to track with premiums as they are earned and taken into revenue.

Statutory Earnings (or Losses). Earnings or losses shown on the NAIC convention blank, in contrast to earnings or losses that are shown if generally accepted accounting procedure statements are used.

Statutory Reserve. A reserve, either specific or general, required by law.

Statutory. Required by or having to do with law or statute.

Step-Rate Premium. Premium is increased at times specified in the policy, based on a predetermined attained age, or number of policy years in force.

Stock. Merchandise held in storage or for sale, raw materials and in-process or finished goods, including supplies used in their packing or shipping, as distinguished from furniture, fixtures or equipment.

Stock Bonus Plan. A profit sharing plan whereby contributions to the plan and benefits derived from the plan are in the form of the company's stock.

Stock Insurer. An incorporated insurer with capital contributed by stockholders, to whom the earnings are distributed as dividends on their shares. Contrast with Mutual Insurer.

Stock Option Plan. Surviving stockholders have the option to purchase or not purchase the shares of a deceased stockholder.

Stock Purchase Agreement. A formal buy-sell agreement whereby each stockholder is bound by the agreement to purchase the shares of a deceased stockholder and the heirs are obligated to sell.

Stock Redemption Agreement. A formal buy-sell agreement whereby the corporation is bound by the agreement to purchase the shares of a deceased stockholder and the heirs are obligated to sell.

Stop Loss. A provision designed to cut off an insurer's losses at a given point. In effect, a stop loss agreement guarantees the loss ratio of the insurer.

Stop Loss Insurance. Reinsurance that is taken out by a health plan or self-funded employer plan. The plan is written to cover excess losses over a specified amount either on a specific or individual basis, or on a total basis for the plan over a period of time such as one year.

Stop Loss Reinsurance. (1) See Aggregate Excess of Loss Reinsurance. (2) A form of reinsurance where the reinsurer reinsures the ceding insurer for an amount by which the latter's incurred losses in a calendar year for a specified class of business exceed a specified loss ratio.

Storekeepers Burglary and Robbery Insurance. A package crime policy for a storekeeper that provides coverage on seven different crime hazards. A specific amount of coverage is purchased and the limits apply separately to each of the coverages. There is very little flexibility in that the insured must buy the package. See also Broad Form Storekeepers Insurance.

Storekeepers Liability Policy. A single limit package policy covering bodily injury and property damage liability claims in the operation of the storekeeper's business. It includes limited coverage on contractual and products liability.

Straight Life Income Option. An option for paying the proceeds of a life insurance policy to beneficiaries that continues to pay for as long as the beneficiary lives, but all obligations of the insurance company end as soon as that person dies.

Straight Life Policy. A whole life policy that stretches the premium payments over the insured's lifetime (to age 100). Also known as continuous premium whole life. See Ordinary Life Policy.

Stranded. A ship that has run aground.

Strict Liability. Usually used when referring to products coverage. The liability that manufacturers and merchandisers may be subject to for defective products sold by them, regardless of fault or negligence. A claimant must prove that the product is defective and therefore unreasonably dangerous. See also Absolute Liability.

Strike-Through Clause. A clause providing that, in the event of the insolvency of a ceding insurer, the reinsurer continues to be liable for its share of losses, which will then be payable directly to the insured rather than to the liquidator of the insolvent ceding insurer. See also Insolvency Clause.

Structured Settlements. The amount of the scheduled installment payments on the policy. This is based on the adjusted age of the payee when benefit payments begin and the remaining life expectancy (calculated by using mortality tables). The younger a person is when benefits begin, the smaller the amount paid—because the insurance company expects to continue paying longer.

Sub-Agents. Agents who report to other agents or general agents, and not directly to the company.

Sub-Broker. An intermediary from whom another intermediary obtains reinsurance business to be placed.

Subchapter S Corporation. A corporate form of business in which all profits and losses are shared by the stockholders and thus the corporation is taxed on an individual basis as opposed to corporate taxation.

Subject Premium (Base Premium, Premium Base or Underlying Premium). A ceding company's premium to which the reinsurance premium rate (factor) is applied to produce the reinsurance premium. In other words, the reinsurance premium is a percentage of the ceding company's premium.

Sublimit. Any limit of insurance which exists within another limit (e.g., special classes of property may be subject to a specified dollar limit per occurrence, even though the policy has a higher overall limit; a health insurance policy may limit certain benefits to fixed dollar amounts or maximum amounts per day, even though the overall coverage limit is higher).

Submitted Business. Applications for insurance submitted to an insurer but not yet acted upon.

Subordination. Putting below in importance. Sometimes the creditors of a contractor subordinate their interests in the obligations owed them until a construction project is completed. This increases the contractor's working capital.

Subrogation. (1) The right of a surety, in its name or in the name of the obligee under a bond, to pursue a course of action against the principal or any other party liable for a loss paid by the surety. (2) The right of one who has taken over another's loss to also take over the other person's right to pursue remedies against a third party. It is never used in life insurance and seldom in health.

Subrogation Clause. A clause giving an insurer the right to pursue any course of action, in its own name or the name of a policyowner, against a third party who is liable for a loss that has been paid by the insurer. This ensures that an insured does not

make any profit from his or her insurance. It prevents collecting from both the insurer and a third
party. It is never part of a life insurance policy.

Subrogation Release. A release taken by an insurer upon indemnifying an insured. It contains a
provision that says the insurer will be subrogated
to the rights of recovery that the insured has against
any person responsible for the loss.

Subrogation Waiver. A waiver by the named insured giving up any right of recovery against another party. Normally a policy requires that subrogation (recovery) rights be preserved. In commercial property insurance, a written waiver of subrogation rights is permitted if it is executed before
the loss occurs.

Subscriber. A person or organization who pays the
premiums, or a person whose employment makes him
or her eligible for membership in the plan.

Subscriber Contract. An agreement that describes
the individual's benefits under a health care policy.

Subscription Policy. A policy where two or more
insurers may subscribe, indicating in the policy the
share of the risk to be borne by each insurer.

Subsidence. Movement of the land on which property is situated. A structure built on a hillside may
slide down the hill after heavy rains. This is different from earthquake damage.

Substandard Risk. (1) A risk not measuring up to underwriting standards. It may still be written but usually at a surcharged premium. (2) See Impaired Risk.

Sue and Labor Clause. A provision permitting and requiring an insured to take all practical measures to protect any salvage, without prejudicing any right to claim against the insurer. The intent of this clause is to ensure that the insured does not fail to use proper care to preserve the property. One effect of it is that in case of a total loss an insurer may pay the loss plus the cost of salvage.

Summary Annual Report. A summary of a qualified plan's operation that is required to be given to each participant annually.

Summary Plan Description. A recap or summary of the benefits provided under the plan. It is used most often with employees covered by self-funded plans.

Superbill. A form that specifically lists all of the services provided by the physician. It cannot be used in place of the standard AMA form.

Superintendent of Insurance. The title of the head of a state or provincial insurance department used in some jurisdictions.

Superseded Suretyship Rider. An endorsement or provision on a new bond under which the new bonding company assumes liability for claims that cannot be recovered from the prior bond because its discovery period has ended. The discovery period of a bond is normally one year, during which it will cover any loss which occurred during the term of the bond.

Supplemental Actuarial Value. A variation of actuarial present value. The value of all benefits expected to be paid under a plan, reduced by the present value of future adjustments (including any contributions by plan participants). See Actuarial Present Value.

Supplemental Contract. A rider usually relating to the method of settlement of the proceeds of a life insurance policy.

Supplemental Dental Plan. See Dental Plan, Supplemental.

Supplemental Extended Reporting Period. An optional "maxi tail" or "full tail" that extends for an unlimited period of time after expiration of a "claims-made" liability policy, and covers claims made after the policy period.

Supplemental Medical Insurance (SMI). Part B of Medicare is a voluntary program that generally covers physician's services and various outpatient services. A premium is charged for electing Part B coverage.

Supplemental Services. Additional services over and above the basic coverage of a health plan.

Supplementary Payments. A provision in most liability policies under which the insurer agrees to pay defense costs, premiums on various bonds, interest accruing after a judgment and other reasonable expenses in addition to the limit of liability.

Surety Association of America (SAA). An association of bonding companies that establishes rules and regulations, rates and rating plans and forms and collects information on rating that is supplied to members.

Surety. One who guarantees the performance or faithfulness of another. A surety can be either a corporation or an individual, but it is usually an insurance company.

Surety Bond. A bond guaranteeing that a principal will carry out the obligation for which he is bonded. A surety bond is most often issued to a contractor, a person seeking a license or permit or someone involved in a court case.

Surety Bond Guarantee Program. A federal Small Business Administration (SBA) program for minority contractors. The SBA agrees to back the surety company in the event of loss under a construction contract bond.

Suretyship. The means by which one person or entity, the surety, guarantees another entity, the obligee, that a third entity, the principal, will or will not do something. It differs from insurance by being a three-party contract, but most sureties today are insurers.

Surgical Insurance Benefits. Health insurance against loss due to surgical expenses.

Surgical Schedule. Part of a basic medical expense plan which itemizes various surgical procedures and the monetary benefit allocated to each procedure. See Schedule.

Surgi-Center. A separate facility (from a hospital) that provides outpatient surgical services.

Surplus. (1) A reinsurer's portion of a risk; that part which remains after deducting the retention established by the ceding company. (2) The amount by which assets exceed liabilities.

Surplus Lines. A risk or a part of a risk for which there is no market available through the original broker or agent in its jurisdiction. Therefore, it is placed with nonadmitted insurers on an unregulated basis, in accordance with the surplus or excess lines provisions of the state law.

Surplus Reinsurance. (1) Pro rata reinsurance wherein the reinsurer accepts that part of each risk written in excess of a specified retention. The part reinsured is usually a multiple of the retention. See also Lines. (2) The amount of any risk that exceeds the net line retained by the ceding company. The reinsurer receives premiums and contributes to the payment of losses in proportion to its share of the risk.

Surplus Release. The use of admitted reinsurance on a portfolio basis to offset extraordinary drains on policyholder's surplus. See also Portfolio Reinsurance.

Surplus Share. See Surplus Reinsurance.

Surplus to Policyholders. See Policyholder's Surplus.

Surrender. To give up a whole life policy. The insurer pays the insured the cash value that the policy has built up if it is surrendered.

Surrender Value. See Cash Surrender Value.

Survivor. The beneficiary of an annuity contract, i.e., the annuitant's survivor.

Survivorship Annuity. See Reversionary Annuity.

Survivorship Benefits. Funds available to pay an annuitant who survives longer than statistically expected from premiums paid by annuitants who died before they had collected amounts equal to their contributions.

Suspension of Insurance Endorsement. An endorsement normally issued after a policy is written that temporarily stops coverage for a vehicle that is not in use. This endorsement states that the premium will be refunded if coverage is suspended for at least 30 consecutive days. But it does not indicate how long the insurance is to be suspended.

Swap Maternity. A provision granting immediate maternity coverage in a group health plan but terminating coverage on pregnancies in progress upon termination of the plan. "Swap" means providing the coverage at the beginning of the policy where it is not usually provided, but not providing it after the end of the policy where it usually is provided.

Switch Maternity. A provision for group health maternity coverage on female employees only when their husbands are included in the plan as dependents.

Symbol. A number assigned by the insurance company to represent the cost of a car when new. Both the symbol and model year (or age) of covered autos are used to determine the policy premium.

Symbol Group. A rating code developed by adjusting a vehicle's price upward or downward to reflect the physical damage loss experience for that particular model. Two automobiles of different makes and models might have the same market value, but be assigned to different symbol groups if one tends to suffer greater damage in an equal crash, or if it is more expensive to repair equal damage in one model because of the cost of individual parts. The rating symbol group code is based on the first eight characters of a vehicle's VIN.

Syndicate. A group of insurers or underwriters who join to insure property that may be of such total value or high hazard that it can be covered more safely or efficiently on a cooperative basis. See also Pool.

T

24-Hour Care Coverage. A health insurance concept that blends occupational and nonoccupational benefits to provide round-the-clock coverage for injuries or diseases whether or not they are work-related.

"3-D" Policy. See Dishonesty, Disappearance and Destruction Policy.

1035 Exchange. A nontaxable exchange of life insurance policies and annuities as provided under Section 1035(a) of the Internal Revenue Code.

Tabular. Of or pertaining to a table. Tabular cost is the cost of mortality, morbidity or other claims, according to the valuation tables and assumptions used by the insurer.

Tabular Plan. A retrospective rating plan, which uses tables to furnish the various values for the rating formula.

Tail. This term describes both the exposure that exists after expiration of a policy and the coverage that may be purchased to cover that exposure. On "occurrence" forms, a claims tail may extend for years after policy expiration, and the losses may be covered. On "claims made" forms, tail coverage may be purchased to extend the period for reporting covered claims beyond the policy period. See Mini, Midi and Maxi Tail.

Tangible Damages. A medical bill or the cost to repair a damaged vehicle. If one driver is liable for an accident, then the other party may be entitled to compensation for injuries or damage or both.

Target Benefit Plan. A qualified plan that is a combination of a defined benefit and defined contribution plan whereby an employer is required to fund a specific targeted benefit for plan participants. Target benefit plans impose defined contribution limitations for plan funding.

Target Risk. (1) Certain high-value bridges, tunnels, and fine art collections that are excluded from an automatic reinsurance contract to permit specific handling of the capacity problem and to release the reinsurer from the potential heavy accumulation of liability on any one risk. (2) A large, hazardous risk on which insurance is difficult to place. (3) A large, attractive risk that is considered a target for competing insurance companies.

Tariff Rate. A specialized insurance rate established by a rating organization, which comes from the tables, schedules and rules found in the tariff of rates.

Tax Basis. Money that has yet to be taxed, usually part of a qualified plan benefit or distribution.

Tax Equity and Fiscal Responsibility Act. A federal law intended to prevent group term life insurance plans from discriminating in favor of key employees, and which amends the Social Security Act to make Medicare secondary to group health plans.

Tax Factor (or Tax Multiplier). A factor applied in retrospective rating to an insurance premium in order to increase it to cover state premium taxes.

Tax Sheltered Annuity (TSA). An annuity program under which contributions reduce the taxable income of participating employees, and the benefits are not taxable until distributed.

Taxable Estate. This equals the adjusted gross estate less the marital deduction property and any charitable deductions.

Tax-Free Rollover. The tax-free transfer of assets from one qualified retirement plan to an IRA or annuity, and vice versa.

TDB. See Temporary Disability Benefits.

Teachers Insurance and Annuity Association. An organization selling life and health insurance and annuities to college and university staff members.

TEFRA. See Tax Equity and Fiscal Responsibility Act.

Temporary Agent. A person licensed to act as an agent for a brief period of time (usually 90 days) without taking a written examination. Temporary licenses are commonly granted to allow someone to continue the business of an agent who has died, become disabled or entered active military service.

Temporary Disability Benefits (TDB). Legislated benefits payable to employees for nonoccupational disabilities under TDB laws in certain states. See also Disability Benefits Law.

Temporary Living Allowance. Coverage for extraordinary expenses that occur when an insured has been displaced from home. Includes boarding a pet in a kennel, renting furniture—or paying to store furniture that survived a loss—and eating at restaurants while staying in a hotel or motel without kitchen facilities.

Temporary Partial Disability. A condition where an injured party's capacity is impaired for a time, but he is able to continue working at reduced efficiency and is expected to fully recover.

Temporary Total Disability. A condition where an injured party is unable to work while recovering from injury, but is expected to recover.

Ten Day Free Look. A notice, placed prominently on the face page of the policy, advising the insured of his or her right to examine a health policy, and if dissatisfied, return the policy within 10 days for a full refund of premium and no further obligation.

Ten Year Funding. Primarily for older individuals, this type of funding requires that premiums be payable for 10 years even though retirement is permitted within 10 years.

Tenancies for Years. Ownership of real property for a specific period of time.

Tenants Improvements and Betterments. Property affixed to an owner's building by the lessee or tenant that may not be legally removed at the end of the rental period.

Tenants in Common. Where two or more persons have undivided ownership and possession of real property, but (unlike joint tenancy) each owner may transfer or dispose of their share of ownership. Contrast with Fee Simple and Joint Tenancy.

Tenants Policy. A homeowners policy specifically designed for people who rent; often called an HO-4 policy.

Term. The period of time for which a policy or bond is issued.

Term Insurance. A life insurance policy that provides protection only for a specified period of time. A common policy period would be one year, five years, 10 years, or until the insured reaches age 65 or 70. It does not build up any of the nonforfeiture values associated with whole life policies. See also Decreasing Term Insurance, Increasing Term Insurance and Term Insurance. Contrast with Whole Life Insurance.

Term Rule. The provision in a rating manual that states the periods for which coverages run, and discounts, if any, that apply to the rates or premiums of policies issued for more than one year.

Terminal Funding. A form of retirement funding by which an employer sets aside a single sum of money when the participant retires. This sum will fund the individual's retirement benefit.

Terminally Ill. A term referring to a person who will normally die within six months of a specific illness or sickness. Often refers to the terminally ill requirement for hospice care.

Terminal Reserve. A percentage of a reinsurance contract set aside to protect the reinsurer in case of an immediate claim.

Termination. (1) The time the coverage under an insurance policy ends, either because its term has expired or because it has been canceled by either party. (2) The cessation of premium paying for a whole life or endowment policy before the agreed upon time. This ends the coverage, and the insured receives one of the nonforfeiture values. The cessation of a policy that does not or has not yet developed a cash value is termed a "lapse."

Territorial Limitation. See Geographical Limitation.

Territorial Rating. In most states, territorial rating of automobile risks is permitted and insurance companies consider the neighborhood in which you live. This means the primary rating factor also depends on the territory where the vehicle is parked.

Tertiary Beneficiary. A beneficiary designated as third in line to receive proceeds or benefits if the primary and secondary beneficiaries do not survive.

Tertiary Care. Services provided by such providers as thoracic surgeons, intensive care units, neurosurgeons, etc.

Testamentary Capacity. The ability to form a legally valid will.

Testamentary Transfer. Transfer of the assets of an estate according to the provisions of the deceased person's last will and testament. Contrast with Inter Vivos Transfer.

Testamentary Trust. A trust created after the grantor's death, according to the provisions of the deceased person's last will and testament. Contrast with Inter Vivos Trust.

Testing Exclusion. In boiler and machinery insurance, a provision that excludes coverage for any object while it is being tested.

Theatrical Floater. An inland marine form used to cover theatrical properties, such as costumes and scenery.

Theft. The act of stealing, including larceny, burglary and robbery. Does not include coverage for theft of materials or supplies to be used for construction of a dwelling. Theft by a member of the insured's household is not covered nor is property stolen from a room rented out.

Theft, Disappearance and Destruction Coverage Form. A commercial crime coverage form covering money and securities against the causes of loss described in its title.

Theory of Probability. The mathematical principle upon which insurance is based. See also Degree of Risk, Law for Large Numbers, Odds and Probability.

Therapeutic Alternatives. Alternate drug products that may be different in chemical content, but provide the same effect when administered to patients.

Therapeutic Equivalence. Different drugs that control a symptom or illness exactly the same as other drugs used to control that illness.

Third Party Administration (TPA). Accounting and actuarial services as well as filing of various reports required by the IRS and the Department of Labor provided by organizations that administer qualified plans.

Third Party Administrator (TPA). A firm that provides administrative services for employers and other associations having group insurance policies. The TPA is also involved with certifying eligibility, preparing reports required by the state and processing claims.

Third Party Beneficiary. A person who is not a party to a contract but who has legally enforceable rights under the contract. It might be a life insurance beneficiary or a mortgagee.

Third Party Insurance. A term for liability insurance. Liability always involves a third party, the one who has suffered a loss, in addition to the insurer and the insured. See also Liability Insurance.

Third-Party Payor. Any organization such as Blue Cross/Blue Shield, Medicare, Medicaid or other commercial insurance company that is the payor for coverages provided by a health plan.

Three-Fourths Value Clause. A clause stating that the maximum loss the insurer will pay is three-fourths of the actual cash value of the property.

Threshold Level. The point at which the insured may bring tort action under a modified No-Fault Auto Plan. Many of these plans prohibit tort action for pain and suffering unless medical bills exceed some figure, like $1,000, or disfigurement or death occurs.

Thrift Plan. Any retirement plan in which an employee savings feature is added.

Ticket Policy. See Transportation Ticket Policy.

Ticket Reinsurance. A note attached to a daily report setting forth the details of any reinsurance that has been effected.

Time Element Insurance. Insurance that covers expenses consequent to damage or destruction by an insured peril. The amount paid depends on the length of time when expenses accumulate (e.g., business interruption insurance pays for the loss of earnings during the time it takes to repair the property).

Time Limit on Certain Defenses. One of the uniform individual accident and sickness provisions required by state law to be included in every individual health policy. It sets a limit on the number of years after a policy has been in force that an insurer can use as a defense against a claim the fact that a physical condition of the insured existed before the policy was issued, but was not declared at that time.

Time Limits. The limits of time within which notice of a claim and proof of a loss must be submitted.

Time of Payment of Claims. A health insurance provision that requires that claims be paid immediately upon receipt of proofs of loss. Some states specify a number of days in place of the word "immediately."

TIRB. Transportation Insurance Rating Bureau. See Transportation Insurance.

Title Insurance. Insurance that indemnifies the owner of real estate in the event that his clear ownership of property is challenged by the discovery of faults in the title. Title insurance is not the same as—or even part of—homeowners insurance. It is a separate coverage designed especially for disputes that may occur over the legal status of the land bought along with a house.

Title XIX Benefits. See Medicaid.

Tobacco Sales Warehouses Coverage Form. A commercial property coverage form used to insure tobacco warehouse operations.

Tort. A private wrong, independent of contract and committed against an individual, which gives rise to a legal liability and is adjudicated in a civil court. A tort can be either intentional or unintentional, but it is mainly against liability for unintentional torts that one buys liability insurance.

Tort Liability. Liability imposed by law in the absence of any contract or agreement.

Tortfeasor. A person who has committed a tort.

Total Disability. Injury or illness that prevents the insured from performing the duties of any occupation for remuneration or profit.

Total Loss. A loss of sufficient size such that there is nothing left of value. The complete destruction of the property. The term is also used to mean a loss requiring the maximum amount a policy will pay. Compare with Partial Loss.

Total Policy Premium. The final line of the Declarations Page includes space for entering this value, which is the total amount the insured pays for all coverages for which limits and premiums are shown and for any additional endorsements that are attached.

Towing and Labor Costs. Coverage for road service, such as jump-starting your car, changing a flat tire and towing.

Townhouse. A group of usually six buildings placed side by side with one contiguous wall between each unit. Units usually have at least two levels and include access to land that may be divided by privacy fences. Each unit has a private entrance. Commonly bought as a fee simple property or condominium.

TPA. See Third Party Administrator.

Trailer Interchange Agreement. An arrangement whereby one trucker transfers a trailer containing a shipment to a second trucker for continued transportation.

Trailer Interchange Coverage. Coverage for the legal liability of truckers for loss or damage to non-owned trailers and equipment that are in the insured's possession under a written trailer interchange agreement.

Trans Union. One of three major credit report companies.

Transacting Insurance. The solicitation, inducement and preliminary negotiations affecting a contract of insurance and the subsequent carrying on of business pertaining to it.

Transfer of Risk. Shifting all or part of a risk to another party. Insurance is the most common method of risk transfer, but other devices, such as hold harmless agreements, also transfer risk. One of the four major risk management techniques. See **Risk Management**.

Transit Policy. A policy that provides coverage for loss to property while in transport.

Transition Program. In commercial liability insurance, rules designed to offset wide differences in premiums for mercantile risks because of a change in the rating base from area to gross sales. It limits maximum and minimum premium changes resulting solely from the change in the rating base.

Transplant and Cosmetic Surgery Benefit. This provides total disability benefits for elective medical procedures, such as donating an organ.

Transportation Expenses. Automobile coverage for transportation expenses incurred by the named insured only in the event of theft of an entire covered auto. Coverage begins after a 48-hour waiting period and is subject to a daily limit and maximum dollar limit, and it applies only when the insured has physical damage coverage for theft.

Transportation Insurance. Usually an open form policy that covers the insured's property in the course of transportation. It can include all modes of transportation, including ocean vessels.

Transportation Ticket Policy. An accidental death and dismemberment and disability benefit policy issued with a common carrier ticket and limited to the risks of travel and the duration of the trip for which the ticket has been purchased.

Traumatic Injury. An injury to a person's physical body caused by an outside source, as distinct from physical disability caused by sickness or disease.

Travel Accident Insurance. A form of health insurance limiting coverage to accidents occurring while the insured is traveling.

Treatment Facility. Any facility, either residential or nonresidential, authorized to provide treatment for mental illness or substance abuse.

Treaty Reinsurance. A contract of automatic reinsurance setting forth the conditions for reinsuring a class or classes of business. Contrast with Facultative Reinsurance.

Trend Factor. The factor applied to rates that allows for such changes as increased cost of medical providers, the cost of new and expensive medical technology, etc.

Trespasser. An individual who enters another person's property without any legal right to do so. The only duty that the owner of the property owes a trespasser is not to intentionally harm or set a trap for him or her.

Triage. A method of ranking sick or injured people according to the severity of their sickness or injury in order to ensure that medical and nursing staff facilities are used most efficiently.

Trial Work Period. An incentive for a disabled worker under Social Security to attempt a return to work. The individual may work nine months in a five-year period without loss of Social Security disability income benefits. If a disabled worker refuses rehabilitation without a just reason, benefits may cease.

Trigger. See Coverage Trigger.

Trip Transit Insurance. Coverage for goods in transit for a specified trip and by a specified mode of transportation.

Triple Indemnity. See Multiple Indemnity.

Triple Option. A plan where employees have their choice among different types of providers such as

HMO, PPO or basic indemnity plan. Usually, their choice depends on how much they want to pay for the coverage.

Triple Protection. Life insurance that combines whole life and twice as much term insurance. The term portion applies until a stated date. This policy might be used to provide maximum protection to an individual at an earlier age when the need for insurance is greater but the ability to pay is less.

Truckers Coverage Form. A commercial automobile insurance coverage form used to insure truckers who are engaged in the business of transporting goods for others.

Truckers Liability. See Motor Cargo Policy-Carriers Form and Interstate Commerce Commission Endorsement.

True Group Insurance. Group insurance issued under a master contract with certificates of insurance that are not policy contracts issued to persons included in the group. This would be in contrast to franchise or wholesale "group" insurance, under which a covered person is issued an individual policy contract.

Trust. A legal arrangement whereby property is held and managed by a trustee for the benefit of beneficiaries.

Trust Agreement. (1) A supplemental agreement attached to and made a part of a life insurance policy setting forth the manner in which the proceeds are to be paid, in lieu of having them paid in a lump sum or under one of the other installment settlement options in the policy itself. (2) An agreement or instrument under which a corpus (fund/property) is given over to the management of the trustee named in a trust instrument for the benefit of the beneficiaries of the trust. (3) A written agreement between two parties—the employer and the trustee —setting forth the provisions of a pension plan.

Trust and Commission Clause. A provision found in some property, ocean marine and inland marine policies enabling a person to insure his interest in the property of another.

Trust Fund Plans. A type of qualified plan in which contributions are made to a plan trustee or a corporate trustee. The trustee in turn provides retirement benefits for plan participants.

Trustee. A person appointed to manage the property of another.

Trustees. Persons who, by entering into trust agreement with the employer, assume the impartial supervision of a retirement plan. They may be employees, a trust company or outside individuals.

"T" Tables. The factors used to properly fund retirement benefits for employees of varying types of industries incorporating the ideas of interest, mortality and turnover.

Tuition Fees Insurance. An adaptation of business interruption coverage. It protects a school against the indirect loss of tuition fees that may result from a fire or other peril covered by the policy that closes the school.

Turnkey Insurance. Insurance coverage that includes General Liability for Contractors and Architects Errors and Omissions.

Turnover. The number of persons hired within a stated period to replace those leaving or dropped; also, the ratio of this number to the average workforce maintained. In pension plans, turnover refers to the ratio of participants who leave employment through quits, discharges, etc. to the total of participants at any age or length of service.

Twisting. Misrepresenting a policy or making incomplete comparisons of policies to induce a policyowner to change or replace an existing policy.

U&O. See Use and Occupancy Insurance.

UAB. Underwriters Adjustment Bureau.

UAC. Underwriters Adjusting Company.

UCD. See Unemployment Compensation Disability Insurance.

UJF. See Unsatisfied Judgment Fund.

UL. See Underwriters Laboratories, Inc.

Ultimate Net Loss. The total sum that the insured or any company as its insurer, or both, become legally obligated to pay either through adjudication or compromise, including among others, legal, medical and investigative costs.

Umbrella Liability Policy. A coverage affording high-limit coverage in excess of the limits of the primary policies as well as additional liability coverages. These additional coverages are usually subject to a substantial self-insured retention. The umbrella policy pays up to a predetermined limit (usually $1 million) for liability claims made against you or your family.

Umbrella Policy. A policy that provides high limits of coverage to protect against catastrophic losses, and provides broader coverage than underlying policies.

Umpire. For property coverage, if a company and a claimant fail to agree on the amount of loss, each may appoint an appraiser, and these in turn select an umpire. A decision by any two of the three is binding.

Unallocated Benefit. A benefit providing reimbursement of expenses up to a maximum but without any schedule of benefits as such.

Unallocated Claim (or Loss) Expense. Expenses of loss adjustment that cannot be charged specifically to any claim. Examples are claim department salaries and office overhead.

Unallocated Funds. Plan contributions are made or pooled for the benefit of all plan participants collectively.

Unauthorized Insurer. See Nonadmitted Insurer.

Underground Property Damage. Refers to damage to underground property, such as wires, conduits or pipes, sewers, etc., beneath the surface of the ground caused by the use of mechanical equipment for the purpose of grading land, paving, excavating, drilling, burrowing, filling, backfilling or pile driving.

Underinsurance. A condition in which not enough insurance is carried to cover the insurable value.

Underinsured Motorists Coverage. A coverage in an automobile insurance policy under which the insurer pays damages up to specified limits for bodily injury damages, if the limits of liability under the liable motorist's policy are exhausted and he cannot pay the full amount for which he is liable. See also Uninsured Motorist Coverage.

Underlying. The amount of insurance or reinsurance on a risk that attaches before the next higher excess layer of insurance or reinsurance attaches.

Underlying Insurance (also Underlying Policy). Any insurance policy that provides the initial or primary liability insurance covering one or more of the types of liability listed in the deductible section of the Declarations Page. Your auto policy and homeowners policy are underlying policies to your umbrella policy.

Underlying Policy. See Underlying Insurance.

Underlying Premium. See Subject Premium.

Underwriter. A technician trained in evaluating risks and determining rates and coverages for them.

Underwriters Laboratories, Inc. (UL). A testing laboratory for manufactured items to determine their safety.

Underwriting. The process of selecting risks and classifying them according to their degrees of insurability so that the appropriate rates may be assigned. The process also includes rejection of those risks that do not qualify.

Underwriting Profit (or Loss). (1) The profit or loss realized from insurance operations, as contrasted with that realized from investments. (2) The excess of premiums over losses and expenses (profit) or the excesses of losses over premiums (loss).

Unearned Income. Rents, royalties, interest, dividends, etc. paid regardless of an insured's disability or work status. If an insured has substantial amounts of unearned income, the insurance company may reduce the benefit amount it sells.

Unearned Premium. That portion of the written premium applicable to the unexpired or unused part of the period for which the premium has been paid. Thus, in the case of an annual premium, at the end of the first month of the premium period, eleven-twelfths of the premium is unearned.

Unearned Premium Reserve. The amount shown in the insurance company's balance sheet that represents the approximate total of the premiums that have not yet been earned as of a specific point in time. See also Unearned Premium.

Unearned Reinsurance Premium. That part of the reinsurance premium applicable to the unexpired portion of the policy reinsured.

Unemployment Compensation Disability Insurance (UCD). Health insurance that covers off-the-job accidents and sickness. It does not cover disability resulting from an injury or sickness covered by workers' compensation insurance. See also Disability Benefits Law.

Unemployment Insurance. Insurance against loss of income due to unemployment. It is funded by payroll taxes and subject to control by both the federal and state governments. Individuals who are willing and able to work qualify for this insurance by working at a job in an eligible classification, earning a minimum amount of money and being subject to involuntary unemployment.

Unfair Claim Settlement Practices Law. State laws designed to protect the consumer against unfair practices in the reporting, investigation, payment and final resolution of insurance claims.

Unfair Trade Practices Law. State laws designed to protect the consumer against misleading, deceptive, monopolistic or otherwise unfair practices in the business of insurance.

Unfunded Plan. Any plan that follows a "pay-as-you-go" method. See Funding, Disbursement.

Unfunded Supplemental Actuarial Value. The excess of the Supplemental Actuarial Value over the Actuarial Asset Value.

Unified Tax Credit. A standard credit that can be used to offset gift and federal estate tax liabilities.

Uniform Billing Code of 1992 (UB-92). This code is a federal directive, stating how a hospital must provide its patients with bills, itemizing all services included and billed on each invoice.

Uniform Forms. Policy documents where the wording has been agreed upon by most companies and standardized. They are printed and distributed by rating bureaus and well-known establishments.

Uniform Premium. A rating system that is used to calculate premiums for all insureds with no distinctions as to age, sex or occupation.

Uniform Provisions. (1) A set of provisions required by state law in life insurance policies. (2) A set of provisions regarding the operating conditions of individual health policies developed in a model law recommended by the National Association of Insurance Commissioners.

Uniform Simultaneous Death Act. State law that states that if the insured and beneficiary die in the same accident and it cannot be determined who died first, the beneficiary is assumed to have died first, and all proceeds then pass to the insured's contingent beneficiary.

Unilateral Contract. A contract such as an insurance policy in which only one party to the contract, the insurer, makes any enforceable promise. The insured does not make a promise but pays a premium, which constitutes the insured's part of the consideration.

Uninsured Motorist Coverage (UM). A coverage in an automobile insurance policy under which the insurer pays damages to the insured for which another motorist is liable if that motorist has no liability insurance. This coverage usually applies to bodily injury damages only. Injuries to the insured caused by a hit-and-run driver are also covered.

Uninsured Plan. Any pension plan that is not maintained or handled through insurance products.

Unintentional Torts. The basis for these torts is usually negligence. In order for negligence to exist, the following must be present: 1) duty to act; 2) breach of the duty to act; and 3) occurrence of injury or damage.

Unit Benefit Plan. A type of pension plan providing retirement benefits as a definite amount or percentage of earnings for each year of service with the employer. If a unit of annuity is purchased each year to fund the ultimate benefit, this may also be referred to as a unit-purchase type of plan.

Unit Investment Trust (UIT). An investment company that invests on behalf of investors in a portfolio of securities such as stocks and bonds. The trust does not have a management function; it merely holds the assets.

United States Aircraft Insurance Group. A group of insurers providing coverage for all forms of aviation insurance.

United States Government Life Insurance (USGLI). Life insurance issued to members of the armed forces during World War I until the end of World War II.

Universal 24-hour Coverage. A package that provides the most complete combination of 24-hour occupational and non-occupational coverage. It includes medical and disability coverage for both accidents and diseases on a 24-hour basis. See 24-hour Coverage.

Universal Life. A combination flexible premium, adjustable life insurance policy. The premium payer may select the amount of premium he or she can pay and the policy benefits are those which the premium will purchase. Or, the premium payer may change the amount of insurance and pay premium accordingly. Many believe this is the only true solution to the "buy term invest the difference" problem.

Unlevel Commission System. A system of commissions under which the first year commission is a higher percentage of the premium than are renewal commissions.

Unoccupied. Property that may be furnished or have furnishings but is not occupied. The standard fire policy prohibits unoccupancy beyond a specified period of time. Contrast with Vacant.

Unpaid Premium Provision. A provision in a health insurance policy that allows deduction of unpaid premiums from claims payments.

Unqualified Plan. Any plan that does not meet the qualifications for special tax advantages as set forth in the Code. Such a plan provides only those deductions that are allowed in the course of normal business operation.

Unreported Claims. A reserve, based on estimates, to set up claims that have occurred but have not yet been reported to the insurer as of the time when either the policy has expired or the insurer is preparing its annual statement. See also IBNR.

Unsatisfied Judgment Fund (UJF). Several states have laws that provide for reimbursement to a person injured in an automobile accident who has been unable to collect from the person responsible.

Unscheduled Personal Property. Property that is not listed prior to a loss. See Scheduled Personal Property.

Unscheduled Premium Payments. In universal life insurance, the policyowner can pay extra premiums in addition to the scheduled premium payment amount. These payments can be made at any time, but are subject to a minimum amount.

Up-Front Payments. These include temporary living costs and other incidental costs paid in advance, which are voluntary to the insurance company. A company can require an insured to incur the expenses first and be reimbursed later.

Upside-Down Life Insurance. See Annuities.

Urban Property Protection and Reinsurance Act. To remedy the growing urban problem, Congress created a federal riot reinsurance program. This Act made riot reinsurance available through the National Insurance Development Fund, which is operated under the Department of Housing and Urban Development (HUD). Residents of high-crime areas who have the required security devices also may qualify for insurance with the Federal Crime Insurance Program. The policy covers only losses due to burglary or robbery.

USAIG. United States Aircraft Insurance Group.

Use and Occupancy Insurance (U&O). Also known as business interruption insurance or business income coverage. U&O may refer to loss of earnings in boiler and machinery insurance, or it may appear in contracts that promise to pay on a valued basis, or fixed amount, for each day the insured is deprived of the use or occupancy of described property because of damage caused by a peril insured against.

U.S. Longshore and Harbor Workers' Compensation Act. This Act protects workers who load, unload, build or repair ships.

USGLI. See United States Government Life Insurance.

Usual, Customary and Reasonable (UCR). See Reasonable and Customary.

Utilization. This refers to how much a covered group uses a particular health plan or program.

Utilization and Review Committee. A committee composed of medical personnel to monitor the health care services and supplies provided to Medicare patients.

Utilization Management. This procedure or process utilizes a review coordinator to evaluate the necessity and appropriateness of various health care services.

Utilization Review. A cost-control mechanism by which the appropriateness, necessity and quality of health care is monitored by both insurers and employers.

Utmost Good Faith. Acting in fairness and equity with a sincere belief that the act is not unlawful or harmful to others. Insurance contracts require that each party is entitled to rely upon the representations of the other without attempts to conceal or deceive.

V

V&MM or VMM. See Vandalism and Malicious Mischief.

Vacancy. Applies to loss or damage at buildings that have been vacant for more than 60 days at the time of loss. A building is considered vacant when it does not contain enough business personal property for conducting customary business operations. Buildings under construction are not considered vacant.

Vacant. A term used in property insurance to describe a building that has neither occupants nor contents. Contrast with Unoccupied.

Vacant Land. Lots and undeveloped land for future building of a dwelling or for investment purposes. Coverage for these lands, commonly found in general homeowners policies, is an extension of personal liability insurance to these lands.

Valuable Papers and Records Coverage. An open perils (all risk) coverage for physical loss or damage to valuable papers and records of the insured. It includes practically all types of printed documents or records except money.

Valuation Assumption. An actuarial estimate of probable future experience of a pension plan with respect to rates of mortality, disability, turnover, age at hiring, age at retirement, investment yield, etc.

Valuation Clause. A clause stating the value of items for insurance purposes, making it a valued policy.

Valuation Reserve. A reserve against the contingency that the valuation of assets, particularly investments, may be higher than what can be actually realized or that a liability may turn out to be greater than the valuation placed on it.

Valuation. (1) A mathematical analysis of the financial condition of a pension plan. (2) Estimation of the value of an item, usually by appraisal. (3) Calculation of the policy reserve in life insurance.

Value Reporting Form. Commercial form designed for businesses that have fluctuating merchandise values during the year. As values are reported (monthly, quarterly or annually) the amount of insurance is adjusted.

Valued. Relating to an agreement by an insurer to pay a specified amount of money to or on behalf of the insured upon occurrence of a defined loss.

Valued Policy. A policy that states that in the event of a total loss, a specific amount will be paid. This eliminates the need for determining the actual cash value of an item of property in the event of a total loss. It is generally used with certain more valuable items, such as fine arts, antiques and furs. See also Valued Policy Law.

Valued Policy Law. A law passed by a state legislature requiring that in the event of a total loss to a building, the insurance company pays the face amount of a valued policy, regardless of the actual cash value of the property that was destroyed. It can allow the insured to recover an amount much greater than the actual cash value of the property. This guards against unscrupulous insurers purposely writing in excess of the value of property in order to collect greater premiums.

Values. Used in life insurance terminology as a shortened term for nonforfeiture values. See Nonforfeiture Values.

Vandalism and Malicious Mischief (V&MM or VMM). Willful damage or destruction to property. Today this is automatically covered by basic commercial and homeowner forms.

Variable Annuity. An annuity contract in which the amount of the periodic benefit varies, usually in relation to security market values, a cost-of-living index or some other variable factor in contrast to a fixed or guaranteed return annuity. As a hedge against inflation, the variable annuity presents investment risks to the annuitant.

Variable Contracts. Contracts such as variable annuities or variable life insurance that contain an element of risk for the investor depending on the performance of the separate account backing the contract. Generally, these contracts are products of insurers but regulated by both state insurance departments and the federal government.

Variable Expenses. These are the unexpected, nonfixed expenses that occur from month to month, such as automobile repairs, medical expenses, prescriptions, home repairs, miscellaneous expenses, etc.

Some estimation of these unexpected monthly obligations must be determined—and the source from which they will be paid.

Variable Life Insurance. A form whose face value varies depending upon the value of the dollar or securities or other equity products at the time payment is due.

Variable Universal Life. A combination of the features of variable life insurance and universal life insurance under the same contract that provides death benefits and cash values that are variable based on the value of equity investments. Premiums and benefits are adjustable at the option of the policyholder.

VEBA. Voluntary Employee Beneficiary Association.

Vehicle Identification Number (VIN). A series of characters—numbers and letters—used to identify an automobile, assigned to the vehicle by the manufacturer. Only the first eight characters are critical to the rating process.

Vehicle Liability. Liability arising from property damage to other people's cars, injury to people occupying other cars, injury to pedestrians and damage to property other than cars (such as a fence).

Vendee. A person who purchases property.

Vendor. A person who sells property.

Vested Commissions. Commissions on renewal business that are paid to the agent whether or not he or she still works for the insurance company with which the business is placed.

Vested Interest. A person has a right to either the present or future enjoyment of personal property.

Vested Liability. The present value of a participant's retirement benefits that are nonforfeitable.

Vesting. The attainment of a benefit right by a participant, attributable to employer contributions, that is not contingent upon a participant's continuation in specified employment. See also Contingent Vesting, Deferred Vesting and Immediate Vesting.

Viatical Settlement. A written contractual agreement under which the policyholder of a life insurance contract covering the life of a terminally ill person assigns, transfers ownership or otherwise irrevocably designates all control and rights in the contract to another person or entity (viatical settlement company) in exchange for the advance payment of a percentage (usually 60 percent to 80 percent) of the eventual death benefit. Under these arrangements, a portion of the proceeds is paid to the insured or policyholder prior to the actual death of the insured person. The settlement company then receives the death benefit when the insured person dies. These settlements are considered taxable income by the government.

Viatical Settlement Company. A company or firm that specializes in negotiating viatical settlements with policyholders of life insurance contracts covering the lives of terminally-ill persons.

Vicarious Liability. Under certain circumstances, a person is liable for the acts of someone else (e.g., a parent might be held responsible for the negligent acts of a child).

Vis Major. An accident for which no one is responsible. An act of God.

Vision Care Coverage. A health care plan usually offered only on a group basis that covers routine eye examinations and may cover all or part of the cost of eyeglasses and lenses.

Void. A term used to describe a policy contract that is completely free of all legal effect.

Voidable. A policy contract that can be made void at the option of one or more of the parties to it (e.g., a property insurance policy can be voided by the insurer if the insured commits illegal acts).

Voluntary Compensation Insurance. A coverage similar to workers' comp used in circumstances where workers' comp coverage does not apply or is not required by law (e.g., an employer wanting to voluntarily pay compensation benefits to members of a company-sponsored athletic team or a church wishing to cover volunteer workers).

Voluntary Employee Beneficiary Association (VEBA). A trust established under IRS Code 501(c)(9) that can be used to prefund health care.

Voluntary Market. The market where people seek insurance on their own—without state or federal help—through an insurer of their own selection. Contrast with Assigned Risk and Assigned Risk Plan.

Voluntary Reserve. An allocation of surplus not required by law. Such reserves are often accumulated by insurers in order to strengthen their financial structure.

Voyage Clause. A clause in ocean marine policies that defines a specific voyage covered.

W

Wage Indexing. A cost of living increase applied to Social Security benefits after a worker has achieved eligibility for benefits.

Waiting Period (WP). The period of time between the beginning of a disability and the start of disability insurance benefits. Also known as Elimination Period.

Waiver. (1) A rider waiving (excluding) liability for a stated cause of injury or sickness. (2) A provision or rider agreeing to waive premium payments during a period of disability of the insured. (3) The act of giving up or surrendering a right or privilege that is known to exist. In property and liability fields, it may be affected by an agent, adjuster, company, employee or company official, and it can be done either orally or in writing.

Waiver of Coinsurance. A provision in a property policy that the coinsurance clause does not apply if the total loss does not exceed a stated amount, such as 2 percent of the sum insured or the amount of $2,500, whichever is greater. This eliminates the need to do a large inventory in order to determine whether or not the insured has complied with the coinsurance clause, especially where very small losses are involved.

Waiver of Premium. A provision in a life insurance policy that provides: in the event of total disability as defined by the policy, premiums for the policy will be waived for the duration of that disability. The rider is temporary, usually expiring at age 65. There's usually a six-month waiting period before the rider's benefits are payable.

Waiver of Restoration Premium. (1) An agreement or decision to forego any premium for reinstatement of the face amount of coverage under an insurance policy after it has been reduced by the amount of a loss payment. (2) A provision, especially in bonds, for automatic restoration of the full amount of protection without cost to the insured.

War Clause. A provision excluding liability of an insurer if a loss is caused by war.

War Risk Insurance. Insurance covering damage caused by war. Most often written by ocean marine insurance companies covering vessels.

Warehouse and Custom Bond. A bond guaranteeing the payment of custom duties.

Warehousemens Legal Liability. Coverage protecting warehousemen from liability claims, common to the business of warehousing, for loss or damage to property in storage.

Warehouse-to-Warehouse Coverage. A clause sometimes found in inland marine coverages that extends the policy to cover from the shipper's warehouse to the consignee's warehouse.

Warranty. A statement made on an application for most kinds of insurance that is warranted as true in all respects. If untrue in any respect, even if the untruth is not known to the applicant, the contract may be voided without regard to the materiality of the statement. By contrast, statements in life and health applications are not warranties except in cases of fraud. Courts have modified the doctrine of warranty to an application only when the statement is material to a risk or the circumstances of a loss. See also Representation.

Warranty, Implied. See Implied Warranty.

Warranty Policy. A policy written by a reputable company. The term is used in cases where additional coverage is needed: The additional policies all state that the reputable company's warranty policy will stay in force and that they provide coverage exactly like that of the warranty policy.

Warsaw Convention. An international agreement setting limits of liability on international flights with respect to payments for bodily injury and death.

Watchman Warranty Clause. A provision often found in a burglary or fire policy providing for a reduced premium if there is a watchman on duty.

Watchperson. Under commercial crime insurance coverages, any person retained to have care and custody of the insured's property inside the premises, and who has no other duties.

Water Damage Clause. A provision affording coverage for certain specified causes of water damage, e.g., damage caused by water leakage, overflow of heating or air-conditioning systems, plumbing, etc.

Water Damage Legal Liability Insurance. Coverage for an insured who suffers a water damage loss that also damages the property of others on the floor below or in adjoining premises.

Wave Damage Insurance. Coverage against damage to property resulting from high waves or tides.

WC. See Workers' Compensation.

We/Us/Our. These words refer to the insurer in many personalized policy forms.

Wear and Tear Exclusion. An exclusion found in many inland marine policies. It excludes loss resulting from wear and tear, which means normal usage over a period of time that reduces the value of the property insured.

Wedding Presents Floater. A form that provides temporary coverage for wedding presents, usually starting shortly before the wedding and ending shortly thereafter.

Weekly Premium Insurance. (1) A policy whose premium is collected weekly by an agent calling at the door. It is usually sold in small face amounts. (2) A form of debit or industrial life insurance. See also Industrial Life Insurance.

Welfare. See Public Assistance.

Wet Marine Insurance. Insurance provided on ocean marine forms, covering ships and their cargos.

"While" Clauses. Clauses that suspend coverage "while" certain conditions exist, such as vacancy.

Whole Dollar Premium. In many insurance contracts, the premiums are rounded to the nearest dollar, rather than carrying them out to the nearest cent. An amount of 51 cents or more is usually rounded up to the next dollar, and any cents amount less than that is dropped.

Whole Life Insurance. Also known as straight life or permanent life, this insurance may be kept in force for a person's whole life and pays a benefit upon the person's death. All whole life policies build up nonforfeiture values, but they are paid for in 3 different ways. Under a straight or ordinary life policy, premiums are paid for as long as the insured lives. A single premium policy is paid for at one time in one premium. Between these two types there are many limited-payment plans, under which the insured pays premiums for a certain period or until reaching a certain age. Contrast with Term Insurance.

Wholesale Group Insurance. See Franchise Insurance.

Widow(er)'s Benefit. An early retirement benefit, at age 60, under Social Security for the surviving spouse of a covered worker.

Will. A legally enforceable declaration of an individual's plan for the disposition of property.

Willful Injury. See Intentional Injury.

Windstorm. Wind of sufficient violence to be capable of damaging insured property. Windstorm coverage is usually included automatically as part of basic coverages.

Wisconsin Life Fund. The system of state underwritten and issued life insurance established by the state of Wisconsin and providing life insurance for citizens who apply. Wisconsin is unique among the 50 states in this respect.

Work and Materials Clause. A provision found in many property insurance policies which states that the insured is allowed to have the typical types of work and materials for his or her business. The clause makes this clear so that the policy cannot be voided later because of the "increased hazard" provision of the standard fire policy.

Work Program. A clause in contract bond reinsurance specifying that reinsurance be attached at a specified level of a principal's total volume of work, rather than on the conventional basis of individual contract or bond amount. See Contract Bond.

Workers' Compensation (WC). (1) A schedule of benefits payable to an employee by the employer without regard to liability, required by state law in the case of injury, disability or death as the result of occupational hazards. (2) Insurance agreeing to pay workers' compensation law benefits on behalf of the insured employer.

Workers' Compensation Catastrophe Policy. Excess of loss reinsurance purchased by primary insurers to cover their unlimited medical and compensation liability under the compensation laws of the several states.

Workers' Compensation Rating. Basic rates for workers' comp insurance are based upon a system of job classifications and manual rates. Job classification codes have been established for each type of job description. Separate job descriptions and classification codes exist for similar types of jobs if there are significant differences in the risk factors present. Each job classification code has a manual rate.

Working Capital. See Net Quick Assets.

Working Cover. A contract covering an area of excess reinsurance in which loss frequently is anticipated.

Wrap-Up. A broad package plan usually found only in large situations that applies to all liability risks (e.g., a wrap-up policy covering all contractors working on a specific job).

Write. To insure, underwrite or accept an application.

Written Business. Insurance on which an application has been taken out but which is not yet delivered and/or the first premium settled.

Written Premiums. The total premiums on all policies written by an insurer during a specified period of time, regardless of what portions have been earned. Contrast with Earned Premium.

Wrongful Abstraction. A term used usually in connection with money and securities coverage. Insurance covering wrongful abstraction protects against all forms of burglary, robbery and stealing.

Wrongful Death Action. A civil suit brought by survivors against someone believed responsible, by negligence or intention, for another's death. Actions for wrongful death may have statutory minimums or maximums.

Wrongful Entry. The resumption of possession (re-possession of real estate) by an owner or landlord of real property by unjust, reckless or unfair means.

Wrongful Eviction. Depriving a tenant of land or rental property by unjust, reckless or unfair means.

X-Y-Z

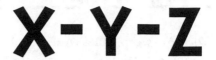

XCU. Explosion, Collapse and Underground Damage. A term used in business liability insurance to indicate that certain types of construction work involve these hazards. Many liability policies exclude them. They can be added by endorsement for an additional premium charge.

X Table. A designation sometimes used to refer to an experimental table or a draft of a table that has not developed to a point of satisfaction or for actual use in rating.

Yacht Insurance. Insurance providing hull coverage and protection and indemnity liability coverage on pleasure boats. It is usually written on an open perils (all risk) basis for hull coverage, although named-perils forms are sometimes used.

Year Plan. A calendar, policy or fiscal year on which the records of the plan are kept.

Yearly (or Annual) Renewable Term (YRT). (1) Term life insurance that may be renewed annually without evidence of insurability until some stated age. (2) A form of life, and sometimes health, reinsurance in which the reinsurer assumes only the mortality risk, which is usually calculated as the face amount of reinsurance minus the terminal reserve.

Years Certain Annuity. See Annuity Certain.

York Antwerp Rules. A set of rules by which ocean marine general average losses are adjusted.

You/Your. Words used to refer to the named insured in many of the personalized policy forms.

YRT. See Yearly Renewable Term.

Zero-Day Qualification Period. When a residual policy has a zero-day qualification period, satisfying the elimination period, it makes the insured eligible for total or residual benefits. When a policy has no qualification period, days of total disability and/or residual disability will satisfy the elimination period.

Z Table. A mortality table showing ultimate experience on insured lives computed from the experienced mortality on life policies issued by major companies from 1925 to 1934. The Z Table was a step in the development of the Commissioners' Standard Ordinary (CSO) Table of Mortality.